House Odds

House Odds

A Joe DeMarco Thriller

MIKE LAWSON

Atlantic Monthly Press
New York

Published simultaneously in Canada
Printed in the United States of America

FIRST EDITION

ISBN-13: 978-0-8021-1995-7

Atlantic Monthly Press
an imprint of Grove/Atlantic, Inc.
841 Broadway
New York, NY 10003

Distributed by Publishers Group West

www.groveatlantic.com

13 14 15 16   10 9 8 7 6 5 4 3 2 1

This book is dedicated to my nephews:
Dan Smaldore, an officer in the Arlington County
Police Department, and Nick Marshall, U.S. Army.
Thank you both for your service.

House Odds

1

"There's something off here," McGruder said as he stared at the monitor, one fat finger tapping the scroll-down key.

Pat McGruder was sixty-four years old, five foot seven, two hundred and sixty pounds, and he had emphysema—and he was scaring the hell out of Greg. He was actually scaring Ted, too, but unlike Greg, Ted wasn't letting it show. Ted sat there sipping his latte, pretending to read *Fortune,* while McGruder studied the spreadsheets. But Greg—the dumb shit—he was fidgeting, wringing his hands, swallowing like he had a golf ball lodged in his throat.

McGruder continued to look at the monitor, wheezing, his thick lips pursed in disapproval. He was sitting in Ted's chair, at Ted's desk, using Ted's computer, while Greg and Ted sat on the couch in front of the desk like two wayward kids called to the principal's office.

"There's something off here," McGruder muttered again.

"Jesus Christ, Pat!" Ted said, tossing the magazine to the floor, acting pissed. "There's nothing *off.* We're down maybe two percent and . . ."

"Two point one," Greg said.

Ted shot Greg a shut-the-hell-up look.

". . . and the books show you exactly where, and we've told you exactly why. We're not trying to hide a damn thing. The economy being the way it is, every casino on the boardwalk lost money this quarter, and profits fluctuate in a business like this."

McGruder didn't answer. He continued to tap the keyboard and squint at the monitor. Finally, he stopped tapping and looked at Ted.

"Don't tell me how things fluctuate, sonny. And I heard what you told me and I can see the numbers. But something's off."

"Pat, can you believe I'd ever try to skim on Al? Come on! Not only is the man like a father to me but . . ."

"Ted, you remember a guy named Pauly Carlucci?" McGruder said.

"Yeah, out in Vegas," Ted said, like he could give a shit.

"That's right," McGruder said. "Out in Vegas. And what do they call Pauly now, Ted?"

Ted didn't answer. He just stared at McGruder, letting him know that he wasn't intimidated.

"They call him Pauly No-Thumbs, don't they, Ted?"

Ted just stared.

"Yep, Pauly No-Thumbs. And you know why they call him that?"

Ted still didn't answer, but McGruder pretended he had.

"That's right," McGruder said. "They call him that because Al hacked off his thumbs. And Pauly just tried to screw Al out of a lousy two grand. Can you imagine what he'd do to a guy who really ripped him off?"

"I've had enough of this," Ted said.

"You've had *enough*?"

"Yeah. I'm sick of you sittin' there, you fat fuck, implying that I'm stealing from Al because you think something's off, but you don't know what."

"You better watch your mouth," McGruder said.

"To hell with you," Ted said.

McGruder stood up with some effort. He looked at Ted for a moment, then nodded. "Okay," he said.

Ted didn't know what that meant.

McGruder waddled away from the desk, over to the coatrack, and shrugged into a suit coat that had to be a size seventy short.

"I'm gonna be back in a couple days," McGruder said. "Look things over again, talk to a few of your people, check out some of these losses you claim you had. I'm coming back because it ain't all about numbers, sonny. It's about my nose." McGruder tapped the end of his broad snout as he said this, then pointed at Greg. "And it's about the way he's sweating and how you're acting so fuckin' cool you're practically whistling."

Ted shook his head like he couldn't believe what he was hearing.

McGruder opened the door to leave, but then he turned back and said, "Oh, I forgot those copies I made."

Greg leapt to his feet and practically ran to the printer. He reached out to pick up the copies, and when he did, McGruder said, "No, Greg, don't pick 'em up like that. Pick 'em up without using your thumb."

———◆———

"We're dead," Greg said. "Absolutely dead. And did you have to talk to him like that?"

Ted didn't say anything. He stood with his back to Greg, looking out a window. His office was on the twenty-ninth floor and there was nothing but ocean as far as he could see, not one boat on the water. He'd never found the Atlantic Ocean, at least this part of it, all that picturesque. The Mediterranean, the Caribbean, the waters off Hawaii—those cobalt-blue and turquoise seas—now, they were lovely. But here, the water was most often a dirty gray-green—and that was on the nice days.

"Ted, are you listening to me?" Greg said. "The guy knows something's wrong. He's going to tell Al."

Ted Allen was the CEO of Indigo Gaming, which meant he ran the Atlantic Palace Casino in Atlantic City. Greg Porter was his head accountant, but called himself the CFO. Whatever. Ted turned away from the window and looked at Greg.

He and Greg had attended UNLV—the University of Nevada, Las Vegas—and they were both thirty-three years old, six feet tall, and tended to dress casually for work: sport jackets over polo shirts, tailored slacks, loafers. But that's where the similarities ended.

Greg's dark hair was beginning to thin and a ring of fat bulged unattractively around his waist. And lately he had stopped wearing his contacts—something about allergies—and had taken to glasses with tortoiseshell frames. Greg thought the glasses made him look intellectual; Ted thought they made him look like the number-crunching wimp that he was.

Ted worked out every day, had broad shoulders, muscular arms, and a washboard stomach. He had a full head of reddish-blond hair, wide-set blue-green eyes, full lips, and a nose that had been worth every penny he'd paid the surgeon. A woman once said that he looked like those Hitler Youth models who pose for Abercrombie & Fitch. He'd never been sure, though, if she'd meant that as a compliment.

"Greg, sit down," Ted said. "And calm down."

"Calm down! I'm telling you, McGruder . . ."

"Have you ever considered that this whole thing could be turned into an opportunity?"

"An opportunity! An oppor—"

"Greg!" Ted snapped. "Quit repeating everything I say. Now, sit down and listen to me. I have an idea."

As Ted spoke, he glanced over at the diplomas on one wall, at his double degrees in business and hotel management. He was proud of those framed pieces of paper. His mother had been a bare-breasted dancer at the Flamingo in Vegas until her tits began to sag, and back in those days she'd also hooked a bit when money was tight. Now she tended bar at the MGM Grand and applied her makeup so heavy she looked like a clown. Good ol' Mom. But she had introduced him to Al, and Al had paid for his education.

That Al now owned him, body and soul, was the price he had to pay.

"I dunno," Greg said. "It might work, but it's risky. I think we should tell Al what we did—what that bitch did—and what you have in mind. I mean it's a good idea but we should come clean first, get everything out in the open. Al will listen to you, Ted. He loves you. He won't do something crazy."

Ted shook his head slowly, not because of what Greg had said, but because of what Greg had become. In college, Greg was the guy you went to if you needed to buy a term paper or the answer key to an exam. He could get you pot, a fake ID so you could drink and, if your girlfriend got knocked up, he knew a lady who could take care of that, too. Back then Greg had balls, which was why he and Ted had become friends, and why Ted had later hired him to keep the casino's books. But not anymore; these days there were mustard seeds bigger than Greg's balls.

Thank God he was a good accountant, though. Or at least a better one than McGruder.

"Greg, we didn't just lose the money," Ted said. "It's the *way* we lost it. Then we cooked the books. No, Greg, I'm not telling Al. I'm going to get the money back and I'm going to get the project financed. I'm going to turn this whole fucking mess to our advantage."

He was going to make lemonade out of lemons, as his dippy mother always said.

But Greg just sat there, head down, looking like he'd just been told that he had colon cancer. Then he reached out to pick up a bottle of springwater. It took Ted a second to figure out what he was doing: he was trying to pick up the bottle without using his thumb. Christ.

"Greg, go find Gus and tell him to come up here," Ted said. "I need to give McGruder something else to think about until I can put everything in place."

2

When DeMarco's cell phone rang, the dental hygienist was jabbing at a tooth with something sharp and painful. He made a noise that sounded like "Waaa" to get her to stop, checked the caller ID, and told the pretty sadist he had to take the call.

"He needs to see you immediately," Mavis said.

"I'm at the dentist's. I can probably be there in . . ."

"Joe, I don't care if they just yanked every tooth out of your head and you're bleeding to death from the holes in your gums. Get back here. Now!"

Mavis glared at him when he arrived, which was unusual because he knew that she had a soft spot for him in that small, hard organ the Boston Irish call a heart. He assumed she was displeased because he hadn't been able to instantly teleport himself from Alexandria to the Capitol, and half an hour had elapsed since her phone call. She shooed him toward Mahoney's office with a brisk, "Hurry up, hurry up." He wondered what the hell was going on.

He entered the room expecting that the big man behind the desk would complain because he, too, had to wait—but he didn't, and this surprised DeMarco. Mahoney was the type who demanded instant gratification, and he whined loud and long when it wasn't forthcoming.

Mahoney gestured with his blunt chin at a young black woman sitting in one of the two visitors' chairs in front of his massive desk. "This is Kay Kiser," he said.

Kiser was wearing a navy-blue suit, a white blouse, and flat-heeled black shoes. DeMarco could tell, even though she was seated, that she was tall. He was five eleven and Kiser was at least that tall, maybe taller. And she looked athletic: good shoulders; flat stomach; shapely, muscular legs. With her height, he wondered if she'd played basketball in college, or maybe volleyball. She was also pretty—and probably even prettier when she smiled—but right now she wasn't smiling. The expression on her face was beyond serious; it was downright grim.

"Ms. Kiser," Mahoney continued, "this is Joe DeMarco. He's a guy who helps me out every once in a while."

Kiser's only reaction to DeMarco's less-than-enlightening job description was to study his face as if she wanted to be sure she could pick him out of a lineup. What she saw was a broad-shouldered, muscular man with a full head of dark hair, blue eyes, a prominent nose, and a big square dimpled chin. DeMarco was a handsome man with a hard-looking face, although he never thought of himself as a hard guy.

"Ms. Kiser works for the SEC," Mahoney said.

Aw shit, boss! What have you done now?

John Fitzpatrick Mahoney had a broad chest, a wide butt, and a substantial gut. His hair was white and full, his features large and handsome, his eyes blue and watery, the whites perpetually veined with red. John Mahoney had the eyes of a committed drinker.

Mahoney was a Democrat and the minority leader in the House of Representatives. He'd represented a district in Boston for decades and had been the Speaker of the House for years, but lost the top job when the Republicans took control a couple of years ago. He was not an easy man to live with even when things were going his way; he'd become even harder to live with since he'd lost the Speaker's gavel. His life these days was devoted to putting his party back in power.

DeMarco had worked for Mahoney for a long time and he knew that his employer skated close to the edge in almost everything he did, but DeMarco had never thought him greedy enough—or stupid enough—to do something that would come to the attention of the SEC.

Rising from his chair, Mahoney said to Kiser, "I gotta go—I gotta go vote on something—but I want you to tell DeMarco everything you told me."

"Sir, I don't have time to . . ."

"Yeah, you do," Mahoney said.

There was usually a life-is-but-a-game twinkle in Mahoney's eyes—particularly in the company of an attractive woman—but not today. And his message to Kiser was clear: no matter what Mahoney may have done, he was still one of the most powerful politicians in the country and she was just a bureaucrat at the Securities and Exchange Commission.

"I'll talk to you later," Mahoney said to DeMarco. "And Ms. Kiser," Mahoney said, his hand on the doorknob.

"Yes?" Kiser said. DeMarco thought the woman's eyes looked like pieces of polished flint—a rock used to start fires and make arrowheads.

"Thanks for doing this thing this way," Mahoney said. "I appreciate it," he added, surprising both Kiser and DeMarco.

"We're arresting the congressman's daughter, Molly, for insider trading," Kiser said.

"What!" DeMarco said. Now he understood why Mahoney had been so solemn. But Molly? No way.

"My boss sent me here as a courtesy to Mr. Mahoney to inform him of his daughter's situation," Kiser said. "Also, as a courtesy to the congressman, we're giving Ms. Mahoney until seven p.m. to turn herself in and be placed under arrest."

Every time Kiser said "courtesy" she spit the word out as if it were something nasty stuck to the tip of her tongue. She clearly resented the preferential treatment Molly Mahoney was receiving and DeMarco could tell if Kiser had had her way, two big federal agents would have marched into Molly's office, slapped handcuffs on her, and hauled her away in full view of her co-workers—just the way they would have handled some coke-snorting young trader on Wall Street.

Kay Kiser wanted to crucify Molly Mahoney on a high hill.

"What makes you think Molly did anything illegal?" DeMarco said.

"I don't *think*. I *know*. Ms. Mahoney works for Reston Technologies in Rockville, Maryland, and she recently purchased ten thousand shares of Hubbard Power stock for fifty-two dollars per share. She . . ."

DeMarco did the math in his head. "She bought half a million dollars worth of stock?"

"Yes. Reston Tech is a research company that works with major manufacturers to improve their products. One of the companies they work with is Hubbard Power and they build batteries used in submarines."

"Submarines?"

Kiser ignored DeMarco's confusion. "Reston came up with a design to reduce the weight and size of submarine batteries by thirty percent. This was a major scientific breakthrough in battery design, and the U.S. Navy is going to spend millions on these new batteries."

"Why?" DeMarco asked.

Kiser kept talking as if DeMarco hadn't asked the question. "Ms. Mahoney worked on the submarine battery project and she bought stock in Hubbard Power a month before the company's shareholders were informed of the breakthrough. And when the company announced the new design, the stock price rose to seventy-eight dollars a share and Molly Mahoney made a profit of approximately a quarter million dollars." Kiser's lips curved upward in a small, humorless smile. "As soon as she sold her shares, her original investment and her profits were seized by the government."

"I still don't get it," DeMarco said. "So what if she bought some stock in this other company?"

Kiser looked at him like he was an idiot. "That's what insider trading is, Mr. DeMarco. When a person has information not available to other shareholders, and this person uses the information to make a profit or avoid a loss, it's called insider trading."

"Maybe she didn't know that what she was doing was illegal."

"She knew. Reston's corporate policies specifically prohibit their employees from buying stock in companies they're working with—to prevent insider trading. In an amateurish attempt to avoid discovery, Ms. Mahoney set up a new e-mail address, a new bank account, and established trading accounts with five different online brokers. Then, over a two-week period, she bought Hubbard stock in increments, buying ten or twenty thousand dollars' worth of stock at a time. She apparently thought that by using multiple brokers and buying the stock in small batches, her half-million-dollar purchase wouldn't be noticed. She sold her shares through these same online accounts and the cash was electronically deposited into her new bank account. In other words, no paperwork, no links to her old e-mail addresses and old bank accounts, no personal checks and, obviously, no visits to the brokers' offices."

"Then how do you know she even bought the stock?"

"Because the brokerage and bank accounts are in her name, with her Social Security number."

"So maybe somebody stole her identity or rigged her computer in some way, and whoever did this set up these accounts."

"It wasn't her computer," Kiser said. "Again, in an attempt to deceive, Ms. Mahoney used a computer at an Internet café."

"Well, hell," DeMarco said. "Then anybody could have done this."

Kiser shook her head as if she felt sorry for DeMarco. "I would suggest," she said, "that her lawyers adopt a different defense strategy."

"Look, there are millions of stock transactions every day . . ."

"*Really,*" Kiser said.

". . . so how'd you happen to spot Molly's trades out of all those other transactions?"

"Because that's what the SEC does, DeMarco. That's our job. That's my job."

In other words, Big Brother is always watching. Or in this case, Mean Big Sister.

"But where in the hell would Molly get half a million dollars?" DeMarco asked. "She's not rich, not that rich."

"I don't know," Kiser said, and she looked momentarily less confident —but she recovered quickly. "And I don't care. Half a million was deposited into this new checking account she established, and she used the money to buy the stock."

"But who deposited the money?"

"Her partners."

"What partners?"

Kiser ignored the question; she was good at ignoring his questions. "And it would be in her best interest to name those partners immediately. It could reduce her sentence."

So Kiser thought Molly had partners but didn't know who they were. "Are you promising her immunity if she cooperates with you?" DeMarco asked.

"The U.S. Attorney will not give her immunity. I'll make sure that never happens. The best she can expect is a reduced sentence."

DeMarco decided that Kay Kiser was more likely to set her own head on fire than show Molly any leniency.

"Has anyone talked to Molly yet?"

"Her father called her while we were waiting for you to get here. And her lawyers have been notified."

Kiser uncrossed her long legs and rose from her chair. DeMarco rose with her. She was taller than him, by at least two inches.

"I'm leaving now," she said, brooking no argument. Her boss may have forced her to kiss Mahoney's ass, but DeMarco wasn't Mahoney. Then Kay Kiser marched through the door without a "goodbye," her back as straight and rigid as a steel rod.

Javert, DeMarco thought as he watched her go.

He'd seen *Les Miserables* in New York a few years ago, and that's who Kiser reminded him of: Javert, the French cop who hounded poor Jean Valjean to the ends of the earth for stealing a loaf of bread.

God help Molly Mahoney.

3

"The driver's name is Gleason," Gus said. "The good news is Donatelli doesn't like him and only uses him when one of his regular long-haul guys is doing something else. He used to work at a government shipyard up there in Kittery, but he's retired now and he pisses away his money on booze and lotto tickets. He lives in a fuckin' shack and most the time, unless Donatelli has work for him, the only thing he eats is fish and crab, and it don't matter to him what fish are legal."

Ted was jogging on a treadmill in the casino's fitness center wearing only shorts and running shoes. A short, white towel was wrapped about his neck. His body glistened with sweat and he knew he looked good; he'd just seen a lady giving him the eye. If she had been closer to twenty than forty, he might have invited her to sit with him in the jacuzzi when he finished his workout. Half the women he slept with he met in the gym.

He glanced down at the heart-rate monitor, to make sure his pulse was staying above one thirty, then looked at Gus and said, "Get to the point."

Ted was convinced the term "knuckle-dragger" had been coined with Gus Amato in mind. He was about forty and he wasn't very tall—only about five foot nine—but he had a broad chest, massive shoulders, and long, powerful arms connected to huge, hairy hands. His nose was broad and his dark hair was curly—so curly that Ted suspected he was the direct descendant of some Moorish invader who'd screwed a Sicilian a few centuries ago. He was wearing gray slacks and an orange golf shirt, which Ted didn't mind, but on his feet were white alligator-skin cowboy boots, and dangling from his left ear was a gold hoop the size of a man's wedding ring. The boots and the earring were something he'd just started wearing, and Ted thought they looked absurd.

"Last week," Gus said, "Gleason got a brand-new pickup—well, almost brand-new, only twenty thousand miles on it—and he bought a new motor for his fishing boat."

"Where'd he get the money? From Donatelli?"

"No, that's the beauty of it. Donatelli would be totally surprised that all of a sudden this loser is driving a new rig."

"So where did it come from?" Ted noticed his pulse was rising, but he didn't think it was because he was running. It was rising because Gus, as usual, was annoying the shit out of him.

Gus laughed. "Two years ago, this useless dick filed a disability claim against the shipyard where he used to work, saying the job had destroyed his hearing. And the government, for whatever fuckin' reason, decided to settle with him. They sent him a check for thirty-eight thousand dollars two weeks ago."

Now, that made Ted smile. "Anything else?"

"Yeah. He has a granddaughter and Gleason takes the little girl fishing with him when he's not drunk and she's not in school."

"Perfect," Ted said.

As Ted had told Greg, he needed something to distract McGruder momentarily, and he needed something to convince him that the casino's books hadn't been doctored the way McGruder thought they had. Ted didn't need a lot of time, just a few days, maybe a week at the outside.

And the good Lord, it seemed, had chosen to drop this poor slob, Gleason, right into his lap.

———◆◆◆———

Mahoney sat, his chair tilted back, his big feet up on his desk. His tie was undone, his suit jacket off, and he held a tumbler of bourbon in his thick right paw. As he talked to DeMarco he looked out at the National Mall, at the protest in progress.

The protesters were as close to the Capitol as the U.S. Capitol Police would allow them to get, but too far away for DeMarco to read the signs they were holding aloft. It seemed to him that there was always someone on the Mall protesting, that hardly a day went by when some group didn't exercise its constitutional right to assemble and complain.

"If it was Maggie, I might believe it," Mahoney was saying. "Even Mitzy, but if Mitzy did something like this, she'd be doing it to save the redwoods or the whales or some fuckin' thing. But not Molly. Molly . . . She's my *mouse*, Joe. She'd never do anything like this."

Mahoney had three daughters: Maggie, Meredith—who went by the nickname Mitzy—and Molly. Maggie, the oldest, was a gorgeous redhead. She was tough, smart, and ambitious—and as tricky as her father if the occasion required it. She was currently an assistant district attorney in Boston, and Mahoney hoped that she'd run for his seat if he ever decided to retire. He and Maggie fought like cats and dogs whenever they were together, but she was clearly Mahoney's favorite.

Mitzy, the youngest, was a free spirit who refused to be shackled by convention or tradition. She dropped out of college her sophomore year, and since then had hopped from one risky, adventurous job to another. She'd been an avalanche maker on the ski slopes of Colorado; a diver on the Barrier Reef filming white sharks in feeding frenzies; and was the only female member of a team that climbed Annapurna II at a record-setting pace. The last DeMarco had heard she was in the Amazon jungle trying to prevent the extinction of some bird whose sole purpose for living was to shit the seeds of some exotic tree.

Molly was the middle daughter. She was pretty, but not head-spinning, knockout pretty like her sister Maggie. And unlike Mitzy and Maggie, she was quiet. When all three girls were in the same room with Mahoney and his wife, Molly would sit there, a small smile on her face, just listening as her parents and her sisters talked and argued. She couldn't compete with Maggie's stories of crime and politics, and no one could match Mitzy's tales of nearly being killed by sea creatures and hostile climates. It was easy to see why Mahoney called Molly his mouse.

"Why'd she go to work for Reston Tech?" DeMarco asked. He knew Molly had some kind of engineering degree, chemical engineering he thought, but that's all he knew about her profession.

"She likes that they do cutting-edge design work," Mahoney said. "That sorta stuff turns her crank. And the outfit she works for is close to D.C., which she also likes, and they pay pretty well."

"Well enough for her to have half a million dollars to invest?"

Mahoney shook his head. "She makes about a ninety grand a year, and her mother told me that she was saving up to make a down payment on a house, but no way has she saved up half a million. She's only twenty-six and she's only been with Reston four years." Mahoney sighed. "This thing's making Mary Pat nuts. She wants to blow up the whole fuckin' government, starting with the SEC. I'm not gonna get a minute's peace until this is settled. Oh, and she wants to see you."

"Sure," DeMarco said. Mary Pat was Mahoney's faithful, long-suffering wife. She had endured her husband's countless affairs, his drinking, his selfish nature. She had raised his children, managed his household, and stayed by his side through political thick and thin. DeMarco would walk barefoot on broken glass carrying a Hummer on his back for Mary Pat Mahoney.

"She probably wants to give you a kick in the ass, make sure you're doing everything you can," Mahoney said.

DeMarco doubted that. Mary Pat wasn't the ass-kicking type. On second thought, maybe she was when it came to her children.

"I need to talk to somebody over at the SEC," DeMarco said. "Somebody other than Kay Kiser."

"Yeah, ain't she a pip," Mahoney muttered.

"And I need to talk to Molly."

"She's a basket case right now, but I'll call her and tell her you're coming over."

"Is she staying at your place?"

"No. Her mother told her she should, but she doesn't want to. Maybe when the press starts camping out on her doorstep she'll move in with us."

"What are her other lawyers doing?"

Mahoney's lips twitched at the word "other." DeMarco had a law degree, had even passed the Virginia bar, but he'd never practiced law. Instead he'd gone to work for John Mahoney—and then did things for the man that he couldn't put down on a résumé. Nonetheless, DeMarco thought of himself as a lawyer and it always pissed him off that Mahoney didn't.

"What they're doing right now," Mahoney said, "aside from charging me six hundred bucks an hour, is chucking big paper rocks at the SEC to slow this whole thing down. And if the case goes to trial, they'll tie Kiser into knots. But it shouldn't ever get to trial, because Molly didn't do it."

He didn't bother to add: *and it's your damn job to prove it.*

Mahoney brooded for a moment, finished his drink, and set the glass down hard on his desk. "Someone's framed my daughter, goddamnit. And when I find the son of a bitch . . ."

"I don't think she was framed," DeMarco said.

"What! Are you saying . . ."

"Boss, you don't frame someone with half a million bucks."

"What the hell are you talking about?"

"I'm saying that if somebody wanted to frame Molly, I don't think they would have thrown away half a million to set the hook. Maybe a few grand, but not half a million. I think there's one of two things going on here. One, somebody's using Molly for cover or . . ."

"For cover?"

"Yeah. Somebody—maybe somebody in her company—was trying to make a killing in the market just like Kiser thinks, but they did it using Molly's identity so if anything went wrong she'd get the blame."

Mahoney nodded. "And two?"

"Two is somebody's out to get you. To get you, somebody might be willing to write off five hundred grand."

Mahoney was silent for a moment; it hadn't occurred to him that he might be the target. "Maybe you're right," he finally said. "So you need to get your ass out there and find out what's going on. You pull out all the stops on this one, Joe. You do whatever you gotta do. You understand?"

What Mahoney meant was that if DeMarco had to break a few laws, Mahoney wouldn't care. DeMarco also knew that if he got caught breaking those laws that Mahoney wouldn't care about that either.

DeMarco looked out at the protesters again. Their signs were waving back and forth in unison like they were singing *Michael Row the Boat Ashore* or some similar Kumbaya-ish chant. Maybe, DeMarco thought, he'd stop working for Mahoney and set himself up as a protest facilitator. All these folks would have to do was step off the bus and there he'd be with permits and face paint and signs emblazoned with clever, rhyming slogans. For a little extra, he'd provide straw-stuffed dummies to hang in effigy—and all the dummies would resemble Mahoney.

Gus Amato drove from Atlantic City to Portsmouth, New Hampshire, where Gleason lived. He didn't like to fly—crammed into a seat built for pencil necks and twelve-year-olds, surrounded by people always coughing and sneezing—and he really didn't like to travel unarmed.

Gleason's place was even worse than he'd expected: a seven-hundred-square-foot shack that hadn't seen paint in twenty years, the front lawn a tangled field of dandelions and weeds, and crap just strewn everywhere: beer bottles, an old toilet, a kid's bike missing a wheel, a rust-covered barbecue tipped over on its side. The only thing that wasn't broken or rusting was a four-door Ford 250 parked in front of the house. On a trailer attached to the Ford was an old fourteen-foot Boston Whaler, and locked to the transom of the boat was a big, shiny Mercury outboard.

The man who came to the door was in his sixties. The little hair he had was thin and gray, and he had an enormous, bloated belly and the bloodshot eyes of a major boozehound. He was wearing a white wifebeater undershirt that showed off flabby arms and blue jeans stained in several places with rust-colored spots that Gus suspected were dried fish blood. He was six-two, which made him five inches taller than Gus, but the last thing Gus was worried about was this guy's size.

"What do you want?" he said when he saw Gus. He didn't say this rudely; more like he was just surprised that anyone would be visiting him.

"You Tom Gleason?" Gus said.

"Yeah. But if you're selling something . . ."

Gus hit him in the gut and felt his fist sink into four inches of fat. Gleason collapsed in the doorway, retching. "Just wanted to be sure," Gus said.

Gus dragged Gleason with one hand across the floor and propped him up against a sofa that was a weird green color, like the color of pea soup. As Gleason sat there trying to catch his breath, Gus looked around the house. *Jesus, how could anyone live like this?* He could practically hear the roaches scuttling over the food-encrusted dishes in the sink.

"You able to hear me okay?" Gus asked. He said this because he'd just noticed that Gleason was wearing a hearing aid in each ear; maybe he really did deserve that settlement money he got from the government.

Gleason nodded, still not able to talk.

"Okay. A couple weeks ago, you were supposed to deliver a truckload of fish to Atlantic City that Marco Donatelli's guys ripped off from Legal Seafoods."

"I did," Gleason said.

Gus wagged a finger. "No, no, listen to me. You gotta get your story straight. Like I was saying, you were supposed to deliver this fish but it never made it. You told the casino buyer that the refrigeration system on the truck crapped out and he was dumb enough to believe you. But then, shit, next thing we know, you got a new Ford sittin' outside your house and new motor for your boat."

"I don't know what you're talking about," Gleason said. "I delivered the fish."

Gus put a hand gently on Gleason's shoulder. "Tom, I don't want to have to hit you again. Now, you got a fat little granddaughter. She takes the bus home from school every day, and it drops her off two blocks from your daughter's place. So what I'm sayin' is, that if you don't get this story straight, a couple of Colombian guys—and these guys are fuckin' animals, Tom—they're gonna pick her up and . . . Well, I don't have to tell you, do I? You've heard what those people do, sell little girls to perverts, put 'em in porno flicks. I mean, it just makes me sick. So I'm gonna start over, to make sure you understand."

DeMarco rapped on the doorframe of an office containing a scarred wooden desk, a high-backed black leather chair behind the desk, four gray metal file cabinets, and two wooden visitors' chairs. Paper was stacked on every flat surface in the room, including the tops of the file cabinets, the floor, and both visitors' chairs. Next to the phone was a pile of pink telephone message slips, and there were at least thirty slips in the pile.

Sitting behind the desk was Perry Wallace—a triple-chinned fat man with small, cunning eyes. His hair was shaved close on the sides but left thick on top, making it appear as if someone had glued a muskrat's hide to his big, round skull. He was as attractive as roadkill. But he was probably the smartest person DeMarco knew and he was definitely the hardest working.

Perry Wallace was John Mahoney's chief of staff.

Making laws requires work, lots of work, and Mahoney was not a hardworking man. Perry Wallace was the one who did the work. While Mahoney gave speeches and posed with Cub Scouts and veterans, Perry managed Mahoney's staff and his reelection campaigns. He read every word in the Bible-size bills making their way through the House, did the research to sniff out the bullshit buried in the bills, and did the math to see how much everything would cost. And not only did he toil until the wee hours on Mahoney's behalf, he knew *everything*. He knew the law and how the federal budget was tallied; he knew the operating rules for Congress, which are harder to interpret than the Dead Sea Scrolls. Most important, he knew every Democratic politician in America and how he or she could be used to advance Mahoney's agenda, whatever that agenda might be.

Wallace's reaction to DeMarco's theory—that somebody was using Molly's legal problems to harm Mahoney—was: "I don't see it. So she's convicted of a crime. Big deal. Everybody has kids, and sometimes their kids do stupid things. Mahoney's numbers wouldn't dip two points if she went to jail. And if they showed Mary Pat crying while they carted Molly off to jail, his numbers would probably rise two points."

By Mahoney's "numbers," Wallace meant Mahoney's standing in the polls, polls that Wallace conducted on every major decision Mahoney made to see how popular or unpopular it might be.

"Okay," DeMarco said, "but what if somebody came to Mahoney and said, 'I have evidence that will get Molly off, but I'll only give it to her lawyers if you'll push the Democrats my way on a particular issue?' Don't you think Mahoney might change his vote to keep his daughter out of jail?"

"Maybe," Wallace said.

"Maybe!" DeMarco echoed. "Definitely. He'd never let his daughter go to jail for a crime she didn't commit."

Or for a crime she did commit.

"Okay, so maybe he wouldn't. So what?" Wallace said.

"So is there some bill out there that's going to make somebody tons of money, so much money that using half a million bucks to frame Molly for a crime would be worth it?"

Wallace laughed. "DeMarco, there's always some bill out there that's going to make somebody a lot of money—or cost somebody a lot of money. You really oughta pay some attention to what those guys do in that big room downstairs every day."

"Yeah, but can you think of something specific?"

"I can think of twenty specific things. The number of bills that involve big bucks is large, but more importantly, the number of people behind those bills is almost infinite. It could be any CEO in America; any millionaire who wants to be a billionaire; any one of a thousand special interest groups."

"Come on, Perry, help me out here. Who's rich enough and hates Mahoney enough to do something like this? Who hates him so much that they'd use his daughter to get to him?"

"Who hates him so much that . . ." Perry Wallace's small eyes suddenly grew wide and a look of shock spread across his broad face.

"My God, Joe, I think I know who it is!"

"You do?"

"Yeah. But it's not a single person. It's a large group, a gang actually."

"A gang? What gang? What are they called?"

"They're called *Republicans,* you moron."

———◆———

"Pat, it's Ted Allen."

"What do you want?" McGruder said, his voice all tight.

"I want to apologize for the way I spoke to you the other day when you came to the casino. I know you were just doing your job."

McGruder didn't respond—he just sat there wheezing into the phone. How long, Ted wondered, could a guy in his condition possibly live? "Anyway," Ted said, "that's not the main reason I called. You remember when you were here, Greg telling you how we lost money on a load of fish?"

"Yeah, almost fifty grand," McGruder said.

"That's right. Marco Donatelli ripped off a truckload of fish, most of it lobster and crab, and we bought it from him. We've dealt with him lots of times, and we've never had a problem in the past, but this time the truck's refrigeration system went out between here and Maine and we lost the shipment. Donatelli gave us back our money, of course, but I had to pay retail for fish to stock the restaurants that week. So, like we told you the other day, it affected the bottom line by almost fifty K."

"Why are you telling me this again, Ted? Are you changing your story now?"

"I'm telling you because I just found out that the driver Donatelli used bought himself a new truck. It looks like this clown lied about the fish spoiling and then sold the load to someone else and kept the money. I'm just letting you know because I'm gonna have Gus take care of the guy."

23

Once again all Ted heard was McGruder breathing into the phone, sounding like those steam irons they use in Chinese laundries. Finally, he said, "I want Delray to go with Gus."

"Aw, that's okay. Gus is already up in Portsmouth and he doesn't need any help with this guy."

"I wasn't asking you, Ted. I was telling you. Delray's going with your boy."

Ted was smiling when he hung up the phone.

4

"Kay Kiser is possessed," Sawyer said.

Randy Sawyer worked for the SEC and DeMarco knew that for him to talk about an ongoing investigation, particularly one this politically charged, meant that Mahoney had either called in a huge favor or had leaned on someone very hard. Or maybe not. Maybe Sawyer had volunteered to help because he was one of those ambitious civil servants who wanted to go from anonymous bureaucrat to presidential appointee. This was Washington: motives were endless—and almost always self-serving.

Sawyer told DeMarco that he was a deputy commissioner in the enforcement division at the SEC, which meant he outranked Kay Kiser. He was a short, chubby-cheeked guy in his forties with a prominent overbite and nervous brown eyes—eyes that kept darting about to see if anybody was paying any attention to him and DeMarco. With his buckteeth, he reminded DeMarco of a paranoid squirrel.

They were at Arlington National Cemetery, walking between two of the seemingly endless rows of white markers. They were there because Sawyer took the metro from D.C. to his home in Falls Church, Virginia, and he'd told DeMarco to meet him at the cemetery metro stop. He said he didn't want to meet in the District—like he was an instantly recognizable celebrity instead of a government pencil pusher.

So they walked between the graves. PFC Harlan Johnson 1899–1918; Corporal Elgin Montgomery 1948–1971; Sergeant Marlon O'Malley 1924–1944. O'Malley, DeMarco noticed, had died on June 6, 1944. A D-day casualty? The headstone didn't say. The headstone just said that O'Malley had lived only twenty years. DeMarco had always thought the cemetery was beautiful and poignant—and a vast, stark reminder of the cost of freedom.

"What do you mean, she's possessed?" DeMarco asked.

"I mean she works about eighteen hours a day. She's not married and, as near as anyone can tell, doesn't have a social life. Or a sex life. All she does is work. It's like she wants to hang every white collar criminal on the planet before she dies. Molly Mahoney is in big trouble if Kiser has her in her sights. She's smart, she's tough, she never quits, and she's hardly ever wrong. In fact, I can't remember her ever being wrong."

Great. It sounded like Molly had pissed off Supergirl.

"What made her investigate Molly in the first place?" DeMarco said. "I don't buy that she just happened to spot Molly buying ten thousand shares of stock out of the trillion shares being traded every day."

"She wasn't investigating Molly. What she was doing was watching Reston Technologies. We—the SEC—have been watching them for years, before Kay Kiser was even hired."

"Why?"

"Because there have been three previous insider trading scams involving Reston—three that we know of—and one goes back to twenty years ago and we never caught the people involved."

"Really!" DeMarco said. This was good news. "What were the other cases?"

"First of all, do you understand what Reston Tech does?"

"Not really. All I know is that Molly's an engineer who works for Reston, and Reston worked with another company called Hubbard to design some super battery the Navy likes. I didn't even know submarines used batteries. I thought they were nuclear powered."

"They are nuclear powered, but they use the ship's battery when they have to shut the reactor down. And reducing the size is a big deal. When you think of a battery, you're probably thinking of the twelve volt battery you got in your car. Well, a submarine battery contains over a hundred cells all wired together and each *cell* weighs over a thousand pounds, and the battery takes up a big compartment in the sub. And on any boat, size and weight are at a premium and if you can reduce the size of the battery you can cram more stuff into the sub: weapons, slick gadgets, whatever. So the Navy is willing to pay a shitload to gain the extra space."

"I get it," DeMarco said.

Sawyer bent over and straightened a little flag that was next to one of the headstones, and DeMarco noticed the name on the grave was Murphy, his mother's maiden name. He doubted he was related to the guy, who'd died during the Korean War, but he found the coincidence spooky.

"And the batteries are just the latest thing that Reston's done," Sawyer said. "Reston Tech was started by a genius named Byron Reston. He was an inventor, kind of a latter-day Thomas Edison, and he's got about a thousand patents on stuff he designed. What he'd do is find some manufacturing company that needed a major improvement in whatever they were making, and he'd come up with the improvement and then he'd partner with the company and share in the profits. The guy was a wizard. He's dead now but the company is run by his son and they still do what Byron Reston used to do but on a larger scale, and they hire the best eggheads they can find.

"Anyway, twenty years ago Reston Tech partnered with a company that made some kind of gizmo for water treatment systems. This was huge because every big city in the country has a water treatment plant and whatever this gizmo was, a filter or some fuckin' thing, was going to make the process a whole lot cheaper, and the company that came up with it a whole lot richer. Well, two months before the company goes public with this new product, an investor buys a million bucks' worth of their stock, when the stock's at an all time low. In fact, it looked like the company was going bankrupt and nobody was buying their stock. Anyway, when the company announced they had a product they could sell to every water district in the country, the stock shot through the roof and the investor made almost five million bucks—and the whole thing just smacked of insider trading. I mean, why would a guy buy so much stock in this failing company unless he knew they were on the edge of a major breakthrough? But in the end, we could never prove anyone was guilty of insider trading and the investor walked away with his five million."

Sawyer stopped and straightened another little flag at another grave, and DeMarco wondered if he had some sort of obsessive-compulsive disorder.

"Six years go by, and this time Reston is working with a company that makes body armor and they come up with a compound that would make the armor lighter but with just as much stopping power as the armor being used at the time. But, just like with the water treatment gizmo, three months before the armor company goes public with a product they can sell to the Pentagon by the boatload, somebody buys a ton of stock, the stock price skyrockets, and the investor makes almost twelve million. But this time we can't even figure out who the investor is."

"What do you mean you couldn't figure out who it was?"

"Just what I said. Whoever did this set up a dummy investment company composed of half a dozen people who didn't exist. The company filed all the right papers with all the right agencies and the people in the company all had Social Security numbers and tax IDs and everything else. On paper, everything looked legit—except the people didn't exist."

"You couldn't follow the money trail?"

"Sure, we could follow it. We followed it from one offshore bank to another to another until it finally disappeared into thin air. Remember, this was fourteen years ago, DeMarco, and it may surprise you to learn that banks in places like Belarus and Nigeria don't follow the same record-keeping practices we have over here, particularly if you tip the banker."

"Earlier, you said *he*. Do you know the investor's a he?"

"No. It could be a she or a they. But the thing is, we now knew the insider had to be at Reston Tech. I mean, when it happened with the water treatment gizmo it could have been somebody at either the water treatment place or at Reston. But when it happened a second time, and with a different company, we knew there had to be a bad guy at Reston."

"But you don't have any idea who he is?"

"Not a clue—and believe me, Kiser's dug hard for him. Anyway, five years ago it happened again. This time it was for a company who was designing an electric motor you connect to the wheels of a jet."

"What?" DeMarco said.

"You know when an airplane is sitting at the gate and they use that little truck to push the plane back? And after the jet is on the runway, it taxis for twenty minutes, using up a bunch of fuel. Well, this electric motor, which operates off a rechargeable battery, hooks up to the airplane's wheels and you can use it to move the plane and taxi. You not only save on fuel, but you can also fire all the guys who drive the little trucks that push the planes around. The thing never got approved by the FAA, but just the idea of it was enough to drive the stock up."

"So what happened?" DeMarco asked.

"What happened is the same thing that happened with the body armor. Right before the company announces their super-duper new electric airplane motor, somebody buys a ton of their stock and makes a mint. This time the investor was a European hedge fund and, once again, the hedge fund was just an empty shell and because it was set up in Liechtenstein or Switzerland or wherever the hell it was, it was even harder for us to figure out who was involved."

"So what I'm telling you is, Reston Tech is a perfect company for insider trading. At any one time, Reston is working with thirty or forty different industries on new technologies and if you can figure out what the next big thing is going to be, the place is a gold mine. And this has happened three times in the past that we're aware of.

"Which brings us to Molly Mahoney and the submarine batteries. The thing that's weird, though, and even Kiser will admit this, is in the previous cases we were dealing with a lot of money. These guys invested millions to make more millions. They weren't screwing around with a lousy half-million-dollar buy-in and a quarter-million-dollar profit. The other thing is, the guy who pulled this off in the past was smart enough not to get caught—unlike Molly Mahoney, who practically hung a sign around her neck saying *I'm a crook*."

"You sound pretty convinced that Molly's guilty."

"Well, I'd like to give her the benefit of the doubt, but frankly . . ."

"Yeah, yeah, but if Molly didn't do it, then it could be the guys that pulled these scams in the past."

Sawyer made a face that said *I kinda doubt that*.

DeMarco chose to ignore Sawyer's skepticism. "The good news about these other cases is they happened before Molly signed on with Reston. She's only been there four years. So it's not unreasonable to assume that whoever pulled these scams in the past could be behind the submarine battery thing. But the big thing is, these past cases *confuse* things, and there's nothing a defense lawyer likes better than confusion."

Before Sawyer could rain on his parade, DeMarco said, "Thanks, Randy. You've been a big help. I'll make sure Mahoney knows."

5

Hardly anyone scared Gus Amato, and he'd never backed down from a fight in his life. He was strong and he could take a punch, and if he couldn't beat a guy with his fists, he'd use a pipe or brick or anything he could get his hands on.

Well, there'd been one guy at Bayside, a psycho named Holloway. He was only five foot eight, skinny as a rail, and had an ugly port-wine stain that covered half his face. He was also a convicted serial killer, doing six back-to-back life sentences. Gus had gotten the last dessert one day at chow, the wacko right behind him in the line, and the guy had said, "I'm gonna kill you if you take that." He said this with no inflection in his voice at all. Gus had told Holloway to go fuck himself, and he took the dessert, but he spent the rest of his time at Bayside looking over his shoulder because Holloway was sneaky and smart. Yeah, he had to admit that Holloway had definitely scared him.

The only other guy who scared him that way was Delray, although he would never have admitted it out loud. And he'd fight Delray if he ever had to, even though he figured he'd probably lose. Delray was just as strong as him, and no doubt he was just as tough; he'd done time in worse places than Bayside. But it wasn't his size or even the stories Gus had heard about him. It was the way he never talked, the way he held himself—and, of course, that fuckin' eye of his. All Gus knew was that he'd have liked it better if McGruder had assigned someone else to come with him to visit Gleason.

He picked up Delray at Logan Airport in Boston, and the whole way to Portsmouth the only thing the guy said to him was, "Pull off over there. I gotta take a leak." When they reached Gleason's shack, Gus said, "This is the place. See the truck?" Delray didn't respond.

Gleason, Gus had to admit, did a good job. It helped that he was scared shitless—so that didn't require any acting on his part—but he also kept the story straight and said just what he was supposed to say. At one point, just to remind him of the box he was in, Gus picked up a picture and said, "This your grandkid?" When Gleason nodded, chin trembling like he was going to cry, Gus added, "She's a chubby little thing, but don't worry. I got a niece who was like this when she was ten or eleven but then, when she was sixteen, she went all anorexic. So there's hope."

He noticed Delray looked over at him when he said this, like he'd said something wrong, but it didn't matter: Gleason got the point. He admitted that he sold the truckload of fish to a couple guys in Manchester and used the money to buy his new truck and outboard motor. And what was left over, he gave to his daughter. Gus had told him to say that; he figured that way the guy wouldn't look like such a greedy prick and, therefore, might get less of a beating.

And he was going to get a beating, or so he thought. Gus had told him on his first visit that he was going to have to smack him around just to make things look right, but promised it wouldn't be too bad unless Gleason fucked up.

Fortunately, he didn't. He stuck to Ted's script like his first name was Jackie instead of Tom.

"Why'd you do it?" Delray asked. So far, that was the only thing he'd said since they'd entered Gleason's house.

"I needed a new truck," Gleason said. "My old one was falling apart and I couldn't get a loan or anything. And I needed a new motor, too. I mean, fish is practically all I eat."

To keep Delray from asking more questions, Gus hit Gleason in the face, knocking him right off his puke-green couch.

"Go get the keys and the title for the truck, you dumb shit," Gus said.

After Gleason handed Gus the keys and the paperwork, Gus pulled out a .22 semi-auto. Gleason said, "Hey, wait a minute." Gus didn't wait. He shot him in the chest, then put one more in his forehead. If Delray was surprised he didn't show it. But then Delray never showed anything.

Gus picked up the shells ejected from the automatic, looked around the room, and said, "I didn't touch anything in here except his face. Did you touch anything?"

Delray ignored the question.

They left Gleason lying on the filthy shag rug in his living room, cockroaches in the blood before they even closed the door. Gus figured the local cops would think that Gleason, after a million years of bad luck, finally fell into some money, bought himself a new truck, and then some asshole came along and killed him and stole it. Which, when he thought about it, was pretty much what happened.

"What do you think?" McGruder asked.

"I don't know," Delray said. "The guy was so scared he could barely talk. But he didn't deny anything."

"What does Donatelli say?"

"He backs up Ted's story."

McGruder snorted. "Marco Donatelli's a fuckin' snake; he ain't like his old man. He might back up Ted's story if Ted comped him a couple nights at the casino."

Delray, of course, didn't answer because McGruder hadn't asked a question.

"Where are you now?" McGruder said.

"Driving back from Portsmouth, we're almost to Boston. Gus is behind me, driving the guy's truck, towing the boat trailer."

"You tell Gus to drop the truck off at my place. My nephew's got a landscaping business, so he can use the truck, but I don't give a shit what he does with the boat. And then after you get back, you and me are gonna go have a talk with Ted's accountant."

6

Molly Mahoney was about two twitches away from a nervous breakdown.

Her fingernails were bitten to the quick, her blue eyes red from crying, and it appeared as if she had lost weight since the last time DeMarco had seen her. He hoped she wasn't sick on top of all her other problems.

Her curly, shoulder-length auburn hair was arranged in a sloppy ponytail and tendrils of hair had escaped the rubber band at the back of her head. She was wearing a Harvard sweatshirt that looked at least one size too big, and unflattering blue jeans that were too short and baggy in the seat. Her thin face was pale and devoid of makeup, and the freckles on her cheekbones stood out starkly.

She had spent one night in jail; her lawyers hadn't been able to keep that from happening. At her arraignment, she pled not guilty and was released on a hundred-thousand-dollar bond. DeMarco had watched on television when Molly left the courthouse with her mother. Molly's lawyers had walked ahead of Mary Pat and Molly, pushing through a mob of reporters, muttering "No comment" like a mantra, while Mary Pat held her daughter's arm and talked to her, smiling occasionally, acting as if the reporters weren't there at all. Mary Pat was made of steel.

DeMarco had met with Mary Pat before coming to see Molly. Mahoney's wife had three things in common with her husband: she had snow-white hair and blue eyes, and was Boston Irish. But that was where the similarities ended. Mahoney was built like a bear; Mary Pat was slender. Mahoney was slowly committing suicide by overeating, overdrinking, and smoking three or four cigars a day; Mary Pat was a vegetarian who practiced yoga. Mahoney was devious, tricky, and dishonest; Mary Pat donated her time to charities and probably wouldn't tell a lie if her life depended on it. How on earth they had ever gotten together in the first place, and then stayed together for forty years, was a matrimonial miracle.

"I'm really worried about her, Joe," Mary Pat had said. "And I don't mean the . . . the SEC thing. I'm worried about her health, her mental health. I don't think she's suicidal but she seems so . . . so *fragile*. You have to find out who's behind this."

DeMarco had promised that he would—and it was a promise he meant to keep because he'd made the promise to Mary Pat.

So DeMarco was now sitting at the kitchen/dining room table in Molly's small, none-too-neat one-bedroom apartment in North Bethesda. He didn't know how long she had lived in the place, but there were still unpacked boxes in her living room and she'd made no effort to decorate—no pictures on the walls, no throw pillows on the sofa, no cute knickknacks on shelves or end tables. The building she lived in surprised him, too: it wasn't in the best of neighborhoods and it didn't have a swimming pool or a fitness center or any of the other amenities you'd expect to find in a place where a well-paid young professional lived.

"Who do you think could have done this, Molly?" DeMarco asked. "I need someplace to start looking."

Mahoney's daughters knew that DeMarco occupied some shady niche in their father's universe; they just didn't know exactly what the niche was. When Molly had asked him if he was working with her lawyers, he'd said, "Well, not directly. Your dad just asked me to poke into this a little on my own."

What DeMarco meant was: your dad expects me to do things your white-shoe lawyers might be disinclined to do, particularly if some of those things might get a real lawyer disbarred. But Molly didn't ask him to clarify his role in her defense. She just sat there staring down at the tabletop, seemingly shell-shocked by everything that had happened to her. She'd never been arrested before. She'd never been fingerprinted or strip-searched by a jailhouse matron. She'd never spent a night in a cage surrounded by crack-addicted prostitutes. That she was in shock was understandable, but DeMarco needed her help.

"Molly, I know you're upset but you have to focus here. The lady from the SEC said that whoever did this used a computer at an Internet café. Have you ever gone to an Internet café?"

Molly nodded. "Yeah, a place called Milo's. It's just a couple blocks from here and whenever I need to go online for something, and if I'm not at work, I go there. It's cheaper than paying for a monthly Internet connection."

Now that surprised him—that a woman of Molly's generation and income level wouldn't have an Internet connection in her home. But maybe she was just frugal.

"Think, Molly," DeMarco said. "Whoever did this knows your habits. He knows you use that café. He knows your address and date of birth and Social Security number. And half a million bucks was deposited into a checking account that supposedly belonged to you, which means this guy is rich or has access to piles of money. So come on, Molly. Who do you know that has money and access to your personal information? The list can't be that long."

Molly just shook her head.

Christ. "Well, do you have any enemies at work, someone who's jealous of you or . . ."

"Jealous!" Molly said, and then she laughed—a short, unhappy bark of a laugh—as if the idea of anyone envying her was absurd.

"Then tell me about people you know who have the computer skills to do this."

"Computer skills?"

"Yeah. Maybe somebody hacked into your computer to get information or installed one of them . . . them *things* that keep track of your keystrokes. And then he got onto this internet café's computer and made it look like you bought the stock and set up the new bank account."

Molly shrugged. "Most the people I work with are scientists or engineers," she said, "and they all use computers. But none of them are hackers, at least not that I'm aware of."

"What about your IT people? There must be some geeks where you work who service your machines."

"We contract out the IT stuff, and I don't even know any of the people who work for the contractor."

"What's the name of the IT company, Molly?"

She told him and DeMarco wrote it down. He was glad to have something to write down.

"What about the people that worked on this submarine battery project with you? Whoever did this had to know about the project and had to know when the battery company was going to announce the breakthrough. So how many people were involved in the project?"

"The main team had five engineers on it, including me, but lots of people in the company knew about it. We'd give the managers and the money guys biweekly updates on how we were doing."

"Give me the names of these other engineers."

Molly did, but added, "They're just people like me. They wouldn't do something like this. And none of them, as far as I know, has any of my personal information."

"Molly, can you think of anything that will help? Anything. Someone snooping around your office, someone asking for your Social Security number, someone asking where you bank?"

Molly started to say something, but then gave a strangled sob and rose from the table and went over to stand by the kitchen sink with her back to DeMarco. She stood there, hunched over the sink as if she might throw up, then finally straightened but didn't turn around.

"What time is it?" she asked.

"Uh, twelve thirty," DeMarco said, checking his watch. *What difference did it make what time it was?*

"Would you like a drink, Joe?" Molly said.

Ah. She didn't want to start drinking before noon, like if you drank in the morning you were an alkie but if the sun was past its zenith, you were okay. And she didn't want to drink alone.

"No, thanks," DeMarco said. "Nothing for me."

Molly opened a cupboard above her sink and pulled out a bottle of scotch. Cheap scotch, DeMarco noted. It probably tasted like paint thinner. While Molly was pouring a drink, DeMarco told her what Randy Sawyer had said about three previous insider trading cases at Reston Tech.

"Molly," he said, "if you can't think of anyone who would want to frame you, can you think of anyone at your company who might be involved in insider trading? If Sawyer's right about these previous insider cases, it has to be someone who's worked there a long time, long before you ever got there. So can you think of somebody who's richer than you'd expect him to be? You know, spending more than you think he should be able to afford. Or how 'bout somebody who always seems especially curious about what you're working on." DeMarco was grasping at straws, and he knew it.

Molly didn't respond; she was still at the sink, her back to DeMarco. She had slammed down her first drink while he was talking and then immediately poured another shot, this time adding ice to her glass.

"Molly," he prompted her. "Do you have any ideas?"

She continued to ignore him while looking down at the drab court-yard outside her window. DeMarco had noticed the courtyard when he walked into the building: a small square of grass that was mostly weeds, a dry birdbath, and a couple of bushes with wilted brown leaves. The whole apartment building had the look of a place that ignored minor maintenance—or a place where the tenants couldn't afford to complain if the maintenance wasn't done.

Molly turned at last to face DeMarco. Her eyes seemed brighter—a by-product of the alcohol, he assumed.

"They said I might go to jail for three years. I'm going to have a criminal record and lose my job and my dad's going to be humiliated by the press. I just feel like . . ."

She started sobbing. She cried so hard that she collapsed into a small heap on her kitchen floor. DeMarco walked over to her, pulled her to her feet, and took her into his arms. He patted her back clumsily, like he was burping a baby; she was so thin he could feel her shoulder blades through her shirt. "Molly, it's going to be okay. We're going to get you out of this, honey. Trust me."

She didn't know a damn thing that would help him and she was too distraught to think straight—but, sure, trust me.

7

---◆◆◆---

Greg Porter walked out of the Public Safety Building on Atlantic Avenue, thinking the meeting with the cops hadn't gone so well—but the cops were the least of his problems.

This thing that Ted was doing—lying to McGruder, hiding stuff from Al, juggling the numbers . . . He had a bad feeling about it, a really bad feeling. It looked as if Ted's latest maneuver, however—convincing McGruder that that guy Gleason had ripped off a load of fish—had worked. Or so Ted thought—but Greg was still worried.

The casino kept two sets of books: one they showed to investors and the IRS and one that showed how much money they really made. The second set of books included Al's cut from the casino, money laundered from some of Al's other operations, bribes they paid to local cops and politicians. It was an intentionally complicated accounting system and hard to follow even if you were familiar with it. Greg was beginning to think, however, that McGruder hadn't seen anything specific in the spreadsheets that had made him suspicious. For one thing, they weren't trying to hide a big loss—only half a million—and Greg had spread the loss out over a lot of things. He couldn't claim they lost the money because a couple of heavy hitters had lucky streaks at the tables; there were just too many people watching the gambling side of things. Instead, he cooked the books on the operations side. He expensed maintenance they didn't do, added in losses for property damage that didn't occur, increased the amount spent to fix a crack in one of the swimming pools, bumped up the cost of consumables that were hard to track. There was no way McGruder could tell if they'd gone through a few dozen more cases of booze than normal.

So he didn't think it was the numbers; it was McGruder's goddamn nose. He just *smelled* that something was off, and probably, just like he'd said, it was because of the way he and Ted had been acting. Whatever the case, whether it was something in the spreadsheets or McGruder's snout, he knew McGruder was going to catch them. He just knew it.

He reached the corner. His car was parked across the street in a thirty-minute loading zone because he hadn't expected to be with the cops more than fifteen minutes. But then it took an hour to come to an agreement with the bastards, and he could see the ticket fluttering on his windshield. He shook his head. Everything in his life these days was turning to shit.

He started to cross the street but before he could step off the curb, a black Lincoln with tinted windows stopped in front of him, blocking the crosswalk. The passenger side window powered-down—and there was McGruder. Delray was driving.

Oh, Lord Jesus, help me.

"Get your ass in the car," McGruder said.

Greg's feet reacted faster than his brain: he ran. He ran right around the nose of the Lincoln, planning to dart across the street and get in his car and . . . And he didn't know what, but no way was he getting in a car with Delray.

He didn't see the city bus that killed him, the bus that dragged him fifty-seven yards, its brakes locked, skidding the whole way.

8

---◆◆◆---

DeMarco was at Clyde's in Georgetown, at the bar, having a vodka martini, admiring the legs of a tall blonde barmaid. He figured he deserved it—both the view and the drink—for toiling diligently on Molly Mahoney's behalf.

After he saw Molly, he had called her lawyer and told him what he'd learned from Randy Sawyer about the previous insider cases involving Reston Technologies. The lawyer was appropriately grateful. When he asked for DeMarco's source, DeMarco refused to tell him. He then gave the lawyer the names of the other engineers who had worked with Molly on the submarine battery project. The lawyer, now sounding a bit snarky, informed DeMarco that he already had the names and was already doing background checks on those people.

DeMarco then wasted the rest of the afternoon at the GU law library. He couldn't remember anything he'd been taught about insider trading in school and thought it might be good to get reacquainted with the subject. After two hours, he hadn't learned anything that would help Molly and his head ached from trying to understand all the convoluted legal bullshit that seemed to be written in some language other than English. So, when he'd looked at his watch and saw it was four thirty—meaning the cocktail hour, or close enough to it—he'd left the library and ambled over to Clyde's to reward himself with a martini.

He was just taking the first sip of his drink when his cell phone rang—the phone call distracted him and he inadvertently allowed ice-cold vodka to stream right over his tooth, the one he'd gone to see the dentist about. The tooth was cracked and every time it was exposed to something cold, the top of his head almost came off. Until he could get back to the dentist, he had to tilt his head to the right whenever he drank, which looked pretty stupid when drinking a martini.

"Shit!" he yelled, reacting to the pain and forgetting he was speaking into the phone.

"Joe? It's Molly."

"Oh, sorry. I just . . . Never mind. What can I do for you?"

"It could be a manager named Douglas Campbell," Molly said.

They were sitting in a small restaurant five blocks from Molly's apartment, and she was picking at a chicken salad, spending more time moving the food around on her plate than eating. The only calories provided by her dinner came from the white wine she was drinking. She was already on her second glass.

"Why him?" DeMarco asked.

Molly hesitated, as if she was reluctant to tell DeMarco what she knew.

"Molly," he prodded.

"Doug is Reston's HR guy. Head of human resources. A couple of years ago, I was standing outside his office, right by the door. I needed to talk to him about a consultant I wanted to hire, but he was on the phone. Anyway, he was using one of those prepaid phone cards to make a call. I could see him looking at the card, reading the PIN number off the card as he dialed. I thought that was odd because he makes long distance calls all over the place, and even if it was for something personal, it wouldn't have raised any eyebrows. Plus, he's pretty senior. It's not like anybody would have questioned one of his calls."

"What's the phone card have to do with . . ."

"Whoever he was calling comes on the line and Doug says, all agitated, like he's upset, 'It failed the solubility test. You better sell.'"

"I don't understand. What's that mean?" DeMarco said.

"At the time, a Reston team was working on a biodegradable plastic bottle. You know how the environmentalists go nuts, saying plastic bottles will be around ten million years from now? Well, the team had come up with a bottle that would essentially dissolve six months after you broke the seal. It would have been a major breakthrough, and the company we were working with would have owned the bottle market for a while. But then, late in the development cycle, they found problems they hadn't seen in earlier tests and abandoned the project."

Yeah, DeMarco could just see it: you're drinking a bottle of pop and suddenly the bottom falls out and you end up with Coke all over your lap. But he didn't say that. Instead, he said, "Are you saying that Campbell was warning somebody who'd bought stock in the bottle company to get out?"

"I don't know, but maybe."

"How long ago was this? What year?"

"Uh, 2010. Maybe the first part of 2011. I just know it was a couple years ago."

"Do you remember the month?"

"No."

"You said you went to see Campbell because you wanted to hire a consultant. Can you get the exact date of the phone call by looking at the consultant's contract?"

"I never hired him. It turned out we didn't need him."

"Shit. Well, other than this one phone call, is there anything else that makes you suspect Campbell?"

Molly took her time responding. She was driving DeMarco nuts the way she mulled over every answer.

"You asked about who would have access to my personal information. The HR office has my Social Security number on file, and since my paycheck is direct-deposited, they know where I bank."

"That's good, Molly. That helps. Anything else?"

Again she hesitated. What the hell was her problem?

"The other thing you asked was if I could think of anybody who seems to live better than they should be able to afford, and that's what really made me think of Doug. I mean, he makes a good salary, at least one fifty a year, but his house must be worth a couple million. It's huge. And he has a beach house and a boat, too. He's always throwing parties and inviting people from work out to his beach place for barbecues and water skiing and stuff. What I'm saying is, he seems to be a little better off than you'd expect, but maybe not. I don't know. Oh, and one other thing. He told me once he was planning to retire when he turned fifty, which is pretty young."

Now, that was enlightening. It was hard to imagine a guy who owned all the things that Campbell owned being able to retire so young. He ought to be up to his neck in debt, and the way the markets had been performing the last few years, his 401K should be in the same shape everyone else's was.

"Is Campbell married?" DeMarco asked.

"Yeah."

"Is his wife wealthy?"

"I don't know."

"Well, maybe she has a good job," DeMarco said.

"I don't think she works," Molly said, "but I don't know for sure."

"Molly, let me ask you something. Why didn't you report Campbell when you heard him making this phone call?"

She didn't answer immediately. She finished the wine in her glass, then looked around for the waitress and signaled that she wanted another. "I don't know," she said. "I guess because it didn't mean anything at the time, not until this happened to me."

She was lying about something, DeMarco thought, but what? And why would she lie?

9

———◆———

Ted parked in front of Al Castiglia's house, then looked at his watch. He was five minutes early. He closed his eyes, centering himself, and rehearsed in his mind how he was going to behave and what he was going to say. His life might depend on how he acted at this meeting.

He checked his watch again. He wanted to be right on time, not a minute earlier, and definitely not a minute later. At 8:59 a.m., he stepped from the car. As he walked up the sidewalk toward the front door, he shook his head, amazed as he always was, at the way Al's place looked.

The house was in a working-class neighborhood in Philadelphia. It was three stories tall, had a big front porch, an expensive oak door, and hurricane shutters on the windows. It was a nice, respectable-looking house; not ostentatious, just roomy and comfortable. The thing that was amazing about it was all the damn lawn statues. There were two big lions by the front door; a doe and two fawns under a tree; a family of plaster rabbits in one of the flower beds. And that was just on one part of the lawn. The backyard looked like a staging area for Noah's ark. Ted knew Al's wife was the nut who bought all the statues, but didn't he ever tell her no?

And it was Al's wife who let him in, a little gray-haired bird of a woman who weighed maybe ninety pounds. She gave him a hug, asked how he was doing, acting oblivious as to why he was there. Ted had always suspected that Al's wife knew a lot more than she let on.

"He's in the kitchen with Pat," she said. "And with that . . . that one with the eye." Then she made the sign of the cross.

Oh, shit. Delray was there. Al's superstitious twit of a wife thought Delray—because of his eye—was a devil. Or maybe *the* devil. And maybe she was right.

Ted put on his game face—an expression that said he was madder than hell—and walked aggressively into the kitchen. Al was sitting at the head of the kitchen table, eating a danish, cream cheese smeared on his upper lip. McGruder sat next to him like a malignant toad, wheezing, his fat hands around a coffee cup. Delray was standing off to one side, arms crossed over his chest, his butt resting against the kitchen counter. His face was expressionless and, as always, regardless of the time of day or the lighting in the room, he was wearing sunglasses. The good thing about the sunglasses was that they hid the eye.

Ted had never been able to figure out Delray's race, and his name didn't give an indication. He had a dark complexion, close-cropped dark hair, a big nose, high, hard cheekbones, and a strong chin. He wasn't huge—only six two or six three—not much taller than Ted—but he was powerful looking, with a serious weight lifter's pecs and biceps. Blue barbed wire tattoos circled his upper arms; he got the tats in prison and the workmanship was crude, the ink faded over time. And prison was where he got the eye.

His right eye was a normal shade of brown but the left one . . . The iris was white instead of brown, about the same shade of white as the normal white part of the eye. And when Delray took off his sunglasses, which wasn't often, you couldn't focus on anything but that dead, milk-colored eye. Delray's eye just creeped Ted out.

"You motherfucker!" Ted screamed the minute he stepped into the kitchen, pointing his finger at McGruder's bloated face.

"Hey! Watch the language," Al said, his mouth full of pastry. "The wife's in the next room."

Yeah, like that would make a difference if Al was the one who lost his temper.

"I'm sorry," Ted said. "But I just can't believe what he did."

"Why was Greg talking to the cops?" McGruder said. "And why'd he run?"

"He was talking to the cops because he was trying to hold down se-curity costs for the ZZ Top show. You know, seeing if he could get the bastards to provide a few more uniform guys for free so we wouldn't have to hire so many off-duty cops. If you don't believe me, call the chief."

"Yeah, but why'd he run?" Al said. His tone was casual, as if Ted's answer didn't matter at all. It was like he'd said: *Is it still raining outside*? But Ted knew better.

"He ran because Pat came to the casino the other day and did this Pauly No-Thumbs number on him. And then he sees Pat with Delray there in the car, and he thinks they're takin' him for a ride, like he's going to end up in landfill somewhere."

McGruder started to say something, but Ted cut him off. "This all happened because you're a paranoid, suspicious prick." Turning to Al, he said, "Did he tell you what he said to me, the other day when he came to look at the books?"

"Of course, he told me," Al said.

Al was sixty-eight years old. He was six foot four, mostly bald on top, had a good-size paunch and the biggest upper arms Ted had ever seen on a man. He looked like a retired stevedore. And he was insane. One minute he'd be perfectly calm, acting like he was getting a big kick out of Ted and McGruder going at it, but in an instant he could turn into a foaming-at-the-mouth fucking maniac.

Ted had seen him go nuts on a guy one time using a stapler. Not the kind you use to staple papers together, but the kind for putting up posters—the kind that sounds like a gun going off when you squeeze the handle. The guy had pissed Al off, so while Delray held his arms, Al started shooting staples into the poor bastard's face. He looked like he had zippers on both cheeks when Al was done.

"Well," Ted said, "did he also tell you that he didn't find anything wrong? Did he tell you that we walked him through where every fuckin' nickel went? But he still gave us this something-don't-smell-right bullshit, and he scared the hell out of Greg."

"But not you," Al said, the corners of his mouth pulled up slightly.

"That's right. Not me. And he didn't scare me because I didn't do anything wrong." Ted hesitated, then with a little catch in his voice, he added, "He killed my best friend."

Then he wished immediately that he hadn't said that; that was maybe just a little over the top.

Al studied Ted for a moment. There was no twinkle in his eyes now. "You know," he said, "when I met you there in Vegas the first time, I was impressed. You were a smart kid, not a fuck-off. A serious kid. And that's why I sent you to school and that's why you got the job you got. But you remember what I told you about being smart?"

Ted nodded.

"What did I tell you?" Al said.

"You said to never start thinking that I was smarter than everyone else."

"That's right." Al paused a beat before he said, "You don't think you're smarter than everyone else now, do you, Ted?"

"No," Ted said.

Al studied Ted's face, maybe to see if Ted would squirm or something, like he was such a wise ol' guinea that he'd be able to tell if Ted was lying. Finally, thank God, he nodded and said, "Good. I'm real glad to hear that."

Al stood up and lumbered over to the coffee pot. "You wanna cup?" he asked. Ted shook his head no.

"A danish, maybe? They're from Costello's. They're good."

"No, I'm all right," Ted said. *Let's just get this over with.*

Al poured himself a cup of coffee then sat back down at the table, the chair creaking under his weight.

"Now, I didn't tell Pat to pick up Greg the other day," Al said, "but I don't mind that he did. Pat's worked for me for a long time. He's got good instincts."

"Jesus, Al! Are you saying you believe him? That you think I'm—"

Al held up his hand. "No, that's not what I'm saying. I'm saying that I don't mind that Pat wanted to have a little talk with Greg, one-on-one. And in a way, maybe it's okay what happened to Greg. It's not good to have a guy around who panics that easy." Then Al chuckled. "But I can kinda understand why he did. Delray, over there, he can be kind of . . . Oh hell, what's the word? *Unsettling,* yeah that's it."

The comment elicited no reaction from Delray.

"Anyway," Al said, "Pat's sorry for what happened to Greg. Ain't you, Pat?"

McGruder, his eyes boring into Ted's, nodded.

Bullshit he was sorry.

"So it's time to move on," Al said, "and here's what we're gonna do. Pat's gonna help out at the casino for a while, you being shorthanded and all."

Ted started to protest but restrained himself.

"You guys will get to know each other better, develop some confidence in each other. That sorta thing. And Pat, he'll help you find a guy to replace Greg."

Oh, this was just great. Not only would McGruder watch him like a hawk, eventually he'd have his own handpicked spy in Ted's casino. This also meant that although Al didn't think Ted had done anything wrong, he wasn't a hundred percent sure. Maybe ninety-nine percent, but not a hundred percent. But what could he do?

"Sounds good to me," Ted said. Looking at McGruder he asked, "You want a room in the casino or do you want me to find you an apartment someplace in town?" Before McGruder could answer, he said to Al, "Oh, but there is one thing."

"What's that?" Al said, his brow wrinkling, thinking maybe Ted was going to give him an argument, maybe want it clarified as to who was in charge.

"If the amount Pat eats affects the bottom line," Ted said, "don't go blaming me."

Al tipped back his head and laughed like that was the funniest thing he'd ever heard.

McGruder just looked at Ted, his eyes narrow slits in the layers of fat, glittering like a pig's.

<hr />

Ted started his car and drove away from Al's house. A block later, he slammed on the brakes and slammed his hands against the steering wheel.

He felt like his head was caught in the jaws of a vice—and McGruder was the one cranking the handle. When McGruder had looked at the casino's books the other day, he'd been skeptical about their losses. So Ted had proved to McGruder—by sacrificing that poor bastard Gleason—that the story about losing money on a load of hijacked fish had been true and, by extension, that everything else they had told him was true as well. And it had slowed McGruder down with the time spent for Delray to go up to Portsmouth, confirm the story, and get back to Philly. But McGruder obviously still believed—data be damned, listening only to his oversize gut—that Ted was hiding something.

On one hand, Greg getting killed—or killing himself—was a blessing. If Delray had just *stared* at Greg for a couple of minutes, Greg would have told McGruder everything. But Greg's death was also a potential disaster. McGruder hadn't been able to figure out how Greg had doctored the books to hide a half-million-dollar loss—a loss that should never have happened—but he'd only spent two hours trying. If McGruder was there every day, and started playing with the spreadsheets. . . . Well, Greg had built a mathematical house of cards and it just might collapse if McGruder pulled at it hard enough.

He was running out of time. He had to get the money back, but more importantly, he needed to get federal funding for the project. If he got the project moving again, Al wouldn't give a damn about how he'd lost the half a million—that is, he wouldn't give a damn provided Ted got the money back. But to do either of those things—to get the money back or get the project restarted—he had to get the politician on board.

He'd go see the lobbyist tomorrow. He'd called the damn guy two days ago but he'd been out of town, plus, after thinking about it, Ted had decided this wasn't the sort of thing he wanted to talk about on the phone. So tomorrow he'd go see him in person, and if the guy didn't come through for him, maybe he'd have Gus give him a beat down. Not that beating the lobbyist would solve his problems; it would just feel good to make someone else feel some pain.

10

"Come on, Emma. Help me out here."

Emma was pulling weeds, her butt pointed rudely at DeMarco, as she uprooted offending flora. She was wearing shorts, an old T-shirt from the New York marathon, and a long-billed baseball cap that had a piece of cloth attached to the back to protect her neck from the sun. On her knees were padded knee protectors, the type carpet-layers wear. She pulled the weeds rapidly, and DeMarco would swear that each time she yanked one she muttered a little curse as if she was condemning the unwanted plant to a hot green hell.

Emma had a large yard surrounding her spacious home in McLean and by early summer her place would look like the grounds at Versailles. But to reach this state of horticultural perfection, each spring Emma went berserk, planting and reseeding and pruning—and doing whatever else it was that fanatic gardeners did. And during this period she reminded DeMarco of the *Star Trek* episode about Spock's sex life.

Vulcans, according to Gene Roddenberry, had sex about every seven years and just before they mated, they went mad—not an unexpected outcome considering the period of abstinence. At the peak of their mating cycle your typical pointy-eared, unemotional Vulcan became this crazed loony who would decapitate his friends if they frustrated his need to procreate. And this was Emma in the spring—except it wasn't celibacy that made her insane; it was the need to revitalize her yard, and she wouldn't return to normal until the job was complete.

"I just told you," Emma said, still not looking at him. "Neil's on vacation and I don't know where he is."

"Yeah, but there must be some way to track him down."

Emma didn't answer. She was frowning at something she'd just pulled from the earth, as if the plant in her hand was some particularly malevolent species, maybe the Ebola virus of weeds.

"Emma!" DeMarco said. "How do I find him?"

Neil called himself an "information broker." The truth behind this ambiguous job description was that Neil, for a substantial fee, could find out anything you wanted to know about your fellow citizens. Most often Neil performed his magic by bribing folks who work in places that stockpile privileged data: the IRS, Google, Social Security, banks, credit card and cell phone companies. But if Neil couldn't find what you needed to know with a simple bribe, he and his small staff were capable of hacking through firewalls and bugging phones and offices. The only reason Neil wasn't the corpulent prison bride of a tattooed man named Bubba was because he was often employed by agents of the federal government, agents who didn't have the patience or the inclination to get the necessary warrants.

"Neil and his wife are on an island somewhere," Emma said, "taking a second honeymoon. He doesn't want to be found. He wants to make love on the sand at sunset."

"Oh, please!" DeMarco said. The thought of Neil naked and having sex was beyond revolting.

"He had to cancel his first honeymoon," Emma said, still examining the wicked weed, "when they arrested him for . . . well, for something. He was never convicted, of course, but he had to postpone his honeymoon to deal with the problem."

He was never convicted, DeMarco thought, because he was probably working for you and Uncle Sugar.

"Well how 'bout that little dweeb he works with?" DeMarco said. "What's-his-name, Bobby something, with the dreadlocks."

Emma stopped pulling weeds and turned to look at him. "Bobby Prentiss is not a *dweeb*," she said. "He's brilliant."

Everyone was brilliant but DeMarco. "Good," he said. "So since he's so brilliant, maybe he can help me."

"Have you ever tried to communicate with Bobby, Joe?"

"Yeah, once." Bobby was a man who could go for days without uttering a word. It seemed as if it was almost painful for him to talk to other members of his species.

"And?" Emma said.

"And it's easier to gossip with God," DeMarco admitted.

Emma stood up and emptied her small box of dead weeds into a larger container full of dead weeds. A genocide, of sorts, was in progress.

Emma was tall and slim and regal—even wearing a goofy hat. She had short hair that DeMarco thought was gray until the light struck it from a certain angle and then he thought it was blonde. She was several years older than him, but she could run him ragged on a racquetball court, which she did every couple of months when she couldn't find anyone else to beat. The marathon T-shirt she wore was from a race she ran in three years ago.

DeMarco wasn't sure he could even walk twenty-six miles.

"I don't understand all this insider trading stock crap," DeMarco said. "You're rich. Help me out here."

"What makes you think I'm rich?" Emma said. "I'm a retired civil servant living on a pension."

"Yeah, right. A pensioner that drives a new Mercedes and has a home in McLean that I'm guessing would sell for about two mil."

"Maybe I inherited my home," Emma said.

"Well did you?" DeMarco asked.

"Maybe," Emma said.

Emma delighted in being enigmatic. She *was* a retired civil servant: retired from the Defense Intelligence Agency. She'd been a spy—and maybe she was still a spy. She'd kept so many secrets during her career that she continued to keep secrets even when they didn't matter; it was habit she could not break.

"So are you going to help me or not?" DeMarco said.

"No. I have to get bulbs into the ground, I have bushes to prune, and this lawn . . . My God, look at it!"

DeMarco thought her lawn looked like one of the putting greens at Augusta National, but then he had fairly low standards when it came to yards and gardens. He wanted to replace the grass in front of his Georgetown home with Astroturf.

Before DeMarco could say that keeping Molly Mahoney out of jail was more important than tulip bulbs, Emma said, "But let me see if I've got all this straight. The SEC says that they have a trail of stock purchases originating from an Internet café. The stocks were purchased using half a million dollars that was mysteriously placed in Molly's new bank account. Molly claims she doesn't know where the money came from, claims she didn't buy any stock, says she never set up a new bank account, and then points the finger at this man Campbell because she heard him make a funny-sounding phone call a few years ago. Is that right?"

"Yeah, but you make it sound like . . ."

"Just for the sake of argument, what makes you so sure that Molly didn't do it?"

"Well, other than the fact that she's not the type of person who'd do something like this . . ."

"Unlike her father," Emma said.

". . . she doesn't have half a million bucks."

"How do you know?"

"Well, I don't for sure. But she lives in this shitty little one-bedroom apartment and her father said she was saving up money to make a down payment on a house."

"Or maybe she lives in a cheap apartment because she was saving her money to invest in the market on inside information."

"Come on, Emma! Whose side are you on?"

"Doesn't the half million bother you?"

"What do you mean?"

"Well, let's say someone was trying to frame Molly. Would you blow five hundred grand on a frame? Don't you think that's excessive? Wouldn't five thousand have worked just as well?"

This was the same conclusion DeMarco had come to earlier.

"I don't think it was a frame, Emma. I think they may have been using Molly for cover. They—*somebody*—set up a new bank account in her name, deposited the half mil in the account, bought the stock, and planned to close the account after they'd transferred the profits back to themselves. If everything had gone right, they would have made a quarter million bucks and nobody would have been the wiser. But if things went bad, which they did, then Molly's the one who ends up with her head on the block."

DeMarco was about to tell Emma his other theory, that somebody was using Molly to get to her father, but before he could, she said, "What happens when Molly gets her monthly bank statement and suddenly discovers she's half a million dollars richer?"

"With a lot of banks, you don't get paper statements these days. You have to go online to look at account activity, and she wouldn't go online to look at an account she didn't know she had. And if they sent her e-mails, she wouldn't see them because whoever did this set up an e-mail address she never used."

"Do you know all this for a fact?"

"No, but it sounds logical—*if* you believe Molly's innocent."

"Humpf," Emma said—and DeMarco didn't know what that meant.

"How 'bout for now," he said, "you assume she's not a crook. What would you do next?"

Emma shrugged. "See if the SEC has anything on this guy Campbell, I guess. See if he's really living large the way Molly says. And see if someone close to Campbell sold off a bunch of stock in this bottle company right after Molly heard him talking about it."

"How the hell would I do that?" DeMarco whined. "I don't have any way to find out if a guy dumped a bunch of stock. But if Neil was here . . ."

"Then let's just assume that Campbell's richer than he should be. Go accuse him of insider trading and see how he acts. Better yet, tell him Molly has given him up to the SEC, that she knows he's guilty, and she's going to trade his butt for a reduced sentence. Do that, and see if he runs to his partner."

"What partner?"

"You said that the SEC has been watching Reston Tech for years. If Campbell was making money illegally off stock tips related to Reston's research, I imagine the SEC would have nailed him by now, just the way they nailed Molly. So if he's involved with some kind of insider trading scheme, he *has* to have an accomplice not connected with the company. All you have to do is find the accomplice. Now, where did I put my pruning shears?"

Emma found the shears. They had blades sharp enough to decapitate gophers. Emma opened and closed the jaws of the tool a couple of times as if she were warming up for an athletic event: full-contact gardening.

11

Preston Whitman was a lobbyist, a very good one, and his job was to convince politicians to vote the way his clients wanted. And Whitman's clients paid his outrageous fees primarily for one thing: his ability to gain access to those in power. Access was everything. Once Whitman had slithered through a legislator's door, he had a small arsenal with which to persuade: a pledge to contribute generously to the lawmaker's next campaign; a position on a board after the pol retired; a special deal on an Aspen condo. He also had at his disposal think tanks staffed with experts—generals and geniuses and ex–cabinet members—and they could develop a viable, well-reasoned argument for any position. They could demonstrate why it was acceptable—hell, even patriotic—to sell flammable pajamas for toddlers if that's what Whitman's clients sold.

And that's why Ted Allen had hired Preston Whitman. He'd paid the man a hundred thousand dollars to get something done in Congress, but so far the lobbyist had failed to deliver. Whitman had warned him in advance that he couldn't promise to accomplish what Ted wanted, but Ted didn't care. In Ted's world, if you give a guy a hundred Gs, you expect to see results. And Al wasn't happy either. Al thought Ted had used the money to bribe a congressman; Al approved of a bribe because he could understand a bribe. What he couldn't understand was paying a lobbyist to influence several congressmen in a legal—or mostly legal—manner. Al was a dinosaur, but one with a heavy tail and very big teeth.

Ted had been working on the project for over three years and had spent over a million dollars of Al's money on it, including Whitman's fee. If he pulled it off, Al would think that the sun rose and set with him—and *fuck* McGruder. But if he didn't pull it off . . . well, he didn't know what the consequences would be, but he knew they wouldn't be good. Maybe fatally not good. You could just never tell with Al.

The project. Atlantic City currently had a convention center that was less than fifteen years old, but the place was already falling apart. And separate from the existing convention center were bus and railroad terminals that brought the suckers in from New York and Philly and D.C. Ted had managed to convince the right people that AC needed a new convention center, and it should include terminals for trains and buses and the terminals should be connected to a retail mall like Union Station in D.C. To get support for the project, he'd bribed a few folks and blackmailed others, but mostly he'd just sold the idea—just the way any legitimate businessman would do. He'd convinced the city council guys and the mayor and state representatives that a new convention center was good for AC, good for the people, good for jobs and taxes.

The hardest guy to convince had been Al—convincing him that he'd have to invest a little money to make a lot of money. McGruder, of course, had been against him every step of the way, telling Al that he'd just be pouring money down the drain. But in the end Ted won. Yep, he lined up all the ducks, and it hadn't been easy.

The project benefited Al's operation in multiple ways. The site for the new structure would require two lots that Ted had acquired, and they'd pay Al ten times what he'd paid for the lots. The work itself would go to a certain construction company—they had an absolute lock on that—and Al would get a big kickback from the company. The construction company would also be forced to use union labor, and Al had his fingers in two of the biggest unions—carpenters and electricians—and he'd get a percentage of the money collected for dues and pensions. And it didn't end there. Al was a legitimate partner in a cement factory located outside Trenton, and Ted made sure that the ground rules specified using products made in Jersey if they were available—and it was going to take a lot of cement to build the convention center. The Jersey politicians, of course, had backed him on this. The icing on the cake was the project included a moving walkway to get the suckers from the new bus and train terminal to the boardwalk, and the first place it would stop would be the Atlantic Palace.

Yes, it was a terrific plan, and it was Ted's plan, and they wre going to make millions off the deal—and then six months ago, it had all fallen apart.

The governor of New Jersey, a guy they'd been paying off for years, went and had himself a stroke. The bastard now had as much brain activity as a radish, and the lieutenant governor, who'd be in the job the next two years, was a rich, righteous son of a bitch and Ted didn't have anything he could use to force the man to play ball.

The lieutenant governor wasn't opposed to the project—he could see how it would benefit Atlantic City and the good people of New Jersey—but he got it into his thick head that the federal government should kick in a little money. His logic was that the convention center should be part of all those other federal stimulus programs designed to get the economy moving, and he decided—arbitrarily—that the Fed's portion should be a hundred million. Why a hundred million, nobody knew, but the guy was adamant the Feds had to share in the cost.

The problem, of course, was that other than the New Jersey delegation, very few people in Washington were inclined to give the state a hundred million bucks, so now the project wasn't moving forward. And that had been Preston Whitman's job: to get a rider attached to some bill—any fuckin' bill—that would send a measly hundred million to Jersey, but Whitman hadn't been able to make it happen.

Which was why Ted had decided to pay Whitman a visit. He needed to get the damn guy moving, and he needed to get things back under control before McGruder sniffed something out.

———◆———

To make sure Whitman understood the possible consequences of failure, he brought Gus Amato with him. Ted had told Gus to wear a suit—and to leave the suit jacket unbuttoned so Whitman could see the gun in the shoulder holster. He'd also told Gus to take the damn earring out of his ear, but the idiot was still wearing his alligator skin cowboy boots. In spite of the boots, Gus had the intended impact: The entire time Ted was talking to Whitman, Gus stood behind Ted, staring dead-eyed at Whitman, and Whitman's eyes kept straying over to look at the gun.

As Gus stared and Whitman fidgeted, Ted explained the situation with Molly Mahoney. Molly was his ace in the hole; she was the pry bar he needed to get things unstuck. He didn't tell Whitman everything, but he told him enough.

"Wow," Whitman said when Ted was finished.

Wow? And this guy depended on his tongue to make a living. No wonder he hadn't made any progress.

"So do you think this will work?" Ted said.

"Maybe," Whitman said. "If we could get Mahoney behind the project, he'd be a huge help. But I have to warn you, Ted, John Mahoney can be very unpredictable."

"Just set up the meeting," Ted said. "And do it quick. You gotta be good for something."

———◆◆◆———

Preston Whitman sat at his desk for several minutes after Ted Allen left his office, thinking about Ted—and what Ted had told him.

Taking on Ted as a client had been a mistake—a huge mistake. The man just didn't understand how things worked in D.C. He particularly didn't understand the *pace* at which things worked. Ted dressed well, he spoke like an educated man, but underneath all that Whitman sensed that Ted had been raised rough and poor. He was a thug with a diploma. And that ape that he'd brought with him to the meeting . . . What the hell was that all about? What was Ted going to do? Break his legs if he didn't do what Ted wanted?

Unfortunately, the answer to that question was: Maybe.

But all Ted wanted him to do was set up a meeting. He could do that, or at least he thought he could. Like he'd told Ted, John Mahoney was unpredictable. Then it occurred to him that what Ted had told him could benefit several people, people much more important to his business than Ted Allen. The information Ted had given him, if properly exploited, could be used to hurt John Mahoney—and he could think of ten people in ten seconds who would like to hurt John Mahoney. If Ted's information was shared with too many people, however, it would dilute its value. So it was a matter of deciding the single best person to share it with, a person who would be of use to Preston Whitman not just today but in the future. He let his mind wander through the political landscape for a few minutes and made a selection.

There was a problem, however, and it was significant. If Ted found out that he had shared his information with someone else, Ted would be quite unhappy. But what would Ted do if he found out? Kill him? Maybe.

"Preston, I have to leave in about ten minutes, so you're gonna have to be quick, son."

"Of course, Congressman," Whitman said, "and I appreciate you taking the time to see me." He found Robert Fairchild calling him "son" a little annoying, as he and Fairchild were about the same age.

Big Bob Fairchild was one of the most influential Republicans in the House. He was forty-nine years old, six feet five inches tall, and slim as a whippet. His dark hair gleamed with whatever grease he applied to keep it in place and his eyes were small and black and cold. He would have been a handsome man if he'd had a chin.

Fairchild had never struck Whitman as a person of staggering intellect, but he did have other attributes that made him a good politician: he could be quite charismatic when he made the effort; he was an above-average speaker, particularly if someone else wrote the speech; and he was good at forging alliances. His constituents liked him because his first loyalty was to his home state—versus the country—and thus lots of federal dollars, whether needed or not, ended up in his district.

The most significant thing about Big Bob, however, was that he was popular with Hispanics, more popular than any other white Republican. He couldn't actually speak Spanish but he could give a short speech in the language if the words were spelled out phonetically on a teleprompter, and a number of people on his staff were Hispanic. The real force behind Fairchild, however, was his wife. She could speak Spanish fluently and devoted considerable energy—and money—to Hispanic causes to increase her husband's popularity with that demographic. It was a well-established fact that Fairchild had a seat in the House only because of his wife's money and influence; it was unconfirmed rumor that she totally dictated her husband's political agenda.

Because of his potential ability to pull in Hispanic voters, and regardless of whether it was due to his wife's acumen or his own, there was a very good possibility that Robert Fairchild would be his party's choice for vice president in the next national election—a situation that didn't bother Preston Whitman as a lobbyist but which did bother him as a private citizen. Whitman had always felt that the man who sat in the Oval Office—and the man who was a heartbeat away from the Oval Office—should be significantly smarter than the folks who had elected them, although history had shown this was often not the case. In fact, it was rarely the case.

"So get to it," Fairchild said. "You said on the phone you had something that could help my nephew." Fairchild wasn't looking at Whitman when he spoke; he was answering e-mails on his BlackBerry, pecking away with two clumsy thumbs.

"Yes, I believe I do, sir," the lobbyist said, speaking to the top of Fairchild's oily head. "And as I told you when I called, I believe this information can do more than just help your nephew. I know he's one of your primary concerns right now, but if this information is, uh, properly handled, I believe it could not only help Little Bob but could also be used to assist you in other legislation you're working on." Whitman meant legislation that was important to his paying clients.

Whitman was hoping Fairchild would ask him to be more specific about how the information should be handled, but Fairchild didn't. Instead he snapped, "Don't call him Little Bob. He goes by Evans now. You know that."

"Sorry," Whitman muttered.

Big Bob Fairchild represented Arizona's 7th congressional district. His nephew, Robert Evans Fairchild, was the congressman from the adjoining 8th district, and was known as Little Bob although he was almost as tall as his uncle. The reason for this was that Big Bob actually represented *two* congressional districts because Little Bob did whatever his uncle told him to do. The last couple of years, Little Bob, in an attempt to distinguish himself from his uncle, had taken to calling himself R. Evans Fairchild instead of Bob or Robert—but nobody called him Evans. That just sounded too stupid.

The other thing about Little Bob was that he was currently up to his neck in shit with a certain special prosecutor.

Whitman told Fairchild what he'd learned from Ted Allen. He also told him of Ted's desire to get federal funding for a new convention center in Atlantic City.

"And you think this Allen person has connections to organized crime?" Fairchild said.

"I think so, but I don't know for sure."

"And does the SEC or Justice know about any of this? Allen, his ties to Molly Mahoney, any of it?"

"Again I don't know, but if they do, it shouldn't be too hard to find out."

"No, it won't be," Fairchild said. "But I would assume they don't know. That sort of information would have been leaked by now."

"That would be my guess, too, sir," Whitman said. He was being so obsequious he was almost disgusted with himself. Almost.

Fairchild licked his lips. Maybe it was because of Fairchild's southwestern roots, but Whitman instantly thought of a gila monster—those orange and black toads with a poisonous bite. So when Fairchild moistened his upper lip, Whitman imagined a reptile's tongue flicking out, tasting the air for prey.

"I want you to know I appreciate you telling me this, Preston." Fairchild said. He paused a beat, then added, "You may consider that I owe you one."

For a lobbyist, having a man who might become the next vice president of the United States "owe you one" was a good day's work.

Fairchild pushed a button on his phone. "Call my wife and tell her I'm going to be a few minutes late for the party."

His secretary hesitated, then said, "If you leave right now, Congressman, I think you can be there on time."

"Damn it all, Dolores, just make the call."

It really pissed him off that his own staff thought he was intimidated by his spouse. He also knew that when he saw her, he'd have to endure his wife's sarcastic comments about his tardiness, but right now he didn't care. He needed to be alone, he needed to think. Information was like a hot cup of coffee—it cooled off quickly—and he had to figure out the best way to use the information that Whitman had given him.

A few years ago a lobbyist named Jack Abramoff had taken a ton of money from a tribe of Native Americans. He spent a large portion of the Indians' money on himself and then took another large portion and flung it at various congressmen to influence their votes on things unrelated to what the Indians wanted. Abramoff was eventually caught and a few congressmen and their aides were jailed or forced to resign. Those politicians not indicted made speeches about corruption in government, and then tweaked a few laws to limit how brazenly a lobbyist could bribe a legislator.

And then life went back to normal.

Six months ago, it appeared as if Abramoff's soul had left Jack's body and magically inserted itself into the corpus of another lobbyist, named Lucas Mayfield. Mayfield, thus possessed, then repeated Abramoff's transgressions as if he were making a sequel to Jack's shoddy life. And, as had been the case with Abramoff, a special prosecutor had been assigned to hunt down the stupid and avaricious, and one of the people currently being investigated—one of the stupid—was Little Bob.

Fairchild could have strangled his nephew for having become involved with a man like Mayfield, but the person he really blamed for Little Bob's problems was John Mahoney. When it became apparent that most of the congressmen that Mayfield had bribed were

Republicans, and right after it became known that Little Bob was one of those Republicans, Mahoney had pressured the president, via the press, to assign a special prosecutor. Had a bunch of Democrats been involved, Mahoney would never have done this, but since it was Republicans, and since one of those Republicans was Fairchild's nephew, Mahoney made speeches about the need to sweep *his* House clean. The damn hypocrite.

Big Bob Fairchild had always envisioned a political dynasty, like the Bushes or the Kennedys, but unfortunately his wife gave him only one child, a daughter, and then had her tubes tied to make sure that her fugure would not be ruined by subsequent offspring. And his daughter, also unfortunately, had neither the inclination nor the temperament for politics, so all Fairchild had was his nephew. By now he knew that Little Bob would always be *Little* Bob, and that the Fairchild dynasty would never be, but his nephew was kin and he'd be damned if he'd let a conniving bastard like Mahoney destroy him.

12

Mahoney was thinking that this had to be the dumbest system of government ever invented.

The Democrats wanted to raise taxes on poultry products to make sure chickens didn't have some kind of bug that was killing people all over China, and a congresswoman from Mississippi had been going on for almost ten minutes about how she was outraged—*outraged!*—by the proposal. According to her, the tax was going to put poor Mississippi chicken farmers out of business, and she said this knowing, as did everyone else in the chamber, that a giant conglomerate based in Delaware reared almost all the chickens in America.

Mahoney at this point, however, didn't care who the chickens killed or who would be affected by the tax. His right knee had been lacerated by a grenade in Vietnam and it ached when he sat too long. His back ached as well, but the cause of that pain was less glamorous than a combat injury: his back hurt because of the stress placed on it by the weight of his gut. He just wanted this woman to shut up so he could vote, then go back to his office, take a leak, have a drink, and put an ice pack on his knee.

The congresswoman also knew—as did every other member present —that no matter what she said, folks were going to vote the way they'd already decided to vote—and straight down party lines. God forbid that anyone on either side of the aisle should be bold enough to stray from the herd. So the politicians made speeches, not because they expected to change anyone's mind, but so the folks back home might see a clip of them on the local news battling for home state pork.

What a dumb system of government.

Finally, the congresswoman stopped talking. Thank God. But now another guy—a Democrat—Christ, what the hell was his name?—was jumping up so he could tell the cameras how wrong the congresswoman was. *Finally*, the time for debate expired, stopping all the nonsense, and everybody cast their vote as they'd intended all along. Mahoney rose from his chair, in a hurry now, as his bladder was about to burst.

"Sir, do you have a moment?"

Mahoney turned to see who was speaking. It was a lobbyist named Preston Whitman.

Whitman had always reminded Mahoney of that actor Liam Neeson: he was a tall man with large hands and *enormous* feet—those puppies had to be size 15s—and he had a big nose and a wide mouth and hair that always looked windswept, as if he had just stepped from a convertible.

It really pissed Mahoney off that Whitman was on the floor of the House. Whenever he saw lobbyists on the floor he felt the same ire that Jesus must have felt when He saw the money changers in the Temple. Well, maybe that was a poor analogy, but it still pissed him off.

"Sorry, Preston, but I'm expecting a call from the White House," Mahoney lied. "If you need to see me, just make an appointment." There was no way Whitman—whose clients didn't contribute to Mahoney—would get an appointment, and both men knew it.

"I need to talk to you about your daughter, sir. About Molly. I have some information you need to hear."

"My daughter?" Mahoney said, and he felt his face begin to redden. "You listen to me, Whitman. My family is off-limits to you and every other snake on K Street, and if you ever . . ."

"Mr. Speaker, I'm going to be at the Hay Adams at seven p.m. For your daughter's sake, I'd suggest you meet me there for a drink. You need to hear what I know before anyone else finds out. I'm trying to *help* you, sir."

"What?" Mahoney said, but he was speaking to Whitman's back as Whitman was already walking away.

Goddamnit, Molly, you're killin' me.

13

DeMarco had been waiting outside Kay Kiser's office for twenty minutes; she wasn't about to interrupt her schedule just because he had decided to drop by. As he waited, he dripped oil of clove from a small bottle onto his index finger, then stuck his finger in his mouth and rubbed the oil against his fractured tooth. This crude remedy had been suggested by his mother, and it seemed to help, but he was a little concerned. The label on the clove-oil bottle said the product was meant to be used to "flavor potpourri" and to "avoid contact with skin, lips and tongue," none of which sounded good for a dental anesthetic.

Kiser finally opened her door and made an irritated motion for him to step into her office. Today she was dressed in a short-sleeved white blouse with an open collar and formfitting slacks. The only jewelry she wore was small gold studs in her ears. The woman just glowed with good health: high, hard cheekbones; clear eyes; perfect muscle tone. He was willing to bet that she kept to a regular . . . no, make that a *rigid* workout schedule: gym four times a week, jogged every other day, avoided junk food, and went to bed at the same time every night. He'd wager there were robots less disciplined than Kay Kiser.

On her desk was a framed photograph of her when she was younger, standing between a middle-aged couple. Relaxed and with a smile on her face, Kiser was stunning. The people in the photo were probably her parents; they looked like nice people. Other than the family portrait there were no other personal touches in the room: no executive toys, no plants, no poster of that Tuscan vineyard she'd once visited. Completely obsessed with her job, as Randy Sawyer had said.

"I have a meeting in fifteen minutes," Kiser said, cramming papers into a briefcase as she spoke. "And I'll tell you nothing about our case against Ms. Mahoney other than what I told you the other day. Now, what do you want?"

DeMarco felt like giving her the punch line of an old, raunchy joke: *So I guess a blow job's out of the question*. But he didn't.

"I want to know if you've ever investigated a guy at Reston Tech named Douglas Campbell."

"I don't know who you're talking about, and if I did, I wouldn't tell you anyway."

But DeMarco saw something in her eyes—this *flick*. Kay Kiser was a species rarely encountered: a lawyer who was a poor liar.

DeMarco had not really wanted to talk to Kiser about the Douglas Campbell phone call that Molly had overheard. He had wanted to talk to Randy Sawyer, but when he called Sawyer's office, he was informed that Sawyer was attending a conference in Las Vegas. It had become fashionable for government agencies to hold conferences in Vegas, not because the bureaucrats wanted to gamble and see bare-breasted showgirls, but instead because the city gave them good deals on hotel rooms. Yeah, you bet. So because Sawyer was on a taxpayer-funded boondoggle, and since Neil wasn't available to help him, he was forced to talk to Kiser.

"I got it from a pretty good source," DeMarco said, possibly selling Randy Sawyer right down the river, "that somebody over at Reston Tech was involved in three big insider swindles in the last twenty years, and that the SEC never caught the folks involved. And since I know from this source that you've probably looked at everybody working at Reston, I was just wondering if Douglas Campbell was ever a person of interest."

"Who told you about those cases?" Kiser said.

"I probably shouldn't tell you," DeMarco said, "but it was a guy over at Justice."

DeMarco was a much better liar than Kiser. In fact, if lying ever became an Olympic event, DeMarco figured he had a pretty good chance of making the American team. Mahoney would get the gold medal, of course, but still . . .

"And if you don't tell me what I want to know," he said, "Molly's lawyers are going to ask the same question in a long, formal subpoena. And you know what a hassle that can be."

Lawyers would submit a subpoena asking for the contents of an entire library when all they wanted was one book.

Kay Kiser stood a moment without moving, her teeth clenched, a little muscle jumping in her jaw. DeMarco could tell that she was the type who hated to compromise—and she didn't like being threatened either.

"So give me a subpoena," she finally said. "I'm not going to help Molly Mahoney's lawyers develop their case."

"Oo-kay," DeMarco said. "But you've already confirmed the main thing my source told me, which is that something screwy has been going on over at Reston for a long time—long before Molly ever worked there. And I think you've investigated Campbell before, too."

Kiser's dark eyes flashed, emitting enough heat to melt steel.

"You people make me sick," she said. "Molly Mahoney is a privileged little brat who's committed a crime. But she has a big shot for a father who can afford a high-power defense team, and her lawyers are going to throw up a smoke-and-mirrors defense. They'll say that somebody stole little Molly's identity and opened accounts in her name, and that somebody else over at Reston is *really* the bad guy. And maybe they'll win, DeMarco, but I'll be damned if I'll help them. I'm going to do everything I can to put Molly Mahoney in a federal prison."

DeMarco was stunned by the force of her anger; she was acting like Molly had mugged her grandmother. "Jesus, Kay," he said, "can't you concede that it's even remotely possible that she could have been framed?"

"No! She wasn't framed. She did it!"

"Then what was her motive? Why would she do something like this?"

Kiser laughed. "You need to get to know your client a lot better, DeMarco."

What the hell did she mean by that?

DeMarco returned to his office, which was in the subbasement of the U.S. Capitol. Not the basement, the *sub*basement—and his work space was smaller than some walk-in closets. Located down the hall from him were the janitors, and across the hall was the emergency diesel generator room. His was not a power office. He did have a title, though. The flaking gold paint on the frosted glass of his office door proclaimed him *Counsel Pro Tem for Liaison Affairs.*

The title was John Mahoney's invention—and complete nonsense.

DeMarco had worked for Mahoney for a long time but there was no organizational chart that showed this to be the case. Mahoney preferred this in part because of DeMarco's family history and in part because he sometimes asked DeMarco to do things that he didn't want traced back to his office. This meant that if DeMarco was ever caught doing something inappropriate on his boss's behalf,

Mahoney could—and would—deny any connection to DeMarco's position.

DeMarco had a small refrigerator in his office, one just large enough to hold a six-pack of beer. He pulled a Coke out of the fridge—it was too early in the day for beer—popped the top on the can, took a careful sip to avoid cold liquid touching his temperamental tooth, and booted-up his computer. He wanted to know about Douglas Campbell.

If Neil had been available, DeMarco would have called him and Neil would have charged him—meaning the U.S. Treasury—a mind-boggling amount of money, but he would have turned Campbell's financial and personal life inside out and upside down. For Neil, most computer security systems were a weak joke, and within a couple of hours he would have examined Campbell's bank accounts, tax returns, and credit card statements; he would have learned about every investment Campbell had ever made and if the investment had turned a profit or not.

But Neil wasn't available—he was off with his bride, wallowing in pleasures of the flesh—so DeMarco did about the only thing he could do: he googled Douglas Campbell, and since the name was only slightly less common than John Smith, he got about two zillion hits. An hour later he found one article about the Douglas Campbell he cared about. The article was in the *Charlottesville Daily Progress* and was about the reunion of a University of Virginia football team that had gone to the Florida Citrus Bowl twenty four years before—where they lost. The reason the reunion made the papers was that a couple of the UVA players had gone on to play in the pros and one was a Hall of Famer. Campbell wasn't the Hall of Famer. He had played defensive tackle for the Cavaliers and his football career ended after college.

Having learned nothing other than the fact that Campbell had once played college football, DeMarco called a neighbor in Georgetown.

The neighbor lived across the street from him and worked at the IRS, and he answered DeMarco's questions every year when DeMarco was grappling with his tax return—usually at ten o'clock at night on April 14. The accountant liked DeMarco because his wife had become a teetotaler and wouldn't allow alcohol in their house, so if the poor guy wanted to enjoy the simple pleasure of drinking a beer, he'd find some excuse to visit DeMarco.

So the IRS accountant was a pal and a neighbor—but he wasn't exactly thrilled with the idea of giving DeMarco Campbell's Social Security number, which DeMarco needed. DeMarco, consequently, had to resort to pleading and lying. His neighbor knew he worked for Congress and the lie DeMarco told was that his interest in Campbell was related to a classified security issue, but he couldn't say exactly what the issue was.

"Look," he said, "I just need to check a few records related to this guy but if I call Homeland Security—which I could, of course— they'll take forever. Plus, if I get those guys involved, the next thing you know Campbell's on the no-fly list and he's got federal agents interviewing him. I don't think the guy's done anything wrong so I don't want to screw him like that, but I need to look into a few things and for that I need his DOB and his SS number. I mean, come on, you know me. It's not like I'm gonna steal the guy's identity or some-thing. Oh, hey, I forgot. The Nats are playing Pittsburgh tomorrow. Maybe you oughta drop by and watch the game with me and have a couple of beers."

His neighbor finally gave him what he needed, but he wouldn't give him any other information off Campbell's tax returns, so DeMarco's second call was to a company that performed credit checks.

Molly Mahoney had told him that Campbell appeared to live above his means, and DeMarco wanted to see if there was any evidence of this. Specifically, he wanted to know how much Campbell owed on his credit cards, the size of the mortgages on his two houses, and any outstanding loans he might have on cars and boats. The company he called worked mostly for banks trying to avoid lending money to folks trying to buy a home, and all they needed to do their job was Campbell's name, date of birth, and the Social Security number wheedled out of his neighbor.

The next thing DeMarco wanted to know was if Campbell had a criminal record—which he thought was pretty unlikely—and what he needed was some law enforcement agency to run Campbell's name through their database. DeMarco knew a few cops but he met almost all of them while working for Mahoney, and not under circumstances where they became his friends. One of them had wanted to arrest him. Neil, once again, could have obtained what he wanted, but since Neil wasn't there he called Perry Wallace, Mahoney's devious chief of staff.

Perry Wallace knew several cops who had political ambitions, like the desire to be appointed to a high-profile job in some federal law enforcement agency. Politics was all about connections and favors, and Perry Wallace had the connections. Normally, Perry would have refused to do DeMarco's legwork for him, but since DeMarco was working on something involving Mahoney's daughter, he reluctantly called a cop and asked him to do a record check on Campbell. The cop he called turned out to be the deputy chief of the D.C. Metropolitan Police Force, and he called DeMarco half an hour after Perry Wallace talked to him.

The deputy chief, a guy named Foster, sounded like he was irritated that he was having to waste his time on grunt work like a background check. He told DeMarco that Campbell had no convictions and, except for a couple of traffic tickets, hadn't had a brush with the law in over twenty years. But twenty-four years ago—the same year the Cavaliers lost in the Citrus Bowl—Campbell was arrested for drunk and disorderly, which for a college football player wasn't exactly earth-shattering news. But at the same time, he was also arrested for obstructing a homicide investigation—and that went way beyond your normal frat boy prank.

"But nothing ever came of it," Foster said. "He was never formally charged or indicted and the whole thing was dropped. And I can't tell from the records I was able to access what the whole thing was all about. All I've got here is a Charlottesville PD case number and the name of the detective who worked the case. And one other thing. The record is cross-referenced to another record involving a guy named Russell Mc-Grath who was arrested at the same time and for the same things but, like I said, nothing ever went to trial. It sounds like they just arrested these guys to rattle their cages, but since this all happened more than twenty years ago, I doubt if anyone will remember anything. Do you want the case numbers and the detective's name?"

"Yeah, I guess," DeMarco said, and wrote down the information.

DeMarco turned back to his computer and looked again at the article on the team reunion in Charlottesville. Russell (Rusty) McGrath had also been on the team. He was one of the guys who made the pros.

DeMarco sat for a moment, trying to decide if he should call the Charlottesville police department, and decided not to. Maybe he'd call them later if there seemed to be a reason for calling them, but he agreed with Foster that he'd most likely be wasting his time trying to find someone who remembered an arrest that happened almost a quarter century ago.

He looked at his watch. It was almost six—time to knock off for the day—and that's when the phone rang. It was the credit checkers, and the news they gave him wasn't what he'd expected at all.

He decided to go see Douglas Campbell.

14

―――◆◆◆―――

Douglas Campbell lived in Chevy Chase, Maryland.

His house was a behemoth with a three-car garage and had a front yard about as big as a soccer field. One of the garage doors was open, and DeMarco could see a Lexus SUV, this year's model, which sold for seventy or eighty grand if you got all the bells and whistles. And Molly had said that Campbell also owned a boat.

The credit checkers had told DeMarco that Campbell had an excellent credit rating. In fact, other than a couple of credit cards that he paid off monthly, he didn't owe anybody anything. He'd purchased his Maryland home for one point seven million ten years ago, and his "cottage" on Chesapeake Bay had cost six hundred grand, and neither place had an outstanding mortgage. Molly had told him that Campbell made around a hundred and fifty thousand a year; he couldn't imagine how he owned all the things he owned and was debt free. He either had an excellent financial adviser or a very rich wife—and DeMarco hoped this wasn't the case. If Campbell was completely legitimate that wouldn't help Molly.

DeMarco rang the doorbell. The woman who answered was a forty-something blonde wearing white shorts and a pink Izod T-shirt. She had a cute, upturned nose and was fashionably thin, but her skin was leathery from too much unprotected exposure to the sun. Ex-cheerleader was DeMarco's first impression. She'd probably been as cute as a button twenty years ago but her looks were fading, like a photograph left sitting too close to a window.

"Is Mr. Campbell available?" DeMarco asked.

"Doug?" she said, as if confused that DeMarco would be asking to see her husband in his own house. The woman swayed a bit as she stood in the doorway and DeMarco thought she might be drunk. The glass in her hand was another clue.

"Yes," DeMarco said.

"Oh. Well, he's out back, barbecuing. Ha!" she added, as if the idea of her husband cooking was hilarious. Not funny hilarious, but pathetic hilarious. "Why do you want to see him?" she then asked, her eyes narrowing, maybe thinking DeMarco was selling something.

"I work for Congress, Mrs. Campbell. I need to ask your husband some questions about an ongoing investigation."

"Is that right?" she said, but she was already losing interest and looking back at the television in the room behind her. *Entertainment Tonight* was on, and Nancy O'Dell was asking some teenage actress with arms the diameter of spaghetti if she might possibly have an eating disorder.

"Yes," DeMarco said. "May I come in please?"

"Nah, the place is a mess. Just walk around the side, that way, and you'll find the master chef. Ha!" she said again and closed the door.

DeMarco walked around the house as directed and saw Campbell—and the kidney-shaped swimming pool behind him. The patio he was standing on was constructed from stone that looked like granite, and Campbell's barbecue was big enough to roast a luau pig.

83

Campbell, as might be expected of an ex-college lineman, was a big man, at least six five. Also, as might be expected, twenty-plus years after his playing days, he was packing forty or fifty pounds he didn't need. He had thinning blond hair combed forward to provide the most coverage for his scalp, and his complexion was ruddy from drink, sun, and lack of exercise. He was wearing a blue apron over Bermuda shorts and a white T-shirt; the apron had a picture of a big red lobster lying on its back with X's for eyes. Campbell was using his two-thousand-dollar barbecue to grill two hot dogs.

"Mr. Campbell?" DeMarco said.

"Uh, hi," Campbell said. "What . . ."

"Your wife told me to come back here. My name's Joe DeMarco. I work for Congress and I need to talk to you."

"At this time of night?"

It was only seven p.m. "Yeah," DeMarco said. "When a situation involves the daughter of the highest ranking Democrat in the House, folks like me tend to work overtime."

"Oh, it's about Molly." Campbell shook his big head. "It's really a shame about her. I just can't believe it."

"That's good, Mr. Campbell, because nobody else believes it either."

"Well, that lady from the SEC sure as hell does. Man, I'd hate to have her down on my ass."

"I'm gonna let you in on a little secret, Mr. Campbell," DeMarco said. "The SEC knows that somebody at Reston Tech has been leaking insider information for twenty years. In other words, a long time before Molly Mahoney began working there."

But as long as you've been there.

"You're kidding," Campbell said.

DeMarco just stared at him.

"Hey, where are my manners?" Campbell said. "You wanna drink?"

"No," DeMarco said.

"Well, I'm gonna make myself another one. I'll be right back."

Campbell's reaction to DeMarco's statement about something criminal going on at his company hadn't been right. Too nonchalant. No big surprise. No big denial. Just *off.*

DeMarco looked through the sliding glass door that allowed entry to Campbell's kitchen from the patio. Campbell was mixing his drink, head down, his back to his wife, trying to ignore her, while she made angry, jabbing gestures at his back as she yammered at him.

Two drunks in an unhappy marriage, DeMarco thought.

Campbell came back to the pool, a gin and tonic in his hand. He took a gulp of his drink then turned the hot dogs on the grill. He had the heat up too high and the hot dogs were scorched black on the side that had been facing the flame.

"Does your wife work, Mr. Campbell?"

"Not unless you call hitting tennis balls work," Campbell said. "Anyway, what does my wife working have to do with . . ."

"You didn't seem particularly surprised when I told you that the SEC has been trying to find a criminal at Reston Tech for twenty years."

"Sure I'm surprised," Campbell said, "but if something like that's really going on, I sure as hell don't know anything about it."

"That's not what Molly says."

"What's that mean?"

It was time for DeMarco's big lie. "Molly overheard a conversation between you and another person in two thousand . . . Well, I'm not going to go into the details—we'll save those for the trial—but when the SEC finds out what she knows, they're going to start looking at you again, and this time they'll find something."

"Are you saying Molly's accused me of doing something illegal? Well, if she has, it's bullshit and she's lying to take the heat off herself. And I'll tell you something else, pal: this discussion is over. Right now. I'm not saying another word to you without a lawyer present."

"Now, I know you have a partner, and . . ."

"A partner? What are you . . ."

"And when Kay Kiser hears what Molly has to say, she'll find your partner."

"What in the *hell* are you talking about?"

"Do you know how the government makes most of its cases, Mr. Campbell? By rolling one of the people involved. WorldCom, Enron, Madoff—in all those cases, one guy rolled and told the government what all the other guys did. And the reason the one guy always rolls is the government grants him immunity. The trick is, you have to be the first guy to turn over. But if you wait, and if somebody else talks first, then you get nothing but time in the pen. In your case, a federal pen."

"This is outrageous! You get the hell off my property," Campbell said, glowering down at DeMarco. Ordinarily, DeMarco would have been concerned goading a guy Campbell's size, but Campbell was not only drunk, he also looked pretty foolish in his barbecue apron, his big gut pushing out the cloth.

DeMarco didn't move. "I think you live far above your means, Mr. Campbell. There's no way you can afford this place, your beach house, your boat, and all your cars and not be up to your neck in debt. But I did a credit check on you, and you're debt free."

"You gotta lotta goddamn nerve doing credit checks on me. Wait'll my lawyer hears about that. And I know my rights. It doesn't matter if you're from Congress, you can't interrogate me without a lawyer present."

"Sure, I can. I'm not a cop. I'm just the guy who's going to get Molly Mahoney off the hook—and if that means packing you off to prison for a dozen years, that's fine by me."

"I don't know what the fuck you're talking about!" Campbell shrieked. "I haven't done a damn . . ."

"Your hot dogs are burning, sir. And remember what I said: only the guy that rolls first gets a pass. Now, here's my card," DeMarco said and placed his business card—the one that had nothing on it but his name and phone number—facedown on the patio table.

And bon appétit, motherfucker.

15

———◆———

Mahoney ordered a Wild Turkey on the rocks and then looked around the bar of the Hay Adams Hotel. Oh, great. In one corner, a Republican senator was sitting with Ray Suarez, the PBS *NewsHour* guy. Three tables away was an assistant to the president's chief of staff talking to one of the White House lawyers—Mahoney wondered if someone at the White House was about to be indicted—and at the bar was a lady who was an undersecretary over at State. The State gal was patting the hand of a guy who wasn't her husband, and who looked about ten years younger than her. Ordinarily this would have piqued Mahoney's interest, but not tonight.

He hated meeting Preston Whitman in a place where Washington's political elite tended to eat and drink, but Whitman knew it would be a feather in his hat to be seen in a social setting meeting one-on-one with Mahoney, and he was taking full advantage of the situation.

Mahoney felt like he'd been kidnapped.

Whitman finally walked into the bar, his tardiness adding to Mahoney's mounting irritation. He gave Mahoney his Liam Neeson smile, waved cheerfully to another man in the room, and then strode over to Mahoney's table. One of his big feet bumped a table leg when he sat down, almost spilling Mahoney's drink. Out of the corner of his eye,

Mahoney could see the assistant to the president's chief of staff and Suarez both staring at him. Goddamnit.

After Whitman had ordered his drink, he said, "Thank you for meeting with me, sir, and I promise I won't waste your time. I asked to see you because a client I represent wants to help your daughter."

"You mean help with these false charges against her."

"Well, not exactly."

"Then why the hell are we here?" Mahoney said. If this meeting wasn't about his daughter's legal problems, Mahoney was going to string Preston Whitman up by his balls.

"Sir," Whitman said, "I represent a number of people in the gaming industry and . . ."

"The gaming industry? You mean *gambling*."

"It's not just gambling, sir. Gambling's a small part of it. The gaming industry is about entertainment, lodging, restaurants, retail stores. They provide jobs—union jobs—for thousands of people."

"Goddamnit. What the hell does this have to do with my daughter?"

Whitman grimaced and shook his head, as if something pained him deeply. "Congressman, your daughter owes one of my clients, the Atlantic Palace Casino in Atlantic City, over one hundred thousand dollars."

Mahoney had played political poker all his life and his face remained expressionless—but he felt like throwing up.

"In addition to the hundred thousand Molly owes my client, she also has an additional one hundred thousand dollars in credit card debt. I would assume the SEC knows about her credit card situation, but her obligation to the casino is not known to anyone but my client and myself."

"Let's just cut to the chase here," Mahoney said. "What the hell do you want?"

"My client wants to find some way to work this out, sir."

"What's to work out? If my daughter owes someone money, she'll pay it back."

"Well, in case she can't do that, my client feels he may be able to help in that regard," Whitman said.

"Oh, yeah," Mahoney said. "How's that?"

"He was thinking he might be able to, uh, consolidate her debt—pay off the credit card companies for her then give her a very generous interest rate."

"How generous?"

"Two percent."

"Just two," Mahoney said, making no attempt to hide his skepticism.

"Yes, sir. Which is certainly better than the eighteen or twenty percent that credit card companies charge. Furthermore, my client might be willing to defer payment on the debt for some period, say three months, if that would help. So how does that sound to you, sir?"

"Why that sounds just peachy, Whitman. Now get to the part about what I have to do to make all this happen."

"I'm afraid I can't do that, sir. My client is insisting on a meeting with you. He feels it would be best that there be no middle man—meaning myself—involved in all this. And I think he's right. We all want to do what's best to protect Molly's privacy."

"Is that some kind of threat?" Mahoney said, then realizing he was speaking too loudly, lowered his voice. "Are you saying that if I don't meet with this guy you'll talk to the press?"

The media coverage for Molly's arrest had actually been fairly quiet. She made the news, both print and television, the day she was arraigned—photos included, of course—and there were follow-up stories the next day, but after that the media turned to other more entertaining matters. Fortunately, at least for Molly, the day after her arrest another Hollywood star managed to ingest enough cocaine to kill himself and the president's wife made a comment about slave labor at a state dinner that had the Chinese all fired up. But if Molly's gambling problems became known, the newsies would swing back into action and for his sake, as well as his daughter's, Mahoney didn't want that.

"Of course not, sir," Whitman said. "I would never talk to media about something that affects a member of your family."

The hell you wouldn't, you oily-mouthed prick, but Mahoney didn't say that. He drained his drink and crunched down on the ice cubes in his glass. He pretended he was crunching down on Preston Whitman's bones. Finally, he spoke.

"I'm gonna pass. I can handle a couple hundred thousand, so I don't need the loan or a meeting with your client. And if the media finds out about my daughter's gambling, so be it. But if they do, life for you in this town will become hell on earth, Whitman. You won't be able to get access to a janitor in the Capitol, much less a politician."

Mahoney rose to leave, acting as if he didn't have a worry in the world. But he'd actually lied to Whitman. In his current financial situation, coming up with two hundred grand might not be that easy.

"Uh, Congressman," Whitman said. "I'm afraid Molly's problem is bigger than two hundred thousand dollars. Much bigger."

Mahoney sat back down.

Jesus, Molly, what have you done?

16

———◆◆◆———

When Alice walked into the restaurant, DeMarco was so shocked his mouth dropped open.

Alice was a short, big-busted woman who was pushing fifty, and the last time DeMarco had seen her, her hair was dyed platinum blonde and she probably weighed a hundred and sixty pounds. The woman walking toward his table had honey-colored hair that perfectly framed her narrow face and she weighed, maybe, a hundred and twenty pounds. And there was something different about her face—her jaw was firmer, or something.

"Wow!" DeMarco said when she sat down. "You look great."

"Divorce will do that to you," Alice said, obviously pleased by DeMarco's reaction. "After twenty-two years, I finally divorced the asshole, got a face-lift, and joined Weight Watchers and a gym. I also got a boyfriend, this cute little Nicaraguan guy who lives down the block. I think he just wants to marry me so he can become a citizen but I don't care. He's a tiger in bed."

DeMarco winced when he heard this. He didn't want to hear about Alice's sex life.

"What about you, DeMarco? Are you married yet?"

"No."

"Girlfriend?"

"Not at the moment. I was going with this woman who worked for the CIA but she got transferred to Afghanistan. Actually, she asked to be transferred to Afghanistan."

"Why? Were you cheating on her?"

"No. She just . . . No, I wasn't cheating on her."

Alice shook her head. "How many serious girlfriends have you had since I've known you, since your divorce?"

DeMarco had to think about that. "Three," he said.

"Three—and you're still single. What's wrong with you?"

"Nothing's *wrong* with me."

"Well, something must be wrong. You need a wife, DeMarco. You're the kind of man who needs . . . You need *direction*."

"I don't need . . . Never mind. Did you get what I asked for?"

Alice, in addition to providing unwanted counseling regarding De-Marco's personal life, worked for a telephone company. He'd met her on one of the first assignments Mahoney gave him, but since he'd met Neil through Emma, he now rarely called to ask for her help. And she helped him, of course, because he paid her—and because she liked him in a pushy, aggravating, big sister way.

"Yeah," Alice said.

DeMarco wanted to know if Campbell had called anyone after he visited him last night—and Alice with her job and her contacts could tell him. DeMarco figured that if Campbell actually was the insider at Reston, he had to have a partner, as Emma had said—a partner who made investments on the basis of the information Campbell provided and then hid the trail from the SEC. What DeMarco was hoping was that after he had lied to Campbell about Molly Mahoney having information she could pass on to the SEC, Campbell might panic and call his partner—assuming he even had a partner and was doing anything illegal. DeMarco had confronted Campbell solely because Campbell appeared to live above his means and because of a phone call Molly had overheard two years ago that might have been perfectly innocent. He'd also confronted him because he couldn't think of anything else to do.

"At seven thirty-five last night," Alice said, "Campbell called a liquor store in the District that delivers."

"Shit," DeMarco muttered. So much for his big plan.

"At seven fifty-two, he called a cell phone belonging to a man named Russell McGrath. McGrath lives in Myrtle Beach, South Carolina."

"And he didn't call anybody else? Just McGrath and the liquor store?"

"Nope. Not last night. And he didn't make any calls from his home phone this morning."

"Thank you, Alice. What would you like for breakfast?"

"I'd like a stack of blueberry pancakes swimming in maple syrup, but since I just bought a new negligee for my short Latin lover, I'm gonna have coffee and half a grapefruit. And while we're eating, I want to tell you about this friend of mine. She's got two kids but . . ."

"Oh, great."

"No, listen to me. The kids are twin girls, seniors in high school, and they're going to college next year. They're basically grown up, and almost out of the house."

"College? How old is she?"

"She had the kids when she was really young. She's younger than you. You want to see her picture?"

"Nah, that's okay."

Alice ignored him and took out her cell phone. "I took this the other day when we were at the gym together."

She handed DeMarco the phone.

"Whoa!" DeMarco said when he saw the picture.

"Yeah, that's what I thought you'd say. I told her you might give her a call."

"What did you tell her about me?"

"That you're a nice guy. You just need direction."

———◆———

After breakfast with Alice—he got her friend's phone number even though he hadn't decided if he was going to call her—and went to his office. It was time to check out Russell McGrath.

Foster, the D.C. Metro deputy chief, had told DeMarco that when Douglas Campbell was arrested twenty-four years ago, the other person arrested with him was Russell McGrath. McGrath had been one of Campbell's teammates at UVA. So DeMarco googled McGrath—he was becoming an expert googler—and learned that McGrath had been drafted in the sixth round as a linebacker by the New York Jets, played for one year, and then his football career ended one fine Sunday when he was blindsided by some mammoth lineman who destroyed his left knee.

But why would Douglas Campbell, after being threatened by De-Marco, call an old football buddy? DeMarco realized he was probably being prejudiced, but he had a hard time imagining an ex-football player being the mastermind behind an insider trading scheme. Football players usually weren't that bright—and they usually didn't major in things like economics or business. But then again, maybe he was being biased just because they were guys with bigger-than-average-size necks.

He looked at the yellow legal pad lying on the corner of his desk, the pad on which he'd written down the information about Campbell's and McGrath's two-decade-old arrest, and saw the name of the cop who arrested them.

It took him almost an hour to track down retired Charlottesville detective Dave Torey.

DeMarco told Torey he was a lawyer—which was true—and that he was working with the SEC on an insider trading case—which was sorta true.

"I realize this is a long shot, detective," DeMarco said, "but you arrested a UVA lineman named Douglas Campbell and another football player named Russell McGrath more than twenty years ago, and I'm just wondering if you remember the case."

"Hell, yeah, I remember it," Torey said, surprising DeMarco. "I got so much shit dumped on my head after I arrested those two knuckleheads that I'll never forget that case."

"So what happened?"

"What happened is a kid named Jimmy Sweet either fell or got thrown out a dormitory window and died, and Campbell and McGrath lied about what happened."

Then Torey explained. This was the year UVA was going to the Citrus Bowl and Jimmy Sweet was a second-string wide receiver for the Cavaliers. Torey was working night shift at the time, and when the 911 call came in about a kid falling from a fourth-floor dorm window, he was dispatched.

"When I got there," Torey said, "Sweet was on the sidewalk, his brains all over the place, and the campus security guys had these three kids in their office, the dumb shits."

"What do you mean?" DeMarco said.

"I mean the college rent-a-cops put all three kids in the same room and left them alone for half an hour so they had plenty of time to agree on a story. You understand?"

"Yeah," DeMarco said. "But you said three kids. The info I got says you only arrested two."

"That's right. I only arrested McGrath and Campbell." Before De-Marco could ask why, Torey said, "Anyway, after I looked at the body, I went up to the dorm room where Sweet fell from. It was an old dorm—it was knocked down a dozen years ago—and it had these big casement windows, and the window in the room was totally busted out. Now, Sweet was a big kid, six six, over two hundred pounds, and I could see him tripping and smashing through that old window, but the thing I couldn't understand was the position of the body. If he'd tripped, the body should have been right under the window. But it wasn't. It was on the sidewalk about five feet away. So what I'm saying is, it would have taken some . . . some *momentum* for him to go out the window and land where he did, which means he either ran at that window and dove out or he got knocked through the window, maybe even thrown through it."

"You mean you think these guys killed him?"

"No, I never thought they killed him. I mean, not intentionally. McGrath and Campbell were both drunk that night, really drunk, but when the doc checked Sweet's alcohol level during the autopsy, he was sober as a judge. So I think what happened is these football players—who were all big guys—were playing grab ass, goofing around, and Sweet got accidently pushed through the window by either Campbell or McGrath. But they denied it. They insisted he just tripped over some books on the floor and fell.

"Well, I knew they were lying to me, but it wasn't just that. It was their goddamn attitudes. I mean, they were sorry Sweet died, but they weren't about to admit they were responsible and maybe get into some kind of legal trouble. And because this was the year UVA was finally going to a bowl game, these guys thought they were king shit. They figured no matter what they'd done, the university was going to protect them—and it turned out they were right.

"But when they weren't straight with me, I got pissed and arrested them. I slapped cuffs on them and charged them with drunk and disorderly, and then, just to get their attention, charged them with obstructing a homicide investigation and threw them into a cell. The obstruction charge was bullshit, but they were young, stupid, and drunk, and I figured if I scared them they'd come clean with me. All I wanted was the truth."

"So, did they come clean with you?"

"No. The university, which is about the largest employer in Charlottesville, had a lawyer in my boss's face twenty minutes after I arrested them. The lawyer made it clear that if I fucked up Rusty McGrath's chances of playing in the Citrus Bowl, me and my boss should both start looking for new jobs. I mean, Campbell was just an average player, maybe below average, but Rusty McGrath was a big deal. Everybody knew he was gonna go pro, and the Cavaliers coach wanted that kid out of jail that night and ready for practice the next day. The lawyer said what happened to Sweet was just a tragic accident and I had no right to act like some kind of storm trooper, so my boss read me the riot act and I had to let them go before I found out what really happened. And it still pisses me off."

"Why didn't you arrest the third guy?"

"Because he was a fuckin' basket case. He couldn't stop crying and shaking and throwing up, and I couldn't make any sense out of what he was saying. I mean, it looked to me like he was going into shock and I even asked one of the EMTs if he should give him a sedative or something. What I'm sayin' is, this kid was so out of it, I didn't even try to question him and focused totally on McGrath and Campbell. I probably would have gone back later and talked to him after he'd calmed down, but by then my boss had made it clear that if I did anything that screwed up UVA's chances in that bowl game, I'd be handing out parking tickets for the rest of my career."

"Was the third kid a football player, too?"

"No, he was just some little geek, and that's the other reason I didn't spend much time on him. He wasn't big enough to toss Jimmy Sweet out a window. And if he'd been on the team, I'd probably be able to remember his name, which I can't right now. But it was his room Sweet fell from, which also surprised me. I mean this kid—what the fuck was his name?—wasn't the kind of guy these ball players would have hung around with."

"Then why were they in his room?"

"According to McGrath—he's the one who did all the talking—it was just your typical college dorm thing. You know, the kids are all drinking, going from room to room, bullshitting with each other, and somehow they just ended up in . . . Praeter! That was his name. Richard Praeter."

DeMarco's shoebox-size office—no windows, inadequate ventilation, and an air-conditioning system that hadn't worked for years—was a place where he spent as little time as possible. A couple of years before, an earthquake had struck D.C.—one that measured 5.9 on the Richter scale and damaged the Washington Monument—and DeMarco had been in his office at the time. He was sure he was going to die that day. He knew the statue of Freedom on the Capitol's dome—a statue that weighed fifteen thousand pounds—was going to plummet through the Rotunda's painted ceiling, then through two floors, and land right on his head.

Since the quake he'd discovered that he couldn't spend more than a couple of hours in his claustrophobic work space before he had to go out and gulp fresh air. He actually wondered if he had a minor case of PTSD, but he was too embarrassed to tell anyone for fear of sounding like a wimp. He walked outside and stood on the side of the Capitol facing the Library of Congress, and while standing there, began bullshitting with one of the guards, an old-timer named Leary.

DeMarco dreaded to think that Leary and his brethren were the last line of defense protecting him from terrorists.

For some reason, he and Leary started talking about the Redskins. They didn't agree on much but they did agree on one thing: Billy Kilmer may have been the best quarterback the Skins ever had. Kilmer had stumpy legs, a potbelly—in fact, he looked a bit like Leary—and he couldn't run or throw for shit, but man, could he win games.

DeMarco returned to his office—like a reluctant mole descending into its burrow—and googled Richard Praeter. He was starting to think that he was like Billy Kilmer when it came to googling: slow, but he got the job done.

Richard Praeter lived in Manhattan.

Richard Praeter was a financial consultant.

DeMarco didn't know exactly what a financial consultant did but he'd finally found somebody connected to Douglas Campbell who might know how to use inside information to make a lot of money. Which made him feel like saying something silly like "hidey-ho."

So he did.

DeMarco spent another hour searching for more information on Praeter, trying to see if the magic Internet could link him directly to Reston Tech or past insider trading cases. The Internet failed. He needed Neil. He decided to call it a day and go someplace where there was air and sunlight, humans and alcohol—and maybe when he got there he'd call Alice's good-looking friend—and that's when Kay Kiser's comment about Molly Mahoney popped into his head.

When he'd asked Kiser what motive Molly could possibly have for committing a crime, Kiser had said: *You need to get know your client a lot better, DeMarco.* What had she meant by that?

And then he thought about the way Molly lived.

And then he thought, *Aw, shit.*

DeMarco called Mahoney's office, obtained Molly's Social Security number and date of birth from Mahoney's secretary, then called the company that had performed the credit check on Douglas Campbell. He asked them to do a credit check on young Molly Mahoney.

Thirty minutes later he learned that Molly was in debt up to her pretty chin. She had four credit cards and every one of them was maxed out, and all she was doing was paying the minimum balance on the cards. She was frequently late paying her rent, her utilities, and her phone bill. And DeMarco now realized why she lived in a dump: a dump was all she could afford. Molly Mahoney's motive for committing a crime wasn't greed—it was *necessity*. If she didn't get a large infusion of cash pretty soon, she was going to be living out of her car.

But what the hell had she spent the money on? He needed to get Molly's credit card statements—or maybe just do the simple thing and ask the woman what the hell was going on.

He called Molly's number and got her voice mail. "Molly, it's Joe DeMarco. Call me as soon as you get this message." He paused before he added, "Molly, you should have told someone."

17

─────◆─────

"Okay, okay. I'm coming, for Christ's sake!"

Denny Reed was fifty-two. He was wearing sandals, black socks, blue Bermuda shorts, and a red sleeveless T-shirt that exposed two skinny arms. His ex-wife had told him one time that he shouldn't wear sleeveless shirts because his arms looked like those tube-balloons street artists twisted into the shape of dachshunds. His ex was a vicious, sharp-tongued bitch.

Denny flung open the door, intending to say: "What the hell's wrong with you, leaning on the fuckin' buzzer like that," but then he saw who was standing on his porch. "Oh, hey, Gus," he said. "How you doin'? Good to see you. You wanna come in?"

Gus Amato stared at Denny for a long moment then snapped his gum, the sound like a twig being broken in two. "Sure, Denny, I'll come in," he said.

Gus strolled past Denny and then stood in the middle of his living room, looking around the house. The house was a two-story Cape Cod that faced the waters off Ocean City, New Jersey, and it contained hardly any furniture. The only items in the living room were a recliner, a cheap television set, and a TV tray that Denny used for a table. The dining room was completely empty, not even a picture on the walls.

Denny had sold almost all his possessions at an impromptu yard sale one day so they wouldn't repossess his car.

"You want something to drink?" Denny asked, speaking to Gus's back. "I don't have any booze but I got some Pepsi."

Gus turned to face him. "I saw the sign on the lawn, Denny. I guess that means you still haven't sold the house."

"Yeah, but I will. I just need a little more time. I been thinking about switching real estate agents, getting somebody who really knows what the hell he's doing."

"This place has a mortgage on it, right?" Gus said.

"Yeah. It didn't have one when I first moved in, but, well, you know."

"So that means you gotta make a pretty good profit to get straight with us."

"I will," Denny said. "The market's a little cool right now, but it'll pick up. You just gotta give me . . ."

"How'd you get this house in the first place? I think you told me once but I can't remember."

"My brother," Denny said. "It was his summer place. He was always such a prick to me, I couldn't believe it when he left it to me in his will."

Gus laughed. "He was probably a prick because you were always trying to borrow money from him."

There wasn't anything Denny could say to that.

Gus walked toward the kitchen, speaking as he went, Denny trailing along behind him. "How long were you in, the last time you were inside?"

"What?" Denny said. "You talking about prison?"

"Yeah. How long were you in last time?"

Denny's kitchen cabinets, the ones above the counter, had glass doors, and the only items in them were two plates, three glasses, and a single coffee cup. Another glass and a coffee cup were in the sink. That was all the dishes Denny owned, and he wished the cabinets had regular doors so Gus couldn't see his stuff.

"Eighteen months," Denny said. "I mean, I never shoulda been there at all. This goddamn lawyer I had . . ."

"And why were you there? Something about credit cards, right? Getting credit card numbers off the Internet, something like that?"

"Yeah. I . . . I needed the money at the time."

Gus laughed. "You fuckin' guys. You just never learn."

There wasn't anything Denny could say to that either.

Gus opened Denny's refrigerator. A half-empty jar of jelly, two cans of Pepsi, and a greasy bucket from KFC. He shook his head as if what he saw was pathetic, and closed the door.

"And you did your time in the joint okay?" Gus asked.

"What do you mean?"

"I mean, you didn't go nuts, try to slash your wrists, nothin' like that?"

"No."

Gus smiled. "Which means you were probably someone's bitch from the day you got there."

"Hey! I wasn't no one's . . ."

"Denny, I don't care. Inside, a guy does what he has to do. I've been there. I understand."

"Why are you asking about . . ."

Gus took a step toward Denny, backing him up so his skinny butt was touching the stove. "Denny, Ted Allen has decided he's gonna let you keep your house and . . ."

"What?"

"Mr. Allen's gonna let you keep your house, Denny. He's gonna write off what you owe him, including the vig, so you won't have to sell the place."

The vig was the interest Denny paid on the money he owed Ted Allen. The vig was murder, and about the same as the interest rate the bastards at Visa charged.

"Why would he do that?" Denny asked.

"Because you're gonna do him a favor."

"What kind of favor?"

Gus told him.

"No way!" Denny said. "No fuckin' way. Tell Mr. Allen I'll sell the house next week. I swear to Christ, I will. And then I'll be able to pay back everything."

Gus nodded as if agreeing with Denny—then hit him in the throat, a short little jab, his right fist traveling only six inches.

Denny fell to the kitchen floor. He lay there, clutching his throat, kicking his feet, flopping like a trout out of water, saying "Gaa, gaa, gaa." He couldn't breathe and he was trying to get air into his lungs but was too panicked to relax and take short breaths.

Gus bent over so he was closer to Denny's face.

"Denny," Gus said, "when I said you were gonna do Mr. Allen a favor, I wasn't asking if you *wanted* to do it."

18

Mahoney walked slowly down the Atlantic City boardwalk.

He walked past Ripley's Believe It or Not! and the place where the old Steel Pier used to be, and past souvenir stores that sold T-shirts and rubber dice and vendors hawking funnel cakes cooked in vats of grease. As he walked, garbage-eating seagulls scuttled out of his way. He passed one guy pulling a rickshaw that contained a couple too overweight to walk to the next all-you-can-eat casino buffet.

Mahoney hated Atlantic City.

He was wearing a red windbreaker over an old Patriots sweatshirt, navy-blue chinos, and tennis shoes. On his big head was a Red Sox baseball cap, the bill pulled down, partially obscuring his face. It was the sort of outfit he wore when Congress wasn't in session and he was home in Boston, walking around the Back Bay, stopping in neighborhood places for a beer or two. He liked the Back Bay, particularly in the fall, when the weather was crisp and the trees had some color and you could see Harvard's crew team sculling on the Charles.

He missed Boston, especially today.

The Atlantic Palace Casino was bigger than the pyramid at Giza and flashier than a New York pimp. As Mahoney walked through it, he glanced at the players hunched over their cards at the blackjack tables. Whenever they showed casinos in television commercials, all the players were young and beautiful, laughing and grinning like they were having the time of their lives. Some of the folks he could see were young, but gray-haired pensioners bused in from New York and Philly far outnumbered the youngsters, and none of them, old or young, were particularly beautiful. More to the point, none of them looked happy; they sat there—grim, tense, humorless expressions on their faces—just hoping—just *praying*—that they wouldn't bust on the next card they were dealt. Yeah, gambling was a lot of fun.

Mahoney presented himself at the security desk and said he had an appointment with Ted Allen. Mahoney could tell the guard thought it pretty unlikely that someone dressed like Mahoney would have an appointment with the man who ran the casino, but he politely asked Mahoney's name.

"Just say it's Molly's dad," Mahoney said.

Mahoney wasn't surprised that the security guard didn't recognize him, and that had little to do with his half-assed disguise. Although he'd been on the political stage for decades—posing with presidents at news conferences, making guest appearances on TV shows, not to mention having been the Speaker of the House for more years than he could remember—he knew that half the people in the country didn't pay enough attention to national politics to recognize him. Hell, half the people in the country didn't even bother to vote.

Five minutes later Mahoney was ushered into a penthouse office. Through the windows he could see the ocean to the east, but not the ugly low-rent district to the west. He figured he might be high enough to see England on a clear day.

Ted Allen turned out to be a pretty-boy with reddish blond hair and chiseled features, and he introduced himself as the CEO of Indigo Gaming, Inc. Mahoney had a hard time believing that anyone would make this arrogant young squirt the chief of anything.

"Would you like a drink, sir?" Ted asked.

"No," Mahoney said. He wanted a drink—actually he *needed* a drink—but he wasn't going to drink with this guy. "What I want is to hear what you have to say about my daughter, and I wanna hear it quick."

"Okay," Ted said. He paused a beat, then said, "Molly owes me—the casino, that is—one hundred and nine thousand dollars for gambling losses."

Mahoney didn't say anything; Preston Whitman had already told him this.

"She likes to play craps," Ted said. "Not usually a woman's game, but . . ." Ted made a gesture indicating to-each-her-own-poison. "She's been a regular here for about a year, a good customer, so when she came to me one day and asked me to extend her some credit, and considering who her father was, I decided to accommodate her. In retrospect, not one of my wiser decisions."

Bullshit, Mahoney thought. She didn't come to him; he went to her. He saw she was losing and running out of money, and he offered Eve the apple. And he did it *because* of who Mahoney was. Like most people, Ted Allen figured Mahoney was wealthy—which, at the moment, he wasn't. Ted had thought that Mahoney would pay off his daughter's debt to avoid the embarrassment, which he probably would have, scraping up the money somehow, if he had known about her problem.

"A hundred thousand's a fairly large number," Ted said, "but not an insurmountable one. Unfortunately, Molly has significantly compounded her problem."

"And how did she do that?" Mahoney said. He just wanted to *smack* this guy.

"When she said she couldn't pay the hundred she owed, I said I was going to have to discuss the situation with you, and that's when she came to me with a proposal."

"A proposal?"

"Yes. She told me she had information on a particular stock—a stock for some company that makes batteries—and that if I would loan her just a bit more, I'd get back all she owed."

Oh, Jesus.

"Molly's an intelligent, educated woman," Ted said, "and she made a very effective presentation. She had charts, historical performance data. That sort of thing." He glanced over at the university diplomas on his wall, letting Mahoney know that he was a man who could appreciate a well-reasoned business proposition. "She was very persuasive and I was quite impressed.

"Molly figured the stock's price would rise anywhere from twenty to thirty percent. That's quite a bump. So I loaned her two hundred and fifty thousand so she could invest it and pay down her debt, and gave her another two fifty to invest for the casino. Twenty percent on two hundred and fifty grand would not be a bad day's work."

"You're saying that you knowingly abetted my daughter in an illegal insider trading scheme."

Ted gave a little shrug. "I'm not a lawyer, Mr. Mahoney. I didn't know that your daughter was doing anything illegal."

"Bullshit," Mahoney said. He was also thinking that if Molly's scheme had worked, Ted would have used her over and over again in the future to do the same thing. He would have had his hooks into her for life.

"Be that as it may," Ted said. "Right now I have a problem: my half million dollars has been frozen by the government—and I want it back."

"Tough shit," Mahoney said. He also noticed that Ted hadn't said anything about consolidating Molly's debts and giving her a low interest loan, as Preston Whitman had said he would.

"The other problem I have," Ted said as if Mahoney had spoken, "is that someplace down the line Molly may think it's a good idea to implicate me in this crime for which she's been arrested. And that's why I thought we should have this little chat. To make sure that

Molly—and you—understand that if she was to do such a thing it could have some very grave consequences. For one thing, Molly's gambling problem would become public knowledge, but that would be the least of her problems."

"Are you threatening my . . ."

"You see, Mr. Mahoney, there's no way to prove that I gave her the money. The money was direct-deposited to her account by a late associate of mine and there's no banking trail leading to him, much less to me. But . . . well, I think my next point would be best illustrated by a small demonstration."

"A demonstration?" Mahoney said. What the hell was this guy gonna do? Show him PowerPoint slides?

Ted hit a button on his phone and said into the speaker, "Tell Gus to bring Mr. Reed in."

A moment later two men entered Ted's office. One was a wide-shouldered thug in a bad-fitting suit wearing white cowboy boots. The other guy was in his fifties and scrawny-looking, particularly standing next to the other guy. The scrawny one looked scared to death.

"This is Denny Reed," Ted said to Mahoney. "The one that looks like he's about to puke all over my rug. If Denny pukes, Gus, I want you to rub his nose in it."

The thug just popped the bubble gum he was chewing; it sounded like a rifle shot going off in the room.

"Now then, Denny," Ted said, "did you deposit five hundred thousand dollars into Molly Mahoney's bank account?"

Reed hesitated for a second then said, "Yes."

Reed's voice was kinda froggy, Mahoney noted, like there was something wrong with his throat. Or maybe it was fear that caused him to croak.

"And are you willing, Denny," Ted said, "to admit that you put this money into her account without her knowledge and that you then used the money to buy a certain stock."

"Yes," Reed said.

"And are you willing to testify that Molly had nothing to do with this illegal transaction, that some person who you are unwilling to name, gave you the stock tip?"

"Yes," Reed said.

"Very good, Denny," Ted said. "But now let me ask you this: are you also willing to admit that Molly was the one who told you about the stock and that you and she conspired together to buy it?"

"Yes," Reed said.

"Wonderful, Denny. You gave the right answer every time. Gus, why don't you take Denny back to his room."

After the two men left his office, Ted said, "Did you get the point of that demonstration, Congressman?"

Mahoney nodded. "Yeah, I got the point. Denny will say whatever you tell him to say."

"That's right. Denny, who has a criminal record by the way, is willing to do the time for your daughter's crime all by himself or he's willing to testify that your daughter was his accomplice. In one scenario, your daughter avoids a jail sentence and in the other, she and Denny both go to jail, but Denny gets a reduced sentence for giving up Molly, she being who she is."

"So what do you want?"

"The first thing I want is my half million back, plus the money Molly owes the casino. That's a total of six hundred grand. The second thing I want is for the U.S. government to provide a hundred million dollars for a certain construction project here in Atlantic City."

"A construction project? What in the hell are you talking about?" Mahoney said.

Ted explained about the new convention center, and how the acting governor of New Jersey was being a prick by insisting on supplemental federal funding.

"As I understand it from talking to Preston Whitman," Ted said, "all you have to do is attach the funding as a rider to some bill, something Preston says you can do if you set your mind to it."

Mahoney didn't say anything for several seconds. He felt like throwing Ted through the window and watching his brains splatter all over the boardwalk. But he didn't. Instead he rose from the chair where he'd been sitting and said, "I'm gonna need a little time to think this over."

"I'm afraid that won't do, sir. I need an answer. Right now," Ted said.

"Okay, then I'll give you one," Mahoney said. "Kiss my ass."

Mahoney needed a drink, but he wasn't going to drink in Ted's casino, so he left the Atlantic Palace and walked over to the next casino on the boardwalk, which meant he had to walk about half a mile.

It was only eleven a.m. and the casino wasn't all that full, but the slot machines were still making their nerve-jangling, god-awful racket. He found a lounge that had a stage in the middle, a place where they probably had some kind of free show at night, but at this time of day the stage was dark. There were only two people in the lounge, a man and a woman sitting at separate tables, and they both looked as if they'd been up gambling all night—and lost. They were staring down into their drinks, the looks on their faces saying that they'd lost more than they could afford and had no idea what they were going to do. God-damn idiot gambling junkies—and it appeared that his daughter was one of them. He could just imagine Molly sitting here at some earlier date, looking just like these two losers.

Mahoney ordered bourbon from the bartender and took a seat at a table the size of a Frisbee. He wasn't worried about having walked out on Ted; Ted wasn't going to do anything immediately. No, he'd give

Mahoney a day or two to think things over and either contact him again or have Preston Whitman do it. The problem was, he didn't have any idea what he was going to do.

But Molly was screwed if he didn't do something. She would either go to jail for a crime which he now knew she'd committed or he had to pay Ted Allen six hundred thousand dollars—six hundred thousand that he didn't have. Plus there were Molly's legal expenses, which would be at least another hundred grand. Finally, as if he didn't have enough on his plate, he also had to get a law passed that would give the state of New Jersey a hundred million bucks. Oddly enough, the hundred million was the least of his many problems.

A hundred million dollars sounds like a lot of money, but in terms of federal spending it's a drop in the bucket. Or maybe half a drop. Getting that amount tacked onto some bill was something he thought he might be able to do, but to get his hands on seven hundred grand . . .

But there was something else going on here. It was obvious that Ted had some scheme where he thought he could make a ton of money if this convention center was built, and six hundred thousand dollars had to be pocket change for an operation the size of the Atlantic Palace. The casino could lose that much in a single night if some whale got lucky at the tables. Yeah, Ted should have been willing to simply *give* Mahoney the money in trade for his influence. So why didn't he? Ted Allen might just be a greedy prick, but Mahoney didn't think that was it. No, there was something else going on, something he was missing.

There was one thing he wasn't missing, though: Ted was connected. At least he thought he was. He had a white-bread name and diplomas on the wall, and he didn't say "youse guys" or "fuckin' this" and "fuckin' that" in every other sentence, but no doubt about it, Ted was Mob. Mahoney thought at first that Ted was just a crooked businessman who had tried to make a fast buck in the market, but when that palooka Gus hauled that pathetic bastard Denny Reed into the room . . . Well, that's when Ted had shown his spots. It was obvious Ted had told Denny that if he didn't agree to do the time for Molly he was going end up with a thousand feet of Atlantic Ocean over his head.

So he had three problems: he had to come up with a boatload of money he didn't have; he had to get his daughter off for a crime that he now knew she'd committed; and he had to divert a hundred million dollars of the taxpayers' money to a construction project that would benefit organized crime. That's all.

No, wait a minute. He didn't have three problems. He had four problems.

The fourth problem was that Ted might kill his daughter if he thought she might testify against him.

19

Big Bob Fairchild needed his wife's advice.

Fairchild had met Barbara Jane Evans at the University of Arizona when he was a junior and she was a freshman, and he decided the day he met her that he was going to marry her.

Barbara Jane's father was dead now, but he'd been a real estate mogul, one of those guys who would—repeatedly—buy a seemingly useless vacant lot in a run-down neighborhood. The next month, Hilton would decide to build on that very spot or the state would decide it needed the land, and offer him a hundred times what he originally paid for the lot. At the time Fairchild met his bride-to-be, there were four Arizonans richer than Sinclair Evans—but being the fifth richest man in the state was still a pretty good thing to be. And Barbara Jane Evans was an only child and her mother had died when she was sixteen.

Barbara Jane was a gold mine.

She was a tall girl, and she had the broadest shoulders that Fairchild had ever seen on a woman. Her breasts were small—at least then they were—but she had a nice ass and good, long legs. And she wasn't exactly ugly; *homely* was probably a better word. She had mousy brown hair, her nose was a bit too long, and her ears . . . Well, she didn't look too good when her hair was short. And although she had the misfortune to have inherited her daddy's face, she'd also inherited his brains, and she'd always been Robert Fairchild's principal adviser.

"You say his daughter owes this casino a hundred thousand?" Barbara Jane said.

Barbara Jane was now forty-seven, and maybe the best-looking forty-seven-year-old woman in Tucson. Hell, maybe she was the best-looking forty-seven-year-old woman in the entire Southwest. The reason she now looked so good was because at the age of thirty, she overcame her fear of cosmetic surgery in a major way. Her hair was now ash blonde and perfectly suited to her face—a face that she'd picked from a catalogue in her doctor's office: *I'll have those cheekbones, and that chin, and ooh, give me that cute little nose, too.* And her body, now that she had the same-size breasts as Marilyn Monroe and sag-proof implants inserted into her butt, was flawless.

They were seated by the pool of Barbara Jane's D.C. mansion. (Barbara Jane had lavish homes in half a dozen places around the world—and all the property was in her name alone.) Fairchild was dressed in a suit that was too hot for the weather; his wife was wearing a white one-piece bathing suit and painting her toenails as they talked. The polish she was applying was a garish, candy-apple red.

Fairchild didn't know why his wife painted her toenails. She had a lady that gave her manicures and pedicures, but for some reason she liked to put the polish on herself. All he knew was that it was irritating talking to the top of her head, and the little balls of cotton stuck between her toes looked stupid.

"Yeah," Fairchild said, answering her question. "And right now the SEC and Justice don't know that. They think Molly's motive was credit card debt and they've probably figured out from her statements that she spent a lot of time and money in Atlantic City, but they don't know about the money she owes the casino."

"So if you leaked that she owes the casino money, all that would do is *confirm* she's a gambler," Barbara Jane said. "Sounds bad, but so what?

I don't see how her being a gambling junky hurts Mahoney any more than the insider trader charges against her have already hurt him—which is to say that they haven't hurt him at all. And the fact that she owes money to a casino doesn't really make the prosecutor's case any stronger, I mean, not really."

"But there has to be some way to take advantage of . . ."

"How do you like this color?" Barbara Jane asked.

"What?" Fairchild said.

"This nail polish. How do you like it?"

"Uh, it's fine. It looks great."

"You know what it's called?"

Now, how in the hell would I know that?

"No," Fairchild said. "Look, there has to be some way . . ."

"It's called *I'm Not Really a Waitress.*"

"What?"

"The name of this color is: I'm Not Really a Waitress. Don't you just love that?"

"Goddamnit, Barbara Jane, will you . . ."

"And you say the casino's connected to some mobster in Philadelphia?"

"Yeah, a man named Albert Castiglia."

"How did you find out about him?"

"I talked to a guy in the Bureau. He said that when Ted Allen was a kid he worked for Castiglia in Vegas, and Castiglia took a shine to him and sent him to college. The FBI figured that a nice-looking, college-educated yuppie like Ted would be the perfect front for Castiglia. There was no way Castiglia was going to get a gaming license, but Ted could. The bottom line is that the Atlantic Palace Casino is probably laundering money for the Mob, but there's no proof of that. And Ted Allen almost certainly works for Castiglia but there's no proof of that, either."

"Well, sugar," Barbara Jane said, "journalists don't need proof. You know that."

"Yeah, but so what? How does leaking that Ted Allen is tied to the Mob hurt Mahoney?"

"Baby, baby, you just gotta learn to think outside the box."

Fairchild just hated that expression. "What box? What are you talk—"

"What if the casino was to cancel Molly Mahoney's debt?"

"What?" Fairchild said again. She just confused the shit out of him.

"Now, I don't know about you, honey, but I can see the headline right now: *Mob Controlled Casino Absolves Mahoney's Daughter's Debt.* And the sub-headline, or whatever it's called, would say: *Is Mahoney Tied to the Mob?*"

"But why would the casino cancel . . ."

"And you said that this Ted person wants federal funds for some project?"

"Yeah."

"So even if Mahoney can't get a rider attached to a bill, all you need is someone willing to say that Mahoney is *trying* to get one attached."

"I still don't see . . ."

"Can't you just see the next headline? *Mob Controlled Casino Cancels Mahoney's Daughter's Debt for Federal Funding.* Well, maybe that's kind of a long headline, but you get the idea, don't you? That kind of press just might be enough to get his big butt bounced right out of the House."

"But why would Ted Allen cancel the girl's marker?" Fairchild asked again.

"Why, he wouldn't, of course. But if someone was to give him a hundred grand, and maybe just a little more as sort of a . . . a service fee, he'd probably be willing to *say* that he did."

Before Fairchild could say anything else, Barbara Jane wiggled her toes and laughed. "That just cracks me up! I'm Not Really a Waitress."

20

"I'm sorry, Mr. DeMarco, but the doctor doesn't have another opening on his schedule until August."

"August! That's four months from now! This tooth . . . Look, I'm not kidding you. I'm in agony here."

"Sorry."

"You're pissed, aren't you? You're doing this because I walked out on you."

"I am not . . ."

"You know I work for Congress. I can't tell you why I had to leave because it's classified—you know, national security—but believe me, I had to go. I didn't have a choice."

"Sorry."

The woman was a rock—and she had a heart of stone. Not an ounce of compassion in her entire body.

"Well, is there some sort of dental emergency room somewhere?"

"Not that I know of, but I believe there's a free clinic in Southeast. A place where dental students practice on the underprivileged."

DeMarco had seen *All the President's Men,* the Watergate movie starring Redford and Hoffman as Woodward and Bernstein. He figured Randy Sawyer had seen the movie, too, because Sawyer had decided to re-create the scene where Woodward meets Deep Throat in an underground parking garage, a cavernous space of eerie shadows with concrete pillars to hide behind. DeMarco thought the meeting place Sawyer had picked was not only overly dramatic but downright uncomfortable. Any bar in the District would have been safe enough—and a lot more pleasant—but apparently Randy Sawyer didn't think so.

"I'm telling you," Sawyer said—or whispered, to be precise, "if Kiser finds out I looked at her case files, she'll have my nuts."

"I thought she worked for you," DeMarco said.

"Have you ever supervised people, DeMarco?"

DeMarco figured that Alice at the phone company didn't count, so he said no.

"Well, let me tell you how it is. You have two kinds of people. First, there are the ones who are afraid of you and always do what you tell them. That's most of them. Then you have people like Kay Kiser who aren't afraid of anybody and do any damn thing they please."

"I don't get it," DeMarco said. "You sound like you're afraid of her."

"I am afraid of her. And it's because she would hand me my head on a platter if I did anything that she construed as preventing her from doing her job. She'd go over my head, she'd go to the press, and she'd call the cops if she thought I did something illegal."

"But looking at her files isn't illegal and is certainly within your purview as a manager," DeMarco said.

"But leaking information to Molly Mahoney's lawyers *is* illegal."

"Randy, nobody is ever going to know that we talked."

"You better be right about that," Sawyer said.

"So what did you find out?" DeMarco said. He was tired of hiding behind a concrete pillar like he and Sawyer were two guys having a quickie.

"Kiser checked out Douglas Campbell's finances five or six years ago. There's hardly anybody at Reston Tech she hasn't looked at, but Campbell was on her list because she thought he lived above his income."

"She thought?"

"Yeah. But then she found out that Mrs. Campbell has a trust fund that was established by her late father and whoever manages the trust is doing a pretty good job. Kiser didn't have all the numbers in the file, but from her notes it looks like the annual proceeds from the trust more than double Campbell's salary."

"Who manages the trust?"

"Ah, shit, who is it? A local bank. Oh, yeah. Riggs."

"So after she found out about the trust, she quit looking at Campbell?"

"I guess. The other thing with Campbell is that he's a personnel guy not a scientist or an engineer and he's not involved with the research Reston Tech does with other companies. So if Reston came up with some kind of big breakthrough that was gonna drive somebody's stock through the roof, I'm not sure he'd even be in the loop."

DeMarco thought Sawyer might be wrong about that. According to Molly, Campbell was a social creature, always inviting folks out to his beach house. And one thing DeMarco knew for sure: people talked. They always talked. DeMarco could envision Campbell chatting with engineers and company executives, subtly pumping them for information, and these days, with everything stored in computers, maybe he had a way to access whatever databases contained the right info. So Campbell may not have been an engineer but he was probably bright enough to listen to corporate scuttlebutt and figure out which big deals were in the company's pipeline.

But DeMarco didn't bother to say any of this to Randy Sawyer.

"Regarding this guy Praeter," Sawyer said, "Kiser had a file on him too. A big one. Remember I told you that twenty years ago we looked at Reston Tech for insider trading on that water treatment thing and how one investor made about five million bucks? Well, the investor was

Richard Praeter, but we could never prove he had any connections to anybody at Reston Tech or did anything illegal."

"You're shittin' me! And what do you mean you couldn't tie him to anyone at Reston? He went to UVA with Campbell and they were both involved in the case of that kid falling out a dorm window."

"I know that *now*, but only because of you," Sawyer said. "There's no record of Praeter being involved in the kid's death. You told me that yourself. You said the only way you found out was because you talked to that cop in Charlottesville. And Praeter never graduated from UVA. He left UVA a couple months after that kid died and he eventually graduated from George Mason. So just going through standard databases—you know, financials, tax returns, criminal records—there's nothing that connects Praeter and Campbell. Kiser even subpoenaed phone records, and I'm sure if Praeter and Campbell ever talked to each other, she would have found out about it and made some note in her files."

DeMarco remembered Molly telling him how Campbell used a prepaid calling card the time she overheard him talking to somebody in his office. He wondered if that's why there was no record of Campbell ever talking to Praeter.

"How 'bout the other insider trading cases," DeMarco asked, "the ones involving the body armor and those electric airplane motors? Did you look at Praeter for that?"

"Kiser did. But it's like I told you before, we could never figure out who bought the stock so she couldn't prove it was Praeter or anybody else. All I could tell was that she spent a lot of time looking at him."

"How could you tell that," DeMarco asked, but Sawyer had just heard a car door slam somewhere in the garage and his head spun about like he was a bucktoothed version of Linda Blair in *The Exorcist*.

"Randy, how do you know she spent a long time looking at him?"

"She did lots of record traces, reviewed the data on dozens of trades he'd made. I could tell by all the notes in the margins of the files. But like I said, she didn't find anything. He's either clean or he's smart—and you have to be damn smart to hide anything from Kiser."

"Did you see anything in Kiser's files linking Praeter to McGrath?"

The garage elevator dinged, Sawyer's head whipped around again. The elevator was empty. "What?" he said.

Randy Sawyer was not your ideal undercover operative.

"I asked if she ever saw any connection between Praeter and McGrath?"

"No, McGrath wasn't in her files at all."

"Shit," DeMarco said.

"So what's this all mean, DeMarco?" Sawyer said. "And does anything I've told you help Molly Mahoney?"

"I don't know."

"Well, that's just great," Sawyer said. There was a pause and he added, "My friend, this is the last time I'm meeting with you. You are on your own from this point forward. Got it?"

"Yeah, I got it," DeMarco said. He didn't bother to tell Sawyer that Molly's lawyers would probably subpoena him, however, if they felt it would help her case.

21

---◆---

DeMarco wanted to talk to Mahoney, to give him an update on what he'd learned, but no one knew where Mahoney was—and that was really strange. A politician of his rank can't just disappear for a whole day, but it seemed as if he had.

Since DeMarco couldn't talk to his boss, and since he couldn't think of anything else to do, he decided to look into Mrs. Campbell's trust fund. Sawyer said the trust was managed by Riggs National Bank but DeMarco learned that Riggs had been taken over by an outfit called PNC Financial Services in 2005. After a few minutes on the phone, telling a tight-lipped PNC VP that the entire weight of the federal government was going to land on his pointy head if he didn't help, DeMarco was informed that Kathy Campbell's trust was managed out of the Georgetown branch of the bank by a woman named Gail Martin. But that's all the helpful banker would tell him.

DeMarco's first impression of Gail Martin—*Mrs.* Gail Martin—was: sharp lady. She had a trim body, wavy dark hair, a narrow foxy face, and these incredible gray-blue eyes. And there was a twinkle in her eyes that said that even though she worked for a big stuffy bank, she found life pretty darn funny. DeMarco wanted a wife like Mrs. Martin: someone pretty, with a sense of humor, and smart enough to make him rich.

"Now you don't really think I'm going to tell you anything about Mrs. Campbell's trust, do you?" she said to DeMarco. She smiled when she said this; apparently DeMarco was one of those people who made life so darn funny.

"Like I said, Mrs. Martin, I'm from Congress and . . ."

"Honey, if you were my sweet ol' mama, I wouldn't give you information about a customer's account without a subpoena."

"Well, speaking of subpoenas," DeMarco said—he just hated to get tough with someone as cute as her—"that's what this may come down to. I'm working on something involving a very powerful congressman and his lawyers will subpoena your records—and you know what pain that can be."

"Not for me," smart Mrs. Martin said. "There's a company we use that employs a bunch of college kids, and whenever we're subpoenaed or audited, the kids print out and box up the records. No work for me at all."

"So a college kid can look at Mrs. Campbell's records but a representative from Congress can't?"

"You got it," Mrs. Martin said.

So much for the tough approach.

"Look," he said, "we can save everybody a lot of work here. You, me, and the college kids. I only want to know one thing."

Mrs. Martin shook her pretty head. "Sorry."

Ignoring the head shake, DeMarco said, "All I want to know is if either a Russell McGrath or a Richard Praeter is involved in the trust in any way. That's it."

The twinkle in Mrs. Martin's lovely gray-blue eyes disappeared like someone had thrown water on a camp fire. "Has Richard Praeter done something illegal?"

"So you know him," DeMarco said.

"Yes. He calls me every once in a while and screams at me, and if I disagree with him, he swears and calls me names."

"What? Why would he do that?" DeMarco asked.

"You didn't answer my question," she said. "Has he done something illegal?"

"I'm not sure," DeMarco admitted. "But he may be mixed up with some past insider trading cases, and that's why I'm asking questions about him."

"I see," Mrs. Martin said, and then she paused as if she were trying to make up her mind about something. Finally she said, "Well, I don't know who Russell McGrath is, but Mr. Praeter, per Mrs. Campbell's verbal authorization, essentially controls her trust. Even though the bank—meaning me—is paid to manage it, all the trust's investments are directed by him."

"So Praeter pulls the strings but he's not officially tied to the trust."

"That's correct. Mrs. Campbell told me Mr. Praeter was her financial adviser and that I was to do what he said. When I objected and asked for something in writing, her husband went over my head, threatened to move his wife's money to some other bank, and my boss told me to stop being so persnickety. So Praeter in reality directs the trust's investments, but I always get Mrs. Campbell to personally authorize any actions I take, which I'm required to do by law. And when I call her, she says, 'Well, if that's what Dickie says you should do, it's fine by me.' What I don't like about the situation is that if something goes wrong, I have no documentation to show that Mr. Praeter is the one responsible and it will appear as if Mrs. Campbell was making decisions based on my advice."

DeMarco could see why she didn't like the situation from a legal standpoint, but he suspected that she also didn't like Richard Praeter for personal reasons. He figured that Praeter had to be one obnoxious SOB to alienate a woman like her.

"I must say, however, that Mr. Praeter is very shrewd when it comes to the market. Or based on what you've just told me, maybe he's not so shrewd; maybe he just has access to information the general public doesn't. In any case, the trust was established by Mrs. Campbell's father when she was eighteen. Its value was two hundred and fifty thousand at the time and her father stipulated that his daughter wouldn't have access to the principal until she was thirty. And for a number of years, the trust's annual payout was just a few thousand dollars. We're a conservative institution, and I'm personally very conservative when it comes to my clients because I don't want them to lose their money. But when Mr. Praeter became involved, this was about fifteen years ago, we started to take huge risks—and they paid off. Handsomely. Mrs. Campbell's trust is currently valued at one point six million, and the Campbells have made substantial withdrawals from it several times since Mrs. Campbell turned thirty."

"Wow!" DeMarco said, thinking that if he couldn't marry Mrs. Martin that Richard Praeter would do. "But you don't have anything that *officially* links Praeter to the trust? A memo? An e-mail? Something like that?"

"No." Then Mrs. Martin smiled. "I do, however, record all my phone calls with Mr. Praeter so in case I'm ever accused of making bad investments related to the trust, my little butt is covered."

"Does Praeter know you record these phone calls?"

"No."

Sly Mrs. Martin.

She then added, "I imagine a correctly worded subpoena would produce those recordings."

22

"Who was that big white-haired guy you had in your office yesterday?" McGruder said.

The son of a bitch, Ted thought. He had spies everywhere, and one of them must have seen Mahoney leaving his office.

"A jackass named Dohenny," Ted said. "He owes us eight grand. You must have seen his name in the book."

"Yeah, I saw it. He hasn't made a payment in three weeks."

"Well, that's what we had a little chat about."

"You talk to these deadbeats personally? You don't have Gus do that for you?"

"Usually Gus does, but this guy pisses me off."

"Huh," McGruder said, as if he was impressed that Ted was willing to get his hands dirty.

"Anyway, he's gonna pay tomorrow."

Which meant that tomorrow Ted was going to have to pay off Dohenny's debt with his own money. Goddamn McGruder. Tonight he'd have Gus beat the livin' shit out of Dohenny, an auto parts dealer who lived in Camden.

"Good," McGruder said. "You can't let these guys stall you too long."

No shit, Ted almost said. But actually, having McGruder around hadn't been that bad. The guy was constantly bugging him with questions, but every day he seemed less suspicious, and he still hadn't figured out how Greg had doctored the books. Ted also discovered that McGruder had a thing for little Asian chicks, so every other night he sent him one.

The other thing he'd found out was that if he played up to McGruder, pretended he was asking for his advice, that made the asshole happy, too. But he had to get the money out of Mahoney and he had to show he was making progress on the convention center project.

And it looked like Mahoney was cooperating. Mahoney had walked out on him the other day, but Ted had found out from Preston Whitman that Mahoney's chief of staff was quietly exploring options to get federal funding for the convention center. But Ted needed to get Mahoney moving faster, and he wanted his five hundred grand back in case McGruder eventually found something in the books.

It was time to send Mahoney a message.

23

Richard Praeter's office was on the twenty-second floor of a building two blocks from the New York Stock Exchange. DeMarco opened the door and found himself standing in a small waiting room with a desk where a receptionist or a secretary would sit, but the desk was empty. Behind the receptionist's desk he could see a larger room and a man in the room, standing, talking on the phone.

Praeter didn't see DeMarco immediately because he was staring out his office window as he talked, so DeMarco walked up to the open door, planning to rap on the frame to get Praeter's attention. He noticed that Praeter's office contained a glass-topped table for a desk; a matching conference table; a multiline telephone; three flat-screen computer monitors; and an enormous wall-mounted TV tuned to some channel devoted to business news twenty-four hours a day. There were also several large, unattractive metal file cabinets against one wall. The cabinets were bolted to the floor and were locked with oversize padlocks, ugly industrial looking things that would have been more appropriate barring the gates to a factory than inside a wealthy investor's office.

Praeter was saying into the phone, "Who's banking the takeover?" and just then he turned and saw DeMarco. "What the hell?" he said.

Into the phone he said, "I'll call you back." He hung up and said to DeMarco, "Who the hell are you?"

Before DeMarco could answer, Praeter noticed that DeMarco was able to see one of the monitors on his desk and he lunged at the monitor and pressed the power button to darken the screen.

"Who are you?" Praeter asked again.

Praeter was about five feet seven and maybe weighed a hundred and thirty pounds. He had dark hair combed straight back, a longish face, and jittery black eyes. In fact, everything about him was *jittery*. He reminded DeMarco of the actor James Woods playing one of his manic, hyperactive, fast-talking roles.

Praeter was wearing a suit—the jacket on even though he was alone in his office—a monogrammed shirt, and suspenders. The suit fit him well and probably cost a lot of money, as did Praeter's watch and every other object in the room: the professional espresso machine, the ultra-thin TV, his ergonomic executive's chair. But no matter how expensively Praeter was attired, and regardless of the cost of the furnishings in his office, DeMarco's initial impression was: immature, insecure nerd. This was the kid in high school who got straight As in math, wore high-water pants and owlish glasses, and pined hopelessly for girls who laughed at him.

"Mr. Praeter, my name's Joe DeMarco. I'm from . . ."

"How did you get into my office?" Praeter said.

"The outer door was unlocked," DeMarco said.

"Janet!" Praeter screamed.

"Your secretary's not out there," DeMarco said. Before Praeter could say anything else, he said, "Mr. Praeter, I'm an investigator from Congress and I . . ."

"Did you hear what I said on the phone?"

"No. Now, as I was saying . . ."

"Are you recording this conversation?"

"What? No. Look, I just want to know if . . ."

"I'm not talking to you."

Then Praeter sat down in his big, black chair, crossed his arms over his chest, and closed his mouth in a tight line—a virtual parody of a kid zipping his lips shut.

"Mr. Praeter, I'd just like to know about your relationship to Douglas Campbell."

Praeter just shook his head. Stubborn little kid refusing to talk.

"You can be subpoenaed, Mr. Praeter."

Praeter shook his head again, then pointed at the door, directing DeMarco to leave.

This was hopeless. The guy was a nut.

DeMarco left.

———◆———

"Crazy Dickie," Sal Anselmo said, shaking his head. "What a piece of work."

DeMarco was in Lilly O'Brien's on Murray Street drinking Grey Goose martinis with Sal. He and Salvatore Anselmo met freshman year in college, and while DeMarco was obtaining mediocre marks in pre-law, Sal was getting equally lackluster grades in business. As undergraduates, studying had not been a priority for either of them.

Sal now worked at the New York Stock Exchange, thriving in the screaming frenzy of the trading floor. And, judging by his suit, he was doing okay. Maybe not as well as Richard Praeter, but okay. Sal had already called his wife and told her that he wouldn't be home until the wee hours because he'd been invited to play poker with some guys from work—and the fact that he had used a poker game as his alibi was an indicator of Sal's wife's feelings toward DeMarco. Mrs. Anselmo had met her future husband in college and she had always thought that DeMarco had some sort of Rasputin-like hold over her boyfriend, as if DeMarco periodically hypnotized poor, gullible Sal and forced him to drink until he puked.

"But the sucker's a genius," Sal said regarding Praeter. "A damn legend on the Street."

"What do you know about his background?"

"Not much. He came here twenty-some years ago and hired on with Morgan Stanley, where he lasted about six months. He was a whiz kid and he was making money for the firm, but he was such a prick, both to the clients and the people he worked with, that they fired him. And when you think about that—about Morgan Stanley firing a guy who was making them money because of his personality—that means Praeter had to be a complete and total asshole. After that, or so the story goes, Praeter ran around town trying to get people to loan him money so he could invest on his own, but naturally nobody would because he had no track record, no assets to put up for collateral, and was an asshole who couldn't hold down a job."

Sal took a big sip from his martini—and expensive vodka dribbled down his chin and onto his tie. "Then something happened, nobody knows what, and suddenly Dickie's rich. He got some seed money from somewhere, invested it, and made a bundle. And then he just took off from there. Now, of course, Morgan Stanley wants him back no matter how big a jerk he is, to which Crazy Dickie naturally says 'Go fuck yourself.'"

"But you don't know where he got the start-up money?"

"Nope. All I know is he made a killing on some company but I have no idea where he got the money he invested. And, of course, Dickie won't say." Sal laughed. "I talked to a guy who went to a meeting with him one time. Praeter gets a cab, goes uptown. Stops the cab, gets another cab, goes downtown. Stops again, gets a *third* cab, and goes back uptown. The guy said Praeter was convinced someone was trying to follow them to the meeting. Another thing I heard is that he can't keep a secretary because he's always firing them because he thinks they're spying on him. He's a fuckin' Grade A, certified nut."

DeMarco ordered another martini, his third—or maybe his fourth. He should have kept the swizzle sticks to keep track of the number since his brain was no longer capable of simple addition. He did notice that his tooth wasn't bothering him as much; martinis were apparently a better anesthetic than oil of cloves and, come to think of it, they tasted about the same. After his drink arrived, he spent a few more minutes asking questions about Richard Praeter for which Sal had no answers. DeMarco finally gave up. "So," he said, "all you really know is that twenty years ago this guy comes into some cash, invests it, and now he's richer than shit because he's so good at what he does."

"Well, yeah," Sal said, "but that's more than you knew before you talked to me—and which is why this Bud's on you." Then he held up his empty martini glass for the bartender to see so he could order another fourteen dollar drink. *Bud, my ass.*

"Let me ask you this," DeMarco said. "Could this guy buy stock in a company and somehow disguise the purchase so the SEC or the IRS or whoever couldn't figure out that he'd bought the stock?"

Sal's attention was momentarily captured by a woman built like a Victoria's Secret model, wearing the archetypal little black cocktail dress that reached midthigh. DeMarco knew Sal was faithful to his thick-ankled, nagging wife, and devoted to his three kids, but like most men he couldn't help but dream.

"I don't know. Maybe," Sal said, finally taking his eyes off the woman. "Dickie's smart as a whip, but why would he do something stupid like that? He's already rich; why would he break the law?"

Shit. None of this was helping—and DeMarco was beginning to suspect that drinking martinis with Salvatore Anselmo wasn't the way to make progress. He began to reach for his wallet to pay a bar tab that had to be over a hundred bucks, when Sal said, "Hey, there's a fight at the Garden tonight. A couple of heavyweights and some Puerto Rican kid who's supposed to be the next Sugar Ray. I know a guy who can get us tickets. You wanna go?"

"Boxing is a barbaric sport," DeMarco said. "And the people who watch it are depraved, sitting there cheering while two men try to beat each other to death."

"That's right," Sal said. "So you wanna go?"

"Sure."

24

An unmarked white envelope was sitting in the middle of Robert Fairchild's desk when Preston Whitman walked into the congressman's office. Fairchild pushed the envelope toward the lobbyist using the eraser-end of a pencil.

"There's a cashier's check for a hundred and twenty five thousand dollars in that envelope, son," Fairchild said. "The amount that Molly Mahoney owes the Atlantic Palace casino plus a little more, kind of like a tip. You see, I want Ted Allen to tear up her marker. In other words, I want their records to show that the casino has absolved her debt. Do you understand?"

"No," Whitman said. "Why are you paying off Molly's gambling debt?"

"I'm not paying it off. Didn't you hear what I just said? The casino is going to *cancel* her debt."

"But why do you want that to happen?" Whitman asked, and Big Bob explained.

Whitman was impressed. He'd never thought that Fairchild was bright enough to think of a plan like this, but apparently he was. But Whitman still had a problem—a major problem.

"Congressman," he said, "I can't just give Ted Allen that money. He'll want to know where it came from. More important, he's going to want to know whom I've talked to about his connection to Molly Mahoney. I'm concerned, sir, that Mr. Allen's reaction to any perceived indiscretion on my part might be rather, uh, violent."

"So figure something out," Fairchild said. "You're a smart guy."

25

The morning after drinking martinis with Sal Anselmo at Lilly O'Brien's, then attending a boxing match at the Garden where he drank beer with Sal, DeMarco woke up at seven a.m. with a hangover so bad he thought he should be in an intensive care unit connected to life support. But, stalwart soldier that he was, he made a reservation for a flight leaving at ten for Myrtle Beach, South Carolina.

DeMarco sat at the bar sipping iced tea through a straw, the straw being the best way to keep cold liquid from cascading over his fractured tooth. As he sipped, he looked out at the marina, then beyond the marina, at the sailboats maneuvering on the water. There were eight boats all clustered together, having some sort of mini-regatta, and all the boats were flying brightly colored spinnakers. What a picture.

He could get used to this: an ocean view and sailboats and cute bar-maids in short shorts. And he'd picked up a little brochure at the airport while waiting for his rental car and it said that there were about eight zillion golf courses in the area, and except for the occasional hurricane, the weather was usually perfect.

DeMarco wished that Mahoney had some sort of field office in Myrtle Beach, South Carolina.

He had decided he needed to see Rusty McGrath. Well, he didn't exactly have a need to see him; he just couldn't think of anything better to do. But when he discovered that McGrath wasn't home—or, to be precise, when he discovered that McGrath was out motoring about *on* his home—he was forced to sit in a bar and enjoy the scenery while waiting for sailor McGrath to return to port.

As DeMarco waited, he thought about calling Alice's good-looking friend, the mother of two, and asking her out for dinner. He'd just placed his hand on his cell phone, when the bartender said, "Hey, McGrath's coming in."

"Where?" DeMarco said, standing up and searching the sea like he was looking for Ahab's whale.

"Right there," the bartender said, pointing his index finger. "That boat that's about the size of an Aegis cruiser, just off the breakwater."

DeMarco finished his iced tea and walked slowly over to the marina. He could understand a potential relationship between Campbell and Praeter: Campbell was the insider at Reston Tech and Praeter was the sharp investor who bought the stock. But he couldn't figure out where Rusty McGrath fit in—and yet it was McGrath, and not Praeter, whom Campbell had called the night DeMarco threatened Campbell. So DeMarco just wanted to put his eyeballs on the guy.

He waited at McGrath's slip and watched as McGrath maneuvered his sixty-foot boat into its space as easily as if he were parallel parking a car. DeMarco didn't know if the boat had those side-thruster things like they have on cruise ships or if he was just very good at the helm.

The boat's hull was sleek and gleaming white, and although DeMarco's knowledge of expensive hardwoods was limited, he was pretty sure the deck was teak. On the bow of the boat, lying on a striped cushion, was a young woman in her twenties. The woman wore a white bikini and had a body that would not have been out of place on the cover of *Sports Illustrated*'s annual swimsuit issue.

"Mr. McGrath?" DeMarco said to the man who had just climbed down a ladder from the bridge.

"Yeah. Here, be a pal and tie me off up forward," McGrath said and tossed DeMarco a white nylon rope. DeMarco took the rope and looped it uncertainly around a cleat on the dock. While DeMarco was tying up the forward line, McGrath jumped gracefully from the boat to the dock and secured the aft mooring line.

McGrath was a big man, six three, two hundred and twenty pounds. His hair was short and curly—a reddish-brown color, perfect for a guy called "Rusty"—and his face and arms were tanned like those of a man who spent most of his days outdoors. Unlike Douglas Campbell, he was in good shape and had the biceps of a weight lifter.

McGrath walked over to DeMarco and looked down at the line he'd secured. "I can see you're no sailor, partner," he said, and retied the line.

"Mr. McGrath," DeMarco said, "my name's . . ."

"Hang on a second," McGrath said to DeMarco. "Hey, Tammy baby."

"Yeah, sugar," the young woman said without raising her head from the cushion. She spoke slowly, as if she were half asleep, and she had a deep, sexy Southern accent. Rocks would melt in her mouth.

"The ice maker's on the fritz again," McGrath said. "How 'bout goin' on up to the office and gettin' us a bag of ice. A five pounder'll do."

"Oh, do I have to?" Tammy said.

"Yeah," McGrath said. "I wanna cold drink but I gotta talk to this gentleman for a minute." Before Tammy could argue that her primary purpose in life was to be decorative, not to fetch and carry, McGrath added, "And when I'm done we'll go get us some dinner at that steak place you like."

Tammy rose languidly from the cushion where she'd been reclining, stretched, and slipped on a pair of flip-flops. The stretch was a show worth watching. McGrath helped her descend from the boat, and then he and DeMarco both stood silently for a moment admiring her ass as she walked slowly up the dock toward the marina office.

"I gotta tell you, sir," McGrath said to DeMarco, his eyes still fixed on Tammy's backside, "the good Lord is one helluva engineer."

"Mr. McGrath my name is Joe DeMarco. I'm from . . ."

"Yeah, I know who you are. Dog told me all about you."

"Dog?"

"Dog Campbell. That's what we called him, back in the day, *Douglas* being kind of a pussy name for a defensive tackle. I used to crawl right up ol' Dog's fat ass when we played together. I'd use his big butt like a launchin' pad to bring down them sneaky little runnin' backs. Anyway, he said you came out to his house the other night and tried to scare him. Shame on you, DeMarco. His wife's already givin' the man ulcers; he doesn't need you puttin' pressure on him too."

"Did Campbell tell you what we discussed?"

"Yeah. He said you're trying to get some big shot's daughter off the hook with the SEC, so you accused him of pulling some kinda insider trading scam. Pure bullshit, but you got the boy's attention."

"Why did he call you?"

"Cuz we're teammates, best buds from way back." McGrath winked then added, "Good thing he doesn't know I nailed his old lady a few times when she still had some juice in her."

"What do you do for a living, Mr. McGrath?"

"You know, I feel like tellin' you to kiss my ass, but since you're with the G you'll just go check my tax returns. Anyway, I'm an investor." Jerking a thumb in the direction of his boat, he added, "And a pretty darn good one, if I say so myself."

"Is Richard Praeter your financial adviser?"

"Dickie? Hell, no! Dickie's crazier than a shithouse rat. I use a couple boys down here, got offices over in Charleston."

"But you do know Richard Praeter."

"Yeah, I just said so. He went to school at UVA for a while with me and Dog." McGrath laughed. "I used to make him do my homework so I wouldn't lose my eligibility. But so what if I know Dickie? Why are you here, DeMarco?"

"I'm here because Douglas Campbell called you about twenty minutes after I talked to him."

"You know the time of the call? What'd you do, tap his phone or something?" When McGrath said this he was grinning. Apparently, everything was a game to this guy.

"Maybe," DeMarco said, his expression dead serious.

For just an instant, DeMarco saw concern in McGrath's eyes as he thought about the possibility of DeMarco having recorded his conversation with Campbell, but then he laughed. "You government guys, you crack me up," he said.

"McGrath, the SEC knows that somebody at Reston Tech, on three separate occasions, made a killing in the market based on insider information. The first time, the information was most likely leaked to Richard Praeter, although the SEC could never prove this. The second and third times, information was leaked to someone who set up phony investment companies, made a ton of money, and then disappeared before the SEC could get him. Well, I'm pretty sure Campbell is the inside guy, and I think you and Richard Praeter are the ones buying the stock. So I'll tell you the same thing I told Campbell: the first guy who testifies gets a deal for a reduced sentence, and if you explain how and why you set up Molly Mahoney, you'll probably get immunity."

DeMarco had no authority to promise immunity to anyone, but he didn't care.

McGrath just shook his head, a small smile playing on his lips. "You're barkin' up the wrong tree, bud. You check my records and you'll see that every year I make a lot of investments. Some win, some don't, but all of them are completely aboveboard. And I've never had anything to do with Reston Tech because I figured any company that would hire Dog Campbell couldn't be worth a shit. And I'll tell you one other thing. If . . . Ah, here comes Tammy. Damn, that girl's slow."

"What else were you going to tell me?"

"Oh. I was gonna say that if the SEC had anything on me, they'd be down here instead of you. Tammy!" he shouted down the pier. "Come on, baby, move that fine ass. Daddy needs a nice cold drink after talking to this scary man."

McGrath placed a canvas deck chair on the aft end of his boat, took a seat, and put his feet up on the rail. DeMarco had almost reached the end of the pier, and just before he turned to go up the stairs to the parking lot, he looked back at McGrath. McGrath gave him a jaunty, two-finger salute. DeMarco's only response was to stare a moment longer then turn away. That's one hard-looking bastard, McGrath thought. Not exactly how he pictured them D.C. political types.

Tammy brought McGrath his drink, a gin and tonic with a twist of lime. He took it from her without looking at her and said, "Thanks, baby."

"When are we goin' to dinner, sugar?" Tammy said. "I'm starvin.'"

He looked at Tammy's lush figure, the full breasts, the way her waist flared into her hips. She was a beauty now but McGrath had met her mama, who weighed in at well over two hundred pounds; he was guessing that in ten or fifteen years, Tammy would look just like her mother. But that was ten years from now.

"I just wanna sit here and think a bit, sweetie. Why don't you go get dressed? Put on your war paint, or whatever it is you do."

"Rus-tee," she said, dragging out his name in an annoying, little-girl voice. "I *am* ready. I'll just put on a tank top and a pair of shorts. The steak house ain't all that formal, you know."

He looked at her, letting his eyes go frosty. "Don't go gettin' bitchy on me, Tammy. I'm not in the mood. Just plop your butt down somewhere and I'll let you know when it's time to go."

"Jesus, Rusty, what's wrong with you?" Then she did the hair flip thing and flounced away, down a ladder, and into the living section of the yacht.

McGrath looked out at the water, at the whitecaps bouncing on the surface, at the sailboats half a mile away. The wind had picked up a bit and the sailboats were at a forty-five-degree angle to the water as they tacked.

Dog and Dickie, what a pair. The SEC had been trying to get a lock on them for years and had never come close, and yet here was this guy DeMarco asking everybody questions. But DeMarco wasn't the SEC and he wasn't Justice and he wasn't the FBI. Dog said he worked for Congress, but nobody knew what he did over there. All Dog knew was that this gal at Reston, this Molly Mahoney, had gotten her ass nabbed by the SEC and the next thing you know, out of the blue, DeMarco's asking questions. It just didn't make sense. They had no connection to this Mahoney broad; Dog said he barely knew the woman. Which made him wonder if his ol' Dog was lying.

Dog and Dickie. Dog was a marshmallow and Dickie was a squirrel. If they squeezed Dog, he'd cave in like a house of cards. If they squeezed Dickie, he was liable to start throwing his own shit at the walls.

McGrath realized that he was humming a song, that gambling song by Kenny Rogers, the one that said you had to know when to hold 'em and when to fold 'em. In other words, when to stop playing and just walk away from the table. Damn, the subconscious mind was a wonder. It truly was.

McGrath rose from the deck chair and tossed the ice cubes from his drink into the water. He looked around—at his beautiful boat, at the postcard perfect picture of the racing sailboats, at the cushion where Tammy had been sunning herself. He was a lucky man. He had it all.

He had too much to lose.

Well. Time to go down and give Tammy a little jump, get her head right again, then go get a steak for dinner. A good, rare rib eye dripping blood.

DeMarco didn't return immediately to his rental car. He went back to the bar overlooking the marina and ordered a drink—this time a Corona—and gazed down at Rusty McGrath sitting on his boat.

A picture was beginning to emerge, albeit a blurry one. Twenty years ago, Douglas Campbell had been a low-level personnel weenie at Reston Tech probably making an adequate but not spectacular living; Richard Praeter was the leper-genius of Wall Street, a guy who couldn't hold down a job or get the financial backing he needed to make big investments; and Rusty McGrath's career in the NFL had ended prematurely thanks to some other monster shattering his knee. In other words, two of these young men were going nowhere and the third was barely moving.

Then, out of the blue, Praeter gets his hands on a million bucks, invests it, and makes a fortune.

So, DeMarco thought, here's one possible scenario. The three men pool the money they have. Praeter and Campbell wouldn't have much but Rusty McGrath would have whatever was left over from his NFL signing bonus, his first year's salary, and maybe even an insurance settlement for a career-ending injury. Ergo, McGrath was most likely the money guy. Then, based on an insider tip from Campbell, Praeter makes his first major killing in the market—and shares his profits with Campbell and McGrath. McGrath gets a great big boat and Praeter a high-rent office a couple blocks from the Wall Street bull where he can look down on the tourists rubbing its balls.

Campbell, however, has to maintain a lower profile than Praeter and McGrath; to do otherwise might make some government watchdog like the SEC or the IRS wonder why he's suddenly rich. To allow Campbell to at least have a taste of the good life, Praeter uses his expertise to steer Mrs. Campbell's trust fund and deposits the rest of Campbell's ill-gotten gains in some offshore account. Campbell's ultimate plan, however—as he told Molly—was to retire early so he could really enjoy all that money that Praeter had socked away for him.

The final thing, DeMarco concluded, was that they didn't go back to the Reston well too often, just three times in a twenty year period, but when they did go there, they made a bundle. And the reason they didn't tap Campbell's insider position at Reston more than three times was because they didn't need to. Richard Praeter, according to Sal Anselmo, was actually a very good investor and he'd made his two pals even richer with legitimate trades.

Yep, that was DeMarco's theory—and it had several problems.

The biggest problem was that he didn't have one shred of evidence to support it. Second, he couldn't understand the relationship between Campbell and McGrath and Praeter. Campbell and McGrath were old football buddies, but as far as he could tell, they hadn't been close to Praeter. Randy Sawyer had told him that Praeter hadn't even graduated from UVA and the only thing he appeared to have in common with Campbell and McGrath was that he was in the same room with them when another football player flew out a dormitory window. And if McGrath was the money guy like DeMarco thought, he'd have to have a lot of faith in Praeter's ability before he'd give him his savings to invest. Or maybe it wasn't faith; maybe it was fear. Maybe Praeter was blackmailing McGrath over the other football player's death. Hmmm. Maybe. It was hard to imagine a guy like McGrath being afraid of Crazy Dickie Praeter.

Whatever the case, DeMarco liked his half-baked idea: McGrath was the one who gave Praeter the start-up money he needed, Campbell was the insider, and Praeter was the one with the brains. Then DeMarco realized something. His three-man conspiracy theory might explain why Praeter, McGrath, and Campbell were all so wealthy—but he had learned absolutely nothing that connected their activities to Molly Mahoney.

DeMarco finished his beer. He had no idea what he was going to do next, but he was pretty sure that doing what he wanted to do—which was stay in Myrtle Beach for a couple of days playing golf—would not suit Master Mahoney. He rose reluctantly from his bar stool, took a final look at McGrath sitting content on the stern of his yacht—and trudged wearily to his rental car.

26

"There's a hundred and twenty-five thousand dollars in that envelope," Preston Whitman said. "Enough to pay off Molly Mahoney's gambling debt and a little extra to compensate you for your trouble."

"What?" Ted Allen said. "Why are you paying off the girl's marker? And where the hell did the money come from?"

"Calm down, Ted. Let me explain. You see, there are a lot of people who don't like John Mahoney. Some don't like him for personal reasons, and some don't like him because he's a Democrat. I went to a number of these people . . ."

"You what! Goddamnit, if you've . . ."

The lobbyist held up his hand. "Ted, just listen to me. I've been in this business a long time. I know what I'm doing. Anyway, as I was saying, I went to these people and said I was collecting money, just small donations, five or ten thousand dollars—and believe me, that's a *small* donation to these people—and I said the money would be used to cause Mahoney a significant political problem. When they asked exactly how it would be used, I said 'You don't want to know.' It was easy."

"What will these people say when nothing happens to Mahoney?"

"With Mahoney, there's always the possibility that he'll do something to damage himself without any outside help, and if he does, I'll whisper to these donors that they had a hand in his misfortune. If nothing bad happens to him in the near future, then I'll say: be patient, these things take time. If nothing happens after a long period has passed, I'll say: I'm sorry, I tried. These people understand that plans don't always work out and for the amount of money it cost them, they won't be terribly upset. And if they are upset, it will be with me and have nothing to do with you."

Ted Allen thought about everything the lobbyist had said—then he smiled. "You're a tricky bastard, Whitman."

"I'm glad you approve, Ted."

"But I still don't see why telling Mahoney I canceled his daughter's marker is a good thing."

Preston Whitman almost said: *Think about it, you arrogant twit.* But he didn't. Instead he said, "Canceling the girl's debt is a two-edged sword, Ted. On one hand, it's a goodwill gesture on your part. You want Mahoney's help on your project, and by canceling the girl's marker, you're essentially giving him—or his daughter—a hundred grand."

"So it's a bribe."

"On one level. But Mahoney will think: what if the media finds out that the casino canceled my daughter's debt? The media will make it look like you have Mahoney in your pocket. Yes, it would look very, very bad if the media was to learn of this."

"No, shit," Ted said. "And I'd get in trouble for bribing a politician. There's no way . . ."

"Ted, you still don't understand. You didn't give the money to *Mahoney*. You gave it to his daughter by canceling her debt. You haven't done anything illegal. But Mahoney will understand how the media will make things look." Before Ted could say anything else, Whitman said, "Look, no one is ever going to know that you canceled the girl's marker except you, me, and Mahoney—but him knowing puts pressure on him, which is what you want, and it didn't cost you a thing."

Ted sat back in his chair and mulled things over.

To Preston Whitman, Ted Allen looked like a little kid sitting at his daddy's desk, a junior mobster who had the illusion he was playing in the same arena as the big boys. Ted Allen didn't realize that he was just a pawn. He'd always been Al Castiglia's pawn and now he was Big Bob Fairchild's pawn. But Whitman sat there, trying to look respectful and appropriately awed as he awaited Ted's decision.

"I like it," Ted finally said. "And it's about time you started to deliver for me. But I still think I need to do something to make sure Mahoney understands I'm serious."

"What does that mean?" Whitman said.

Ted just smiled.

27

Molly looked through the peephole, then closed her eyes and leaned her head against the door. She recognized the man standing in the hall outside her apartment. She couldn't remember his name, but she knew he worked for Ted Allen—and she just wanted him to go away. Her head hurt something awful. She'd drunk way too much white wine the night before; she had to stop doing that.

The man knocked again. Harder. She knew he wasn't going to go away. Molly opened the door.

"Hi, sweetheart," the man said.

"Hi," Molly said. She knew she looked terrible, dressed in a ratty old bathrobe, her hair not combed, her face all puffy. She probably smelled bad, as well; she couldn't remember the last time she'd showered. But she didn't care. She didn't care about anything these days.

"I'm Gus Amato. Remember me?"

Molly nodded.

"Mr. Allen sent me, honey. He wants to talk to you."

"Oh," Molly said. "Well, I'll call him."

"No, honey. In person. He wants to talk to you in person. He sent me to get you."

"I . . . I can't go right now. I have an appointment with my lawyer this morning."

"I think that's one of the reasons he wants to talk to you. You know, so you understand what to say to your lawyer the next time you see him. So why don't you go get dressed. Okay?"

"Can't I just talk to him on the phone?"

"I'm sorry, sweetheart," the man said, shaking his head. The expression on his face was the same—still friendly, looking a little amused, a little bored—but Molly knew he'd make her go with him if she didn't go voluntarily.

"Can I take a shower first?" she asked.

"Sure, honey. Go take a shower. And I'll make us some coffee while you're doing that."

Daniel Caine—of Caine, Connors, and White—was a well-preserved sixty. His gray hair was cut short, his complexion tanned, his belly flat and hard. He wore wire-rimmed aviator glasses over hard blue eyes. He had the kind of eyes you wanted your lawyer to have—not the other guy's—and he was Molly Mahoney's lawyer.

On the wall behind Caine's desk was a picture of him on a racing bike rounding a curve. He was wearing spandex shorts, a bright green-and-red cycling shirt, and one of those little caps with an upturned bill. The bike, DeMarco figured, was a model with a titanium frame that weighed less than air and probably cost ten grand. In another picture, Caine was straddling his bike, this time wearing an aerodynamic helmet, and shaking hands with another cyclist. The other cyclist was Lance Armstrong.

People like Daniel Caine always depressed DeMarco. DeMarco had graduated from law school the same year his father was killed, and his timing couldn't have been worse: there were very few law firms that wanted the son of a Mafia hitman on their legal team. Fortunately—or maybe not so fortunately—he landed a job with Mahoney before he was forced to change his name. But every time he met the Daniel Caines of the world he had to wonder what he might have accomplished had he not been burdened with his father's legacy. Maybe he could have had an office the size of Caine's and his name on the letterhead of a prestigious firm. Maybe. It troubled him to think that it was more likely that he wasn't as smart and ambitious as Daniel Caine—a man who rode bikes with Lance Armstrong.

In Caine's office were Mary Pat Mahoney, DeMarco, and two other lawyers who worked for Caine, lawyers whose names DeMarco had already forgotten. The purpose of the meeting was for Caine to give all concerned an update on Molly's case.

"How much longer do you think we should wait for Molly, Mrs. Mahoney?" Caine asked, checking the expensive watch on his wrist, reminding her that he billed for tenths of hours.

"I'm sorry," Mary Pat said, "but I don't know where she is. I called her before I came here, but she didn't answer." She reached into her purse and took out a cell phone. "Let me try one more time."

DeMarco couldn't believe that Molly wasn't here for this meeting and he wondered if anyone else in the room was thinking about the bail that Mary Pat had posted to get her daughter released from jail. Nah, Molly wouldn't do that, not to her mom. But why the hell would she miss the meeting? This was her future they were about to discuss.

———◆———

Gus held open the rear door of the town car for Molly to enter, and then got behind the wheel, but he didn't start the car. At that moment, Molly's cell phone rang and Gus said, "Don't answer that! And turn your phone off." He spoke so harshly he scared her, and she did what he said.

Gus still hadn't started the car. He pointed down the street and said, "Honey, is that your car over there? The blue one?"

"What?" Molly said.

"The Subaru. That's yours, right?"

"Yeah," Molly said.

She could see the mud and grime caked onto the car even as far away as they were, and she was embarrassed it was so filthy. She'd bought it three years ago and she remembered her sister, Mitzy, laughing because it was a station wagon and looked like a soccer-mom's car. But Molly liked it. It had all-wheel drive and got good mileage, and she could take it skiing—although she couldn't remember the last time she'd skied. She couldn't remember the last time she'd washed the car either, and now it looked, for some reason, like the sort of car a homeless person might live in.

"Is it insured?" Gus asked.

"What?" she said. He was confusing her with all these questions about her stupid car.

"I want to know if your car's insured."

"Of course, it's insured," she said. But the truth was, it wasn't insured. She hadn't made the last payment. "Why are you asking . . ."

"Watch," Gus said.

At that moment Molly saw a man walking down the street. He was dressed in jeans and a hooded sweatshirt, the hood pulled up over his head, obscuring his face. The way he walked—this arm-swinging, bouncy kind of walk—he looked young and athletic.

He stopped next to Molly's car, looked around, then pulled something out of the little pouch in his sweatshirt. A bottle. He did something with the bottle—unscrewed the top or something—then stuffed a rag inside the mouth of the bottle. Then he pulled something out of his back pocket and smashed the driver's side window of Molly's car.

"What's he doing!" she said.

"Watch," Gus said.

The young man lit the rag, flung the bottle hard into Molly's car, and a second later, the interior of the vehicle was engulfed in flames.

Molly screamed and lunged for the door handle, but before she could open the door she heard the door locks click.

"Calm down, honey," Gus said. "You said it was insured. Plus, you know, a cute girl your age, you probably oughta drive something a little flashier anyway."

<hr />

"Mr. Caine, I think we should get started," Mary Pat said. "I'll fill Molly in when I see her. I just don't know where she could be."

"Well, okay," Caine said, and opened a file on his desk. He studied the file for a moment then said, "Actually, we're in pretty good shape." Caine spoke softly but confidently; he whipped the government's lawyers every day of the week. "The fact that the stock and banking transactions were done online is a good thing. In case our jury has never heard of hackers, computer fraud, and identity theft we have several experts lined up who will instruct them." Caine smiled—a shark showing its teeth. "We may even arrange a small demonstration, like depositing ten bucks into the judge's bank account to prove our point."

Caine waited for everybody to laugh, but the only ones who did were the people who worked for him.

"The second part of Molly's defense has been provided by Mr. De-Marco," Caine said, and nodded graciously to DeMarco to show his appreciation. "Thanks to him, we know that the SEC has suspected someone at Reston Technologies of insider trading for quite some time—someone other than Molly, that is—and Mr. DeMarco has identified three men who might be involved. I'll argue that these people were afraid that the SEC was getting close to them, so they decided to conduct their illegal business under Molly's name."

"Can you prove this?" Mary Pat asked.

"No, and I don't have to," Caine said.

"What do you mean?" Mary Pat said.

"Mrs. Mahoney, I need to create reasonable doubt. I need to show that it's possible that someone other than Molly could have committed the crime she's been accused of. So I don't have to prove these men did anything illegal. I just need to show that they *could* have."

Mary Pat looked skeptical but before she could say anything, Caine continued, "We'll subpoena all of the SEC's records involving persons of interest at Reston Tech for the last twenty years. If the SEC claims that providing these records will jeopardize future prosecutions, we'll argue for dismissal of the charges and we'll win. Also working in our favor is the fact that the crime Molly has been accused of committing involves half a million dollars that was directly deposited into her account. This helps us in two ways. First, the SEC has been unable to determine who deposited the money. This is good because it supports our argument that some unknown person, someone unconnected to Molly, put the money in her account to set her up and then this same person took the money out of her account and bought the stock in her name.

"The other advantage we have, although this might be somewhat embarrassing for Molly, is we can show that with her financial situation, she didn't have half a million to invest."

"Well, of course she doesn't have that kind of money," Mary Pat said. "She's only been out of school four years."

Apparently, no one had told Mary Pat about her daughter's credit card debit—and DeMarco didn't want to be the one to tell her.

"The government is going to say that Molly has a rich partner," DeMarco said.

Caine smiled at DeMarco. The smile said: leave the lawyering to us real lawyers, sonny. "They can say that," Caine said, "but they can't prove it."

DeMarco hated to say it front of Mary Pat but he had to. "And the fact that Molly's in debt also gives her a motive."

"What?" Mary Pat said, her head spinning in DeMarco's direction. "What are you talking about, Joe? What debt?"

"Molly owes a rather large amount on her credit cards, Mrs. Mahoney," Caine said.

"She does?" Mary Pat said.

"Yes, but that's not really a problem," Caine said, waving the issue away with his right hand. "So she owes some money? Big deal. If a jury is impanelled—I mean if this case ever goes to trial—I'll do credit checks on all the jurors and say: I know that at least four members of this jury have significant debts, but you're not criminals, are you?"

Mary Pat nodded but DeMarco could tell she was still thinking about her daughter's credit card situation.

"So what we're going to do," Caine said, "is subpoena Misters Campbell, McGrath, and Praeter."

"Are these the three men you mentioned earlier?" Mary Pat asked.

"Yes. Three men who may have been using insider information to buy stock in companies that are clients of Reston Tech, and two of them have been previously investigated by the SEC."

"If the SEC knows these men could have done this, why aren't they . . ."

"The SEC can't prove they've done anything illegal, Mrs. Mahoney," Caine said, "but as I've told you, that's irrelevant. That just shows how smart these people are. So we'll subpoena their financial records, and we'll subpoena them to testify at the trial. We'll subpoena PNC Financial and show that Praeter's and Campbell's finances are linked via Mrs. Campbell's trust fund. That is, we'll show that Campbell, who works for Reston Tech, and Mr. Praeter, a very clever investor, have a connection."

"You can subpoena them," DeMarco said, "but you need to understand that I didn't find anything connecting them to Molly. They just look . . . well, funny to me."

"Exactly!" Caine said, as if DeMarco had just made his point. "We'll put these three on the stand and ask them questions about their wealth and their success in the market and point out that Campbell, unlike Molly, has been at Reston Tech during the time the SEC has noticed a pattern of insider trading."

"But if you can't prove these men have done something illegal . . ." Mary Pat said.

"They provide a plausible *alternative*, Mrs. Mahoney," Caine said, his impatience showing just a bit. "I need to give a jury someone else to consider—someone other than Molly, someone who owns a sixty-foot boat like Mr. McGrath or a two-million-dollar home in Chevy Chase like Mr. Campbell. Juries tend not to like people who own two-million-dollar homes, not unless they own one, too."

"I understand all that," Mary Pat said, "but if these men are innocent you could unjustly damage their reputations."

Caine shrugged—and the message was clear: Molly was his client and whatever should befall Campbell and his pals was not his problem.

"Okay," Caine said, rubbing his hands together, wrapping things up, "we'll keep plugging away. We've asked for time to file motions and review the material we've subpoenaed. With the court's calendar being the way it is, I don't expect we'll go to trial—assuming we ever go to trial—for at least six months."

"But Molly's been suspended from her job," Mary Pat said.

"Suspended with pay," Caine said.

"Still, it makes it look like she's guilty. This will set her back professionally."

"I'm sorry, Mrs. Mahoney," Caine said, "but I can't do anything about Molly's suspension from work. However, after the criminal case is settled in her favor, we may be able to sue Reston Tech or the SEC for damages. Molly might never have to work again."

"Oh no, I don't want that," Mary Pat said. "I just want this to be over with."

Caine made another small shoulder shrug that could have meant anything. "Well, that's something we can always discuss later," he said.

As Mary Pat and DeMarco were leaving Caine's office, Mary Pat said, "You need to find Molly, Joe. Something's wrong. She should have been here."

"I will," DeMarco said.

"And this credit card stuff, Joe. Do you have any idea what that's all about?"

"All I know is she owes a lot of money but I don't know why."

"How much?"

DeMarco hesitated. He hadn't even discussed Molly's credit card situation with Mahoney. "About a hundred thousand."

"Oh my God."

28

A fire truck and a police car were blocking the street near Molly's apartment building, so DeMarco had to park a block away. As he walked toward Molly's, he saw a burnt-out car on the other side of the street, looking like something you'd see on the streets of Baghdad. The lights on the emergency vehicles weren't flashing and the car was no longer burning; it had been soaked down thoroughly by the firefighters and water was streaming toward the gutter drains. The incident must have happened recently, however, because there were still a few gawkers at the scene.

As DeMarco walked toward the entrance to Molly's building, he asked one of the gawkers—a young woman pushing a baby in a stroller —what had happened.

"Someone bombed that car," she said.

"Bombed it?" DeMarco said.

"Fire-bombed it." Pointing at a short Hispanic woman in her sixties who was talking to one of the cops, she said, "Mrs. Gomez saw him do it. She was looking out her window like she always is, and saw this kid throw something into that car. It just exploded, she said, and then the kid took off, running like Carl Lewis. I just don't understand what's wrong with people these days."

"Huh," DeMarco said. Probably some kind of gang thing, he thought.

DeMarco entered the apartment building and because the elevator wasn't working, took the stairs up to Molly's floor. He knocked on the door, and no one answered. He thought about the way Molly had been drinking the last two times he saw her and wondered if she was inside, passed out, and if that was why she'd missed the appointment with her lawyer. He hammered on the door long and hard. Molly didn't answer, but the old woman who lived in the apartment across the hall stuck her head out to see what was going on.

"Have you seen Molly Mahoney?" he asked the old woman.

"No. But she's obviously not home, you beating on the door hard enough to wake the dead."

"Sorry," DeMarco muttered, wondering where the hell Molly had gone and why she wasn't answering her cell phone.

As he left the building, he looked over at the burnt-out car again. Station wagon. Then he remembered when he met Molly the other night and he'd walked her to her car, she'd been driving a station wagon, but he hadn't paid any attention to the model. All he remembered was that it looked like it hadn't been washed in a year. He couldn't tell if the smoking pile of scrap metal on the street was the same car, but it could be.

He walked over to the cop who was still chatting with Mrs. Gomez.

"Excuse me," DeMarco said.

The cop turned to look at him. "Yeah?" he said.

"Do you know who that car belongs to?" DeMarco asked.

"Why are you asking?" the cop said.

"Because I think it may belong to a friend of mine, but I'm not sure. So do you know . . ."

"Who's your friend?" the cop said.

This guy was starting to piss him off, answering every question with a question.

"Her name's Molly Mahoney," DeMarco said.

"Well, that's who the car belongs to," the cop said. "We ran the plates. You got any idea why anyone would want to do this to your friend's car?"

"Was Molly hurt?"

"I asked you . . ."

"Yeah, I heard what you asked. And I want to know if Molly was hurt."

Mrs. Gomez answered before the cop could turn pissy. "She wasn't hurt," she said. "I saw her leave with a man just before it happened."

"Do you know who the man was?" DeMarco asked.

The cop started to say something, but Mrs. Gomez talked right over him. "No. Just what I told this policeman. He was a short, strong-looking guy wearing fancy white cowboy boots. I didn't really notice his face. Just the boots."

"Do you have any idea why somebody would want to destroy Ms. Mahoney's car?" the cop asked DeMarco.

"No. I don't have clue," DeMarco said and turned to walk away.

"Hey, wait a minute," the cop said. "Who are you and what are you doing here?"

Aw, shit. DeMarco pulled out his congressional ID. "My name's DeMarco. And like I told you, I'm a friend of Molly's and I just stopped by to see her."

Five minutes later, after the cop pestered him with a dozen questions he couldn't or wouldn't answer, DeMarco left. The car bombing could have been some sort of random act of vandalism, he thought, although destroying someone's car went way beyond tagging a wall with graffiti. Or maybe somebody saw Molly on television as she was leaving the courthouse after her arraignment, and decided to use a Molotov cocktail to express his displeasure at folks who engage in insider trading. Maybe—but unlikely. The good news was that Molly wasn't hurt. But why did she miss the appointment with her lawyer and run off with some guy wearing fancy cowboy boots? Before he could guess at an answer to this question, Mahoney's secretary called and told him the man wanted to see him.

29

The lights were out in Mahoney's office and the blinds were closed. DeMarco wondered if Mahoney was having one of his migraines, the headaches usually occurring when he smoked too much and didn't eat anything but bourbon. Mahoney refused to believe, however, that there was a connection between his habits and his headaches. But this time it wasn't a migraine; it was just a father sitting in the dark brooding about his daughter.

"Boss, I just came from Molly's apartment and someone . . ."

Mahoney cut him off. "What did her lawyer have to say?"

"Didn't Mary Pat tell you?"

"She called while I was in a meeting and I haven't called her back yet. I wanted to hear what you had to say first."

"Well, according to Caine, things are looking pretty good," DeMarco said, and he told Mahoney about the discussion in Caine's office and Caine's strategy for creating reasonable doubt. Mahoney didn't interrupt once while he was speaking, which was surprising, and he wondered if Mahoney was paying attention. DeMarco concluded by saying, "But there is one problem, though."

"Oh, yeah. What's that?"

"Molly has a motive," DeMarco said. "She's carrying a lot of debt. She's maxed out every credit card she has."

"How do you know this?" Mahoney asked. He didn't sound shocked by DeMarco's pronouncement. It was more like DeMarco had confirmed something Mahoney already knew and Mahoney's question was literal: how did *DeMarco* know about his daughter's debt?

"I ran a credit check on her," DeMarco said.

DeMarco waited for Mahoney to blow up at him for having the balls to check out his daughter's credit rating, but Mahoney didn't say anything. He just nodded his big head, a white blur in the darkened room.

"The other thing is, Mary Pat knows about Molly's credit card situation. Caine brought it up during the meeting and I had to tell her how much she owed."

"Aw, shit," Mahoney muttered.

"So the SEC is going to argue that Molly's motive was all the debt she's carrying, but like I said, Caine still thinks he has a pretty good defense. The other good news is that Caine's managed to kick the trial downstream at least six months. I'm going to need the time to figure out who deposited the money in Molly's account. I know a guy, a computer guy. He's out of town right now, but when he gets back . . ."

"Molly did it, Joe," Mahoney said.

"What?" DeMarco said, not sure he'd heard what he'd just heard.

"I said, she did it. She's guilty. So don't bother with the computer guy."

"But what makes you think . . ."

"And she not only maxed-out her credit cards, she's in hock to a casino for another hundred grand. My daughter's a gambling junky, Joe."

Those two words—*gambling junky*—answered a host of questions. They explained Molly's credit card debt and why she lived in a dump. But instead of saying what he was thinking, DeMarco tried to comfort Mahoney. "She may owe some money, but that doesn't mean she . . ."

"And the half million deposited into her account?" Mahoney said. "It came from the same casino she owes the hundred K to. She went to the head of the casino and *pitched* him the insider trading scheme."

"How do you know all this? Did Molly tell you?"

"No, the guy who runs the casino told me." And Mahoney told DeMarco about the meeting he had with Ted Allen in Atlantic City.

Neither man spoke for a minute, then DeMarco said, "So what does he want?"

"What the hell do you think he wants?" Mahoney shouted. "He wants his money back. He also wants the federal government to give the state of New Jersey a hundred million bucks to help build a convention center in Atlantic City."

"A convention center?"

"Yeah."

"Why?"

"I dunno for sure, but I'm guessing he'll make a bunch of money if it's built."

"Is there anything else?"

"Yeah, there's one other little thing. I think the guy who runs the casino is connected to the Mob."

Before DeMarco could react to this news, the phone on Mahoney's desk rang. Mahoney tapped the speaker button and said, "What is it?"

"Your wife's on line two," Mavis said. "She said she needs to speak with you urgently."

"Tell her . . . Oh shit, just tell her I'll have to call her back." He disconnected the call and said to DeMarco, "I'm gonna catch hell for that."

"It sounds like the smart thing to do is give Ted Allen his money and let Molly take her chances at the trial," DeMarco said. "Caine thinks he can win and . . ."

"I don't want a trial, Joe. Going to trial when you're innocent is one thing, but going to trial when you're guilty is a whole other thing. And as for the money . . . Counting her credit card debt and her legal bills, we're talking about seven hundred grand. Seven hundred! I don't have that kind of money."

This surprised DeMarco; he'd always thought that Mahoney was rich.

"I'd have to sell the house in Boston and maybe Mary Pat's boat to raise that kind of cash. God would that ever break her heart, if we had to sell that boat." He started to say something else but stopped and just shook his head.

"You have a lot of friends, boss," DeMarco said. "And there are a lot of other people out there who I'm sure would be willing to help you out." What DeMarco meant, but didn't say, was that a lot of people would be happy to give Mahoney the money in return for his influence.

"No!" Mahoney said, banging his fist down on his desk.

Aw, shit. DeMarco knew what was coming next. He knew because he didn't work for a reasonable man.

"I'm not giving these people a fucking thing!" Mahoney said. "You got that? These bastards got my daughter hooked and then they coerced her into committing a felony."

DeMarco wasn't too sure about any of that, but he knew it was a distraught father talking.

"Well?" Mahoney said. "Do you understand?"

"Yeah," DeMarco said. "I understand. You want me to get Molly off for a crime you now know she's committed and you want to get the Mob off her back without paying them."

"That's right," Mahoney said. "And I don't want this case going to trial and I don't want her mother to find out what she did."

30

DeMarco was on the Atlantic City Expressway, a straight-as-an-arrow drag strip designed to reduce the time people spent driving and thereby increase the time they spent giving the casinos their money.

When he had told Mahoney how Molly's car had been firebombed, the blood had drained from Mahoney's normally red face. That was the first time DeMarco had ever seen John Mahoney looking scared.

Mahoney's first question had naturally been: "Was she hurt?"

Before DeMarco could answer, Mahoney's face turned back to red again, like a chameleon dropped onto a Chinese flag, and he screamed, "Why the hell didn't you tell me this the minute you walked in here?"

DeMarco didn't bother to say that he'd tried. Instead he said that Molly hadn't been in the car and that before the bombing she was seen leaving her apartment with a guy wearing white cowboy boots.

Mahoney stood up and his big hands clutched the edge of his desk, and for a moment DeMarco thought he was going to flip it over.

"That guy works for Ted Allen. Are you telling me they kidnapped my daughter!" Mahoney screamed.

They finally decided that Molly hadn't been kidnapped. Ted Allen wouldn't be that stupid, and if even he was that stupid, he wouldn't have kidnapped her in broad daylight. They concluded that Ted was doing two things: one, he wanted to meet with Molly and tell her what would happen to her if she testified against him. He'd trot out Denny Reed, as he had for Mahoney, and make sure Molly understood that Denny could be either her salvation or her demise. The second thing they concluded was that Ted was sending Mahoney a message, and not a very subtle one. The message was: Your daughter could have been in her car.

Mahoney said, "I'm gonna kill that son of a bitch."

DeMarco had never considered it his job to protect Mahoney; he'd always figured that Mahoney was the last guy who needed his protection. But maybe that wasn't the case right now. In the frame of mind he was in, Mahoney just might kill Ted Allen. And that's when DeMarco had said: "Look, boss, Molly's okay. I'll drive up to Atlantic City and bring her back. And I'll have a talk with Ted."

The last thing Mahoney said to him before he left was: "When you find her, Joe, bring her to me. I want to talk to her before her mother does."

So DeMarco was on his way to Atlantic City to get Molly—and to have a chat with Ted Allen. He was now driving by all the giant billboards on the expressway that proclaimed that the slot machines in every casino just *spit* out money. They used the term "loose"—the "loosest slots on the Boardwalk."

He pulled into the Atlantic Palace's parking garage and took the elevator to the main casino floor. The sound of all the loose slot machines almost deafened him when the doors opened. He walked over to the security desk and told a man standing there that he wanted to see Mr. Allen. The guard asked if he had an appointment and DeMarco said no. "Tell Mr. Allen I'm from Washington, D.C., and that a very pissed off politician sent me."

When DeMarco entered Ted's penthouse office, Ted was sitting behind his desk wearing a black sport jacket, a maroon T-shirt, and grey slacks. His tasseled loafers were up on the desk. He was a portrait of a relaxed, confident man—a man who had no doubt that he had the world by the balls.

With Ted, standing off to one side, was a short, wide guy wearing a dark suit over a white polo shirt. On his feet were white alligator-skin cowboy boots. He was also wearing a shoulder holster containing a big black automatic.

"Where's Molly?" DeMarco said.

"Who are you?" Ted said.

"My name's DeMarco. I work for John Mahoney. I'm the guy he sends to deal with people like you."

"People like me?" Ted said, and smiled.

"That's right, Ted."

"So you know about the problem I currently have with Mahoney and his daughter."

"Yeah. You got your hooks into Molly, then fucked up big time when she was arrested and your money was frozen."

"That's one way to put it," Ted said. "Has Mahoney decided to cooperate?"

"He's still thinking about it," DeMarco said.

Ted took his feet off the desk and stood up. He didn't look so relaxed now. He looked like he was about to have a little hissy fit.

"You need to make it clear to Mahoney," Ted said, "that I'm not screwing around here. Either he does what I want, or his daughter goes to jail. And that's the *best* scenario."

"Is that why you firebombed her car and dragged her up here? To scare Mahoney?"

"I don't know what you're talking about. I didn't firebomb anything. And I didn't *drag* her up here. I sent a car for her. I even gave her a couple hundred in chips so she can play for a while." Ted barked out a laugh before he added, "But with her luck, I doubt she'll be playing all that long. The last time I checked she was having lunch, and when she's finished playing, Gus," Ted said, pointing at the guy with the boots, "will take her back to D.C."

"No, she'll be going back with me," DeMarco said. "Now I want you to listen to me, Ted. You're screwing around with one of the most powerful politicians in this country. Do you understand that? He's not some small-time city councilman. He can have the FBI climbing all over your dumb ass with one phone call. The smartest thing you can do right now is to write off your losses and let Molly take her chances at a trial. In return, I promise we'll keep your name out of it."

"No, you listen to me," Ted said. "I'm gonna give Molly a little break and cancel her gambling marker, but . . ."

"What?" DeMarco said.

"I said, I'm canceling her gambling marker. Tell Mahoney he can consider that a gift, a gesture to show that I'm a reasonable man. But I want the five hundred grand back that's been frozen by the SEC, and I want federal funding for my convention center. And if I don't get what I want, Molly Mahoney's bony ass is going to end up in prison. Or worse. Now toss this asshole out of my casino, Gus."

Gus said, "Let's go, pal," then he made the mistake of grabbing DeMarco's shoulder to move him out of the room.

DeMarco had a punching bag in his Georgetown home. He liked to hit it when he was frustrated—and right now he was very frustrated. He was mad about what Molly had done and the way she'd lied to him and her parents. He was also pissed at Ted Allen for trying to take advantage of the situation. And his tooth hurt. So when Gus Amato grabbed his shoulder, he spun around and hit him on the chin harder than he had ever hit his punching bag.

In a fair fight, Gus would most likely have beaten him. He looked stronger than DeMarco and he was probably used to hitting folks. But it wasn't a fair fight. DeMarco punched him when he wasn't expecting it, and Gus collapsed to the floor, landing hard on his butt, legs sprawled straight out in front of him. His eyes had the glassy, unfocused look of someone on the verge of unconsciousness. But then he shook his head like a dog shaking off water, and his limbs began to move in slow, un-coordinated movements as he struggled to get to his feet—so DeMarco pulled the automatic from Gus's shoulder holster and hit him on the side of the head with the barrel of the heavy weapon.

Then Gus was unconscious.

Molly Mahoney was not eating lunch as Ted had said. She was at a craps table and it looked like she was winning. The rack in front of her was filled with chips—green and black chips. A green chip is worth twenty-five dollars; a black one is worth a hundred. Her face was flushed and her eyes were shining as if she'd just had the best sex of her young life.

DeMarco wanted to grab her by the nape of the neck and shake her.

Molly had the dice in her hand and she was rolling—and judging by the chips in front of her, she'd been rolling for a very long time. She was making money for herself and the other ten men standing at the craps table, and if DeMarco interrupted her roll they'd take him outside and feed him to the seagulls.

At that moment, Molly hit her point, a four. The men at the table all roared and Molly high-fived the guy on her right, then the one on her left. She threw a green chip to the stickman as a tip.

It was her turn to roll again. She put five hundred dollars on the pass line, the table limit. She shook the dice, then stopped, and tossed a hundred dollar chip to the stickman. "Boxcars," she said.

Boxcars is the number twelve, six dots showing on each die, and if Molly hit the number on her next roll her she would collect three thousand dollars because the bet paid thirty to one. But she had to throw the twelve on the next roll, and the next roll only. And the reason the bet paid thirty to one was, of course, because the odds of hitting the number were practically nil. It was an absolutely stupid bet—but Molly rolled a twelve and won.

The guys at the table all roared again. Molly was their queen.

She rolled again. She threw a nine, then three—then a seven. Her roll was over. All her new friends congratulated her on the fine job she'd done as if skill had been involved instead of dumb luck, and then immediately forgot about her as the dice were passed to the next guy.

DeMarco walked up behind her and whispered in her ear, "Pick up your fuckin' chips and cash out. Now."

Molly spun around and saw it was DeMarco. She started to say something, but before she could, DeMarco said, "I swear to Christ, Molly, I'll drag you away from this table by your hair."

DeMarco's feelings toward Molly Mahoney had changed. At first he'd felt sorry for her, the way Kay Kiser had refused to give her the benefit of the doubt. And later, when he saw the way she was living and discovered how much money she owed, he still felt sorry for her. He had wanted to defend this frail young woman who was being assaulted from every side. But now he knew she was guilty of the crime that Kiser had accused her of, and that wasn't the worst part. There was something devious and manipulative about Molly. She'd been clever enough to pitch Ted Allen the stock scheme to get out from under him, and then, after she was caught, she'd been smart enough to point DeMarco at Douglas Campbell. The only good, unselfish thing she'd done was try to solve her gambling problem without involving her parents, but that had backfired so horribly that her father was now in more trouble than he would have been if she had just gone to him in the beginning and asked for his help. DeMarco didn't feel sorry for Molly anymore; she just pissed him off.

DeMarco followed her over to the cashier's cage and watched as she exchanged her chips for cash. The cashier paid her almost seven thousand dollars.

"I've never had a roll like that in my life," she said, her eyes glowing.

DeMarco didn't say anything. He took her arm and marched her toward one of the casino's bars—the place was so damn big it had five bars—and as they walked, the flush of victory began to drain from Molly's face. From the bartender, DeMarco ordered a cup of coffee, a white wine for Molly—and a champagne bucket.

The bartender looked confused. "You want a champagne bucket for a glass of wine?"

"Just give me a bucket and fill it with ice."

The bartender did, and DeMarco led Molly over to a booth where they could talk. He put the champagne bucket on the seat next to him and shoved his right hand into it, the hand that he'd used to hit Gus Amato.

"Is something wrong with your hand?" Molly said.

"Do you know who Ted Allen is, Molly?" DeMarco said.

"Yeah, he owns the casino."

"No, he doesn't own the casino. The fucking Mob owns the casino, Molly. Ted just works for them." DeMarco started to scream something else at her but he took a breath and said, "How'd this ever happen, Molly?"

And Molly Mahoney began to cry.

———— ◆◆◆ ————

"It started about a year ago," she told DeMarco.

She came up to Atlantic City with a guy she'd been dating, a physics professor at GW. The professor introduced her to the game of craps and then the very worst thing that could have possibly happened, happened —she won. She won almost two thousand dollars. She was hooked.

She explained to DeMarco that what she liked about craps was that a player who understood the odds had an advantage. The game of craps looks complicated to most people, she said. All those numbers all over the table—hardway bets and field bets, pass and don't pass bets—but it was actually quite simple once you understood the mathematical probability of the dice rolling a seven versus any other number.

As she was saying all this, DeMarco was thinking that this was how even smart people, people like Molly Mahoney with an engineering degree, got into trouble. The odds always favored the house. Always. And sometimes the biggest losers were bright, educated people who thought they were brighter than the guys who the built the casinos. The other thing was that for some people gambling was addictive—it could be just as addictive as alcohol or cocaine—and a person's IQ was often no defense when it came to addiction.

After she won that first time, she started going to Atlantic City almost every weekend and within ten months her savings account was bare and her credit cards were maxed out. It wasn't long before she had to find a cheaper place to live and her salary—the part she didn't gamble with—went for paying her rent and utilities and the minimum balance on her credit cards. Like any gambling junky, she always figured the next trip to the casino was going to be *the* trip, the one where she'd hit it big. It really didn't take long at all before her standard of living had more in common with single moms on welfare than with professional women who make almost a hundred grand a year.

She always came to the Atlantic Palace because this was where she won the first time—and because Ted Allen was such a nice guy. Once, when she lost ten thousand dollars in less than four hours, he comped her dinner, a show, and a room. And then Ted said that if she needed money to play some more that weekend, he could give her an advance, and he took a little card out of his wallet and wrote something on the back of it. "Just take this to any cashier in the casino whenever you're up here," he had said, "and they'll give you whatever you need." Then he said, "But you do understand that these are loans, Molly. Right?" Before she could answer, he laughed and ordered her a glass of Dom Pérignon.

"I didn't even know how much I'd borrowed until two months ago," Molly said. "I went to the cashier's cage one day with my magic card and the next thing I know a security guy is taking me up to Ted's office. I knew I owed a lot but when Ted handed me a statement that I had borrowed a hundred and nine thousand . . . I threw up, right there in his office."

Bet Ted had really liked that.

"They told me . . ."

"They?"

"Ted and this other guy, Greg, his accountant. I heard Greg got killed in a traffic accident. Anyway, they said I either had to pay back the money in a week or they were going to talk to my dad and maybe the press. That's when I came up with the stock idea. I knew Doug Campbell was doing something like that—that phone call I told you about really happened—so I figured I could, too, and I knew that when the submarine battery design went public . . . Well, it was a sure thing."

"So that's when you went to Ted," DeMarco said, "this guy who has a degree in business, and he pretends that he's never heard of a little thing called insider trading. He says: Sure, Molly, here's five hundred grand. Make us a little money, too, while you're at it."

"Yeah," Molly said. "I didn't think anybody would notice me buying such a small amount of stock. It's not like I'm Martha Stewart; I'm not famous or anything. And I was careful. I did everything online and . . . Oh, God, what am I going to do, Joe?"

It was apparent that Molly hadn't known that the SEC had been keeping an eye on Reston Tech for past problems. Maybe if she'd known, she wouldn't have taken the risk. Or maybe not. Maybe she was so desperate she felt she had to take the risk.

He didn't necessarily believe her about Douglas Campbell, though. DeMarco had unwittingly pointed her at Campbell when he asked: Who do you know that has access to your personal information and lives above his means? And that's when she thought of Campbell.

Maybe she really did hear the call she claimed to have heard—and maybe that's what gave her the idea for the insider trading scheme—but Molly Mahoney, this person he thought was a victim, was clever enough to point DeMarco at a viable alternate suspect.

"I don't know what you're going to do," DeMarco said, answering her question. "Right now there's about a fifty-fifty chance of you going to jail. The odds of you being convicted would normally be higher, but your lawyer's a shark and he's going to throw up a smoke screen saying that Campbell and a couple of his buddies are the real insiders and not you. And it might work. And Kay Kiser still wants to know where you got the half a million you invested. So if it looks like you're going to lose at trial, you could give her Ted, and maybe the people behind Ted—they're bigger fish than you—and you might get a reduced sentence. But then you'd have a problem."

"What problem?"

"For starters, Molly, and I'm sure Ted told you this, they have a guy who's willing to testify that he gave you the money and that Ted didn't have anything to do with it. But that's not your biggest problem."

"What is?" Molly said.

"Your biggest problem is that Ted might have you killed."

———————◆◆◆———————

DeMarco drove Molly back to D.C. It was a four-hour trip and almost nine p.m. when they arrived at the Capitol. Mahoney had said that he wanted to talk to his daughter before she spoke to her mother, and he was waiting in his office.

The rest of Mahoney's staff had left for the day, except for Perry Wallace. When DeMarco arrived with Molly, Wallace was sitting in front of Mahoney's desk with a six-inch stack of paper on his lap, briefing Mahoney on a dozen different political matters. The wheels of government hadn't stopped spinning just because Molly Mahoney had been arrested.

Mahoney dismissed Wallace and said to Molly, "Sit your ass down. I'll be with you in a minute." Molly started crying again.

DeMarco told Mahoney about his meeting with Ted—leaving out the part where he beat Ted's bodyguard unconscious. "Ted also told me he's canceling Molly's marker."

"Why the hell would he do that?" Mahoney asked.

DeMarco shrugged. "I don't know. He said it was a goodwill gesture. But he still wants the funds for his convention center and he still wants his half million back."

"Something's going on here," Mahoney muttered. Then when he couldn't figure out what it was, he added, "Anyway, you can take off. I'll talk to you tomorrow."

As DeMarco was leaving, he heard Mahoney scream at his middle daughter: "How in the fuck could you do something like this?"

He almost felt sorry for Molly again.

31

The same day DeMarco met with Ted Allen in Atlantic City, subpoenas, as Attorney Daniel Caine had promised, were delivered to five people.

The subpoenas asked Douglas Campbell, Richard Praeter, and Russell McGrath to provide tax returns and other financial records going back seven years.

Mrs. Martin of PNC Financial was directed to provide all documentation—including tape recordings, should there be any—associated with Mrs. Campbell's trust.

And lastly, Kay Kiser of the Securities and Exchange Commission was ordered to produce all records generated in the last twenty years related to SEC investigations associated in any way with Reston Technologies. In addition, she was ordered to provide any files she had concerning Misters Campbell, Praeter, and McGrath.

All the people subpoenaed acted differently.

Pretty Mrs. Martin smiled, tossed the subpoena in her out box with a brief note attached, and then went back to the account she was working on.

Kay Kiser went to her gym and kickboxed a punching bag for an hour.

Richard Praeter threw a coffee mug at a wall in his office, putting a small dent in the plasterboard.

Douglas Campbell screamed at his wife and got very drunk—but then he did that almost every night.

Rusty McGrath sat on the bow of his yacht, enjoying the sunset, humming a Kenny Rogers song.

32

U.S. Supreme Court Justice Stanley Brandon was eighty-four years old and dying of cancer. He'd been dying for two years. The last time Mahoney had seen the man, Brandon had looked like an anatomy-class skeleton covered with a thin layer of brittle parchment. He had to be wheeled into his office each day, couldn't stand without someone helping him, and couldn't sit at the bench for more than a couple of hours before he had to be taken back to his chambers for medications and a nap. And for two years, half of Brandon's time had been spent getting chemo or radiation or just sitting in a hospital bed stubbornly battling death. But would he resign so a sprightly youngster of sixty-five could take his place? No way. He had a lifetime appointment and, by God, and he was going to stay for life.

Today, however, word had come that Brandon was finally on his way to meet that Big Judge in the sky. The head doc at Walter Reed had personally assured the president that the old bastard wouldn't make it through the night. Thank God, the president had most likely said, and since he'd had plenty of time to prepare for this moment, he was ready to begin the painful process of selecting Brandon's replacement.

The president invited a dozen members of the House and Senate to the White House to talk about a number of things. Mahoney and Big

Bob Fairchild were among those present. The president was in one of his optimistic, I-know-we-can-all-work-together moods, so he served a mixed group of Republicans and Democrats lukewarm coffee—a group that couldn't agree on what day of the week it was—and chatted about a number of things: a tax reform proposal that Mahoney knew didn't have a snowball's chance in hell of passing in the House; a half-baked idea for slowing down the exodus of American jobs to places where people still used oxen to pull their plows; and lastly, that a certain distinguished jurist wasn't going to be alive tomorrow morning and he wanted to acquaint the politicians with his short list.

The president realized that his nominee could have the wisdom of Solomon and it wouldn't make any difference. No matter who he nominated, half the people on the Senate Judiciary Committee would find reasons why his candidate was unacceptable. The folks on his short list turned out to be three middle-of-the-road federal judges who'd never been accused of judicial activism; in fact, none of them had ever been accused of having had an original thought. The president extolled each person's virtues basically by saying: *How could you possibly have any objection to these guys?* Three of the senators present said they thought the president's potential nominees sounded like fine choices; three others murmured that they'd give whomever the president selected their serious consideration—which was code for: *You've got to be kidding.* The president could see that he was in for the usual dogfight, and on that happy note, the meeting ended.

Following the meeting, Fairchild and Mahoney stood silently outside the White House, waiting for their cars to return them to the Capitol. God forbid they should have come together in the same car. Fairchild's car arrived first, which annoyed Mahoney. Fairchild's driver opened the rear door for him, but Fairchild didn't move toward the car. Instead he turned to Mahoney and said, "John, I was thinking about stopping by your office later today to explain a few things to you, but I might as well talk to you here."

"Oh, yeah?" Mahoney said. He and Big Bob Fairchild rarely spoke face-to-face; they preferred to snipe at each other via the media.

"Yes," Fairchild said. "I'd like the president to tell Terrance Wheeler that his so-called investigation has gone on long enough. I also want you to tell your people to quit opposing my water bill."

Terrance Wheeler was the independent prosecutor appointed to investigate congressmen who may have been bribed by the lobbyist Lucas Mayfield, the Jack Abramoff clone. The "water bill" was a bill that Fairchild had introduced to help the state of Arizona with one of its biggest resource issues: Arizona was a state that didn't have a whole lot of water. The bill not only threw some federal money to Fairchild's home state, it also helped out some of his cronies there. Mahoney was against the bill only because Big Bob was for it, and consequently every other Democrat in the House was against it, too.

Mahoney smiled in response to Fairchild's comment. He was having a rotten week, all the shit going on with his daughter, and torment-ing Big Bob would be a small ray of sunshine beaming down onto an otherwise dismal day.

"You'd like all that, would you?" Mahoney said. "Well, Bob, I'd like to screw all the Redskin cheerleaders, the point being that we don't always get what we'd like." Before Fairchild could say anything else, Mahoney said, "At any rate, Wheeler doesn't work for me. I can't call him off. And as for the water bill . . ."

"The hell you can't get Wheeler to stop," Fairchild said. "You're the one who got him appointed in the first place. And the only reason you did is you were hoping he'd get something on my nephew."

"Not true, Bob," Mahoney lied. "I had no idea that Little Bob—"

"His name's not Little Bob, goddamnit!"

"—that Little Bob was involved with that lobbyist."

"Bullshit!" Fairchild said. "Wheeler hasn't investigated anybody but Republicans and he's spent more time looking at my nephew than anyone else."

"Not true again, Bob," Mahoney said. "I heard that Wheeler's also investigating Randy Collier."

Collier was a Democratic congressman from Illinois—and a complete idiot.

Fairchild laughed. "He's only investigating Collier because the *Washington Post* mailed him pictures of Collier sitting with Mayfield and two bimbos on Mayfield's boat."

One of the bimbos had actually been sitting on Randy Collier's lap, and in the photo it looked like she was trying to clean out one of Collier's ears with her tongue.

"So there you go," Mahoney said. "That proves that Terry Wheeler is truly independent and not just hunting Republicans."

Mahoney's car pulled up at that moment. "I gotta get back to work, Bob."

"John, if you don't put an end to Wheeler's witch hunt and quit opposing my bill, I'm going to tell the media that the Atlantic Palace casino just canceled the hundred-thousand-dollar gambling debt your daughter owes them."

That stopped Mahoney. "What? How do you know . . ."

"I'm going to suggest that the president's special prosecutor needs to take a hard look at *you* because you're obviously getting some sort of kickback from this casino. I've also heard that you're trying to attach a rider to a bill to give the state of New Jersey a hundred million for some convention center that will benefit this same casino."

Goddamnit, how did Fairchild know all this stuff?

"I'm not doing any such thing," Mahoney said, not quite lying.

What Mahoney had done was ask Perry Wallace, just in case, to look into how to get New Jersey the money, but how did Fairchild know?

"I'll tell you what, John," Fairchild said. "In return for doing what I want, I won't stop you from sending money to your pals in New Jersey."

What Fairchild meant was that the Republicans wouldn't put up a fight if Mahoney wanted to tack the money onto a bill. But that would also mean that Fairchild would have something else to use against Mahoney at some time in the future.

"But," Fairchild continued, "if I don't get what I want, I'm going to tell the press everything. I also have a feeling that if the SEC knew about your daughter's gambling problem, that would strengthen the case against her in so far as motives go."

Mahoney stepped close enough to Fairchild to exhale the odor of the president's bad coffee into Fairchild's face. "You leave my daughter out of this."

"Oh, I see," Fairchild said. "Your daughter's off-limits but my nephew's fair game. I don't think so," he added, then stepped into his car and closed the door before Mahoney could respond.

It took Mahoney about thirty seconds to figure out what was going on. Preston Whitman was working for both Ted Allen and Big Bob Fairchild, and Whitman was Fairchild's source. He also knew why Ted had canceled Molly's marker: because Fairchild had paid him to cancel it and the money had probably come from Fairchild's extraordinarily rich wife. So much for Ted's goodwill gesture. And Molly's marker being canceled was bad news for all the reasons Fairchild had said. Now not only was his daughter in trouble, but Fairchild had information that could possibly destroy his career.

Mahoney stood there on the curb of the White House driveway, his big hands clenched into fists. There had been a time, really not that long ago, when congressmen challenged each other to duels. Mahoney yearned for those times. If he couldn't shoot Fairchild with a dueling pistol, just slapping him with a glove—just slapping the *shit* out of him with a glove—would have been very satisfying.

Mahoney called DeMarco and told him to meet him at Reagan National.

Mahoney was flying to Boston to give the commencement address at Boston College. If DeMarco remembered correctly, BC had given Mahoney an honorary doctorate once upon a time, so he'd wear a robe with a fancy sash and a mortarboard on his big head, and he'd give his standard speech about how the graduates were the bright, shining hope of America. He'd quote JFK half a dozen times—*ask not what your country can do for you*—and urge them to eschew private-sector greed and consider public service. After the ceremony, public servant Mahoney would go to his office in Boston, and like a scene from *The Godfather,* constituents would line up, kiss his ring, and ask for his help on a variety of things.

DeMarco met his boss at a coffee shop in the airport. Mahoney was already seated, a scowl on his face, drinking coffee from a paper cup that had been laced with bourbon from the flask in his pocket. As soon as DeMarco sat down, Mahoney launched into a recap of his White House discussion with Fairchild, concluding with: "So now I know why Allen canceled Molly's marker, and if the press finds out, they'll hang me out to dry just like Fairchild said."

An announcement about a flight to Boston came over the loud-speaker and Mahoney stood up.

"You find a way to get Fairchild off my back. You find some way to neutralize the bastard. You understand?"

"Yeah," DeMarco said. He understood, but what the hell was he supposed to do?

33

Richard Praeter couldn't get the key into the keyhole.

"Man, am I drunk," he said. He placed his forehead against the door to help maintain his balance and continued to jab his key at the keyhole, missing repeatedly, scratching the lock. "This reminds me of the first time I got laid," he said.

"You want me to try?" the big man said.

"Hell, no. You're drunker than I am."

The big man was standing behind Praeter, watching as he poked at the lock. The big man didn't seem drunk at all.

Praeter finally opened the door and stumbled into his office. "I don't know why you wanted to look at this stuff tonight. You'll never remember it tomorrow."

The big man looked down the hallway to make sure it was still empty then followed Praeter into the office.

Praeter shrugged off his coat and threw it at the top of a file cabinet. He missed, and his handmade cashmere topcoat dropped to the floor. He fell into the chair behind his desk and hit the power button on his computer. "This'll take a minute," he said. "Fuckin' security systems slow these machines way down. They oughta chop the fingers off those little hacker bastards when they catch 'em."

The other man stood for a moment then walked over to the window behind Praeter's desk. "I forgot what a view you've got from up here, Dickie," he said.

Praeter glanced behind him. One in the morning and lights blazing everywhere. New York, New York. What a town. "Yeah," he said. "Hey, you want another drink? I gotta bottle of Glen . . . Glen-something."

The big man tapped the window with one finger. "Nah," he said, "but you go ahead and have one."

"Damn right," Praeter said and opened a drawer in his desk and pulled out a bottle. He twisted the cap off and said, "Sure you don't want a hit?" The big man shook his head. "Okee-dokie," Praeter said, and took a drink directly from the bottle.

In front of Praeter's desk was a visitor's chair. It was made of wood and leather. The big man picked up the chair; it was heavier than he'd expected. Good. "I want you to duck, Dickie," he said softly.

"What?" Praeter said.

"Duck," the big man said and swung the chair behind him.

"Jesus Christ!" Praeter said, and dived out of his chair.

The big man threw the chair as hard as he could at the window behind Praeter's desk. The chair bounced off the window, almost landing on Praeter who was lying on the floor.

"What the fuck are you doing?" Praeter screamed.

"Shit," the big man muttered, ignoring Praeter. "Safety glass." The window was still intact but there were a dozen cracks radiating out from the point of impact.

The big man stepped over Praeter and picked up the chair again.

"What are you doing?" Praeter screamed again.

The big man, his legs straddling Praeter's prone form, swung the chair again. More cracks appeared in the glass. He swung a third time, and the glass shattered. Wind roared into the room and the papers on Praeter's desk swirled into the air.

"Goddamnit, are you fucking nuts?" Praeter said. He was lying on his back so he rolled over onto his stomach, then got on his hands and knees. Before he could stand up, however, the big man reached down and grabbed Praeter by his belt and the collar of his monogrammed shirt and dropped him out the window. He didn't *throw* him out; he'd made that mistake once before.

34

The sound of a ringing telephone pulled DeMarco from a deep sleep, and his first thought was: What inconsiderate jackass could be calling so early? His second thought was: Why doesn't she answer the damn phone?

An elbow poked him in the ribs and a sleepy voice murmured, "That's your phone."

"Oh, sorry," he said. He got out of bed, then down on his hands and knees and groped through a pile of clothes until he finally retrieved his cell phone from a pocket.

The jackass calling turned out to be his old college buddy from New York, Sal Anselmo, who sounded bright-eyed and cheerful, as if he'd been up since dawn. "I just thought you'd like to know, since you were asking about him the other night, that Dickie Praeter committed suicide last night."

"What?" DeMarco said, still half asleep, and Sal repeated what he'd just said: Richard Praeter was dead.

DeMarco mumbled a thank-you and looked at his watch. It was only seven a.m.—way too early to do anything. He crawled back into bed, snuggled up against the warm body lying next to him, and cupped her right breast. She pushed his hand away and said, "Too early." He smiled, closed his eyes, and went back to sleep.

Two hours later, DeMarco headed for McLean with a smile on his face. If he'd been walking instead of driving, one might have said that he had a spring in his step.

He'd called Alice's friend the night before and asked if she might like to have dinner sometime in the near future. She surprised him by saying, "Actually, tonight would be perfect. My daughters are out of town."

Tina Burke (née Marino) turned out to be even better looking than the picture Alice had shown him. Short dark hair, dark eyes, slim yet busty—and DeMarco had always been partial to Italian types. Like his ex-wife. She seemed bright and had a sense of humor, but was extremely picky about what she ate. He decided he could overlook that one small flaw. She'd been divorced for four years from a jerk who worked for a think tank, and was seventeen when she had her twin daughters. She made a point of telling DeMarco—twice—that her girls were out of town, checking out William and Mary where they'd be going to school next year, and it had been a long time since she'd had a night to herself.

DeMarco didn't need as much direction as Alice and her friend seemed to think—or maybe he just took direction well.

As DeMarco approached Emma's front door he could hear the sound of a cello. The music was nice and mellow, but nothing he recognized, which meant it was most likely some classical thing composed two hundred years before he was born. He rang the doorbell. The playing stopped and the door was opened a moment later by a pretty young woman, her long blonde hair piled on top of her head in a casual style. She was wearing loose-fitting cotton pants, the waist secured with a drawstring, and a T-shirt with Beethoven's head sketched on the front. DeMarco knew it was Beethoven because it said so on the shirt. She was barefoot and DeMarco thought she had really pretty feet.

The woman was Christine, Emma's lover. She played cello for the National Symphony.

"Is her highness here?" DeMarco asked.

"She's in the backyard." Then Christine leaned forward and whispered, "She had these two guys over yesterday, a couple of Japanese guys, and they spent an *hour* looking at some bug she found on one of her roses. You would have thought the plant had cancer the way she was acting."

DeMarco and Christine had very little in common—in fact, they had nothing in common but Emma—but on one thing they could agree: when it came to her yard, Emma was a nut. He just shook his head to convey his sympathy. As he made his way through the house toward the backyard, the cello began again, this time making edgy, angry noises.

DeMarco found Emma standing on her patio, looking out over her lawn. She was wearing the same sort of outfit she'd been wearing the last time he saw her: a long-billed baseball cap, a grass-stained T-shirt, and shorts. In spite of her attire, she looked like a general surveying a battlefield, trying to decide where to attack the enemy next.

Imagine Patton planning the obliteration of crabgrass instead of Rommel's tanks.

"You got a minute to talk?" DeMarco said.

"No," she said without turning to look at him.

———◆———

Emma put down the phone.

"Like your buddy told you, the cops in New York are treating Richard Praeter's death as a suicide," she said. "They have no reason to suspect he was murdered but they do have a number of reasons to think he killed himself."

The military is a huge club, and its members, active and retired, are spread out all over the globe. And a large number of ex-military personnel become cops when they muster out. This phenomenon—soldiers mutating into cops—gave Emma, a retired superstar from the DIA, contacts in a lot of police departments. Getting an NYPD captain to talk to her had not been hard at all.

"Like what?" DeMarco said.

"First, there were no marks on the body incompatible with a fall. More important, there was no indication that there was anyone with him when he died."

"No indication? Does that mean they're positive he was alone when he died?"

"Not exactly," Emma said, and then she explained.

The building where Praeter worked had a guard in the lobby and there was a security camera in the lobby as well, but there were no cameras in the stairwells or elevators. After normal business hours, doors were secured such that people had to go through the lobby to enter the building but tenants could also enter the building through the parking garage. To enter the garage required a key card, and to get into the elevator from the garage, you needed the same key card. The building security system recorded the time key cards were used. This meant that if Praeter drove into the garage he could take the elevator to his office without being seen by the guard, and Praeter's Jaguar had been found in the garage. According to the guard, no one else was in the building around the time Praeter died, and nor had anyone else used their key card near that time.

"Doesn't seem like much of a security system," DeMarco said. "Praeter was a pretty paranoid guy; I would have thought that the building would have been better protected."

"The building may not be that secure," Emma said, "but his office has a steel door and the best lock you can buy, and the security system on his computers is state of the art. Most of the files on it are encrypted and NYPD's computer guys don't think they'll be able to figure out what's in them unless they get the NSA involved, which they have no intention of doing."

"What time did he die?" DeMarco asked.

"The swing shift guard saw him leave at seven p.m. and NYPD's computer people say he turned off his computer at six fifty p.m. The security system showed he then returned to the building at one a.m. because he used his key card to enter the garage elevator at that time. His computer was turned on five minutes later and was still on when the cops got to the scene. At five a.m., a janitor who works in an adjacent building found his body on the roof."

"On the roof?"

"Yeah, but the roof of the adjacent building is six floors below Praeter's office. Anyway, it appears that Praeter returned to his office about one and turned on his computer for some unknown reason. He then apparently decided that life wasn't worth living, broke a window in his office with a chair, and took a dive out the window."

"But if there was another man with Praeter, he could have gone up the elevator with him and the guard wouldn't have seen the other guy."

"True," Emma said.

"Would the guard be able to tell if someone left the building after Praeter died?"

"Not if he took the elevator down to the garage and left via the garage. To exit the garage, all you have to do is duck under a bar at the entrance."

"So someone could have been with Praeter the night he died. And I think it's a lot more likely that someone killed him than that he killed himself. I mean, he was a rich, successful guy. Why the hell would he commit suicide?"

"According to my NYPD friend, Richard Praeter was not a particularly stable personality," Emma said. "He didn't have any close friends in New York they could find, but they did talk to a few people who knew him. These people all agreed he was, for lack of a better word, a complete fruitcake. And when the cops contacted Praeter's mother to notify her of her son's death, she told them that when he was in college, he tried to commit suicide. So there's a history of suicidal behavior."

"When did this happen, the college suicide attempt?"

Emma told him. It was a month after the wide receiver fell out the dorm window at UVA.

"Well, I didn't know about the previous suicide attempt," DeMarco said, "but the unstable part is definitely true. I met Praeter, and he was a wack job. My pal in New York called him Crazy Dickie."

"So there you go," Emma said. "And Mr. Praeter had a blood alcohol content of .21 the night he died. Most people who commit suicide are drunk or high at the time, and the official thinking goes like this: Praeter was just served with a subpoena for a case involving insider trading. He knows he's guilty, drinks himself into a depressed state, becomes terrified that he'll become someone's prison bitch, and out the window he flies."

DeMarco shook his head. "I don't buy it," he said. "The SEC has never been able to pin a thing on him. He wouldn't have gone off the deep end just because he got a subpoena. I think Campbell or McGrath killed him."

"But *why* would they kill him? And how is Praeter's death tied to Molly?"

DeMarco must have done something—a sideways glance, a guilty facial tic—and Emma noticed. Her cynical blue eyes bored into his. "Are you keeping something from me, Joe?" she said.

Oh, boy.

DeMarco hadn't told Emma that Molly Mahoney was guilty as sin and in hock to a casino for a horrendous amount of money. He hadn't told her because Emma had a righteous streak wider than an eight-lane freeway, and she would have insisted that Molly plead guilty and take her medicine. DeMarco also knew it was a mistake to hold out on Emma—she'd find out eventually—he didn't know how, but she would—and when she did, she'd flay him alive. But for now, he didn't want her to know.

"Of course not," DeMarco said in response to Emma's question. "Let me tell you what I think is going on here. Molly overheard Campbell making a strange phone call related to something Reston Tech was working on a couple years ago. At that time no one, including Kay Kiser at the SEC, had any proof that Campbell was involved in anything shady. But then Molly gets arrested and she tells me about Campbell, and I link Campbell to McGrath and Praeter. So Daniel Caine, Molly's scary, high-priced attorney, then subpoenas all three of these guys, and one of them—Campbell or McGrath—*he's* the one who panics. Campbell and McGrath know that Praeter's not only a loose cannon but he's the linchpin to everything. He's the one who made the insider trades based on tips from Campbell and hid the money trail from the government and . . ."

"And maybe he's the one who set up Molly. He'd be smart enough to set up those e-trade accounts using her identity," Emma said.

"Uh, yeah, right," DeMarco said. "Anyway, if the government can break Praeter, he can provide all the evidence they need to put Campbell and McGrath in jail."

"And you think Campbell or McGrath killed him because one of them was afraid of this?"

"I think it's possible—and a hell of a lot more probable than Praeter committing suicide. I think Praeter made McGrath and Campbell a lot of money, enough to last the rest of their lives, and one of them decided he wasn't going to risk Crazy Dickie cracking under the strain of an investigation."

"Maybe," Emma said, "but there're some things that don't make sense. Why did they decide to use Molly's identity in this latest scheme? Why her, of all people? They had to know that if she was accused of a crime her father would get involved and, with his clout, he could cause them problems. And why were they so . . . so inept this time? You told me in that one case they used a fake European hedge fund to hide the money trail."

"I have no idea," DeMarco said, terrified that Emma's bullshit-detector was about to go off. He should have had a Botox injection before coming here, something to freeze his features into complete immobility. Before Emma could ask another question, he said, "Look, I need some help here. I'm getting stretched too thin to cover everything. I'm still trying to run down some things regarding these old insider trading cases at Reston Tech and . . ."

That was lie.

". . . and some Republican congressman's got his hooks into Mahoney."

"You mean because of Molly?" Emma said.

Whoops. He shouldn't have said that. He didn't want to talk about how Fairchild was using Molly's problems to blackmail Mahoney because then he'd have to talk about Ted Allen and Molly's gambling problems.

"No, over something else," DeMarco said, "but it's urgent and I have to get this guy off Mahoney's back right away. So I could really use some help and I was wondering if you could do some more digging into Praeter's death since you're the one with all the cop connections."

"Now?" Emma said. "Can't you see all the things I'm doing here in my yard?"

She sounded like a surgeon being interrupted during a heart transplant.

"It's Mahoney's *daughter,* Emma. Come on. How would you feel if it was your daughter?"

Now, that was a rotten thing to do, pushing that particular button. Emma had a daughter and she was fiercely protective of her. How she came to have a child was something she had never discussed with

DeMarco. But then there were a lot of things she had never discussed with DeMarco.

He watched her trying to make up her mind. Emma had helped him in the past but the reasons varied. Sometimes she helped because whatever he was working on was something she cared about, but most often he suspected she helped him because she was bored. When Emma worked for the DIA, she'd been a player on the international stage, involved in major military and political dramas. She'd been a spy. And as much as she enjoyed her current lifestyle, he knew she missed the adrenal rush of the good old days, which probably hadn't been all that good. She probably also felt bad that it was Mahoney's daughter who was in trouble; if it had just been Mahoney, she most likely wouldn't have lifted a finger to help.

"All right," she finally said, "as long as it doesn't interfere too much with what I'm doing here."

"Thanks, I really appreciate it, and I'm sure Molly will, too."

She was going to kill him when she found out he was lying.

35

One of the things DeMarco had to do was find out which gangster Ted Allen worked for, and he knew he worked for somebody. Ted was too young to be out on his own, running a place like the Atlantic Palace. He could have asked Mahoney to talk to the FBI's organized crime guys, but then the Bureau would know that something was up, and you could never tell what those headline-hunting glory-seekers might do. So he decided to fly to New York and ask another gangster. And while he was in New York, he'd go visit his mom and spend the night at her place in Queens. He felt guilty that the last time he was in the city he spent all his time drinking with Sal Anselmo and didn't even call her.

DeMarco knew several gangsters and he knew them because his father had been one. Gino DeMarco had been an enforcer, and occasional hitman, for a now dead mobster named Carmine Taliaferro. After Taliaferro died, a man named Tony Benedetto took his place.

Tony had narrow shoulders, a small paunch, a big nose, and hair that had been dyed jet-black, the color contrasting absurdly with his seamed, seventy-four-year-old face. He preferred to wear jogging suits when at home, and today's suit was black with a gold stripe running down the legs. On his feet were tennis shoes designed for marathon runners.

Tony was sitting at the kitchen table of his house in Queens and taking his blood pressure when DeMarco walked into the kitchen. He held up a finger for DeMarco to wait as he squinted through bifocal lenses at the digital readout on the white box in front of him. He raised his head and smiled.

"One thirty-five over seventy-nine. That's not bad. And my cholesterol, it's down to two ten. And my pulse, unless somebody really pisses me off, is usually around seventy-five." He ripped the blood pressure cuff off his arm. "I'll bet I'm in better shape than you are, kid."

"Yeah, I'll bet you are too," DeMarco said.

Christ, had the whole Mob changed? First that yuppie Ted Allen, and now Tony Benedetto acting like Jack LaLanne. Twenty years ago Benedetto would have been sitting in a bar, smoking cigars, and drinking bad red wine. Now here he was checking his blood pressure.

As if reading DeMarco's mind, Benedetto said, "I quit smoking ten years ago, eat red meat only two times a week, and I drink Slim Fast for lunch. And my dick . . . Well, let me tell ya: I don't need no fuckin' Viagra."

Thank God, at least he still talked like mobster.

"How's your mom?" Benedetto asked.

"Tough as shoe leather," DeMarco said.

"Ain't that the truth," Benedetto said, shaking his head. "Man, I think she hates my guts. She acts like it was my fault your dad . . . well, you know."

"Yeah," DeMarco said. DeMarco's father died while working for Carmine Taliaferro, three bullets in the chest, but Tony Benedetto didn't have anything to do with that. At least DeMarco didn't think so.

"One time," Benedetto said, "you were maybe ten or eleven, playing ball down there at the school, and I stopped to watch you bat. Well, your mom, she sees me standing there, and she comes runnin' over and tells me that if I ever come near you she'll cut my heart out. And she was serious. Geez, it was embarrassing. I bet the people who heard her thought I was some kind of child molester."

"I remember that," DeMarco said. DeMarco's mother had done everything she could to keep him out of his father's world.

"Mothers and their kids," Benedetto said. "Doesn't matter if they're ducks or dogs or people, if a mother thinks you're a threat to her kids . . . well, you better watch out."

"Yeah," DeMarco said. Enough of this. "Do you know a guy named Ted Allen? He runs a casino in Atlantic City."

Benedetto shrugged. "Maybe. Why you askin'?"

"I just need to know about him. And I need to know who his boss is." Seeing that this explanation was insufficient, DeMarco added, "He's gotten himself mixed up in something that I don't think his boss would like."

"You tryin' to do his boss a favor or something?"

"No, I'm trying to do *my* boss a favor, and to do that I need to know who Ted works for."

Benedetto mulled this over for a moment, concluded the truth wouldn't hurt him, and said, "He works for Al Castiglia, down in Philly. Ted was a kid, just out of high school, and he impressed Al some way. Plus, I heard Al had something goin' on with Ted's mom at the time. Anyway, the next thing you know, Ted's in college and after that he's working for Al, first in Vegas, then in Philly, now in AC. He makes a good front man and so far he has a clean record. But I'll tell you something. He may look like an Ivy League frat boy, but he's a vicious little bastard."

"You know this for a fact?"

Benedetto shrugged. "Just things I've heard, rumors of stuff he's pulled."

"Tell me about Castiglia. What kind of guy is he? What's he into these days other than the casino with Allen?"

Benedetto stared at him for a second, then said, very softly, "Are you wearing a wire?"

"What! Hell, no," DeMarco said. He stood up, took off his suit coat and turned in a circle so Benedetto could see his back. "You want me to strip down?"

"Nah, that's okay, you wouldn't do something that dumb." Benedetto paused then said, "What's Al like? Well, I guess he's like me. He pulled a bunch of cowboy shit in the old days, like a guy does when he's trying to get to the top, but now he's an old man. And he saw how the FBI got almost everybody up here in New York, everybody rattin' everybody else out, so he's learned to stay a couple steps removed from anything that could land him in the can. I mean, if people are selling dope in Philly and ripping shit off, Al might get a piece, but you won't see him anywhere near a dope deal. But mostly, he's legit. He's got apartment buildings filled with people who pay their rent, a piece of a cement company, a couple restaurants, and a trucking company that probably carries some stuff it shouldn't carry, but he's careful about that. Then there's the casino. I know he gets a slice of that—I know because Ted Allen works for him—but you won't find his name on anything connected to the casino and you won't find a money trail leading back to him. So, I guess you'd say he's just a businessman—like me—but that don't mean he won't cut your fuckin' head off if you mess with him."

"What about insider trading? Do you think Castiglia might get involved in something like that?"

"Insider trading. That's the most bullshit crime they ever came up with. There's always somebody on the inside that makes money because he knows things the yahoos on the outside don't know. That's business."

"Yeah, maybe so," DeMarco said. There was no point having a discussion with Tony Benedetto on the ethics of insider trading. "But is that the kind of thing Castiglia would do?"

"I doubt it. Something like that would be too far out of Al's comfort zone. I mean, insider trading's a Wall Street crime. Now, those are the real fuckin' criminals. Those guys rip off billions and you never see any of them in the can. And how come the fuckin' RICO laws don't apply to them?"

Sheesh. Even the Mafia hated the crooks on Wall Street. Or maybe they were just jealous of them.

"Anyway, why are you asking about Al and insider trading?"

"Because," DeMarco said, "his boy Ted is an accomplice in an insider trading swindle, and the SEC and the Department of Justice and one really pissed off politician might be coming after him. And I'm starting to think that Al doesn't know what Ted did."

DeMarco thought this because Ted was so desperate to get back the half million that the government had confiscated. If Al Castiglia knew what he was doing, he probably would have just written off the loss in return for Mahoney's help on the convention center project.

"What do you think Castiglia would do," DeMarco asked, "if Ted got involved in something like that without getting his approval?"

"Didn't I mention something about Al cutting people's heads off? Well, that wasn't a metaphor."

DeMarco couldn't believe the old goombah had just said *metaphor*.

36

The main reason Emma had agreed to help DeMarco was that the weather forecasters were predicting heavy rains the next few days, and rain would interfere with the things she was planning to do in her yard.

And she was bored.

But she knew DeMarco was holding something back from her—and when she found out what it was, she was going to wring his thick neck. She didn't buy the story that some congressman was trying squeeze Mahoney. Well, she did buy it in the sense that she knew Mahoney was an unscrupulous bastard, so she wouldn't be surprised if another unscrupulous bastard had uncovered some shady thing that Mahoney had done and was now trying to exploit the situation. The part she didn't buy was that whatever was going on wasn't in some way related to Molly Mahoney. Mahoney would have wanted DeMarco completely focused on his daughter's problems, and not off pursuing some other issue. But then again, maybe not. Mahoney was so self-centered that maybe he was looking out for Number One as usual, and allowing his daughter's problems to take a backseat. Whatever the case, she knew DeMarco wasn't telling her everything.

Regarding Molly, Emma did feel sorry for the young woman. She didn't know her, but she believed that DeMarco was probably right and that she hadn't committed a crime. Emma was also intrigued by Richard Praeter's death, wondering if the New York cops had gotten it wrong and if a murder had actually occurred.

Murder wasn't boring.

If either Campbell or McGrath had killed Praeter, they had to get to Manhattan. In Campbell's case, it was only a four-hour drive from Chevy Chase, Maryland, to New York. He could have left his office at five p.m. and been in New York by nine or ten. He would have had plenty of time to meet Praeter, get a few drinks into him, convince Praeter to take him to his office, and, at approximately one a.m., toss Praeter out a window. Then, if he left immediately after Praeter died, Campbell could have been back at his desk in Maryland the next day, tired but on time for work.

For McGrath it was harder. It was a twelve-hour drive from Myrtle Beach to New York. She went online and saw that an outfit called Spirit Airlines had two-hour nonstop flights from New York to Myrtle Beach, which would make things easier, but flying left an electronic trail. That is, there would be a trail if McGrath flew commercial but not if he chartered a private plane or had a pilot's license and had his own plane. Shit. She needed Neil.

If Campbell had driven to New York, she knew from her own experience that it was difficult to drive there from Maryland without going on toll roads, and if Campbell had an EZ-Pass tag on his car, there would be a record of him paying the tolls. But she had no way to find out if he'd paid the tolls without access to EZ-Pass's computers. Likewise for McGrath. Neil could have told her if he'd taken a commercial flight or charged a charter flight to a credit card—but Neil wasn't available.

She thought for a moment then called a man who had once worked for her at the Pentagon and had later transferred to Homeland Security. She asked him to do her a favor and check with TSA to see if McGrath had taken a flight to New York. She also asked him to flex a little muscle and ask the FAA if McGrath had a pilot's license; post 9/11, Homeland Security asking about pilot's licenses was not unusual. Half an hour later he called back and said *no* on all counts. McGrath didn't have a license and he hadn't taken a commercial flight to New York.

So now what should she do? DeMarco felt that of the two men, McGrath was the more likely murderer. He said McGrath gave off a "vibe"—whatever the hell that meant—and that Campbell struck him as being too soft to kill a man. She had no idea if DeMarco was right, but for now she'd trust him, and focus on McGrath. Which meant that what she probably should do next is take a trip to Myrtle Beach and see if she could find out where McGrath was the night Praeter died—but she wasn't sure she felt like doing that.

Then raindrops began to pelt her kitchen window and she said out loud, "Oh, what the hell."

It was a seven-hour drive from McLean, Virginia, to Myrtle Beach, South Carolina. A commercial flight would take four hours because there were no nonstop flights from D.C. A private plane, however, could make the trip in an hour or two.

Which meant that Emma was going to have to risk her life.

A man she'd known for years—he flew jets for the Navy in his twenties—had a Cessna he co-owned with two buddies. He didn't, however, have the money to fly as often as he wanted, and if Emma would pay for the fuel and airport fees, he'd take her anywhere she wanted to go. The problem was that he was no longer in his twenties. He was seventy-two. His eyesight was still good and he was in great shape for a guy his age, but still. . . .

"Ed, I need a ride to Myrtle Beach," Emma said when she called him. "Would you mind giving me a lift?"

"Hell, yeah," Ed said. "When do you want to leave?"

"As soon as you can gas up your plane." Then she thought about the rain. "I mean, I'd like to leave right away, but if the weather . . ."

"Oh, this is nothing," Ed said. "I've flown in weather a hundred times worse than this."

Yeah, when you were twenty-six, wearing a parachute, and flying a multimillion-dollar military jet.

———— ◆◆◆ ————

Lyle Wallace, Chief of Police in Myrtle Beach, hung up the phone and nodded to Emma. "Well, sister," he said, "according to Captain Sutter you can walk on water and play the banjo at the same time. He said if I didn't help you, he might fly down here and give me a whuppin'. So ask your questions."

Captain Sutter was the ex-military NYPD detective Emma had spoken to in New York about Praeter's death, and she asked Wallace to call him, knowing Sutter would verify who she was and convince Wallace to cooperate. She doubted, however, that Wallace was worried about anyone giving him "a whuppin'." He was about the size of a refrigerator.

"It's like I told you, Chief. I just want to know what you can tell me about Rusty McGrath."

Wallace grimaced, as though the topic was painful. "Ol' Rusty," he said. "Well, mostly what I can tell you is that the man's life seems to be devoted to women and play. He's made a hell of a swath through the ladies down here, both the married and the unmarried. And a couple husbands have gotten downright irate with Rusty, and that's always turned out bad for the husbands."

"What do you mean?"

"Have you seen Rusty?" Wallace asked.

"Not yet," Emma said.

"He played linebacker in the pros for a while, and he looks like he could still play the position. He lifts weights, jogs, works out. Anyway, a couple of men have taken, ah, *umbrage* at Rusty screwing their wives, and Rusty beat the hell out of them. He didn't start the fights; he just sat there goading these guys on, telling 'em how fine their wives were in the sack, until they took a swing at him. Then he mops up the floor with the poor bastards. I'll tell you another thing about Rusty, and he and I have had words over this. You know about the big biker week we have down here?"

"No," Emma said.

"Every spring we get a couple hundred thousand bikers down here. Most of 'em are just good ol' boys in their forties or fifties who want to pretend they're Hell's Angels for a week. I mean you gotta have a pretty good-payin' job to afford the motorcycles these boys drive, so most of them are just workin' stiffs who like to ride. Anyway, every spring, for a full week, the town's full of bikers, raisin' hell and drinkin' too much—and every year, regular as salmon spawning, Rusty picks a fight with one of them. He'll go to a bar, pick out a good-size guy, and stare at his woman or kid the guy about being a pussy dressed in leather, and the guy'll be forced to take on Rusty to salvage his pride. And just like with those husbands, Rusty cleans the poor bastard's clock. If it happened once, I could understand it, but like I said, it happens every year. It's like Rusty just likes to stay in practice puttin' the hurt on people. I told him if it happens next year, I'm gonna put his ass in jail for assault even if I have to lie about the charges."

"What does he do when he's not beating people up?"

"He plays. Goes to ball games, cruises around in that big boat he lives on, hunts, rides ATVs, fishes. Hell, the man just plays. He says he's some kind of investor and that's where his money comes from, but I'm not sure he's telling the truth."

"Why's that?"

"I know some guys here, smart guys, businessmen, bankers, those sorts of people. These guys have talked to Rusty about stocks and bonds and such, asking him for advice I guess, and a couple of them have told me that he just doesn't sound too sharp on the subject. Maybe he's just being cagey, playing his cards close to his vest, but the banking guys don't think so. *I* thought he might have been bringing in dope on that boat of his, so, since he pisses me off, I had one of my narcs tail him off and on for a month. Nada."

Emma passed through a stucco archway to enter the apartment complex. It was one of those places where each unit had a balcony overlooking the swimming pool, and it catered to the young and sexually hyperactive. The pool was rimmed with empty beer bottles from the never-ending party.

She rang the doorbell of a third-floor unit. She had to ring twice before a young brunette with a lush figure wearing shorts and a tank top finally opened the door. She was waving her hands in the air; she had just painted her fingernails.

"Yeah?" the brunette said.

"Are you Tammy Doyle?"

DeMarco had told Emma that McGrath's girlfriend's first name was Tammy, and Chief Wallace—with a couple of phone calls to bars near the marina where McGrath docked his boat—had been able to come up with her last name and then her address.

"Yeah," Tammy said. "What . . ."

"I need to talk to you concerning an SEC investigation into a case of insider trading. The Department of Justice, the Federal Bureau of

Investigation, and the attorneys general in three states are involved.
I'm assisting them."

She expected the woman would ask to see her ID—but the airhead
didn't. Instead she said, "Wow. That sounds really heavy."

"It is. May I come in?"

"Yeah, I guess," Tammy said, and stepped aside so Emma could enter
her apartment. The place was a mess; there were clothes lying everywhere, as if the woman had never heard of a closet or a laundry hamper.

"Do you know a man named Russell McGrath?" Emma asked.

"Rusty? Sure. He's, like, my boyfriend. Or I think he is anyway."

Emma didn't know what that meant.

"Do you know where Mr. McGrath was on Monday and Tuesday
of this week? In particular, I'd like to know where he was at one a.m.
Tuesday morning."

"Why do you wanna know? Has Rusty done something?"

"Ms. Doyle, you really don't want to obstruct a federal investigation."

"Obstruct! I was just . . ."

"Do you know where he was Monday and Tuesday?" Emma repeated.

"No. We had a fight on Saturday and I haven't spoken to him since
then. He was being an asshole."

"So you haven't seen him since last Saturday?"

"That's right."

"Have you talked to him on the phone since then?"

"No. I was really pissed. I wasn't about to call him, and he didn't call
me. The jerk."

Tammy Doyle had seemed like a mental midget, but she was an intellectual colossus compared to Gary Fosket, the man who managed the

marina where Rusty McGrath moored his boat. Emma suspected that contributing to Fosket's dullness were both alcohol and marijuana. She could smell the marijuana in his office and the alcohol on his breath.

It took a while for Fosket to recall the days Emma was asking about but he finally did, using a baseball game as a point of reference. "Oh, yeah, right," he said. "Monday the Braves played Tampa. One of them interleague games. Cost me twenty bucks, that asshole reliever they brought in in the eighth."

"So did you see Mr. McGrath that day or the next day?" Emma asked for the third time.

"No," Fosket said. "He was gone both those days."

"Gone where?"

"I dunno. He took his boat out. I gassed him up Sunday morning and helped him load a few supplies on board. He said he was going down the Intercoastal, just gettin' away for a couple of days."

Emma was sure McGrath hadn't taken his boat to New York. Most powerboats don't cruise faster than about ten knots, and it would have taken several days for McGrath to travel by boat to New York City. Her next thought was that maybe he had a friend like her friend Ed, a friend with his own airplane, and maybe McGrath met his friend at some nearby marina. But why take his boat to meet his friend? Why not drive? Whatever the case, she wanted to find out where McGrath was on the day Praeter was killed as that would give her a starting point for tracing his movements.

"Do you have a map showing marinas fifty miles south and north of here?" Emma asked.

"Oh, man," Fosket said, spreading his arms to indicate the chaos in his office. "I must have a couple charts around here somewhere, but it'd take me forever to find 'em."

Emma was seated at a bar near the marina sipping a glass of bad white wine. She didn't know it, but it was the same bar where DeMarco had sat on his trip to Myrtle Beach. And, just as DeMarco had done, she was sitting there looking at McGrath's boat.

As she drank, she tried to figure out what she'd learned about McGrath. Nothing useful, she finally concluded. Just that he was a womanizer living off his investments and had a mean streak. Regarding where he'd been the night Richard Praeter died, she had no idea and didn't know who else to ask, other than McGrath himself. All she knew was what the marina manager had told her: that McGrath had said he was taking a trip on the Intercoastal Waterway.

Emma took out her phone and called a lady who was a vice admiral in the Coast Guard; she and Emma had once served together on a counterterrorism task force. Emma asked her if it was possible to check public marinas on the Intercoastal Waterway in the vicinity of Myrtle Beach to see if McGrath had been docked at any of them the day Praeter was killed. She described McGrath's boat, gave the admiral its name and hull number, and said as big as it was, someone might remember it.

The admiral said if he docked at a marina and paid for a berth, the marina should have a record, although marina record keeping could be pretty spotty. She'd have someone on her staff e-mail the marinas; marina owners were typically very responsive when the Coast Guard asked for something. On the other hand, the admiral said, there were a lot of places where McGrath could have just anchored his boat and taken a dinghy ashore. She'd get back to Emma.

Lastly, she called Chief Wallace and asked him to e-mail law enforcement agencies along the Intercoastal Waterway to see if any of them had encountered McGrath. She knew it was a long shot, but she couldn't think of anything else to do. Chief Wallace agreed, but Emma could tell he was beginning to tire of doing her favors.

She wished she could interrogate McGrath and ask him to account for his whereabouts the night Praeter died, but she didn't have the authority to do that, and unlike his girlfriend, McGrath would be bright enough to know it. But then, sometimes, you get what you wish for.

"I hear you been asking questions about me. Thought maybe I should find out who you are and why you're asking."

Emma turned to look at the speaker.

McGrath was a big, good-looking man. He was wearing a Tommy Bahama shirt, tight-fitting blue jeans, and Top-Siders without socks. Emma could smell his aftershave. He was smiling at her and he looked amused, as if he found the idea of a woman investigating him humorous.

Emma stepped off the barstool.

"Well, are you gonna answer me? You been running all over town pokin' into my private life, and I'd like to know why."

"Where were you on Monday and Tuesday of this week, Mr. McGrath?"

McGrath laughed; he laughed loud enough that other patrons in the bar looked over at him. Then he leaned down so his eyes were level with Emma's. "You can kiss my ass, lady. Now, who are you and why are you asking about me?" As McGrath asked the question, he took a step forward so that Emma was forced back against the bar. He outweighed her by over a hundred pounds and had, at one time, been a professional in a sport where the primary objective appeared to be maiming the opposition.

Emma shifted her position slightly, her arms down at her sides, palms facing outward. She was deciding which part of McGrath's body she was going to strike first. "Step back, McGrath. Get out of my space."

McGrath looked around the bar, casually, to see if anyone was looking at him and Emma. Several people were.

He held up his hands in a gesture of false surrender, took a step back, and said, "Sure, honey. I didn't mean to scare you."

Emma felt like hitting him just for calling her honey. "You didn't scare me," Emma said. "Now, are you going to answer my question? Where were you on Monday night, the night Richard Praeter died?"

McGrath just smiled, shook his head as if she were nuts, and walked away, down toward the end of the bar where two barmaids were waiting for drink orders. "Ladies," McGrath said to the barmaids, "you are both lookin' delectable tonight. Would one of you sweet young things bring me a gin and tonic? Oh, and you see that lady over there, the tall, ornery-looking one? Bring her another glass of wine."

As Emma walked past McGrath's table to leave the bar, he winked at her.

37

The morning after returning from Myrtle Beach—grateful that old Ed had managed to land his plane safely the night before—Emma talked again to her source at the NYPD to see if he'd learned anything new regarding Praeter's death. He hadn't—and she got the distinct impression that the death of an unpopular rich guy with no political connections wasn't high on his priority list. She also pestered her friend at Homeland Security, asking him to check airport surveillance cameras to see if McGrath had been in any of New York's major airports.

"I know he didn't take a commercial flight using his real name," Emma said, "but maybe he has a fake ID, and if the TSA could . . ."

Her friend said, "Sorry, Emma. I love you like a sister, but unless this guy's Al Qaeda there's no way I can vector people off on that."

Well, poop.

It was still raining; indeed, it was coming down so hard Emma was afraid it was going to wash away the new topsoil she'd put in. She wasn't going to get any yard work done today, so she might as well go see Douglas Campbell and find out if he had an alibi for the night Praeter died. But before driving to Chevy Chase, she had a long, leisurely breakfast with Christine.

This delay almost cost Campbell his life.

Kathy Campbell answered the door holding a glass of what appeared to be orange juice, and Emma's first thought upon seeing her was: This woman should use sunscreen.

"Doug isn't here," she said when Emma asked to speak to her husband.

"Do you know where he is? I called his office and they said he took the day off."

"Who are you?"

"A federal agent," Emma said. Emma had—and she knew it—a face and a manner that people tended to believe and were reluctant to challenge. Nonetheless, she took what looked like a badge case out of her pocket and flipped it open, allowing Kathy Campbell the briefest glimpse of a card embossed with a fancy gold seal. The card identified Emma as a retired civil servant who had special privileges at commissaries on military bases.

"You people need to stop hounding Doug," Kathy Campbell said. "He didn't have anything to do with Molly Mahoney."

"I still need to speak with him, Mrs. Campbell. Can you please tell me where he is?"

"He's with his good buddy Rusty."

"Rusty McGrath?"

"Yeah. They're going to a UVA baseball game today. Rusty called him last night and asked him to go, and Doug took a day off work. I mean, really. College baseball. Who gives a shit?"

Maybe she wasn't drinking pure orange juice. A mimosa or a screwdriver seemed more likely.

"Mrs. Campbell, do you know where your husband was on Monday night of this week? Actually, early Tuesday morning, about one a.m."

"I guess he was here," Kathy Campbell said with a shrug. "I drove down to Richmond on Sunday to see my sister and didn't get back until Tuesday afternoon. But where else would he have been? I mean Doug's no Rusty McGrath. He sure as hell wasn't out chasing college girls in Georgetown."

⁘

Emma had a bad feeling about McGrath inviting Campbell to a baseball game the day after she'd confronted him. Maybe McGrath just wanted to enjoy an afternoon with a good friend from college. Or maybe McGrath wanted to get together with Campbell and talk about them having been subpoenaed by Molly's lawyer. Maybe—but Emma didn't think so.

If DeMarco was correct, McGrath had killed Praeter, and after meeting McGrath, Emma now shared DeMarco's bad vibe about the man. She couldn't help but think that maybe McGrath was planning to get rid of the only other man who could implicate him in a crime—and he was going to do it today. Campbell was going to have some kind of accident before he left Charlottesville—a fall down a flight of steps where his neck is broken, a car accident where McGrath walks away and Campbell doesn't. Rusty McGrath was definitely strong enough to break Douglas Campbell's neck, and if that happened, she would be partially to blame for stirring the pot with McGrath.

When Emma had worked for the DIA, she rarely relied on the gut feelings of her subordinates, usually insisting on hard data to support their conclusions. But she relied very much on her own instincts, and had been right often enough to feel justified in doing so. And right now her instincts were screaming at her: she needed to get Campbell away from McGrath. The problem was that she didn't know anyone in Charlottesville she could call to assist her. Well, she knew a couple of professors at UVA—but a professor wasn't the sort of person she needed. She needed a cop.

She thought for a moment then called DeMarco.

"Where are you?" she asked.

"I'm in New York."

"What are you doing there?"

"I'm, uh, . . ."

"Oh, never mind. Who was that retired cop you spoke to in Charlottesville?"

"A guy named Dave Torey."

"Do you have his number?"

"Yeah."

"Well, give it to me."

DeMarco fumbled with his cell phone, then read off the number. "What's going on?" he asked.

"I don't have time to talk right now," Emma said and hung up.

What the hell was he doing in New York?

Emma explained to Torey what was going on with Campbell and Mc-Grath, and told him about Praeter's death. She concluded with, "I think McGrath might try to kill Campbell. So what I need to know is, do you still have any pull with the Charlottesville PD?"

"Well, I got a lot of pull with one guy. He's my son. He's in charge of their SWAT team."

"Do you think you could get him to find McGrath and Campbell? Campbell's wife told me they were going to a UVA baseball game."

"Yeah, if you think this will really stop a murder, I can probably convince my boy to help. He's got enough clout with the department that if he puts out a BOLO for McGrath, the folks in patrol will start looking for him. But what should he do if he finds them?"

"Hell, I don't know. Tell him to just watch them and make sure Mc-Grath sees him watching. He's not going to do anything to Campbell if a cop is looking at him. But I don't have these guys' pictures."

"That's okay. He can get their photos from the Maryland and South Carolina DMVs."

"Thanks. I'll be down there in a couple of hours, maybe quicker if I don't get caught for speeding."

"Okay, I'll call my kid. Call me when you get near town and I'll meet you someplace." Torey paused, then added, "You know, this sure as hell beats sitting here on my ass watching TV all day."

———◆———

Dave Torey turned out to be stocky guy in his sixties with a white mustache. What little hair he had left was also white. His son looked just like him, except he didn't have a mustache; he was losing his hair, however. The good thing about Torey's son, Steve, was he looked tough and strong—at least as strong as Rusty McGrath.

Emma was sitting in back of a Charlottesville PD patrol car. Steve Torey was driving and his father was riding in the passenger's seat. Emma didn't like being in the backseat separated by a screen from the Toreys—and she really didn't like that there were no handles on the inside of the car to open the back doors. Emma didn't like not being in control.

"We spotted them when they left the ball game," Steve Torey said, "and followed them to a bar called O'Grady's, which is where they are now. I've got guy inside the bar watching them—and I can tell you O'Grady isn't too happy about that, having a uniform cop standing in his doorway. Half the people he serves in that place are underage college kids with fake IDs."

"We need to get Campbell away from McGrath," Emma said.

"Well, I'm not sure how I'm supposed to do that," Steve Torey said.

"How long have they been inside this bar?"

"About an hour," Steve Torey said.

"Then Campbell's drunk. And you can . . ."

"I don't know that he's drunk," Steve Torey said.

"Listen to the lady," Dave Torey said to his son.

"Officer Torey," Emma said, "you're going to arrest Campbell for public drunkenness, or whatever the correct legal term is. Later on you can apologize and let him go if he's not really drunk, but I'm willing to bet they've been drinking beer all afternoon at that ballgame and now they're drinking some more. Campbell's drunk."

"I like it," Dave Torey said. "And this time these assholes aren't going to a bowl game and the university's not going to send some lawyer over to get them out of whatever jam they're in."

———◆———

Steve Torey walked into the bar and nodded to the cop standing by the door. The bar was packed with college kids and between the kids and the jukebox, it was noisy in the place. But the kids all stopped talking when a second cop entered the bar.

Campbell and McGrath were at a table by themselves, about thirty feet from the door. McGrath was drinking a beer; Campbell had a colorless drink in front of him that could have been vodka or gin. When McGrath saw Emma come in behind the cop, he looked in her direction and shook his head. He wasn't smiling now.

Steve Torey motioned to the other cop and they walked over to the table where McGrath and Campbell were seated. "Would you gentlemen please stand up," Steve Torey said.

"What?" Campbell said, but he stood up—and almost fell. There was no doubt he was drunk.

McGrath didn't move. "What's this all about," he said.

"Sir, I told you to stand up. I want to see IDs from both of you. Then I want you to go over and put your hands on that wall so I can make sure you're not carrying weapons."

"You're not searching me," McGrath said. "You don't have probable cause."

"Sir," Steve Torey said, "I suspect you don't know shit about probable cause. What I do know is that right now you're resisting a lawful order issued by a police officer. Now, stand up, hand me your wallet, and then go grab the wall."

McGrath sat for a moment longer, then stood up. Unlike Campbell he didn't look or sound drunk. Steve Torey examined both men's IDs, and while he did, Campbell swayed, having a hard time maintaining his balance. Emma thought he looked close to passing out. Then another thought occurred to her: she wondered if McGrath might have spiked his drink so he'd be easier to control.

Torey patted Campbell down first, and while he was doing this, Campbell said, "What the hell's going on here, Rusty? Why are these guys fucking with us?" McGrath didn't respond.

When Torey finished with Campbell, he patted down McGrath, taking his time, doing a more thorough search. He noticed a bulge in the back right-hand pocket of McGrath's jeans. He reached inside the pocket and pulled out a bag of peanuts. The peanuts in the bag were almost pulverized, as if McGrath had sat on them.

"You squashed your peanuts," Torey said, and tossed the peanuts on the table next to McGrath's wallet. McGrath still didn't respond.

"Okay," Steve Torey said. "Mr. Campbell, you are obviously intoxicated and I'm arresting you for being drunk and disorderly in public."

"You can't do that! Can he do that, Rusty?"

"Cuff him," Torey said to the other cop, and Campbell didn't resist as handcuffs were placed on him and he was led out of the bar. He was four inches taller than the cop walking beside him.

As the cops were leaving, Emma walked over to McGrath. He was putting his wallet back into his pocket. The peanuts Torey had taken from him were still sitting on the table.

"Where were you last Monday, McGrath?" Emma said.

"Kiss my ass, you bitch."

———◆———

Campbell was sitting in the back of a patrol car, his head lolled back on top of the seat. He'd passed out.

"What am I supposed to do with him?" Steve Torey said, now wishing he'd never got sucked into Emma's and his father's plans.

"Just toss him into a cell until he wakes up, then let him go," Emma said. "McGrath isn't going to do anything now. In fact, I'm guessing McGrath will head back to Myrtle Beach right away. If he comes by the police station and tries to get you to release Campbell into his custody, tell him Campbell's going to be held overnight, and then you're going to personally escort him out of Charlottesville.

"Oh, and do one other thing for me. Ask Campbell to tell you where he was last Monday night at one a.m. I don't think he'll tell you anything, but if he does, let me know. And thank you for your help, Officer Torey. I'm convinced you just kept a man from being killed."

Actually, Emma had no idea if that was true.

38

DeMarco found Emma in her backyard, arms folded across her chest, watching two Hispanic men aerate and reseed a portion of her lawn that apparently didn't meet her standards. She was wearing a long-sleeved white shirt, jeans, and rubber boots that almost reached her knees. Her jeans were tucked into the boots, and absent a bullwhip, she looked like the overseer of an antebellum plantation watching the cotton being picked. DeMarco felt sorry for the Hispanics.

Emma had asked him to come to her house, saying she had a few things to tell him. Actually, she hadn't asked him; she'd *ordered* him. That was the problem with involving Emma in his cases: she automatically assumed command and pretty much did whatever she wanted.

"What were you doing in New York?" she asked, without taking her eyes off the gardeners.

"Looking into something to get this congressman off Mahoney's back, like I told you the other day. I also spent the night at my mom's place since I hadn't seen her in a while."

Now Emma looked at him—and she looked skeptical—but she didn't say anything.

If for no other reason than to change the subject, he asked, "Why did you want Dave Torey's number yesterday?" and Emma proceeded to tell what she'd learned about Campbell and McGrath and the incident in Charlottesville.

"You had the guy *arrested*?" DeMarco said, amazed at what she'd done. He was also amazed that she hadn't bothered to call and tell him —but that's what happened when you worked with Emma.

"I had to get him away from McGrath."

"And you seriously thought McGrath was going to kill him?"

"I don't know. I just . . . I just had this feeling," Emma said. "I was afraid Campbell was going to have an accident in Charlottesville. He was going to fall down a flight of steps, or get mugged, or get in a car accident where McGrath lived and he died. I think something like that was going to happen."

"But what made you think that?"

"Because I think McGrath's a sociopath, and I think he's getting rid of the people who can put him in jail. I also think he wants them gone before they have to testify at Molly's trial."

She told DeMarco that neither Campbell nor McGrath had a solid alibi for the night of Praeter's death but at the same time she hadn't been able to find any evidence that they'd been in New York. Emma was silent for a moment, pondering their next step. Until now, her interest in the case had been somewhat halfhearted, but DeMarco could tell that McGrath had gotten her competitive juices flowing.

"I wonder if Neil's back yet," she said. "We need some facts. All we have are theories and guesses. I want to get Neil looking into this money that was deposited in Molly's account, and . . ."

No, no, no! That was the last thing DeMarco wanted. Fortunately, at that moment Emma saw something that derailed her train of thought.

"You!" Emma screamed at one of the Hispanics. "Yes, you! Watch the roots of that tree, for God's sake."

"Ruts?" one of the guys said.

And Emma began to yell at the poor man in Spanish.

When she finished instructing her helpers on the degree of care they needed to take with her plants, she turned back to look at DeMarco. He was waving one hand frantically near his face.

"What are you doing?" she said.

"Bee!"

"Oh, for Christ's sake. Quit swatting at it and it'll fly away. It's not going to kill you."

"It might," DeMarco said, relieved that the insect had finally abandoned its vicious attack. "I've never been stung by a bee before. I could be allergic to bee venom, go into analgesic shock or something."

"It's *anaphylactic* shock, you fool, and only about one percent . . . Shit! We need to go talk to Campbell."

"What the hell do you want?" Campbell said when he opened his door and saw Emma and DeMarco on his porch. He was dressed in sweatpants and a white T-shirt and he appeared to be in the final stages of a terminal hangover. His thin blond hair was plastered to his scalp, he was sweating, and his complexion was ash-gray.

"We need to talk to you," Emma said.

"Fuck you," Campbell said. "Fuck you, and get off my property."

"Mr. Campbell, are you allergic to peanuts?" Emma asked.

A person severely allergic to peanuts may experience respiratory distress, fainting, hypotension, urticaria, vomiting—and death. But when Emma suggested that Rusty McGrath had been planning to kill his good buddy Doug Campbell with a small, normally harmless nut,

Campbell said, "You're crazy. So the guy had a bag of peanuts on him. Big deal. That doesn't prove anything."

"The peanuts were *pulverized*, Mr. Campbell," Emma said. "I saw them. And I think they were pulverized so he could mix them into your food more easily. At some point you would have gone to the restroom or been otherwise distracted, and McGrath was going to sprinkle your dinner with peanuts and kill you."

"He bought a bag of peanuts for the game. People eat peanuts at baseball games. And then he sat on them, for Christ's sake. He didn't *pulverize* them."

"McGrath knows about your peanut allergy, doesn't he?" Emma said.

"Sure. I told the guys about it when I was in college, and once, this asshole, this guy who played backup quarterback, put a couple peanuts in this pizza I was eating. He thought it'd be funny to see what happened. Fortunately, the medics got there in time. But just because Rusty knows I'm allergic doesn't mean he was trying to kill me. I've known the guy for twenty years. We were teammates."

"Yeah," Emma said, "Rusty seems like a real team player, all right."

And DeMarco wondered how Campbell would feel about his teammate if he knew that McGrath had screwed his wife.

"Campbell," DeMarco said, "you have to face reality. Richard Praeter did not commit suicide. Rusty McGrath killed him and he's going to kill you next."

"That's bullshit," Campbell said. "Why would Rusty kill anyone?"

"You know why," DeMarco said. "You, Praeter, and McGrath have been involved in a criminal conspiracy for years. You gave Praeter information on your company's research, he bought stock at the right time, hid the trail from the SEC, and then shared the profits with you and McGrath."

Campbell opened his mouth to protest, but DeMarco kept talking.

"When all of you received subpoenas the other day from Molly Mahoney's lawyer, McGrath decided that you and Praeter had become expendable. He killed Praeter and he would have killed you in Charlottesville if my friend hadn't intervened."

"That's what this is all about," Campbell said. "You guys are trying to get Molly off by pinning something on me."

"We're not trying to pin anything on you," Emma said, "We're trying to save your life."

"You need to confess, Campbell," DeMarco said. "That's the only way you're gonna stay alive."

"Confess to what?" Campbell shrieked.

"That you gave insider tips to Praeter, and that you and McGrath were Praeter's partners."

"And we want you to tell us why you set up Molly," Emma added.

Oh, boy, DeMarco thought.

"For the tenth fuckin' time," Campbell screamed, "I didn't have a goddamn thing to do with Molly! And don't you people ever come to my house again."

39

"Thanks for coming by, DeMarco."

Lawyer Daniel Caine was in his well-furnished office riding an exercise bike, the pedals a blur at the rate he was going. As Caine cycled to nowhere, DeMarco sat drinking expensive coffee, thinking Caine would probably put ten miles on the odometer in the time it took him to finish the cup.

"I've got some bad news," Caine said, not even breathing hard. "Actually I have two pieces of bad news."

"Great," DeMarco said. That was just what he needed: more bad news.

"As you know our defense is based primarily on the fact that the e-trade brokerage and bank accounts were established online, and that the people who did this, possibly Campbell and the late Mr. Praeter, stole Molly's identity and used computers at an Internet café to commit their crimes. Furthermore, there is no evidence that Molly ever spoke or met with the brokers, nor is there any direct evidence she used the computers at the café to set up any accounts."

Caine sounded like he was doing a summation for a jury. He was also telling DeMarco things he already knew. "So what's changed?" he asked.

"We've been going through the records we subpoenaed from the SEC," Caine said. "Kiser *buried* us in paper. She filled a FedEx delivery truck with boxes of files, knowing it would take us forever to go through everything.

"Well, yesterday one of my guys, this intern we just hired, found something. I'm going to give that kid a bonus when this is all over. Anyway, a brokerage firm called CoreTrade is one of the firms that Molly allegedly used to buy stock in Hubbard Power, the submarine battery company. Well, now there's some circumstantial evidence that Molly called them."

"Circumstantial?"

"Yes. Before the stock was purchased, someone called CoreTrade and asked how one went about setting up an online account, what information was required, what documents had to be signed, that sort of thing. Well, CoreTrade, clever boys that they are, use their caller ID system to automatically record the phone numbers of callers; they also log some calls they receive, and note the subject of the call. They do this so they can call people back who express an interest in their services but don't sign on with them the first time they call."

"You're not going to tell me that the call was made from Molly's cell phone, are you?"

"No. But the call was made from a phone at Reston Tech, and the phone is in a conference room just down the hall from Molly's office. Kiser must have found out about the broker's call-back system, went through it looking for phone numbers, and finds the number for one of several hundred phones at Reston."

"Was Douglas Campbell working the day the call was made?" De-Marco asked. Even though DeMarco knew it was Molly who'd made the call, Kay Kiser couldn't prove it, and if Campbell was there that day, Kiser couldn't prove that he *didn't* make the call.

"I'm way ahead of you, DeMarco," Caine said. "Campbell was on a recruiting trip to a bunch of colleges in the Midwest."

"Well, shit," DeMarco said.

"Like I said, it's circumstantial. The fact that a phone call was made to a brokerage firm from a phone fifty feet from her desk doesn't prove she made the call, but it doesn't help our case."

"So is that it?" DeMarco said.

"No. I told you I had two pieces of bad news," Caine said. He finally stopped pedaling and climbed down from the exercise bike. He dabbed at the sweat on his face with a towel, though he wasn't really sweating all that hard. Caine reminded DeMarco of the guy who played the robot in the second *Terminator* movie, not Arnold, but the skinny, unstoppable guy made of liquid metal.

"Molly normally used cash at the café but one time she paid for her computer time with a credit card, and the time she used the computer is on the café's copy of her receipt. The time recorded coincides *exactly* with the time one of the five brokerage accounts was established online. Just like with the phone call, Kiser can't prove that Molly established the account—there are ten computers in the place—but her being there at the exact time the account was set up is devastating."

Daniel Caine didn't know about Ted Allen, but DeMarco was beginning to suspect that Caine now knew he was defending a guilty client. The good thing about defense lawyers, however, is that most of their clients are guilty, and guilt or innocence often has very little to do with a lawyer's strategy.

"So how are you going to handle this?" DeMarco asked.

Caine grimaced. "I'll continue to argue that Kiser can't prove beyond a reasonable doubt that Molly made the phone call or that she set up the e-trade account. I'll say the people who are trying to frame her are so smart and devious that they established one of the brokerage accounts *knowing* she was in the café that day, that they obviously followed her there."

"I'm not sure that's going to fly," DeMarco said.

"Well, if you have a better idea, I'm listening," Caine said.

"I don't," DeMarco said.

40

DeMarco caught up with Mahoney in a hearing room at the Rayburn Building.

He'd been part of a group of lawmakers who spent the last four hours beating up a couple of bankers, the bankers having been given multimillion-dollar bonuses while simultaneously losing several billion dollars of their shareholders' money. Beating up investment bankers was one of the recurring Punch and Judy shows in D.C. The only point of the hearings, as far as DeMarco could tell, was for the politicians to be seen on television *pretending* to be outraged by the bankers' greedy behavior; he knew they were pretending as they never passed any laws to truly change that behavior.

"I just got out of a meeting with Molly's lawyer," DeMarco said. "Things have gone from bad to worse."

"What the hell are you talking about," Mahoney said, and his face began to flush to an unhealthy shade of crimson—and he hadn't even heard the bad news. Mahoney saw nothing wrong with shooting the messenger, particularly when there was no one else to shoot.

DeMarco relayed what he'd learned from Caine: that Kiser now had more evidence, albeit circumstantial, that she could use to convict Molly. DeMarco concluded by saying, "Caine's good and she still has a chance at trial but I'd say the odds of her being found guilty have gone up substantially."

As DeMarco watched Mahoney absorb the bad news he couldn't help but think of the old saying about never backing a dangerous animal into a corner, which is what Robert Fairchild and Ted Allen were doing. Mahoney was just sitting there, glowering, but what DeMarco saw was a white-haired bear—a bear with yellow fangs and long sharp claws. What Big Bob and Ted didn't realize was that Mahoney wasn't the type of man to go down without a fight, even if he *knew* he was going to lose the fight. Somebody, very soon, was going to feel the bear's claws.

"I'm starting to think," DeMarco said, "that the only way to get free of Ted and keep Molly out of jail is to give Ted his money and let that guy Denny Reed take the fall for her."

"Don't forget," Mahoney said, "that I also have to move a hundred million dollars from the U.S. Treasury to the State of New Jersey."

"Yeah, well," DeMarco said, "someone's going to have to tell Ted that even you can't make that happen."

"But I can," Mahoney said, and then he explained.

Every year the Congress of these United States appropriates a pile of money for the Department of Defense, a green stack so high it reaches the clouds. And every year DOD spends all the money it's been given and then comes back to Congress with its hands held out, like an Oliver Twist clad in olive drab asking for more porridge. After a suitable period of haggling, Congress inevitably gives the military more money, and the additional monies given are termed a "supplemental," meaning that Congress will increase, or supplement, the staggering amount already provided in the original appropriations bill. It just so happened that the annual defense supplemental was currently winding its way through the hallowed halls of Congress.

Now, the average citizen, naïve schmuck that he is, thinks that the Pentagon is being given the extra money to buy more soldiers, tanks, planes, and guns—and of course the average citizen is completely wrong. The military supplemental is, in reality, just another mechanism for Congress to distribute pork, and the fact that some of the money is actually used to help our fighting forces is often coincidental or, at best, tangential. Last year, for example, Mahoney—that great grandmaster of pork distribution—used the supplemental to build a parking garage for union workers at a defense plant in Massachusetts. The stated rational for this expenditure was that erecting said garage would make the workers more efficient at producing whatever they produced; the reality was that the parking garage created happy voters and made a certain construction company—one that contributed heavily to Mahoney—even richer than it was before. And it appeared that this year, if he had to, Mahoney was going to use the defense supplemental to help Ted Allen get his convention center built.

The way Mahoney planned to do this was to include in the supplemental one hundred million dollars for the state of New Jersey—mere chicken feed in terms of defense spending—and the money would be earmarked for military recruitment and homeland security. The deal was this: when the new convention center retail mall was built, it would include rent-free space for military recruiters—like there was a chance in hell that the slot machine grannies coming down from New York were going to stop by the recruiting office. In addition, the state had to agree that in the event of a disaster—hurricane, tsunami, terrorist attack—the convention center would become a place for the public to cower until the threat had passed.

"Won't the Republicans in the House try to stop you?" DeMarco asked.

"No," Mahoney said. Mahoney didn't bother to explain but DeMarco figured that Perry Wallace, Mahoney's diabolical chief of staff, had cut deals with key Republicans over other provisions in the bill and that New Jersey's Republican congressional delegates were all backing Perry, of course, as the bill benefited their home state and supported New Jersey's Republican governor. The Democrats would go along for the simple reason that Mahoney would make them. In other words, Perry had worked his backroom magic, all the politicians were perfectly aligned, and he was just waiting for Mahoney to give him the go-ahead.

"But I'm not gonna do it," Mahoney said. "Goddamnit, I'm not."

DeMarco knew Mahoney didn't really care about the hundred million—it wasn't *his* money—what the bear cared about was allowing Ted Allen to win.

"So what the hell are you gonna do next?" Mahoney said.

Somehow all this had become DeMarco's problem.

"Well," he said, "the first thing I'm going to do is try to get Big Bob Fairchild's hooks out of your ass. I've got a guy—you know, that computer guy I've used in the past—and he's finally back in town. I'm going to get him digging into Fairchild's past, trying to come up with something to use against him."

"Good," Mahoney said. "What else?"

Good? Only Mahoney would consider it good that DeMarco was trying to find a way to blackmail a member of Congress.

"I got the name of Ted Allen's boss and I'm trying to come up with some way to use that to our advantage."

"Shit, I thought you would have done that by now," Mahoney whined. "And what about those guys, Campbell and the other one?"

"McGrath," DeMarco said. "But I don't see how they're going to help since we know they didn't have anything to do with Molly. I mean, Caine can still trot McGrath and Campbell out during Molly's trial to confuse things, but with the evidence that Kiser has, I don't think it's going to work."

Mahoney's Machiavellian mind groped desperately for a solution. "Yeah, but if you can prove that Campbell and McGrath did something illegal then maybe you can trade them to Kiser for Molly."

"The problem with that," DeMarco countered, "is that Kay Kiser, who's a whole lot smarter than I am, has been trying to get these guys for years. So I kind of doubt, in the time remaining before Molly's trial, that I'm going to do better than Kiser. And with Praeter dead, it's going to be even harder to pin something on them."

This was not what the bear wanted to hear. It stood up on its hind legs and roared.

41

DeMarco wished that he were a billionaire media mogul. If he were, he'd not only be rich but he'd have thousands of sneaky journalists at his disposal—including the type willing to hack into computers and wiretap phones—and they would help him dig up the dirt on Big Bob Fairchild. And that's what DeMarco needed: dirt. Since Fairchild had something sharp to hold over Mahoney's head, DeMarco needed something equally lethal to dangle over Fairchild's greasy scalp to balance the scales.

Unfortunately, he was not a media mogul and he didn't employ any sneaky journalists—but he did have Neil, who had finally returned from his second honeymoon. Neil was a fat man who wore his thinning blond hair in a short ponytail and typically dressed in Hawaiian shirts, shorts, and sandals. As DeMarco talked to him, Neal sat in a chair designed to accommodate his substantial girth, slurping a fruit smoothie. He looked tanned, relaxed and sexually sated—all by-products of his belated honeymoon.

Normally, DeMarco would have been jealous of Neil, but he was actually feeling somewhat sated himself, thanks to Tina, Alice's lovely friend. And he'd been invited to dinner at Tina's house so he could be introduced to her twin daughters—an occasion that smacked of feminine manipulation and made him somewhat apprehensive. The good news, however, was that the daughters were supposed to leave right after dinner to attend a concert, leaving DeMarco and their mother time to themselves. But that was later—and right now he needed to focus on the problems caused by Mahoney's middle daughter.

"There's probably not much point looking for funny-money stuff," DeMarco said to Neil. "Not with his wife."

What DeMarco meant was that Fairchild's wife was so damn rich that Neil probably wouldn't find evidence of illegal kickbacks, or outright bribes, or illicit campaign contributions.

"Maybe I can tie him to his nephew's problems, you know, Little Bob's connections to that lobbyist Mayfield," Neil suggested.

"I don't think so," DeMarco said. "Mahoney has had the president's special prosecutor digging into that for months. So look for the usual stuff. Affairs. Twisted perversions. Illegitimate children. Maybe he e-mailed pictures of his dick to a bunch of women like that yahoo from New York. All I know is that right now Big Bob comes across as a sanctimonious paragon of virtue—family values and all that crap—so you just *know* there's gotta be something sordid he's been hiding for years."

"This could get expensive," Neil said. Then he smiled. Neil's retail rate was extremely dear.

But DeMarco said, "Don't worry about the money."

When Mahoney set up DeMarco's position those many years ago, he had to provide the operating funds that DeMarco needed to ply his trade. And Mahoney, being an expert at diverting the government's money to causes of his own choosing, had no problem at all supplying the small amounts that DeMarco needed. Imagine the federal budget as the planet Jupiter; by comparison, DeMarco's budget was the size of a chickpea and the amount he would pay Neil, a sesame seed. This meant that Neil's bill, no matter how large and outrageous it might be, would be virtually invisible to those organizations tasked with monitoring how the taxpayers' dollars are squandered. So when DeMarco said don't worry about the money, this time he meant it.

"Then I'll begin my endeavors immediately," Neil said, rubbing his chubby hands together, already thinking of ingenious ways to pad his bill.

"Good. Call me as soon as you've got something."

"If I can't get a hold of you, do you want me to pass on whatever I get to Emma?" Neil said.

"Definitely not," DeMarco said. Then realizing how that sounded, he added, "Uh, she's real busy right now. Her yard work, you know."

DeMarco was starting to feel like Richard Nixon trying to hold down the lid on Watergate—and he just knew that at some point his own John Dean was going to come along and spill the beans to Emma.

42

DeMarco dialed the next number in the yellow pages.

He had just finished calling five dental offices near his house in Georgetown, asking if any of the dentists could see him immediately. None could. One of the receptionists had actually laughed out loud. He was beginning to believe that everyone in the dental profession was a direct descendant of the guys who ran the Spanish Inquisition. He dialed the sixth number, going immediately into his desperate spiel. To his surprise, the woman said: "Ooh, you poor thing." She sounded like somebody's sweet grandmother and acted as if she actually cared. Then she said, "And you're lucky, too. The doctor just had a cancellation. So if you can get here in the next ten minutes . . ."

"I'm on my way!" DeMarco cried.

DeMarco's John Dean turned out to be Neil.

He was backing his car out of the driveway when Emma pulled up in her Mercedes. He got out of his car to see what she wanted, and saw her coming toward him, taking long aggressive strides, lips set in a tight line, hands clenched into fists. He immediately envisioned a terrified gopher looking up and seeing an eagle dropping from the sky, talons extended—and he was the gopher, not the eagle.

"I want to know what the hell's going on, and I want to know now!" Emma said.

"What?" DeMarco said, trying to look innocent, knowing that too many years of working for Mahoney made that impossible.

"I called Neil today to see what you had him doing," Emma said. "I thought he'd be trying to find out how the money got into Molly Mahoney's bank account. And that's when I learned that you have him trying to get something on Robert Fairchild and that he's not doing anything related to Molly. So do not give me that '*What?*' crap. You tell me what's going on."

DeMarco considered his options—and then he gave it all up. He told her everything.

When he finished, Emma just stared at him for what seemed a lifetime, her blue eyes colder than an arctic winter. "So all the time that I've been running around trying to clear Molly's name, you knew she was guilty and didn't tell me. I could just . . ."

"Emma, I didn't know she was guilty when this all started, then . . ."

Emma raised a hand to stop him. "No! I don't want to hear whatever excuse you're about to make up for lying to me."

"I wasn't going to make up an excuse," DeMarco said. He would have, but he couldn't think of one. "I was going to say that this thing has become a whole lot more complicated than Molly just taking a guilty plea."

"No, it's not. She's guilty. She should go to jail."

"It's not that simple, Emma. Ted Allen will have her killed if he thinks she'll testify against him. Then you have both Ted and Fairchild blackmailing Mahoney. I mean . . ."

"What do Campbell and McGrath have to do with Molly?" she said.

"Nothing," DeMarco said. "Molly got the insider trading idea when she heard that phone call of Campbell's, but other than that, there's no link between Molly and those guys. But I know that Campbell and his friends have been making money illegally for years and I'm about ninety percent sure that McGrath is a murderer. He killed Praeter and you know he tried to kill Campbell in Charlottesville."

Her voice dripping sarcasm, Emma said, "And that's why you're still investigating Campbell and McGrath, because you want to bring them to justice for all the crimes they've committed."

"No," DeMarco said, "but if I can prove they've done something criminal then maybe I'll have something Molly's lawyers can use to get her a better deal with the SEC."

Emma just shook her head in disgust.

"Come on, Emma," DeMarco said. "Molly's the lesser of two evils. You must see that."

"The lesser of two evils," Emma repeated. "I *despise* that saying. The lesser of two evils is still evil."

Emma turned her back on him and walked away—and he wondered if he'd ever see her again.

By the time DeMarco arrived at the dentist's office, thirty minutes late—naturally, he hit every red light on the way there—the sweet grandmother he'd spoken to had morphed into a nagging hag, lecturing him on the inconsiderate behavior of people who make appointments and fail to keep them. And, no, the doctor did not have another opening on his schedule.

This was turning out to be a really shitty day.

43

Casey Maynard shut off the engine and looked around. It was two a.m. and he didn't see anyone on the street or any lights on in nearby homes. He stepped out of his pickup and stretched—it had been a long drive—and looked around again. Nobody.

He got down on one knee with some effort. He was a shaggy haired, bearded man, six foot four, two hundred and seventy pounds. A lot of the weight was fat. He reached under the driver's seat and pulled out the Glock. He'd bought the Glock from a dealer in Virginia on his way up from South Carolina. The dealer had told him that the weapon was untraceable but Maynard didn't care if it was or not. After he finished the job he'd toss the gun in the first river he came to.

He looked around one more time; he was in no hurry. There were only a few cars parked on the street—in this kind of neighborhood people parked in their garages—but none of the cars had anybody in them nor did any of the vehicles look like something a cop would drive. The problem was there were shadows everywhere—pockets of darkness where somebody could hide. But why would someone be hiding? He shoved the Glock into the back of his jeans.

He reached into the pickup again and took a plastic bag off the passenger seat. Inside the bag was a penlight he could hold in his mouth, a roll of duct tape, a glass cutter, a pair of leather gloves, and a black ski mask. He put on the gloves and the ski mask and left everything else inside the bag.

He walked slowly around to the back of the house. There was a swimming pool and a barbecue big enough to roast a side of beef—and the sliding glass door he'd been told about. With his penlight, he could see the little latch you pulled up to open the door. He put a piece of duct tape on the glass so the glass wouldn't fall down and shatter when he cut it, then took the glass cutter out of the plastic bag.

"Freeze! Put your hands on top of your head. If you make any kind of move, I'll blow your ass to kingdom come."

Aw, shit.

———— ◆◆◆ ————

Maynard was sitting on the parking strip in front of the house, next to his pickup. His hands were secured with plastic zip ties.

Standing behind him were two guys in their thirties, both of them wearing jeans, black T-shirts, and low-topped black boots. They also had black and green camo paint smeared on their hands and faces. *Military* was Maynard's first impression. They looked more like soldiers than cops: hard muscles, flat stomachs, short hair. Not an ounce of fat on either of them.

"I wanna lawyer," Maynard said. That was the third time he'd said that. This time he got a response.

"Shut up," one of the guys said.

He'd been expecting that five minutes after they collared him, a squad car would show up and haul him off to the nearest jail, but he'd been sitting on the curb almost twenty minutes.

"I want you guys to tell me what's going on," he said. He was starting to get a little scared.

"If you say another word, I'm going to take that duct tape you brought with you and tape your mouth shut."

Man, there was something wrong here.

Ten minutes later, a Mercedes drove up and double-parked next to his pickup. A woman—a slim, older gal with short blonde hair—stepped from the vehicle. She spoke to the two young guys quietly—he couldn't hear what she said—then walked over to him and said, "Who hired you?"

Maynard thought about the question, and it took him two seconds to figure out he wasn't going to tell her a damn thing. If he told her that Harvey Samuels had hired him to kill the two people in the house . . . well, that wasn't going to do him any good at all. And he'd only committed two crimes. The first one was trespassing: he'd snuck into somebody's backyard and put a little duct tape on a window. He hadn't even broken the window, so he didn't think they could get him for attempted robbery. Well, maybe they could. The glass cutter might be enough to make an attempted robbery charge stick. But the real problem was the gun. They were going to throw him back into prison because he was a convicted felon carrying a weapon. He was going to prison for at least five years, maybe longer, with his record.

But if he gave up Samuels . . . Well, nothing good would come of that. He'd be admitting to attempted murder or conspiracy to commit murder—and Samuels would, of course, deny that he'd hired him to do anything. And then, after he was in prison, Samuels would have someone kill him. There was no doubt about that.

"Tell me who hired you and I might be able to get you some kind of deal," the woman said.

"Fuck you," he said—and one of the young guys kicked him in the ribs.

"Watch your mouth," the guy said.

"It's okay, Buddy," the woman said.

The woman walked away, made a phone call, and five minutes later a squad car showed up and two cops chucked him into the car.

<hr>

DeMarco was sound asleep when the phone next to his bed rang—the kind of deep sleep where the ringing telephone became part of the nightmare he was having. In the nightmare, he was being chased by a faceless woman. She was holding hedge clippers in her bony hands, except the blades of the clippers were about six feet long, shaped like scimitars, and dripping blood. The ringing telephone became a banshee's shriek coming from the place where the faceless woman's mouth should be. The phone rang six times before he answered it.

"Hello?" he croaked.

"Meet me at the Montgomery County police station. They're located on Wisconsin Avenue in Bethesda," the caller said and hung up.

The caller was the faceless woman in his dream.

<hr>

DeMarco found Emma and two very fit-looking young men sitting in a room at the police station that looked like it might be a briefing room. The young guys had camo paint on their faces and empty holsters on their belts. When DeMarco asked Emma what was going on, she said, "You'll find out in a minute. I don't feel like going through the story twice."

"Okay, but who are these guys?" DeMarco asked, jerking a thumb at the two hardbodies.

Emma ignored him, and the two young guys just stared at him for a moment, then looked away.

Sheesh.

Ten minutes later a gray-haired uniformed cop in his late fifties entered the room. He had sergeant's stripes on his right sleeve and his name tag said "J. Farris." He pulled a chair around to face them and took a seat. "Who's this?" he said, speaking to Emma.

"He's my lawyer," Emma said. "In case we need one." DeMarco knew Emma's real lawyer and he was in the same class with Daniel Caine—or maybe in a class above Daniel Caine.

"All right," Farris said. "Tell me what's going on." Pointing at the young guys, he said, "These two obviously aren't part of some neighborhood block watch, so why were they watching Campbell's house?"

"I'll tell you everything I can, Sergeant," Emma said, "but would you mind telling us about the man we caught trying to break into Douglas Campbell's house?"

Farris hesitated for a moment, then said, "Sure. Why not? We took his prints and found out that he's a subhuman piece of shit who has a record that's about ten miles long. His name is Casey Maynard. He's thirty-nine years old and has spent half his life in prison. He started out in a biker gang, committed the usual drunken mayhem, and got sent to prison the first time on an assault charge for almost stomping a guy to death. Prison, of course, didn't rehabilitate Casey. Instead it provided him with an undergraduate education in being a criminal.

"After his first hitch, he hooked up with a few other lowlifes in Richmond, manufactured and distributed meth, pulled off a few robberies, got caught for one of the robberies and went back inside. While he was in prison the second time, he ganged up with morons just like him and was suspected of killing another inmate.

"When he gets out of prison, he goes to work for a guy named Harvey Samuels who lives in Myrtle Beach, South Carolina. Samuels owns a strip club there and a couple of auto body shops, but he's essentially a small time Mob boss. He employs several geniuses like Maynard who deal drugs for him and steal cars and motorcycles, and if someone needs somebody killed, Samuels acts as a middleman and gets people like Casey to do the job for him."

"How did you find out about Samuels?" Emma asked.

"When I saw that Maynard had a South Carolina driver's license and a Myrtle Beach address, I called the cops down there to see what they could tell me about him. Now it's your turn."

"I suspected that a man in Myrtle Beach named Russell McGrath was going to try to kill Campbell," Emma said, "so I hired Benton Security to watch over him. Buddy and Brian work for Benton."

DeMarco had heard of Benton Security. They were essentially mercenaries for hire and worked mostly overseas. He figured Emma probably knew somebody in the company, like Benton himself, the ex–Marine general who owned the company.

"And based on what you've just told me," Emma said, still speaking to Farris, "it sounds like McGrath went to this Samuels person and paid him to have Campbell and, I'm guessing, his wife killed. Maynard would have broken into the house, shot them with the gun he had, and then stolen a few things to make it appear like a robbery."

"Why does McGrath want Campbell dead?" Farris asked.

"It's a long a story," Emma said, "but it involves insider trading and McGrath is afraid that Campbell is going to testify against him."

"Okay," Farris said, "but we can't get Maynard for attempted murder because your guys caught him outside the house and he's not going to admit that Samuels told him to kill anyone. What he will do is go back inside for carrying a weapon, and with his record, he'll probably be in his fifties when he gets out."

"He won't deal Samuels for a reduced sentence?" Emma said.

"No, because according to the Myrtle Beach cops, Harvey Samuels would have him killed."

"Shit," Emma said. "Can we leave now, Sergeant? All Buddy and Brian did was make a citizen's arrest and they've given your people a statement. And when Maynard goes to trial, they'll testify—assuming they're still stateside."

"Yeah, they can go. And so can you. But I don't ever want to see them again in Montgomery County, lurking around some neighborhood armed to the teeth. If you're concerned about some citizen's life being in danger, you call us."

DeMarco followed Emma out of the police station and watched as she shook hands with Buddy and Brian. After they left, she turned to him and said, "Let's go talk to Campbell."

"Yeah, sure, but why did you . . ."

Emma ignored him and walked toward her car.

Campbell and his wife were in bed when Emma and DeMarco arrived at their house. The police had woken them up after they arrested Casey Maynard and asked if Campbell knew the man. Campbell said he didn't and thanked the cops for catching the guy—having no idea that two mercenaries hired by Emma had actually apprehended Maynard. After the cops left, Campbell went back to bed, telling his wife how lucky they were and how they needed to start setting the security system at night before they went to sleep.

Campbell answered the door when Emma rang the bell at six a.m. He was dressed in a blue T-shirt and white pajama bottoms with red stripes. He looked like an overweight Uncle Sam. His big feet were bare.

"What in the hell do you two want?" he said when he saw Emma and DeMarco standing on his porch. "And what are you doing here at this time of day?"

"Campbell," Emma said, "the man the police arrested trying to break into your house was hired by Rusty McGrath to kill you."

"What?"

"Let us in. We need to talk to you."

They took seats in Campbell's living room and Emma told him how she had hired people to protect him and who Casey Maynard was. "Do you believe me now, Mr. Campbell?" she said. "McGrath tried to kill you in Charlottesville with a bag of peanuts and he tried to kill you again tonight. If I hadn't had people watching over you, you and your wife would both be dead."

"You don't know that," Campbell said. "The guy could have just been trying to rob the place. I mean, this is a wealthy neighborhood and . . ."

"Get real!" Emma said. "That man didn't drive all the way from South Carolina to rob you. Like I told you, the cops said he works for a gangster in Myrtle Beach and he's a contract killer. And can you think of anyone, other than Rusty McGrath, who lives in Myrtle Beach and might want you dead?"

Campbell just shook his big head and DeMarco didn't know if that meant he didn't believe Emma or was just in denial over everything that was happening to him.

"Campbell, you dumb shit," DeMarco said, "McGrath killed Praeter and he's going to kill you. He's afraid you're going to give him up. And he's willing to kill your wife, too. Your wife! You need to testify against him now, because the next time he tries, somebody might not be here to stop him."

But Emma and DeMarco couldn't move him. Campbell just sat there looking down at the floor—a hulking, brooding form on the couch—obviously scared and trying to figure out what to do next, but refusing to cooperate. Emma and DeMarco gave up.

As they were walking toward their cars, DeMarco said, "I thought you weren't helping me anymore."

"I'm not," Emma said. "I hired Benton Security to watch over Campbell before I found out you lied to me. I couldn't let McGrath kill that imbecile." Emma stopped walking and gave DeMarco the full force of her eyes. "You've set something in motion to clear Molly Mahoney of a crime you know she's committed, and now you're getting people killed. Do you understand that?"

"I didn't set anything in *motion,* Emma. I didn't have some sort of master plan when this all started. All I did was ask Campbell a couple of questions."

"And one other thing, genius," Emma said. "McGrath didn't kill Praeter. He has an alibi."

"What! What alibi?"

"The guy who ran the marina in Myrtle Beach said McGrath was taking his boat out for a couple of days. Remember?"

"Yeah. You thought he parked it somewhere and flew up to New York using a fake ID."

"Well, I was wrong," Emma said. "I had asked a Coast Guard friend of mine to contact marinas near Myrtle Beach, and the day Praeter was killed, McGrath's boat was docked in Georgetown, South Carolina. When I called the marina operator, he said McGrath was there the whole time entertaining a local woman. The woman confirmed McGrath was with her the night Praeter died."

"I'll be damned," DeMarco muttered.

"Without a doubt," Emma said.

"So maybe McGrath hired someone to kill Praeter. Maybe this guy Maynard was the one who did the job."

Instead of responding to DeMarco's latest theory, Emma said, "Don't call me again regarding any of this, Joe. If fact, don't call me period. And Campbell's your responsibility from this point forward."

After Emma drove away, DeMarco stood on the curb feeling . . . What? Shame? No, not so much shame as a sense of loss. One of the few good friends he had no longer trusted him.

Molly Mahoney wasn't worth what he'd just lost.

44

"Why would Rusty want to kill us, Doug?" Kathy Campbell said.

Campbell had made the mistake of telling his wife what Emma and DeMarco had told him, and now she was yammering at him, asking questions he couldn't answer.

The fact was, he didn't know why Rusty wanted to kill him. With Praeter dead, both he and Rusty were safe. Praeter was the weak link—he was the one who bought the stock, hid the trail from the SEC, and set up the offshore accounts—but the SEC had never been able to connect him leaking information to Praeter. With Praeter gone, they didn't have anything to worry about—so why did Rusty want him dead? Was Rusty afraid that he'd crack under the pressure if people kept investigating? Did he think this whole thing with Molly Mahoney was going to lead back to them? It just didn't make sense.

Well, one thing made sense. Rusty McGrath was a cold-blooded son of a bitch who loved nobody but Rusty McGrath and he'd do anything to protect himself. *And* he was a fuckin' psycho. When they'd played together at UVA, the one thing he learned about his pal, Rusty, was that he was not only willing to hurt people, he liked to hurt people.

"Doug, answer me!" Kathy Campbell shrieked, her voice piercing his skull. "What are we going to do?"

Campbell was still wearing the pajama bottoms he had on when Emma and DeMarco woke him. He left his wife—she was still yammering at him as he walked away—went to his bedroom, put on a pair of battered loafers and a lightweight jacket, and shoved his wallet and his car keys into one of the jacket's pockets.

"Where the hell are you going?" his wife asked.

He ignored her and walked out of the house.

———◆———

It took him fifteen minutes to find a pay phone. He called Rusty's cell phone and said, "It's me, you cocksucker. I'm still alive."

"What?" McGrath said. "What are you talking about?"

"You know what I'm talking about, you demented fuck. Now, go find a pay phone and call me back. I don't want to talk to you on your cell. Here's the number I'm at."

He read the number off the phone and ten minutes later McGrath called.

"So what's going on, buddy," McGrath said. "What are you all riled up about? You're not drinking this early in the day, are you?"

"You know what's going on. You sent a guy up here to kill me but the cops caught him trying to break into my house."

"I don't have any idea what you're talking about," McGrath said.

"You lying son of a bitch! Look, I have as much on you as you have on me but I'm not going to say anything to the SEC or anybody else. I don't have any intention of testifying against you or telling anybody what we did. All I want to do is enjoy the money Dickie made us. But here's what I am going to do. I'm going to put a letter in a safe deposit box and tell my lawyer if anything happens to me, anything at all, he should send the letter to the cops. You hear me, Rusty? You kill me and you'll go to jail."

McGrath didn't say anything for a moment, then finally said, "I hear you, Dog. But let me tell you one little thing. If you do talk to anybody about what we've done, I know people who can get to you even if I'm in prison. So we'll call it a draw for now and just hope that Dickie didn't leave any kind of trail the feds can follow."

———◆———

McGrath hung up the phone and walked back to the marina. Goddamn Campbell. He wasn't the brightest guy in the world but he may have been the luckiest guy in the world. First that gal Emma keeps him from sprinkling peanuts on Campbell's dinner in Charlottesville and then the idiot Samuels sends to kill Campbell gets caught by the cops. Dog Campbell oughta be buying lotto tickets.

So what should he do now?

Well, the answer at this point was obvious: he should do nothing. Campbell might be lying about putting a letter in a safe deposit box but he probably wasn't. So he'd just have to hope that this whole mess surrounding Molly Mahoney didn't lead to anything, and if it did, that Campbell would have the brains and the balls to keep his mouth shut.

He had used a pay phone a couple of blocks from the marina and as he walked back to his boat, he looked up at the sky. It was gonna be a good day. Hot, not a rain cloud in sight. Yeah, it would be a good day to go fishing. He'd heard that a guy caught a good-size tarpon yesterday, and there was nothing more fun than getting a big ol' tarpon on the line.

45

Mahoney pulled into the gravel parking lot of a tavern. The tavern was on the outskirts of Manassas, about thirty miles southwest of D.C., and Mahoney knew before he entered the place that it would have country western songs on the jukebox, long-necked bottles of Bud, and pickled things in jars behind the bar. At eleven a.m., there were only two cars in the parking lot: a new Ford pickup with a Romney bumper sticker and a severely dented Mazda with red tape over one taillight. Mahoney was willing to bet that one of the vehicles belonged to the bartender and the other to some guy who'd gotten too shitfaced the night before to drive home—a predicament that Mahoney had found himself in more than once.

An hour earlier DeMarco had called and told him that Rusty Mc-Grath had made another attempt on Campbell's life. And that's why Mahoney had gone for a drive—because there was just too much information to process.

Al Castiglia and Ted Allen. McGrath and Campbell. Big Bob Fairchild's machinations. Molly's legal problems. It was all just too much, and his head felt like it was about to explode. Finally, unable to get any work done, he changed clothes, told his secretary a lie, sent Perry Wallace to a meeting that he should have gone to himself, and left the Capitol.

He started driving, no particular destination in mind. He just wanted to get out of D.C. as if he might be able to think better if the distance between him and all the politicians were greater. When he saw the tavern, he decided to stop for a drink, thinking that the way he was dressed, no one would recognize him. He was wearing beige chinos, a short-sleeved white polo shirt that was tight across his gut, and a blue baseball cap with "USS *Boston*" emblazoned on the crown. The USS *Boston* was a nuclear sub—now decommissioned and dismantled—and the Chief of Naval Operations had given Mahoney the hat at the decommissioning ceremony. It was one of Mahoney's favorite hats.

The bartender was a woman in her fifties. She was wearing jeans and a turquoise shirt with pearly-looking snap buttons. She had a good figure, dyed blond hair, and a face that said she didn't take crap from anyone. She was reading the *Wall Street Journal,* looking at the mutual fund section, and she looked up in annoyance when Mahoney walked through the door. This was the quiet time of her day and she wasn't thrilled to see a prelunch boozer. She stared at Mahoney's face for a moment when she brought him a Wild Turkey on the rocks but didn't say anything to him. After she handed him his drink she took her *Journal* down to the far end of the bar to read, leaving Mahoney to drink and brood alone.

A lot of Mahoney's cronies in Congress were very wealthy people. They had large family fortunes and vast real estate holdings or had run successful businesses before turning to politics. But neither Mahoney nor his wife came from money; they didn't have a fat family trust to fall back on. Prior to 2008, Mahoney was doing okay, however, and his net worth had been around three million bucks. He'd made most of the money off investments—investments where, during the normal course of his job, he learned which stocks to buy and sell. In other words, he'd profited from insider trading, which, ironically, was legal for members of Congress until a law was passed in 2012 banning them from doing what the general public—including his daughter—wasn't allowed to do.

But in 2008, the recession hit him as hard as anyone—which was one of the reasons he beat up bankers whenever he got the chance. Money he had in mutual funds was reduced by over forty percent, but that wasn't the big problem. In 2007, some smart guys who were supposed to know what they were doing talked him into putting a ton of dough into a development down in Florida. It was a sure thing, and he figured to make maybe five or ten million off the deal—until the housing market collapsed and he lost all the money he invested. Mary Pat was still steamed about that. On top of that disaster, he had to put more of his own money into his last two campaigns because the economy was pissing everybody off and he was more nervous than usual that he might lose his seat. The bottom line was, his net worth was now nowhere near three million bucks. He wasn't sure how much he had in the way of liquid assets—he'd have to talk to his accountant—but it was probably in the range of two or three hundred grand.

The other problem Mahoney had with money was that he spent it quickly and in large amounts. It seemed to run through his hands the way bourbon ran down his throat. He made over two hundred thousand a year, which wasn't bad, but he dressed well, he ate well, and he was always entertaining someone. And last year they had to give some dough to their youngest daughter, Mitzy, who still didn't make enough to support herself, and Mary Pat's mom, who had Alzheimer's, was in a facility that was costing them a mint. He had a big house back in Boston, a condo in D.C., and his wife's boat. The house and boat were paid for, but they were still paying on the condo. If all that wasn't burden enough, now Molly's lawyers were bleeding him dry.

There was no way he could pay off Molly's credit cards, her lawyers, and the five hundred grand she owed Ted Allen unless he sold the house back in Boston and maybe Mary Pat's boat as well. He supposed he could also sell the condo in D.C. and find someplace cheaper to live. . . . Aw, screw that; he wasn't going to live in a dump.

He could get a loan, of course. There were plenty of people who'd be willing to lend him the money—or for that matter, who'd be willing to just give him the money. Mahoney was hardly a virgin when it came to trading to his influence for some sort of compensation, but there were two things he didn't do. The first of those was that he didn't take large amounts of cash; money just left too much of a trail. Instead, his house would be remodeled for an extraordinarily good price, his cars would cost him significantly less than the sticker price on the windows in the dealer's showroom, a vacation in Hawaii . . . Well, it was amazing how little it cost him to travel first-class. Most often though, his compensation came in the form of campaign contributions, and when you had to run for office every two years, you needed all the help you could get.

The other thing he didn't do was approach people asking for something in return for his vote. They always approached him, asking for a favor, and he made sure they understood he couldn't guarantee results in the unpredictable world of partisan politics. But if he went to somebody now and *asked* for money . . . Well, they would basically own him, and he wouldn't allow that. It wasn't a matter of integrity—it was a matter of being in charge of his own destiny. But if he didn't do one of those things—get a loan, sell the house in Boston, or sell his vote—where in the hell was he going to get the seven hundred grand he needed?

Then on top of the money problem, which was huge, there was Big Bob Fairchild, who knew about Molly's gambling and thought he could force Mahoney to do whatever he wanted. What he could do with Fairchild was tell the special prosecutor to back off on Little Bob and vote on a couple things to make Big Bob happy, but he knew that even if he did those things, Fairchild wouldn't stop. He'd eventually leak to the media that Ted Allen had canceled Molly's marker, and that could ultimately destroy his career. But he'd worry about Big Bob later; right now getting the Mob off Molly's back and keeping her out of jail was his major concern.

He stirred the bourbon in his glass with one thick finger and thought about what DeMarco had told him, about this gangster, Al Castiglia. And he thought about Douglas Campbell and that maniac, McGrath.

And he came up with an answer.

A really ugly answer.

"Would you like another drink, Congressman?" the bartender said.

Aw, shit. She *had* recognized him.

"Yeah, maybe just one more," Mahoney said.

"Kinda surprised to see you here, during the middle of the workday," the bartender said, and then, jabbing a finger at the *Journal*, she added, "I mean, with the economy being all screwed up the way it is."

Aw, shit.

Mahoney told DeMarco to meet him at a park that sat on the Virginia side of the Potomac River. Why he wanted to meet there, DeMarco didn't know. Or maybe he did know.

During the time he'd worked for Mahoney, he'd observed that when Mahoney wanted him to do things that were borderline illegal —or just plain illegal—he liked to meet outside. He'd always been a bit paranoid about somebody bugging his conversations, but as time went on—and as technology improved and Homeland Security planted even more cameras around the Capitol—he'd become even more paranoid. Even meeting outside wasn't a guarantee that some eavesdropper, using the kind of high-tech gadgets the NSA employed, wouldn't be able to hear him. The park seemed safe, however. There were lots of trees around to disrupt lines of sight, and it wasn't a likely terrorist target, so there wouldn't be cameras hidden in the bushes.

DeMarco arrived at the park before Mahoney. There were no other cars in the parking lot, and he walked down to stand on the bank of the river and stare at the city on the other side. When he heard a splash in the water to his left, he discovered that he wasn't alone. There were two kids fishing, one black, one white, ten or eleven years old. It was like a scene from a Mark Twain novel until one of the kids pulled out a cell phone and started texting someone. The kids hadn't seen DeMarco, and he walked away from the riverbank and back to the parking lot before they did.

Mahoney arrived a moment later. He was dressed in casual clothes, a Navy ball cap on his big head, and DeMarco wondered where his boss had come from and why he was dressed the way he was. His security guys weren't with him, either, which meant that Mahoney had ditched them—another indication that Mahoney didn't want anyone to know about this meeting.

He jerked an arm at DeMarco, and DeMarco joined him in a small stand of trees where they weren't visible from the parking lot or to anyone looking across the river. He thought about telling him about the two kids fishing but didn't for fear that Mahoney would insist they drive to some other place. DeMarco just wanted to get this meeting over with and go home and go to bed, since he'd been up most of the night.

The first words out of Mahoney's mouth were: "Here's what you're gonna do."

When he finished talking, DeMarco was so shocked that for a moment he couldn't speak, and when he could speak, he was dumb enough to say, "Are you serious?"

"Does it look like I'm serious!" Mahoney yelled. And then seeing the expression on DeMarco's face he added, "And one thing I don't need right now is you turning into a fuckin' Boy Scout on me."

The last thing DeMarco was was a Boy Scout. And the fact that Mahoney's plan was illegal and included the subversion of two, maybe three, government agencies wasn't what shocked him.

What shocked him was the cold-blooded brutality of Mahoney's plan.

Ted Allen should never have cornered the bear.

46

Mahoney returned to the Capitol, changed back into a suit and tie, and lit a cigar. No one was going to tell him that he couldn't smoke in his own office.

So. What could he give these guys to get them to do what he wanted? He called Perry Wallace to his office; Perry's big brain would produce the answer.

Perry came in, looking like he'd slept in the suit he was wearing—and maybe he had. It wasn't unusual for Perry to pull an all-nighter to bend politicians to Mahoney's will.

They concluded that Randy Sawyer would be easy because there was an undersecretary of Treasury position opening up in a couple of months. Perry had read that the guy currently in the job was going back to investment banking; he figured two years of public service had cost him about twenty million—and that was enough.

"Sawyer wants to be considered a big financial guru and he's tired of the SEC," Perry said. "He wants to appear on CNN and tell folks how if the administration would just listen to him, things would be different. If he could get his ticket at Treasury punched, and if somebody over at one of the networks would even *hint* that they might call him the next time they need a so-called expert, Sawyer would drool all over himself."

"Do we have a TV guy that'll whisper in his ear?"

"We got a TV gal. You remember how we leaked the story on the Fed chairman to Marsha Turner last year?"

"Yeah."

"So Marsha owes us. And she's bright enough to make it sound like she's promising Randy something without really promising him anything."

"How do we get Treasury to give Randy the job?"

"That's easy. HR 2019."

HR 2019 was a bill currently passing through the House that expanded the powers of the secretary of the Treasury in a very subtle way. Mahoney had promised to vote against the bill and make every other Democrat vote his way.

"Aw, shit," Mahoney said. "Do I gotta give him that one?"

Perry shrugged. "It's your daughter."

"All right. And how do we tell Sawyer what we want him to do?"

"We just tell him," Perry said. "We don't have to be subtle with Randy. And I'll talk to him. You want some distance between yourself and him."

"Okay, now what about the guy at Justice? He's going to be a lot harder to move than Randy. Plus, I don't trust the fucker."

"Harvard," Perry said.

"Harvard?"

"He wants to teach. He wants to pontificate to a bunch of kids and write the book he's been talking about writing for the last twenty years."

Harvard was easy, Mahoney was thinking. They owed him so damn much that he could get the president of Harvard to kiss the guy's ass in Harvard Square if that's what he wanted.

"But it may take more than Harvard to get him to relocate to Boston," Perry said. "I think you need to have something in your back pocket if it looks like Harvard won't be enough."

"Like what?"

"I was thinking a position on the board of Paul Anderson's company. He pays board members a hundred and twenty-five grand a year to agree with him."

Yeah, Anderson would do it, Mahoney thought. He didn't owe Mahoney as much as Harvard did, but he owed him enough. The helicopter pad at Anderson's headquarters had been paid for with federal funds—thanks to John Mahoney.

"I'll talk to Anderson and Harvard," Perry said, "but you'll have to talk to the guy at Justice. And you're going to have to be really, uh, *subtle* with him. I mean, he'll figure it out but you can't just go straight at him and tell him it's tit for tat, Molly for Harvard."

"I can handle him," Mahoney said.

Perry raised an eyebrow—meaning: *Are your sure?* Subtlety wasn't one of Mahoney's strong points.

"I can handle him," Mahoney said again. "But are you sure the White House isn't going to be a problem?"

Perry shrugged. "An undersecretary position at Treasury is pretty low on the radar. And they can't stop the guy at Justice from leaving. But I don't know. Now, if you'd go to Pakistan like the president wants . . ."

"Goddamnit," Mahoney said. "Do I have to do that?"

"It would help," Perry said.

The secretary of state—a gal who could piss off Santa Claus—had just pissed off the Pakistanis again. The president knew that Mahoney had a good relationship with the prime minister of Pakistan—he had known the guy for thirty years—and he wanted Mahoney to fly over there and smooth things out.

When the president asked him to do this, they'd just arrested Molly and he'd told the president it wasn't a good time for him to leave town.

The other thing was, there was always a good chance of somebody killing you when you went to places like Pakistan. So now what he'd have to do was agree to go there, and would probably have to leave tonight. But if he was gone for a couple of days, that was all right. It'd give De-Marco a chance to go talk to the gangster.

"Okay," Mahoney said. "But Pakistan. Goddamnit."

Mahoney picked up the phone. "Mavis, see if Jim Steele over at Justice can meet me for a drink around five, and then get me an appointment with Horrigan. I need to see him this afternoon."

Fuckin' Tommy Horrigan. He was the president's chief of staff and a political wolverine and as smart as anybody Mahoney knew. As soon as Mahoney told him he was willing to do the president a favor and go to Pakistan, Horrigan would know that something was going on.

But what else could he do? Surviving in this town was hard. It became really hard when your daughter was a crook.

47

Driving toward Philadelphia, DeMarco tried to sort out how he felt about last night.

Dinner with Tina and her daughters had been—for lack of a better word—an ordeal. The girls were eighteen-year-old carbon copies of each other—and their mother—and they had decided it was their job to determine if DeMarco was suitable boyfriend material. They started off, like all good interrogators do, with a few soft questions to put him at ease, then started to bore in. They probed, and not very subtly, about whether or not he was steadily employed and likely to remain so. He could see them checking off little boxes on a mental questionnaire when he told them he had his own home and government-subsidized health insurance. Since when did eighteen-year-old kids give a damn about health insurance?

Then there was his past as it related to women. One of the twins—he still wasn't sure which one was Kathy and which one was Karen—said, "I understand you've been married before." He figured this bit of intelligence had been passed on to Tina from Alice and then Tina passed it to the inquisitors.

"Yeah, once," he said—and didn't say more—which, of course, was not tolerated. By the time the smart little brats left for their concert he felt as if he'd been sitting on the witness stand for two hours.

Sex after dinner with their mother was almost compensation for the grilling—but now he was beginning to have his doubts. He liked Tina, but he wasn't really thinking beyond the next date. He certainly wasn't thinking, at least not yet, in terms of a long-term relationship—but he could tell she and her daughters were. And he could see his future— being triple-teamed by Tina and the bookends, being molded into whatever shape they wanted to mold him into—and it was a future too frightening to contemplate.

Maybe.

As he approached Al Castiglia's front door, DeMarco was amazed by all the statues on the lawn. He was particularly surprised to see the little black lawn-jockey by the mailbox, surprised that some member of the African-American community hadn't knocked its head off. But then, considering who Al Castiglia was, maybe that wasn't so surprising.

He found Castiglia playing three-cushion billiards in the basement of his home. Castiglia was a big guy, six-four, gray-haired, potbellied, massive upper arms. With him was a dark-complexioned man built like a light-heavyweight. The man was wearing sunglasses, which was odd as Castiglia's billiards room was dimly lit, only a single lamp over the billiard table. The guy with the shades was definitely muscle—muscle that could apparently see in the dark.

Castiglia didn't look at DeMarco immediately. He was hunched over his cue stick, studying his next shot. "You play?" he asked.

DeMarco shook his head. "No, never played billiards. Just pool."

"Yeah, nobody plays billiards anymore. Everybody plays eight ball. Shit, anybody can play eight ball. This takes real skill."

On the billiard table were two white balls, one with a yellow spot on it, and a single red ball. Castiglia took his shot, the tip of the cue stick making solid contact with the spotted white ball. The spotted ball hit a rail, then another rail, then a third rail before it hit the other white ball, and then just *kissed* the red ball. DeMarco didn't know if that was a good shot or not, but Castiglia seemed to think so. "Now you show me some Minnesota Fats wannabe that can do that," he said. Turning to the guy in the sunglasses, he said, "Right, Delray?"

Delray didn't say anything. Delray was scary.

Castiglia put the cue stick down on the table and looked at DeMarco for the first time. "I can't believe how much you look like your dad," he said. "I knew him when he worked for Taliaferro. Did you know that?"

"No," DeMarco said.

"Well, I did. And you look just like him. It's kinda spooky."

There wasn't anything to say to that.

"Anyway, so what do you want?" Castiglia said. "I checked you out after you called, but all I learned was that you're some kinda lawyer who works for Congress. So if you're here to talk to me about some legal thing, one of those fuckin' hearings you clowns in D.C. are always holding, you can haul your ass on outta here. Even if I did know your dad, I don't talk about legal shit without my lawyer."

"This has nothing to do with Congress," DeMarco said. "I'm here to talk to you about a guy who works for you. I thought you might want to hear what he's been up to."

"Who's that?" Castiglia said.

"Ted Allen."

"Allen doesn't work for me. I heard he works for some outfit called Indigo Gaming. Ain't that right, Delray?"

Again Delray didn't respond. DeMarco was starting to wonder if he was mute.

"Fine," DeMarco said, "Ted works for Indigo Gaming and you have nothing to do with that company. But let me tell you what he's been doing anyway."

Castiglia made a suit-yourself face.

"Do you know who Congressman John Mahoney is?" DeMarco said.

"You mean that fat, white-haired guy from Boston?"

"Yeah, that guy. He's one of the most powerful politicians in the country."

"So what?" Castiglia said. "What's he got to do with me?"

"Well, Ted Allen, this guy who doesn't work for you, the first thing he did was notice that Mahoney's daughter was spending a lot of time in his casino, losing her money playing craps. So, nice man that he is, Ted extended her a hundred thousand dollar line of credit which she also lost."

Castiglia shrugged. "If people are gonna gamble, they oughta know their limit. So is that why you're here? You want Ted to tear up her marker because her old man's a big shot in Congress?"

"No, the marker's already been torn up."

"What!" Castiglia said, unable to stop himself.

DeMarco could tell that the idea of absolving a gambler's debt didn't appeal to Al Castiglia; more important, it was apparent that Castiglia had no idea what Ted had done.

"But we'll get to the marker later. You see, after Mahoney's daughter couldn't pay what she owed, she came to Ted with a proposition."

Then DeMarco proceeded to tell Castiglia how Ted Allen had advanced Molly half a million bucks on an insider-trading scheme, that Molly had been arrested, and the money was now frozen by the federal government. He also explained how Molly's marker had been bought by Congressman Robert Fairchild, and that now Fairchild was essentially blackmailing Mahoney.

As DeMarco talked, Castiglia struggled to keep his face in a neutral position. He was struggling so hard it looked like a big blue vein in his forehead was about to rupture. DeMarco could tell that Al Castiglia wasn't used to restraining himself in any way.

"Son of a . . . ," Castiglia said. "And you say some lobbyist knows about all this, too? A fuckin' lobbyist!"

"Yeah. I don't know about you, Mr. Castiglia, but I think Ted fucked up pretty good. You're old school. You would never have authorized something like this, and now, whether you like it or not, the SEC and the Department of Justice are involved and they just might end up tracing this whole thing back to your boy. And the money that's been frozen by the government? Well, you're not going to get that back, not the way things stand right now."

"The hell I won't," Castiglia growled, apparently deciding to drop the pretense that he was unconnected to Ted's affairs. Turning to Delray again, Castiglia said, "Can you believe that fuckin' guy would do something like this?"

Delray didn't respond.

To DeMarco, he said, "All right. So what do you want, money for telling me this shit? Your dad would have been ashamed of you."

DeMarco shook his head. "I don't want your money. I just came here to tell you that John Mahoney wants to talk to you. Privately."

"Why? Why does he wanna meet with me?" Castiglia said.

"He has a proposition for you, a way for you to get your money back and get his daughter off the hook at the same time."

48

Neil was sitting at his desk, eating a twenty-four-inch pizza—all by himself—and laughing as he watched something on one of the three computer monitors on his desk. When he saw DeMarco, he said, "Come here. You gotta see this."

DeMarco helped himself to a slice of pizza and went to stand behind Neil. On the monitor he could see a woman in her fifties dressed in a black bra, black panties, and a black garter belt with black stockings. She did a strange little dance move—like a mamba move without a partner—then took a seat at a makeup table and snorted a line of cocaine. When the drug hit her, she tipped back her head and screamed, "Yo Mama!"—and Neil started laughing again.

"Who is that?" DeMarco asked.

"That is Madame Marie de Villiers. She represents France on the Board of Governors of the World Bank. She's getting ready to meet her lover, a thirty-nine-year-old ex–soccer player turned embezzler, from Nigeria. Madame de Villiers doesn't realize it but in addition to getting her hooked on cocaine and cuckolding Madame's husband—a member of the French parliament, by the way—he's using her to siphon off approximately fifteen million euros from the bank."

"You stuck a camera in her bedroom in France?"

"No, on both counts," Neil said. "She's in New York and I didn't sneak a camera into her room. The picture is coming from the camera in her laptop. And in case you're wondering, I'm not trying to blackmail her. I'm helping some guys from Interpol."

Neil scared the shit out of DeMarco. George Orwell's Big Brother was not a bunch of government agents wearing gray suits and fedoras—it was a fat guy in a Hawaiian shirt stuffing his face with pizza.

Neil turned off the monitor and said, "Where's Emma?"

"She's mad at me."

"Ooh. You don't want Emma mad at you."

"Tell me about it. So what did you find out about Fairchild?"

"I found out," Neil said, "that he's a model citizen, a pillar of society, a veritable paragon of virtue."

"I don't want to hear that, Neil. I wanna hear that he spent a weekend in Reno screwing a goat."

"Sorry, Joe."

"Well, shit." DeMarco sat there for a moment, sulking, trying to figure what to do next. Finally he said, "So how much do I owe . . ."

"I said the man's a paragon of virtue, but he has a family."

DeMarco stared at Neil's smiling face for a moment. "Why do you do that, Neil? Did you pull the wings off flies when you were a kid?"

Neil's only response was to increase the width of his smile.

"So what about Fairchild's family?" DeMarco said.

"He has a daughter, Patricia. She's now twenty-five years old, happily married, and the mother of two. She sings in the choir at her church. When the girl was sixteen, however, I think she had an abortion."

"Big Bob's daughter had an abortion?"

Fairchild was, supposedly, a pro-life champion—a very outspoken champion who placed abortionists in the same category with serial killers.

"Correct," Neil said.

"How did you find this out?"

"I looked at the family's medical records, of course. You know, patients had a lot better chance of keeping their medical problems private before doctors started putting every little thing into a computer. Anyway, I was actually looking to see if Fairchild or his spouse had ever had a recurring case of the clap or some other nasty STD, which might mean that Bob had been doing a little fishing off the wrong pier. Unfortunately—for you, that is—Bob's sexual plumbing appears to be in pristine condition. I did learn that Fairchild's wife has had more cosmetic surgery than Joan Rivers."

"Get to the abortion. How do you know his daughter had one?"

"In her medical records, the ones with her regular doctor in Tucson, I noted she had a problem with her uterus."

"What kind of problem?"

"DeMarco, did you become an OB-GYN when I wasn't looking? It doesn't matter what kind, but since I saw the word *uterus,* and since I'm not a doctor either, I called a doctor I know and he said it looked like the girl's problem might have been related to complications following an abortion."

"*Might* have been?"

"Right. I also noted that the girl's regular doctor consulted by phone with a Dr. Aarini Kumur in San Francisco. The records don't indicate why she consulted with Dr. Kumur, but the good doctor works for Family Planning Associates—an abortion clinic.

"Furthermore, credit card records show that Fairchild's daughter and his wife were in San Francisco about a week before the two docs talked to each other. So it appears that the girl got knocked up, told her mom, and she and her mother went to San Francisco where the girl had an abortion. A few days later there were complications and the girl went to see her own doctor."

This was why people tolerated Neil and paid his outrageous fees.

"I couldn't find any record of payments to the clinic in San Francisco, so I'm guessing they paid with cash instead of using their insurance or a credit card."

"Does Fairchild know about the abortion?"

"I don't know. But while his wife and daughter were in California, Fairchild, per the Congressional Record, was in D.C."

"I'll bet he doesn't know about it," DeMarco said. "I don't think he'd be so vocal on the subject of abortion if he did."

Neil shrugged. There was no reason to comment on the hypocrisy of politicians.

"Well, this is good, Neil," DeMarco said. "Anything else."

"Maybe. Do you remember, it must have been seventeen, eighteen years ago, right before Fairchild's first term in the House, that he shot a man? He was the Tucson city prosecutor at the time and a mugger attacked him and a woman who worked for him."

"Yeah, I do remember that. In fact, I think one of the main reasons he was elected was because he'd taken the expression "tough on crime" to a whole new level. So what's the problem?"

"Well, the woman who was with him . . ."

"You think Fairchild had an affair with her?"

"No, no. Get your mind out of the gutter."

"So what about the woman?"

"A week after the incident, she stopped working for the prosecutor's office, and other than retail sales jobs during the Christmas season, it appears that she hasn't worked since. Every month, however, she gets a check for twenty-five hundred dollars. Actually, the check is for two thousand, five hundred and twenty dollars and eighty-three cents—a weird amount— and it's made out to the Saguaro Cactus Preservation Society."

"You think she's being paid off by Fairchild for something?"

"I can't tell. The check is actually written by the Sinclair Evans Foundation."

"Sinclair Evans?"

"Fairchild's wife's late father. He was a developer, and he didn't hold environmental organizations in high esteem. He sued the Sierra Club twice in one year. What's even more ironic is that a group in San Xavier, Arizona, once forced Sinclair Evans to redesign a portion of a hotel he was building because two saguaro cacti would have been destroyed. The saguaro cactus, in case you didn't know, grows at a rate of about one inch per year, and so when you see one of them big saguaros in some Western movie, them things are a couple hundred years old and folks get all upset if you knock one down."

"This is fascinating, Neil, but what does this have to do with Bob Fairchild?"

"I don't know. The Evans Foundation donates buckets of money to all the usual places: Red Cross, United Way, hospitals, research centers for various diseases, but the Saguaro Cactus Preservation Society is the only environmental group. So I just found it odd that this woman gets a monthly check from an organization founded by a guy who would have fed every cactus he ever saw into a wood chipper."

Mahoney was exhausted. In the last thirty-six hours he'd been to Pakistan and back. While in Pakistan, he met with the American ambassador and the CIA's head of station in Islamabad to get an update on the latest developments, then had dinner with the Pakistani prime minister and several of his cabinet members. During dinner, the only drinks served were water and fruit juice. After the dinner, he and the prime minister retired to the prime minister's home where they smoked Cuban cigars and drank a bottle of Maker's Mark that Mahoney had brought with him. The prime minister was a strict Muslim until behind closed doors. After the United States' relationship with Pakistan had been temporarily restored, Mahoney flew back to Washington and when DeMarco rang the doorbell, he answered it.

DeMarco was surprised that Mahoney had wanted to meet at his condo, because he knew Mary Pat would be there. DeMarco had no idea how much Mahoney had told his wife about Molly's problems, but he knew for sure that Mahoney had not talked to her about what he was planning with Al Castiglia.

Mary Pat was a person who was almost always cheerful, and more than that, she always seemed serene to DeMarco, content with her place in the universe and confident she could handle whatever cards she was dealt. And having lived with John Mahoney for over forty years, she'd been dealt more than a few bad hands. Tonight, however, she didn't seem the least bit serene. She sat twisting a Kleenex in her hands and it was apparent that she'd been crying earlier. Mary Pat wasn't usually a crier, either.

Mahoney began by saying, "You can talk in front of Mary Pat, Joe. I've told her everything." Mahoney was standing behind his wife when he said this, adding vodka to a glass of orange juice, and as he made the statement he looked at DeMarco and shook his head violently.

"I told her all about Molly's gambling and how she owed Ted Allen a hundred grand until that shithead Fairchild bought her marker. She also knows how Fairchild is twisting my nuts."

What Mahoney was saying was that Mary Pat did *not* know that Molly was guilty of insider trading and in hock to the Mob for another half million.

Now clear on what he could say in Mary Pat's presence, DeMarco briefed Mahoney on what he'd learned from Neil, the principal finding being that Fairchild's daughter had had an abortion. When he finished, Mahoney said, "This is good. What I want you to do . . .

"No!" Mary Pat said. "You will not use this information, John. Do you hear me? That girl is married now and a mother and I won't allow you to drag her past through the mud."

"I didn't say I was going to tell the press," Mahoney said, "I'll just threaten Fairchild with that."

"No," Mary Pat said.

"Honey, I gotta do something," Mahoney said. "I can't let that son of a bitch . . ."

"John, you will leave his daughter out of this. Do you understand? If Fairchild doesn't know the girl had an abortion when she was sixteen, he doesn't need to know now. And the press had better not ever hear a word about this. What about this other lead you got, Joe?" Mary Pat said. "This cactus woman?"

"I haven't followed up on that yet," DeMarco said. "And it might not pan out, Mary Pat. The woman could be legitimate and the abortion's a known quantity."

"Damnit, Joe!" Mary Pat said, slapping her hands on her thighs. "Didn't you hear what I just told John? I am not going to allow you two to hurt some other woman's child just because my child's in trouble. You find some other way to deal with Fairchild."

It would be a different world, DeMarco thought, if everyone were like Mary Pat.

<hr />

Mahoney walked DeMarco to the elevator so he could speak without his wife hearing.

"Delay the meeting with Castiglia," Mahoney said, "and head on down to Arizona and look into this cactus thing some more."

"You sure that's smart?"

"Yeah. Molly's case doesn't go to trial for months, and I've hired a couple of ex-Capitol cops to watch her in case Ted tries something. More money goin' down the fuckin' drain. So go to Arizona and when you get back, I'll meet with Castiglia."

The elevator arrived and DeMarco stepped inside. Before the door closed, Mahoney said, "And don't you dare come back empty-handed, Joe."

And thank you, sir, for your encouragement and support.

49

Melinda Stowe lived in a trailer park in a suburb of Tucson called Flowing Wells. She had a double-wide; the siding was white and clean, and there were spiky plants near the concrete block steps leading up to her door. Behind her trailer, in an open desert area that didn't appear to be part of the trailer park, was a single, small saguaro cactus, one no more than three feet high.

Before flying to Arizona, DeMarco had called Neil and asked him to find out more about the Saguaro Cactus Preservation Society. Neil said that there wasn't anything to find out; the organization didn't even have a website. To Neil, it looked like the society was a society of one, Melinda Stowe being its president and only member.

Melinda was a good-size woman with dark hair and bright red lipstick. She was overweight but seemed vigorous and healthy. She wore flip-flops and a shapeless dress that DeMarco thought was called a muumuu. Her toenails were painted cobalt blue.

When DeMarco knocked on her door, she smiled but then she said, "If you're a salesman, cutie pie, and you ignored that NO SOLICITATION sign at the gate, I'm afraid I'm gonna have to call J.B. and have him turn the pit bulls loose."

He thought she was joking about the pit bulls, but he wasn't sure. "I'm not a salesman, Ms. Stowe. I'm from Congress and I'd like to talk to you."

"Congress? You doing a poll or something? Well if you are, I don't mind. I was just watchin' *Ellen* on TV but talking to a good-lookin' man has gotta be more fun than watching her dance."

The interior of the trailer was as nice as the exterior. The furniture was inexpensive but tasteful and her appliances and television appeared relatively new. It appeared that Melinda Stowe spent the little money she made well and wisely. According to Neil, she didn't pay taxes on the money she received from the Sinclair Evans Foundation.

"Would you like a Diet Coke, or maybe some lemonade?"

"No thanks," DeMarco said.

"So," Melinda said, "what did you want to talk about?"

"Ms. Stowe, eighteen years ago . . ."

"Oh, call me Melinda."

"Fine, and you can call me Joe. But as I was saying, eighteen years ago you quit your job with the Tucson prosecutor's office, and since that time you've been getting a steady paycheck as president of the Saguaro Cactus Preservation Society."

"You want to talk about that?" Melinda said.

"Yeah," DeMarco said.

Melinda frowned, but then pulled herself together, and smiled brightly. "Well, Joe, I just decided that I didn't like sitting in an office all day, typing and filing and answering phones. I wanted do something to, you know, help the environment. So I applied for a grant."

"Can you show me the grant?"

"I would, but I'm not sure I know where it is. I mean that was a long time ago, sugar, and I've moved a couple times since then."

DeMarco shook his head. "Melinda, as near as the federal government can tell, there is no Saguaro Cactus Preservation Society, and I'm willing to bet that the only cactus you're preserving is that runt I saw out in the desert behind your trailer."

"That's not true! We go out every couple of days, a bunch of us girls, and check on plants all over the city."

"Give me the names of these other women and I'll leave right now and let you get back to watching *Ellen*."

"I can't. It's a privacy thing, you know. And I think you should leave. I don't want to talk to you anymore."

"Melinda, you can either talk to me or to an IRS agent with a badge and handcuffs."

"What are you talking about? I haven't done anything illegal."

"You haven't been paying taxes on the money you've been getting. You can go to jail for income tax evasion."

"I was told I didn't have to pay taxes, being a charity and all."

DeMarco shook his head gravely. "Melinda, I'm a lawyer and I know what I'm talking about. You not only owe the IRS a shitload in back taxes and interest, you're guilty of a felony." DeMarco had no idea if that was true; the only thing he knew about tax law was whatever information came with the TurboTax program he used.

Melinda sat there a moment staring down into her lap. She muttered, "Goddamnit," then looked DeMarco in the eye. "All right. What do you want? You didn't fly out here all the way from Washington to catch a nobody like me for not paying taxes."

"I want to know why Bob Fairchild has been sending you a check every month for the last eighteen years."

"So it's Big Bob you really want?"

"Yep," DeMarco said.

"Well, if the only choice I got is me or Bob . . ." She got out of her chair and said, "You want a beer, Joe? I'm gonna need a beer to talk about this."

"I'd love a beer," DeMarco said.

"We were taking some things to Bob's car," Melinda said. "Records for a trial, two big boxes, and I'd been told to stick around and help Bob lug the boxes. And by the time he was ready to leave that day, it was dark outside.

"Anyway, Bob parked his car in the alley behind the building then came back up to the office and I helped him carry down the boxes. Just as we were approaching his car, this guy jumps out at us. He was big and dirty and all bug-eyed jittery. And he had a knife, not a great big one, but a knife, and he told Bob to give him his wallet.

"But Bob, he was the city prosecutor back then, and he was real impressed with himself. So instead of just giving the man his money, he says, 'Do you know who I am?'—like he was Tom Cruise or some-body famous. The junkie, of course, says he don't give a shit who Bob is and if he doesn't take out his wallet, he's gonna slit his throat. Well, Bob, the jackass, he starts to say something else and the next thing you know, the guy had that knife right up against Bob's neck."

Melinda laughed, a big, rich laugh that boomed within the confines of the trailer. "You know what happened then?"

DeMarco shook his head.

"Big Bob pissed his pants. I mean, I couldn't blame him, the guy was scary. I was scared, too. But when he saw what Bob did, he started laughing. So Bob finally gives him his wallet and then the junkie turns to me and asks for my money, and I start to hand the guy my purse—now he's looking at me instead of Bob—and Bob takes out his gun and shoots the guy."

"Jesus. In the back?"

"Sorta in the back, but more like in the side than in the back. Any-way, Bob's standing there with a big old piss-stain on the front of his pants and with this shocked look on his face, like he can't believe what he's just done. I mean, it was like he didn't realize until *afterward* that he didn't have to shoot the guy at all, since he had a gun and that man only had a knife. I think Bob shot him because the guy made him wet his pants."

"Why didn't he pull his gun as soon as the guy threatened him with the knife?"

"He was holding a box, remember? And he kept his gun on his belt at the back of his pants, so you wouldn't see it if his coat was open. He couldn't pull the gun until he put the box down, and before he could do that the guy had the knife to his throat."

"What happened next, after he shot this guy?"

Melinda took a long swallow of her beer. "He called a detective he knew—he didn't call 911—and the detective was the first guy on the scene. Him and Bob talked things over a bit, then a bunch of other cops showed up and an ambulance and whoever else is supposed to show up when somebody gets shot.

"The thing is, nobody asked me what happened. Not the detective or any of the other cops. Not then and not later. Everybody just milled around for a while, and finally Bob shakes hands with the detective and offers to drive me home. And while we're driving to my place, Bob asks me about a dozen times if I'm okay, and I say yeah, it wasn't me who got shot, and then Bob says we'll talk about what happened tomorrow.

"The next day, I read in the paper that Bob was forced to shoot that junkie in self-defense. According to the paper, the junkie put a knife to Bob's neck, and because he was holding this box, he put the box down and gave the junkie his wallet. And then when the guy was moving toward me to get my purse, Bob pulled his gun. And that part was all true. But the next thing the paper said was that Bob told the junkie to drop the knife and he went all crazy and lunged at Bob, and Bob was forced to shoot him.

"The next day, Bob calls me into his office and hems and haws for a while and says that it would be best if I didn't talk to the press and just left things standing the way they were."

"And that's when you decided to blackmail him," DeMarco said.

"No, it wasn't like that. I might have decided to just go along with everything—I mean, I thought what Bob did was kind of chicken shit—but I hadn't really made up my mind. You gotta remember, I was only twenty-two years old. And if Bob had just explained to me that he panicked and how it wouldn't be good for his career if people knew what really happened, I probably would have just gone along. But that's not what he did. He threatened me. He said if I contradicted his story, everybody would think I was just this little confused secretary, so scared I couldn't remember accurately, and that nobody would take my word over his. And then, I'd most likely be fired.

"Well, I don't like bullies and it pissed me off, him threatening me like that. So I told Bob that he could just kiss my big butt. I told him I didn't want to work for him no more and that I was quitting. And then I guess I sort of blackmailed him. I told him if the prosecutor's office didn't keep paying me until I found another job, then I was going to tell the papers what really happened. Bob, of course, he backed right down—just like bullies always do when you punch 'em in the nose."

"And that's when you became president of the Saguaro Cactus Preservation Society."

"Yeah. Bob said the prosecutor's office couldn't pay me if I quit and he didn't have a bunch of cash to pay me, either. And I figured he was probably telling me the truth since I knew Bob's wife was the one who had all the money. But Bob said what he could do was arrange to have the Evans Foundation pay me if I was some sort of charity. I guess he could do that without his wife finding out, particularly as my salary was so small, and the next month I got a check in the mail for the exact amount of my salary."

"And they just kept coming for the next eighteen years?" DeMarco said.

Melinda finished her beer and crushed the can with her fat hands. "Yep, and I didn't expect that. I figured at some point Bob or somebody would call and tell me that I'd had enough time to find a job, but nobody ever did. I think Bob was afraid to stop paying me. And the Sinclair Evans Foundation gives away millions every year. Who was going to notice the tiny amount Bob was giving me?"

DeMarco almost said: *Well, a guy named Neil noticed.*

"And that's what happened, Joe. That's the whole story. So what's going to happen to me now?"

50

---·◆·---

Mary Pat Mahoney dipped her fingers into the holy water font and crossed herself. According to Mahoney, his wife had been attending early morning mass ever since their daughter was arrested, and De-Marco was waiting for her at the back of the church. She saw him and gave him a small smile. She looked tired.

"Joe, what are you doing here?" she said. "And so early too." She knew DeMarco was neither a churchgoer nor an early riser.

"Your husband wanted me to tell you what I learned about Congress-man Fairchild, Mary Pat."

"Let's walk," she said, and took DeMarco's arm and they left the church together.

DeMarco quickly told her what he'd uncovered in Tucson.

"Good, Joe," she said. "So I imagine John will be talking to Fairchild soon."

"No, but I will, Mary Pat."

Mary Pat shook her head. "You must get tired of doing John's dirty work."

"It's my job, Mary Pat."

"I'm not so sure about that, but right now Molly's the only thing I care about. Have you found anything else that will help her when she goes to trial?"

"No," DeMarco said. "But you heard what Caine said the last time we met with him. He still thinks he can get her acquitted."

DeMarco said this only to make Mary Pat feel better; he couldn't tell her that if Mahoney's plan succeeded there wouldn't be a trial. He also noticed that Mary Pat had said: *Have you found anything that can help Molly?* She didn't say: *Have you found the people who framed my daughter?* He wondered if Mary Pat now knew—or at least strongly suspected—that her daughter had committed a crime to pay off her gambling debts.

They walked a few more paces, her so small next to DeMarco's broad-shouldered bulk. "I just can't believe it, Joe. My daughter's a gambling addict. And she's probably an alcoholic, like her father. I've been praying all week, trying to figure out what to do."

"What can you do, Mary Pat? She's an adult."

"No!" Mary Pat said, her eyes blazing. "She's my child! And I will do something. I will see her through this. And I've decided to sell the house back in Boston to take care of all the money she owes."

"I don't think you should do that, Mary Pat," DeMarco said. He was trying to come up with a plausible lie to explain why she shouldn't sell the house, but before he could say anything, she said, "It's just a house. We needed that big place when we had three girls and my mother living with us. But now, all that space is more trouble than it's worth. So I'm going to sell it and get us something smaller and I'll make enough off the sale to pay Molly's debts and her lawyers too."

DeMarco didn't know how much she could get for the house; it was a big house with a great view. Maybe it would sell for enough to pay off everything Molly owed, including the five hundred grand that belonged to Castiglia and that had been frozen by the Justice Department. But since Mary Pat didn't know that Molly had lost half a million dollars of the Mob's money, that wasn't included in her calculations.

"Mary Pat, does your husband know you're planning to sell the house?"

"No. I just decided this morning."

And DeMarco could tell from her tone of voice that it was pretty clear that whatever Mahoney wanted at this point didn't matter.

"Mary Pat, please listen to me. Don't put the house on the market yet. Just wait awhile."

Mary Pat looked at him sharply, catching something in his tone.

"Joe, are you and John keeping something from me?"

DeMarco, for some absurd reason, placed his hand over his heart when he lied. "I swear, Mary Pat, I'm not keeping anything from you." *Your husband is.* "I'm just saying wait a few days before you do anything. There's just a lot of stuff going on right now, and it would be better if you waited a bit."

"Okay, but after this is all over," Mary Pat said, "I'm taking Molly someplace to heal. My daughter will survive this."

Neither Molly nor Mahoney deserved this woman.

DeMarco sat in the Sheraton's bar drinking orange juice until people started coming out of the dining room. Above the double doors to the dining room was a twenty-foot banner, and printed on the banner in letters two feet high were the words: LEGISLATION FOR LIFE. Congressman Robert Fairchild was the breakfast speaker for the first day of the conference.

About fifty people walked out of the room before DeMarco saw Fairchild. He was talking to an evangelical minister with a growing reputation. DeMarco—not a big fan of television preachers—hated to admit it, but he liked the minister. He saw him on a talk show one day, promoting a book he'd just written, and the guy came across as intelligent, good-humored, and genuinely filled with compassion for his fellow man. DeMarco waited until the minister and Fairchild separated before he approached Fairchild.

"Congressman," he said, "I need to speak with you."

Fairchild gave DeMarco the insincere smile he used for nobodies who were potential voters. "I'm sorry, sir," he said, "but I need to get back to the Capitol."

"John Mahoney sent me. To talk to you about Melinda Stowe."

"Who?" Fairchild said. He might have pulled off the lie if his head had not been spinning about to see if anyone was near him.

"Melinda Stowe, Congressman, a woman with a story to tell."

"I'm sorry, but . . ."

"This conference, Legislation for Life? Is there going to be a panel discussion on the need for a law against shooting people in the back? Oh, wait a minute. There's already legislation covering that."

"Keep your voice down!" Fairchild said.

Actually DeMarco had barely spoken loud enough for Fairchild to hear him. "Yes, sir," he said, "but we need to find a place to talk. The bar's practically empty. How about over there?"

"I'm not going to have anyone see me sitting in a bar at nine in the morning," Fairchild said.

Geez. "What about my car then?" DeMarco said. "It's in the garage, in the basement."

"No," Fairchild said, "I have no idea who you are and I'm not going to . . ."

"Then what about the lobby of the *Washington Post*? Just pick a damn spot."

Fairchild made an irritated motion for DeMarco to follow him and walked back inside the conference room where the attendees had just eaten breakfast. Waiters were clearing tables and there was one small group of women sitting at one table chatting, but the room was otherwise empty. Fairchild led DeMarco to a table as far away from the women as they could get and sat down.

"What do you want?" Fairchild said. "If Mahoney thinks he can blackmail me . . ."

The irony that Fairchild was blackmailing Mahoney apparently escaped him.

"Listen to this, Congressman," DeMarco said.

DeMarco took out a small tape recorder and hit the play button.

"This is Melinda Stowe speaking, Bob. I'm sorry, but this fella's got me over a barrel. So if you don't do what he wants, I'm gonna have to tell what really happened in that alley all those years ago."

"I know who that woman is now," Fairchild said. "And she's lying. She . . ."

"Congressman, I don't care. But you are going to quit twisting Mahoney's nuts over his daughter's gambling problem. You will also have a talk with Preston Whitman explaining to him how his discretion in this matter will be greatly appreciated. You need to be very convincing when you talk to Whitman."

"Who the hell are you?" Fairchild said.

"Now if by some chance a reporter was to ask Mahoney about his daughter's gambling or finds out that her marker has been canceled by the casino, regardless of who leaked the information to the press, I'm afraid I'll be forced to introduce Melinda Stowe to the media."

"I think I've seen you around the Capitol," Fairchild said, his small eyes narrowing.

"Yes, sir," DeMarco said, "you may have. I have an office in the sub-basement next to the janitors, and I do pretty much the same thing they do: I take out the garbage."

51

Setting up a meeting between a gangster and the highest-ranking Democrat in the House of Representatives was a pain in the ass.

The two men couldn't be seen together and the meeting had to be conducted in such a manner that both men would be satisfied that their discussion wasn't being filmed or recorded. Castiglia had assigned his man, Delray, to assist DeMarco in this task and it was Delray who came up with the meeting place. Other protocols for the meeting, such as the time and the right to come armed and methods to be used to ensure privacy, were then discussed and settled upon. By the end of it all, DeMarco felt like the guy in charge of setting up the conference room for the Paris peace talks during the Vietnam War.

DeMarco picked up Mahoney at his condo at the Watergate at nine p.m., and the first thing Mahoney did was light a cigar, ensuring that the odor inside DeMarco's Toyota would never be the same no matter how many of those little cardboard pine trees he hung from the mirror. Next he bitched that the seats didn't go back far enough and then started punching buttons on the radio, screwing up all of DeMarco's preset stations.

An hour later they arrived at a small fitness center in Havre de Grace, Maryland. One car was already there, and five minutes later two other cars drove into the lot. DeMarco exited his car and Delray stepped out of the car that carried Castiglia. From the third car stepped a middle-aged guy wearing glasses and a little flat cap. From the fourth vehicle emerged a slender, narrow-shouldered black man with rust-colored dreadlocks. The black man was Bobby Prentiss, Neil's assistant.

Bobby and the guy in the flat cap were each holding small suitcases and they proceeded into the building together. DeMarco and Delray stood side by side, saying nothing. DeMarco noted that Delray was wearing his sunglasses in spite of the hour; he wondered if the glasses were really night-vision goggles. Fifteen minutes later, Bobby and flat cap exited the building. Bobby nodded to DeMarco and flat cap nodded to Delray, then both men got into their cars and drove away.

The meeting place had just been declared bug-free.

Mahoney exited DeMarco's car. He was wearing a hooded sweatshirt, sweatpants, and moccasins without socks. Castiglia was attired in a similar manner, in a jogging suit and flip-flops. Mahoney and Castiglia went into the building and proceeded to the locker room with Delray and DeMarco following, then Mahoney and Castiglia stripped off their clothes and walked into the steam room.

The sight of the two men—both overweight and elderly—waddling naked to the steam room was almost comical.

———— ❖ ————

"Is it too hot in here for you?" Castiglia said.

"Nah, feels good," Mahoney responded.

"So. You think you got an idea where we both get what we want."

"Yeah. And what I want is that my daughter doesn't go to jail and that Ted Allen never gets his hooks into her or me again."

"Then give me the money," Castiglia said, "and that guy Denny Reed takes the fall for your daughter."

"No. I don't want this thing going to trial and I don't trust Reed not giving everything up at some point. Denny didn't strike me as a guy you can rely upon."

Castiglia laughed. "So what's your idea?" he said.

Mahoney told him, and when he finished, Al Castiglia saw John Mahoney in a totally different light.

"How much money are we talking about?" Castiglia said.

"I don't know for sure, at least a couple million, but probably a whole lot more. Like maybe ten or twenty million more."

"What about the convention center?"

"You give that up. I mean, I don't care if you get the thing built, but you do it without my help. And one thing you have to realize, is it could take years to make that happen. We don't work all that fast in Washington and there are a lot of variables that nobody can control, not even me. But if you want to pursue it with the Jersey delegation, I don't give a shit. I just won't help."

Castiglia sat there a moment, looking at Mahoney, then he got up and poured water over the heated rocks in the corner of the steam room. The water hissed and steam bellowed out and both men winced as hot, wet air seared their lungs.

Castiglia sat back down on the bench and said, "You know, when I was young, moving up in the outfit, I didn't mind all the shit that went with the job. But now, at my age, I just wanna take it easy. I don't really need to get any richer, and I sure as hell don't need to get cross-wired with you and the Feds."

Mahoney nodded; he knew what the mobster meant. At a certain stage of life, enough was enough, and peace of mind was more important than wealth or power. Mahoney had almost reached that point himself. Almost.

"So, we got a deal?" Mahoney said.

"Yeah, we got a deal."

Mahoney sat back and closed his eyes. He didn't feel good about what he'd just done, but he was relieved.

"I think I'm just gonna sit here for a while," Castiglia said. "This steam feels good."

"Yeah, me too," Mahoney said. "Sweat out some of the booze."

Castiglia laughed. "How many kids you got?" he asked after a moment.

"Three," Mahoney said. "All girls. Molly's my middle daughter."

"I got two, a boy and a girl. My boy, he's a veterinarian, if you can believe it. Lives out west in some town that don't have four hundred people in it. He fixes sheep and pigs and shit. But he's a good kid. I'm proud of him. Now, my daughter, that's a whole different story. That girl . . ."

52

"Be in your office at ten," McGruder said. "And make sure Gus is with you."

"I don't work for you, you hog-faced son of bitch!" Ted screamed into the phone, but McGruder had already hung up—and Ted knew it.

Now what? What had McGruder found out now?

Ted tried not to react when he saw that Delray was with McGruder, but he was pretty sure he failed. And with Delray was another guy, Billy something, a total fuckin' lunatic. Delray normally worked alone but when he needed an extra pair of hands—or an extra gun—Billy was the one who helped him. This wasn't good.

Ted had heard a story about Billy. He'd been sent to collect from a guy who owed Al a couple grand, and that same day Billy had seen a movie where a gangster held some deadbeat out a window, threatening to drop him if he failed to pay. So that's what Billy did with Al's deadbeat—except his hands slipped. Billy said, "Oops," when the guy fell five floors and landed on his head. Al wasn't amused, however, as you couldn't get money from a dead man, and he took the money out of Billy's salary.

McGruder sat down in the chair in front of Ted's desk, his wide butt filling up the seat.

"I told you to have Gus here," McGruder said.

"He's on his way. Why? What's going on?"

Gus Amato rushed into the office. "Hey, sorry I'm late. Some doofus electrician's got the elevators all fucked up."

Billy laughed when he saw Gus. McGruder didn't. He rose from his chair with some effort and walked over to Gus. "Goddamn," he said. "Just look at you. I mean, just *look* at you! That fuckin' earring, those stupid fuckin' boots. You look like a goddamn fag that escaped from a rodeo."

"I just like . . ."

"What if you had to do a job? Huh?" McGruder said. "What if you had to pop somebody? I can just see it, this witness sayin', 'Yes, officer, it was this nappy-haired sissy wearing white fuckin' boots who did it.'"

"Hey, I ain't no sis—"

"Shut up!" McGruder screamed.

While McGruder was talking to Gus, Delray had been walking around Ted's office. He was now standing behind Ted, looking at the framed UNLV diplomas hanging on the wall. Ted looked back at him once, not liking Delray behind him, then tried to ignore him.

"I want your ass back in Philly before the day's over," McGruder said to Gus. "You got it?"

"Yeah, but . . ."

"Hey, Pat, what the hell do you think you're doing?" Ted said. "Gus works for me."

Ted noticed the motion out of the corner of his eye and tried to move but he was too slow. Delray had taken one of his diplomas off the wall and smashed it down on Ted's head. The glass in the frame broke and Ted's head punched through the paper. The frame ended up on his shoulders, his face nicked in several places by broken glass.

"Be quiet," Delray said softly to Ted.

Ted started to tremble. No way would McGruder be doing this without Al's permission.

McGruder glanced over at Ted, then resumed chewing out Gus.

"It's like in the majors," McGruder said. "A guy starts to fuck up in the bigs, they send him down to the minors, to get a tune up, to get his head straight again. That's what we're doing with you. Now get your ass out of here and I'll see you tomorrow, give you a job a dumb shit like you can handle. And if you're wearing those boots . . ."

"I won't be," Gus said. He looked once more over at Ted, shrugged an apology, and left the room.

McGruder returned to the chair in front of Ted's desk and sat down, winded just from talking to Gus. He looked at Ted for a few seconds without speaking, trying to catch his breath.

"Smart guy," he said at last. "Such a smart fuckin' guy. It's really too bad about you."

53

---◆---

"You're an idiot," Barbara Jane said to her husband. Then she addressed the snowball-white Pomeranian in her lap. "Isn't that right, Johnny? Yep, Johnny Carson thinks you're an idiot, too."

Fairchild was sitting with his wife on a balcony overlooking the swimming pool. She was dressed in a white tennis outfit, the skirt so short you could see her butt. He didn't say anything in response to the idiot remark. What could he say?

"I just can't believe," Barbara Jane said, "that you never told me about this secretary and what you did. But what I *really* can't believe is that you were dumb enough to leave a paper trail. Can you believe he did something that stupid, Johnny? No, I can't either."

"Look, I need to . . ."

"Tell me something, Bob. I just have to know. Why'd you have the foundation send her checks? Why didn't you give her cash?"

"Because I would've had to come to you for the money!" he cried, making it clear how much he resented the way she controlled the purse strings. Lowering his voice, he added, "Plus, it was such a small amount. I figured with all the money the foundation gives away every year, it wouldn't even be noticeable."

"And I suppose you told the foundation's accountant that I authorized the expenditure."

"Yeah. I mean, like I said, it was such a small amount."

"My God," Barbara Jane said, shaking her head. She was so tired of it all. She was tired of being a politician's wife and she was *really* tired of him. The man just plain wore her ass out.

"You realize," she said, "that you're going to have to do something about this, don't you?"

"Like what?" Fairchild said.

"Bob, Melinda Stowe can do more than just embarrass you. You lied about killing a man in self-defense! You probably won't end up in jail—not with a Tucson jury—but you'll sure as hell be finished in politics, covering this up the way you did."

"I'll have the records deleted."

Cupping the Pomeranian's small face in her hands, Barbara Jane looked into its liquid brown eyes and said, "Did you hear him, Johnny Carson? Did you hear dumb ol' Bob? He's going to have the records deleted." Looking at her husband, she said, "Tell me something, Bob. Are you going to delete the accountant who's been sending checks to Melinda? Are you going to delete this DeMarco person who talked to her? Are you going to delete whoever hacked into the foundation's computers and probably made copies of the records?"

"That's why I'm talking to you, goddamnit! I need to know what to do about all this."

"Did Bob just swear at me, Johnny?"

"I'm sorry, but I'm looking for some advice here. So will you quit talking to that dog and tell me what you think I should do?"

"I really don't know what you should do, Bob. All I know is your political career is over if this ever comes to light. Maybe the best thing to do is call Mahoney and tell him it's a draw. Tell him if he keeps quiet about the cover-up, you won't say anything about his daughter and the casino. Then I guess you're just going to have to hope that none of this stuff with Melinda Stowe ever gets out."

"That's your advice? Trust Mahoney?"

Barbara Jane rose and smoothed the wrinkles out of her short skirt. "I'm supposed to meet some of the girls at the club. We'll bring our tennis rackets, but all we're really going to do is sit around and drink mimosas and check out the butt on the new pro they hired. So I have to get going. What I want you to do while I'm gone, Bob, is just sit here and think. Maybe if you sit here long enough you'll come up with a different solution."

Barbara Jane thrust the Pomeranian at him. "Here," she said. "You can talk it over with Johnny Carson. He's got lots of good ideas."

—◆—

As soon as his wife left, Fairchild dropped the Pomeranian on the ground and gave it a good kick in the ass. The dog yelped and ran back into the house. He'd always hated that little shit.

The last four years he'd done everything he could to get the VP slot in the next election. A lot of politicians scoffed at being the vice president, who played an almost powerless ceremonial role, filling in for speeches and photo ops not worth the president's time. But he wanted a place in the history books, and if he ended his days as just a congressman, he might not even be remembered in Arizona. Not so if he was the veep. And he knew that eight of forty-three American presidents died while in office, turning the White House over to that no-longer-powerless butt of jokes. Those weren't great odds, but they weren't bad either.

His chances of being the number-two man on the ticket had never been higher. He had the support of traditional conservative voters and the big Republican donors and—thanks to Barbara Jane's money and her advice—he was well liked by the Hispanic community. The

Hispanic vote really counted these days. But now Mahoney, that bastard, had information that could sink all his plans.

Mahoney would wait until he got the nomination, and then he'd spill what he knew about Melinda Stowe. He wouldn't go to jail for having shot the bum; the bum *had* pulled a knife. For that matter, he doubted there'd even be a trial. It would be his word and the official police reports against the word of Melinda Stowe. The cover-up was the problem; the cover-up would ruin him.

He's seen what happened when politicians tried to cover up their misdeeds: Nixon, Clinton. Look how they went after John Edwards. If Melinda Stowe told her side of the story publicly—that he'd been paying her off for years to keep quiet about what happened that night in an alley in Tucson . . . Well, he'd be finished in politics. No doubt about it.

So what options did he have?

He could do nothing, as Barbara Jane had said. He had information about Mahoney's daughter that could damage Mahoney's career, so it was possible that Mahoney wouldn't use the information he had regarding Melinda Stowe. But the last thing he wanted was John Mahoney having that kind of hold over him; John Mahoney was just too vindictive and unpredictable. The other problem was that people other than Mahoney knew about Melinda: that thug, DeMarco, and whoever had accessed the foundation's records. He wasn't too worried about the records, however; the records could be . . . finessed. No, the problem wasn't the records; the problem was Melinda explaining what the records all meant.

He could meet with Melinda and offer her an enormous amount of money to deny the story she'd told DeMarco, but that probably wouldn't work. DeMarco had forced the story out of her once, and if someone threatened her with something—tax evasion, conspiracy to cover up a crime, some damn thing—she'd tell everything she knew, and giving her more hush money would just make his situation worse. He could just see it: some hard-nosed *60 Minutes* interviewer pounding away at him and Melinda on television, and if they tried to stonewall the interviewer, the *60 Minutes* guy would make her look like she was lying and he would end up looking guilty as sin. No, just paying her more wouldn't work.

But maybe he could convince her to get on a plane and just disappear. He'd get her a new identity, hand her a suitcase full of cash, and she could go live like a queen someplace where the cost of living wasn't too high, someplace like Ecuador or Panama where she'd be able to afford a cook and a maid and a house on the beach. But that probably wouldn't work, either. Mahoney, with his clout, would get some federal agency to track her down, and then he'd be right back where he was now.

The Pomeranian came back onto the balcony and started barking at him, acting like he was some kind of burglar, like it had never seen him before. He looked around for something to throw at it, but the only things available were the china coffee cups he and Barbara Jane had been drinking from. He forced himself to smile and held out his hand for the mutt to sniff, hoping to lure it closer. "Come here, Johnny, you little shit. Come here." If it came within reach he was going to grab it and throw it into the swimming pool. At least he thought he could throw it that far. And if he missed . . .

There was only one thing he could think to do about Melinda Stowe.

54

"This was a good idea, hoss," Billy said. "Beats the hell out of a pick and shovel."

Billy pulled back on a lever, letting the backhoe's bucket scrape away another foot of dirt. The trench was now seven feet long and about five feet deep.

"Take one more pass," Delray said. "That'll be deep enough."

"You sure?" Billy said. "Operating this thing is kinda fun."

After they'd left Atlantic City, they'd been driving down the Black Horse Pike and Delray had noticed the road construction in progress. They were widening one section of the road—they hadn't paved the new section yet—and on one side of the road they were planting a bunch of trees to make things prettier. Delray had told Billy to stop the car near a yellow Caterpillar splattered with mud. It was Sunday, and he figured if the construction crew wasn't working by now, there was little chance of them showing up later in the day. And people driving by wouldn't think twice about a guy operating a backhoe near a construction project, all those orange road-cones blocking things off. It took him all of two minutes to hot-wire the machine.

"Yeah, that's enough," Delray said.

Billy climbed down from the backhoe and he and Delray went over to the car, and Delray popped open the trunk. They glanced around to make sure no cars were coming and carried Ted's body over to the trench.

"Could you believe that fuckin' McGruder, whacking off his thumb?" Billy said. "I mean, what the hell was the point of that? The guy had already told us everything."

"I dunno," Delray said.

"Jesus," Billy said. "What a fuckin' psycho, wheezin' like he was gonna croak, trying to cut through bone with a goddamn paper cutter. I thought he was gonna have a heart attack."

"Put a couple feet of dirt over him," Delray said, "then we'll get one of them trees."

There were two dozen unplanted saplings, the roots wrapped in burlap, the trees spaced at ten foot intervals. After Billy had partially covered the body, they picked up one of the saplings and placed the root ball into the hole, directly over Ted's chest.

"What kinda trees are these?" Billy said.

"How the fuck would I know," Delray said. "Fill in the hole."

"Well, whatever kind they are, I'll bet you that damn tree grows faster than any of them," Billy said.

55

When Fairchild arrived at Orville Rate's house in Casas Adobes and knocked, Rate didn't come to the door. He called out that the door was unlocked and for Fairchild to let himself in. He didn't rise from the chair where he was sitting to shake Fairchild's hand, either. He just pointed at another chair, and after Fairchild was seated, he said, "I was real surprised you called me, Congressman. It's been a long time."

It had been a long time. The last time Fairchild had seen Orville Rate was eight years ago when he spoke at Rate's retirement party, but Rate still looked pretty much the same. He was a big, gaunt man with crew-cut gray hair. His face was weathered and there were deep furrows on both sides of his mouth, and his dark eyes had as much life in them as marbles. He was wearing a white dress shirt, the top button buttoned, and jeans—but not his cowboy boots. It was the only time Fairchild could recall seeing Orville Rate when he wasn't wearing boots. He was wearing slippers with thick white socks.

When Fairchild was Tucson's prosecutor, he had a good conviction record and Orville Rate was one of the reasons why. Rate knew how to get suspects to confess, and if he couldn't get a confession, he didn't have a problem manufacturing evidence and getting witnesses to commit perjury. Fairchild didn't think he'd ever sent an innocent person to jail—he just figured that Orville Rate had simplified the process of convicting the guilty.

The night he shot the junkie, Orville Rate was the detective he'd called—and Rate was the one who made sure the junkie's death was never really investigated. In return for his help, Fairchild got him the job of chief of detectives and Rate retired from that position.

The other thing about Orville Rate was that he was the only killer that Big Bob Fairchild knew—the only killer who wasn't a convicted criminal, that is. Rate had killed four men while working as a policeman—a higher number than any other cop on the force—and two of those shootings had been questionable.

"How much?" Rate said, after Fairchild explained what needed to be done. If he was surprised, he didn't show it.

"Fifty thousand," Fairchild said. "Half now—I've got the money with me—and the other half when it's done."

Barbara Jane hadn't even asked why he wanted the money. In fact, when he tried to tell her what he was planning, to see if she had a better idea, she just walked away.

Rate smiled after he named the amount he was willing to pay—and that's when he noticed it: the left side of Rate's mouth didn't move right, it sagged kind of funny. And then he noticed Rate's left arm. All the while he'd been talking to Rate the man hadn't moved his left arm, not once; his left hand just sat there on the arm of the chair like something dead.

"Is there something wrong with you?" Fairchild asked.

Rate smiled—or half-smiled—again. "Nah, not really. I had a little stroke a while back, but I get around okay."

Oh, shit. But since he'd already told Rate what he wanted him to do, he couldn't just walk away.

"Show me," Fairchild said.

Rate reached down with his right hand and picked up a cane lying on the floor next to his chair. Fairchild hadn't seen the cane either.

Rate rose from the chair without any apparent difficulty, and using the cane, walked over to a nearby china cabinet. When he walked, his left arm hung limply at his side, but then he used his left hand to open a drawer in the cabinet and took a short-barreled .38 revolver from the drawer. He turned slowly and pointed the gun at Fairchild's head.

"I can pull a trigger just fine, Bob."

56

Preston Whitman lived in a redbrick town house on Capitol Hill. As Delray and Billy approached the door, Delray said, "Stand where he can't see you through the peephole."

Delray figured that as long as he kept his sunglasses on, he could probably pass for a cop. But Billy, with his greasy blond hair falling to his collar . . . Well, he just looked like the dangerous hood that he was.

Delray rang the bell. He waited a moment, then just leaned on it. "Police," he said. "Open the door." He knew the guy was inside; they'd seen him come home just five minutes ago.

He saw the peephole darken.

"Police," he said again. "Open up."

The door opened and Preston Whitman said, "What's this about?"

Delray hit the door hard with the palm of his right hand and it slammed into Whitman, knocking him backward, and he and Billy walked into the house.

Whitman, clearly frightened, but still thinking he was dealing with cops, said, "What in the hell do you think you're doing? You can't . . ."

Delray took out his .45 and placed the muzzle against the end of Whitman's big nose. "Shut up."

Billy ignored Whitman and walked around the house a little. He noticed the big television set that was tuned to a political talk show. "Hey, is that one of them new 3D TVs?"

"What?" Whitman said.

"I asked if your TV . . ."

"Billy," Delray said. Then looking at Whitman, the gun still pointed at Whitman's face, he said, "We're going to leave here together like we're all friends. If you yell to anybody, or try to take off, or give me any kind of problem, I'm gonna shoot you in the spine. You understand?"

"Who are you men? Why are . . ."

Delray had really fast hands. He hit Whitman just above his left ear with the barrel of the .45.

"Do you understand?" Delray asked again.

———— ◆◆◆ ————

"Where to?" Billy asked.

Billy was driving. Delray was sitting in the rear seat with Preston Whitman. Whitman was weeping and a rivulet of blood was trickling down the side of his head from where Delray had hit him with the gun. Delray took out a handkerchief and gave it to Whitman. "Press that against your head." Delray didn't want Whitman's blood ending up in the car.

To Billy, Delray said, "Get on 395, then work your way over to 50 going west. If I remember right, it's kinda farmy out there. We'll find a place."

"Please. If you'd just tell me . . . ," Whitman said.

"Shut up," Delray said.

"Have we got time to drive by the White House, Del?" Billy said. "I've never seen the White House before."

"No," Delray said.

"Whitman," Billy said, "have you ever been inside the White House?"

"What?"

"I asked if you've ever been to the White House?"

"For God's sake! Just tell me what you want," Whitman said.

Forty-five minutes later, Delray said, "Billy, see those trees over there? Go that way."

Billy stopped the car at edge of what appeared to be a small patch of forest, large deciduous trees, not too close together and not that much brush on the ground. It would be easy walking. Delray couldn't tell how deep the woods were, but they went back far enough. Nobody would be able to see them from the road.

"This'll do," Delray said.

"Please. I'm begging you," Whitman said. "Tell me what you want."

"I want you to get out of the car," Delray said.

The three men exited the car. "Get the shovel, Billy," Delray said.

"Oh, God," Whitman moaned.

They walked fifty yards into the woods before Delray said, "This is good."

"Look, I have money," Whitman said. "I'll . . ."

"Take off your clothes," Delray said. "You can leave your underpants on."

"Please. I know there must be some way to work this out."

Billy, who was carrying the shovel, swung it and the handle cracked into the back of Whitman's knees. "I'm getting hungry," he said. "So hurry up and do what you're told."

Whitman started to take off his clothes. As he was doing this, Billy handed the shovel to Delray and gathered up a few small stones, each stone nice and round, just about the size of a golf ball.

"Toss your shirt over here," Billy said to Whitman.

Whitman did and Billy spread it on the ground, underneath a nearby tree, and sat down on it. "Thanks," he said. "Don't want to get the seat of m'pants all dirty. You gotta dry-clean these pants."

"Hurry up," Delray said to Whitman.

"Are you working for . . ."

Billy flung one of the stones at Whitman, hitting him in the back. Billy had pitched in high school.

"Shit!" Whitman said, the blow stinging.

"Speed it up, Slick," Billy said. "I told you I'm hungry, and I get cranky when I'm hungry."

When Whitman was standing there in his underpants and socks, Delray said, "The socks, too."

Whitman stripped off his socks, and Billy laughed and said, "Man, you gotta have the biggest feet I've ever seen. Jesus, Del, look at those fuckin' things. What size shoe do you wear?"

Whitman was crying again and he didn't answer, so Billy flung another rock at him, hitting him in the thigh this time.

"I asked you . . ."

"Size fifteen," Whitman said.

"Fifteen! You gotta special order your shoes?"

"No, I . . ."

Delray tossed the shovel at Whitman. Whitman wasn't expecting it, and the shovel bounced off his chest, the handle hitting him in the nose.

"Start digging," Delray said.

"Please. Don't do this," Whitman said.

Billy threw another rock as hard as he could from his sitting position, again hitting Whitman in the back.

Whitman started digging. While he dug, Billy closed his eyes, like he was napping, although Delray knew he wasn't sleeping, and except for Whitman's sniffling, it was actually quite peaceful there in the woods. He was reminded of a forest in North Carolina where he and his older brother used to play when they were kids. His brother had died in prison; Delray hadn't thought of him in years.

When the grave was two feet deep and Whitman's feet and bare calves were covered with black soil, and his face was shiny with sweat and stained by tears, Delray said, "Now you see how easy this was? We stop by your house, pick you up, and make you dig your own grave. Then we shoot you a couple times in the head. It's not any work for us at all. We're leaving now, but hopefully you got the message."

"What mes—"

"You're never to talk to anybody, ever, as long as you live, about Ted Allen and his connection to Molly Mahoney. If you do, we'll be back and we'll do this again, except next time we'll finish the job. And if my boss ever thinks he needs a lobbyist, you're the guy. You understand?"

That was the only reason they weren't killing him: Al Castiglia liked the idea of having his own lobbyist. He'd never had one before.

"Yes," Whitman said. "I swear to God, I understand."

"Good. Let's go, Billy."

Whitman's legs gave way and he collapsed into the bottom of the grave, in a sitting position, and began to sob.

57

Delray had told DeMarco to meet him for breakfast at the Howard Johnson's in Crystal City on Highway 1. Sitting with Delray was a cheerful-looking, overweight man with long blond hair who was mopping up a plate of French toast and sausage. Delray was just drinking coffee.

"Who's this?" DeMarco said, chin-pointing at the blond guy. Delray didn't answer and the blond guy just smiled at him.

The waitress came to the table and asked what DeMarco wanted. "Just water," he said. "And don't put ice in it and make sure it's not too cold." Seeing the look everyone gave him, he added, "Cracked tooth. I can't get an appointment to get it fixed to save my life."

"He oughta go see your nephew," Billy said to Delray, his mouth full of French toast.

"Aw, that's okay," DeMarco said, imagining Delray's nephew: a trembling junkie with scabby needle tracks running up and down his arms.

As if he knew what DeMarco was thinking, Delray said, "Most my family, they turned out like me. But not my sister, and definitely not her kid. He's smarter than anybody you know and he's good and he's just getting his practice started." Then Delray said, "Look"—and he smiled. DeMarco had never seen the guy smile before; he should have been doing Colgate commercials instead of breaking heads for Al Castiglia. "The kid takes care of me, and I drive down from Philly to see him."

What the hell, DeMarco figured, and he wrote down the dentist's name. Then they talked about the plan, making sure they were all clear on what they were going to do.

"The guy's out of town for the next couple days," DeMarco said. "But his secretary told me he's getting back Friday night. So we'll do it Saturday, around noon."

"Okay," Delray said.

DeMarco didn't like any of this but he was just going to have to trust that these guys wouldn't let things get out of hand. He wasn't too worried about Delray. Delray was a pro, but this other guy . . . He had loose-cannon written all over him.

But those were the risks you took when you became business partners with mobsters.

———————◆◆◆———————

DeMarco spent Saturday morning puttering around his house, just killing time until his appointment with Delray, although the word *appointment* didn't seem quite right. Assignation? Rendezvous? Whatever.

He had one pair of underwear left so he decided that maybe he should wash some clothes while he waited. He was just cramming all the dirty clothes he had into the washing machine, wondering if maybe he should wash two loads instead of one, when his cell phone rang. It was Alice.

"Tina says you haven't called her since you had dinner at her place."

"Well, uh . . ."

"It's the girls, right? They scared you."

"They didn't . . ."

"I want you to imagine your future, DeMarco. You're in your seventies. Your prostate's the size of a basketball. You need a hip replacement, and the way you drink, maybe a new liver, too. But you're all alone. There's no one to drive you to your doctor appointments, no one to push your wrinkled old ass around in a wheelchair."

"Jesus," DeMarco muttered.

"No, Jesus won't be there either. So you think about that, Joe. There are a lot things in this world that are worse than being hooked up with a nice woman with two smart young daughters."

On that cheery note, Alice hung up and DeMarco went back to stuffing clothes in the washer, and the phone rang again. He checked the caller ID, making sure it wasn't Alice calling back to depress him some more, and saw it was Neil.

"You know that woman Melinda Stowe?" Neil said.

"Yeah?"

"Well, I set up Google Alert to let me know if she popped up in the news and I saw this morning that she's dead."

"What happened? Did she have a heart attack?" The woman had been overweight but she'd seemed healthy to DeMarco.

"She was shot. It happened the night before last, but nothing was posted online until today."

"Shot? What the hell happened? Was it a robbery?"

"The article didn't say. All it said was that whoever did it didn't break into her trailer and most likely talked his way in, and they're giving folks the usual warnings about being careful about opening your door to strangers."

DeMarco remembered that when he visited Melinda, she opened her door without asking who was there. And he could picture her clearly: her broad, cheerful face, her cobalt-blue toenails. What he couldn't do was picture her dead. He supposed some random lunatic could have killed her, some wacko targeting women who lived alone in trailer parks, but it was also possible that she was killed because of what he'd learned about her and Bob Fairchild. This, of course, made Fairchild the obvious suspect but it was hard to imagine him killing the woman. You didn't kill people like Melinda Stowe—you bribed them, you intimidated them, you discredited them—but you didn't kill them unless you were a total fool.

But he couldn't deal with Melinda Stowe right now.

He had to get to Douglas Campbell's house.

"Son, could you help an old fella out?" The voice had a strong southwestern accent, what DeMarco thought of as a Texas twang.

He turned and saw a man in his sixties or seventies coming toward him, walking with a cane. His first thought was that the old guy was a hard-looking bastard even with the cane.

"What do you need?" DeMarco said.

The man continued to walk toward DeMarco. When he was about a foot away, he pointed with his cane and said, "That's my car over there and . . ."

DeMarco turned to look where the man was pointing, and when he did, he felt something jam into his rib cage.

"Son," the man said softly, "that's a Smith & Wesson .38 revolver you're feelin'. It's loaded with hollow points, and it'll make a real mess out of your insides if I shoot you."

"My wallet's in my back pocket," DeMarco said. He couldn't believe it. He was being robbed by a senior citizen.

"I don't want your money, son," the man said. "What you're gonna do is walk, real slow, over to my car. We're gonna take a ride together, have a little talk, that's all. I'm gonna let you drive."

"Talk about what?"

"Don't worry about that right now. But you got my word, son. If you talk to me, answer all my questions, I'll let you go. I got no reason to hurt you."

Bullshit.

"Now, let's go. Mosey on over to the car. And not too fast. I'm not as quick as I used to be."

DeMarco hesitated for a moment, and the man prodded him with the gun barrel. He looked around. Not a neighbor in sight. He stepped off the curb and started toward the car across the street.

The old man stepped off the curb after him and the tip of his cane slipped, just a bit, not enough to make the man fall, but enough to make him stagger and momentarily lose his balance. It all happened very fast after that: the man stumbled and DeMarco pivoted and hit him in the throat with his elbow which caused the older man to fall to the ground. As he was falling, he fired the gun, the bullet missing DeMarco by inches, passing under his left arm, and hitting the driver's side window of the old man's car. Before he could fire again, DeMarco was on top of him, grabbing the wrist of the hand holding the gun, then ripping the gun out of his hand—something that wasn't all that hard to do considering the man was over sixty, walked with a cane, and was practically choking to death.

While waiting for the cops to arrive, DeMarco called Delray and told him they'd have to postpone the meeting with Campbell until tomorrow.

58

<hr>

Delray was annoyed. He had tickets for the Phillies, a seat right behind home plate, but he was going to miss the game because DeMarco had delayed the job on Campbell. He was going to take out his annoyance on Douglas Campbell.

He glanced at his watch. Noon. "Let's go," he said to Billy. They exited the car and rang the Campbells' front doorbell. No one answered. Delray knew Campbell was home because he'd seen the guy just an hour ago and knew he hadn't left, so he and Billy walked around the house and into the backyard.

Campbell and his wife were sitting in Adirondack chairs, near a gigantic barbecue, drinking from tall glasses—and arguing about something. Delray could hear the woman bitching about them never going anywhere fun and how she was sick of it. The couple didn't see him and Billy until they were practically standing next to them.

The woman saw them first. "Who are you?" she said. When Delray didn't answer, he could see the fear grow in her eyes. She looked over at her husband and said, "Doug!" Just "Doug," but like *Doug! Do something!*

Delray glanced over at the barbecue. They were cooking steaks, big thick ones, and the idiot had the heat up way too high. That was okay, though; a hot grill could be useful.

He took off his sunglasses so the Campbells could see his eye. He knew the effect his eye had on people, particularly people like this, people who thought they were immune from violence. And that wasn't the only reason he took off the glasses. They were Ray-Bans with special lenses and he didn't want to get them broken.

Campbell got up from his chair with some effort. He was wearing shorts—his legs pasty white—and a baby-blue T-shirt that exposed the underside of his flabby gut. "What I can do for you, gentlemen?" he said, trying to sound confident.

Gentlemen. Like he could bullshit his way out of this, acting polite.

Delray and Billy both ignored him. Billy smiled at Kathy Campbell, not his friendly good-old-boy smile but his see-what-a-fuckin'-lunatic-I-am smile. Delray walked over to the barbecue and picked up the barbecue tongs. He liked the heft of them in his hand.

"I asked what you men wanted," Campbell said, this time trying to put some authority into his voice.

Delray pivoted on his right foot and backhanded Campbell across the face with the barbecue tongs. Slashed him a good one.

Campbell cried out in pain and stumbled backward, tripping over the chair where he'd been sitting. His wife spilled her drink and leapt to her feet, mouth wide open, eyes the size of walnuts.

"Take the bitch in the house and do her," Delray said to Billy.

The woman sucked in air to scream, but Billy, who was amazingly fast for a guy his size, clamped his hand over her mouth and began to drag her toward the house.

Campbell was still on the ground, but now on his knees and trying to get back up onto his feet. Tears were leaking from his eyes. Before he could stand, Delray kicked him in the stomach, knocking the wind out of him.

Delray looked over his shoulder to make sure the woman was under control then reached down and grabbed the back of Campbell's shirt, and, with one hand, dragged the two hundred and seventy pound man over to the edge of the swimming pool. He started to kneel down next to Campbell, but then realized he was going to get the knees of his pants wet and dirty. He kicked Campbell again to immobilize him, and went over to the chair where Campbell's wife had been sitting, took the cushion off the chair, and tossed it near the pool. That was better.

Kneeling down on the cushion, he grabbed Campbell by his belt, pulled him forward until his head was over the edge of the pool, then pushed his head under the water. Campbell's legs started to kick and he tried to get his head out of the water, but Delray was too strong.

After about forty-five seconds, after all the air was gone from Campbell's lungs and he started to ingest water, Delray let Campbell raise his head. He allowed him enough time to cough and hack a bit, then said, "You owe my boss half a million dollars. He wants it back."

"What? I don't know what you're talking about. You're making a mis—"

Delray pushed Campbell's head under the water again.

Man, those steaks smell good. Gonna have to go for a steak after this.

He pulled Campbell's head out of the pool a second time and again had to wait for Campbell to stop gagging. He hoped the fat fool didn't have a heart attack.

"My partner's in there raping your skinny bitch of a wife," he said, "and then I'm gonna have my turn, and then I'm gonna start cuttin' parts off your body until we reach an understanding. Now, what are you gonna do about the half million?"

"I swear to you . . ." Campbell said.

"Hey! What the hell do you think you're doing?"

Campbell and Delray both turned toward the man who had yelled. It was DeMarco.

"Help!" Campbell screamed.

"Oh, shit," Delray said, trying to put a little panic into his voice, and let go of Campbell. He had to get past DeMarco to get out of the backyard. "Billy!" Delray yelled, "Get out of the house!"

DeMarco stepped to one side to allow Delray to get by him, making no attempt to stop him, and Delray smiled slightly—then lowered his shoulder like a running back, hit DeMarco square in the chest, and knocked him into an azalea bush. He chuckled as he moved toward his car.

By the time Delray reached the front yard, Billy was coming out the front door. They walked casually to their car.

"You didn't hurt the broad, did you?" Delray asked.

"Nah. Just ripped her clothes a little and told her all the nasty stuff I was gonna do to her. She's got a pretty nice rack on her, I mean for a gal her age."

"I'm hungry," Delray said. "Let's go get us a steak."

59

"Thank God you got here when you did," Campbell said.

That was about the third or fourth time he'd said that, and DeMarco still didn't say anything to acknowledge his gratitude. He knew the man was going to be much less grateful in a few minutes.

They were sitting at the Campbells' kitchen table. Kathy Campbell was wearing a bathrobe to cover her torn blouse, Campbell was holding an icepack to his face, and DeMarco was rubbing his chest where Delray had smacked into him. The son of a bitch had knocked him ass over teakettle, and his chest hurt, his back hurt, and his pants were a mess. There'd been no reason for the bastard to do that.

It took a while for Kathy Campbell to stop crying and when she finally did, she wanted to call the police. "You don't want to do that, Mrs. Campbell," DeMarco said.

"Why not? That man was going to *rape* me. And look at Doug's face!"

"You need to know what's going on before you talk to the cops. And the cops aren't going to be able to help you, anyway."

"I don't understand," she said. Turning to her husband, she said, "What's he talking about, Doug?"

Campbell ignored his wife. He rose from the table, took a bottle of gin out of a cupboard, and poured three fingers into a glass. When he didn't pour a drink for his wife, she gave him a dirty look and a sarcastic "Thank you, Doug," then got up and poured her own.

Campbell swallowed half the drink before he sat back down at the table. His thin blond hair was plastered over his scalp and his T-shirt was still wet. The one-inch-wide welt on the left side of his face was bright red and that side of his face was beginning to swell. Delray really enjoyed his work.

"The men that attacked you and your wife, Mr. Campbell, work for a crime syndicate."

"A crime syndicate?" Kathy Campbell said.

"Mafia. Mob. Whatever you wanna call 'em."

"But why the did they come here?" Doug Campbell said.

"The half million that Molly Mahoney is accused of investing in that insider-trader scheme, the money that's been frozen by the government? Well, that was Mob money."

"But what hell does that have to do with me?" Campbell said.

"They think you're the one who lost their money," DeMarco said.

"But I'm not!" Campbell shrieked.

"Campbell, I need to talk to you privately."

———◆◆◆———

Kathy Campbell wasn't too happy to be excluded from the discussion, but Campbell told her to shut up—which caused her to start crying again—and then he grabbed the gin bottle and led DeMarco outside onto the patio. Campbell noticed his steaks were still on the grill, now looking like two hockey pucks. "Shit," he said, and turned off the barbecue.

"So what the hell's going on? Why do those guys think . . ."

"First," DeMarco said, "I want to apologize for your wife getting roughed up. I didn't think they'd do something like that."

"What! You knew they were coming?"

"Well, not them specifically, but I knew somebody would be coming to see you."

"I don't understand. How did you know . . ."

"Campbell, those two guys work for a murderous lunatic up in Philly. And the money that was frozen by the SEC when Molly was arrested? Well, the money belonged to that lunatic, and what I did was tell him that you were Molly's partner and it was your fault his money was confiscated."

"You gotta be shittin' . . ."

"I told this gangster if he wanted his money back all he had to do was knock you around a bit."

"This is outrageous!"

"Keep your voice down, Doug."

"But I never had anything to do with Molly Mahoney."

"I know that, Doug, but somebody has to pay this mobster back and I decided you were the guy. You see, I *know* you were the inside guy at Reston and I know you fed information to Praeter. And he made you and Rusty McGrath a shitload of money in the last twenty years. So to keep Molly Mahoney from getting killed by the Mob, I fed you to them. Sorry, but I didn't have a choice."

"This is bullshit. You can't do this."

"Doug, I've already done it. And let me tell you what else I can do. If the Mob doesn't get you, I'll give you to the State of New York."

"New York?"

"Yeah, I'll make sure they arrest you for Praeter's murder because I know you killed him. At first, I thought McGrath killed Praeter, but then I found out he had an airtight alibi for the night Praeter died. But you don't have an alibi. What you have is an EZ-Pass sticker on your car, which means you were recorded going through every tollbooth between Maryland and Manhattan, and you were in Manhattan the night Praeter was killed."

DeMarco knew this because of sneaky Neil.

"I didn't kill Dickie," Campbell said. "I went to Manhattan that night to recruit a guy we were trying to hire. The guy will tell you I was with him."

DeMarco figured Campbell was probably telling the truth; he'd been smart enough to come up with a reason for being in New York the night Praeter died. But he wasn't that smart.

"I believe you, Doug. I believe you met this guy, maybe had dinner with him, then met up with Praeter later that night, got him drunk, and killed him."

"That's not true. I . . ."

DeMarco held up his hand. "Campbell, right now NYPD thinks Praeter committed suicide because he was a wack job who'd tried to kill himself before. The cops don't even know that you knew Praeter. But when I tell them how you were afraid that Praeter was going to testify against you after he was subpoenaed by Molly's lawyer, and after Molly's father leans on the cops with all his political weight . . . Well, they're going to get you, Doug. And they're going to get you because they're good and because you're a fuckin' moron."

"I'm telling you, I didn't . . ."

"They're going to find witnesses that will put you and Praeter together in some bar that night. They're going spot your ugly mug on one of the ten million cameras they have all over Manhattan. They're going to find fingerprints or DNA in Praeter's office. They're going to find *something*, Doug, and then you'll be convicted for murder—assuming the Mob doesn't kill you first, and right now my money's on the Mob."

"So what the hell do you want? Did you just come here to tell me how you've fucked up my life?"

"No. I came here to make you a deal."

"A deal?"

"I want you to take the fall for Molly Mahoney. I want you to confess that Praeter set up a bank account in her name, that you and your pals put up the money she supposedly invested, and that Praeter was the one who really bought the stock through those e-brokers she allegedly used."

"Why the hell would I do that? Why would I admit to committing a crime I never committed?"

"Because it'll keep you alive, Doug, and it will keep you out of jail. And if you do what I want, you can also keep your money. The money that Praeter made you, that is."

"I don't understand."

"You see what I've done, Doug, is I've worked out a deal for you with the Justice Department."

"The Justice Department?"

"Yeah," DeMarco said. Actually, Mahoney and Perry Wallace had worked out the deal but he wasn't going to tell Campbell that. "And the deal is this: You take the fall for Molly, admit you and McGrath worked with Praeter on the Reston insider-trading scams, then you testify against Rusty McGrath—this good friend of yours who's tried to kill you twice. If you do that, then Justice won't put you in jail and you'll go into the witness protection program so the Mob can't get you. And once you're in the program, you can start spending all the money Praeter made you, and that you've got socked away in some offshore account. In other words, Doug, you can start life over with a new identity and a lot of money in the bank and go live in fucking Tahiti for all I care."

"You'll let me walk?"

"*I'm* not letting you walk. The SEC and the Department of Justice are letting you walk in return for testifying against McGrath. Justice knows McGrath hired a guy to kill you even if they can't prove it. So they'd rather have McGrath than you. But if you don't take the deal . . . Well, there's no point in repeating myself."

"Why are you doing this to me? I never did anything to you."

"Because that's my job, Doug. My job is to keep Molly Mahoney out of jail and the only way I can do that is to hang your ass out to dry. So are you going to take the deal or not?"

"I gotta think this over."

"Sure. Take your time. You've got until I reach my car to make a decision, after which you'll never see me again."

"I need time to think! I can't just . . ."

"Time's up, Doug. So which door is it going to be?"

"Which door?"

"Yeah. Door number one is the deal I just offered you. Door number two is the NYPD, a murder conviction, and the rest of your life in a cage. Door number three is a guy from Philly that's going to cut your fucking head off. So pick a door. Now."

Campbell sat there for a bit, looking down at his feet, then nodded. "Okay."

"Okay? What's that mean."

"I'll do what you want."

"Good. There's just one more thing."

"What else could you possibly want?"

"I want to know what happened at UVA twenty-four years ago when that kid, Sweet, went out the window."

"Jesus. You know about that, too?"

"Yeah. I know Sweet died, and I suspect that either you or McGrath killed him. But I don't know why and I want to know."

Campbell looked away, like a man looking for an exit, then, to stall further, picked up the gin bottle, topped off his glass, and took a drink before he started speaking.

"McGrath's a smart guy but he's got dyslexia, and he can barely read. The whole time he was at college he had guys do his homework and take tests for him."

"How could someone take tests for him?"

"It was easy. He was enrolled in all these general courses where there were two or three hundred kids in the class, and the professors didn't know who half the kids were. And when they gave you a test, the professor wasn't even there. Some teaching assistant would pass out the exams and collect them after you were finished. And don't forget, McGrath was a football player. I imagine some professors were told to look the other way. Anyway, senior year, Dickie Praeter was the guy McGrath used."

"What did Praeter get out of this?"

"Money. UVA alumni would give McGrath money, and he'd give some to Dickie. I mean, you gotta realize what a big deal McGrath was back then. All-American linebacker, headed for the pros, and the Cavaliers were going to a bowl game for the first time in ages."

"So where did Sweet come into all this?"

"Jimmy Sweet was a righteous, Bible-thumping prick. Nobody on the team liked him, and he didn't like McGrath, particularly after he found out that McGrath got his girlfriend drunk one night and screwed her. Sweet had been going with the broad since junior high. Anyway, he heard from someone that Praeter was doing McGrath's work for him and he went to see Praeter to see if what he'd been told was true. That same night, me and McGrath were out drinking and McGrath decided to stop by Dickie's room to pick up some essay Dickie wrote for him, and when we got there, Sweet had one hand around Dickie's scrawny neck and was shaking the shit out of him.

"He'd already made Dickie confess to what he'd been doing for McGrath and he was planning to march him over to the dean's house and make him tell the dean, which meant that McGrath wouldn't have played in the bowl game. I mean, the school knew a guy like McGrath couldn't pass his courses without help, and they looked the other way as much as they could, but if Sweet brought it all out into the open, the university wouldn't have been able to cover it up."

"So you guys killed Sweet because of this?"

"No, it wasn't like that. We saw Sweet choking Dickie and asked what the hell was going on, and he tells us he's going to turn McGrath in. We tried to talk him out of it—we begged him to think about what he was doing to the team—but that prick said he had an obligation to God Almighty to tell the truth. Although it probably had more to do with McGrath nailing his girlfriend than God. Anyway, he started to walk out of Praeter's room, and I grabbed his arm. All I was trying to do was stop him from leaving so we could talk to him some more, but I kind of swung him around and he trips and out the window he goes. I mean, I was strong back in those days and pumped up and pissed at Sweet because he was going to screw up the team. And I was drunk. I didn't mean for it to happen."

"Then you guys just covered it up."

"Well, yeah. What else were we supposed to do? I wasn't going to admit I threw Sweet out the window and McGrath sure as hell wasn't going to tell folks that Dickie was taking tests for him. So we said it was an accident, that Sweet tripped, which was actually pretty much the truth."

"Why did Praeter try to commit suicide?"

"Because he was a nut. I mean, he was a genius, but he was the most paranoid son of a bitch you've ever seen in your life, and he was scared of everything. He was convinced that somebody was eventually going to tell the school that he'd been doing McGrath's homework, and that he was going to go to jail for being an accomplice in Sweet's death. He was a fuckin' basket case after Sweet died."

"And that's why he tried to kill himself? Because he was afraid of going to jail?"

"I'm not even sure he tried to kill himself," Campbell said. "The night of his so-called suicide attempt, he drank a fifth of Jack Daniel's at the same time he was taking speed to stay awake so he could finish some paper he was working on. Speed. Not downers or sleeping pills. Anyway, another kid finds him lying in his own puke, sees the pills, and calls 911. After they pumped out his stomach, a shrink talked to him and concluded that Dickie was a depressed nut, which, of course, he was, and that he tried to kill himself. But did he *really* try to kill himself? I don't know. I doubt it. But a couple weeks later he transferred to another school."

"So how'd the insider-trading stuff all start?"

"That was Dickie's idea. At the time, I was the only one who had a job, working in the HR office at Reston Tech. McGrath had just been let go by the Jets because of his knee and Dickie was up in Manhattan with all these hotshot investment ideas but he didn't have any money to invest. But McGrath had money, over a million from his signing bonus and the insurance he collected when he was injured. So I passed on to Dickie all the stuff that Reston Tech was working on at the time, and he picked the company to invest in, this water-treatment company. We only did it three times."

This was just what DeMarco had thought the first time he met McGrath.

"So why did you kill Praeter?"

"McGrath forced me to. He was afraid if the SEC or Justice started squeezing Dickie, he'd give us up. I mean, I don't know how many different ways I can say it, Dickie was a genius but he was a total flake. He wasn't a guy you could rely on and McGrath wanted him gone, and he said if I didn't take care of Dickie, he was going to tell what happened at UVA with Jimmy Sweet."

"Bullshit," DeMarco said. "I don't think McGrath made you do anything. I think you killed Praeter because you and McGrath decided together that he was a liability and you drew the short straw to get rid of him."

"No, it wasn't that way. Rusty said . . ."

"I think you're lying, Doug, but it doesn't really matter at this point. The only thing that matters is that you take the fall for Molly Mahoney."

60

It was a big meeting: DeMarco; Douglas Campbell; Molly's lawyer, Daniel Caine; Randy Sawyer from the SEC; and a lawyer from the Justice Department, Dave something or other—a young guy with a bad haircut and a yellow bow tie. DeMarco had always thought bow ties were a pretentious affectation, the poster boy for this particular fashion being George Will. And Dave, before too long, proved that DeMarco's bow-tie prejudice had some merit.

They were all sitting in Daniel Caine's swanky conference room at a table that was bigger than DeMarco's office. But it was DeMarco's meeting, not Caine's.

"So here's the deal," he said. "Campbell will testify that he, Richard Praeter, and Russell McGrath have pulled off three successful insider-trading scams involving Reston Tech clients. He will also testify that Richard Praeter, based on a tip from him, bought ten thousand shares of stock in a company that makes submarine batteries and Praeter used Molly Mahoney's identity to buy the stock. In return for his testimony, Justice and the SEC will recommend that the judge give Mr. Campbell a suspended sentence and a big fine. All charges against Molly will, of course, be dismissed since Campbell's testimony fully exonerates her. Finally, Mr. Campbell and his wife will go into the witness protection program."

Randy Sawyer started to speak, but Dave, the bow-tied man from Justice, jumped in first. "You know, there're some things here I don't understand. Like why's this guy confessing, and why does he get witness protection?"

Whoa! This was not good. Dave was supposed to have known all this *before* he got to the meeting. Dave was supposed to be a human rubber stamp and not say a fucking thing.

"He's confessing," DeMarco said, "because he can see the handwriting on the wall. He knows you guys will get him and McGrath eventually, and he knows if he testifies now against McGrath, he'll get a deal he can live with. He's also confessing because he fears for his life. McGrath has tried to kill him twice and he knows McGrath's a psycho who will keep on trying, even from a jail cell—which is why he's insisting on witness protection."

"Huh," Dave said, still looking skeptical. He was *really* starting to make DeMarco nervous.

"And you're saying that this guy Praeter, who's dead so we can't confirm the story, is the one who bought ten thousand shares of Hubbard Power stock using Molly's identity?"

"That's right," DeMarco said.

"Well, Praeter may have bought the stock," Dave said, "but Molly Mahoney was the one who set up those brokerage accounts. We *know* she did, and we want her, too."

DeMarco looked pointedly over at Randy Sawyer, a look that said it was time for him to slap a muzzle on Dave. Mahoney had greased the skids with Sawyer and with Dave's boss. Sawyer was going to slide into a soon-to-be-vacant undersecretary's chair at Treasury, and Dave's boss was getting a job at Harvard and a hundred and twenty-five grand a year position on a corporate board. And all Mahoney had asked these men to do was accept Campbell's confession. Just *accept* it—and don't probe any deeper. But Dave, the little twit, was probing.

It appeared that Dave's boss, to make sure that his fingerprints were nowhere on this deal, had sent Dave to the meeting instead of attending himself, and then, to make matters worse, hadn't fully explained to Dave that his only reason for being here was to nod.

Daniel Caine chose that moment to step into the breach. He smiled graciously—at this point he could afford to be gracious—and said, "Dave, get serious. Your case against Molly was weak before this happened. Now, with Campbell's confession, you have no case at all. So please, son, save my client the hassle and the Justice Department the embarrassment."

Dave's bow tie quivered; he didn't like being called son.

"But *why'd* they set up Molly?" persistent Dave now wanted to know. "I thought in the past when these guys pulled off one of their insider scams they developed some kind of bulletproof cover."

"We don't know," DeMarco said. "And we'll never know. Praeter handled all the financial transactions. We think he may have been doing some kind of dry-run for something bigger. You know, a test to see what he could get away with. All we know, and as Mr. Campbell has stipulated, is that Praeter did it."

"What happened to your face, Mr. Campbell?" Dave asked.

"Tripped," Campbell muttered. DeMarco had made it clear to Campbell that Al Castiglia and his men would in no way be part of the discussion during this meeting.

Dave sat a moment, looking confused and stubborn. Mostly stubborn. "I don't know about all this," he said. "Ignoring the evidence against Molly, Campbell getting off without doing any time . . . This just doesn't sit right with me. People are going to think Molly's getting a break because of who her father is. There's no way we'll agree to this. Right, Randy?"

Randy Sawyer didn't respond. He was doodling furiously on a legal pad, refusing to make eye contact with DeMarco.

"Dave, take the deal," DeMarco said. "Take away all of Campbell's money and relocate him to bum-fuck Idaho. Get him a job pumping gas. His life turns to shit, you clear three cases that the SEC's been trying to solve for twenty years, and you put a killer in jail. Isn't that enough?"

"A killer?" Dave said. "Who'd McGrath kill?"

"Richard Praeter."

"Can you prove that?"

"No, which is why you need to throw the book at McGrath. But without Campbell's testimony, you'll never get McGrath, you'll have a damn hard time getting Campbell, and Campbell won't testify against McGrath unless he gets the deal."

"I don't think so," Dave said. "Now that we know . . ."

"I agree with Mr. DeMarco." Randy Sawyer had spoken at last. "Our chances of convicting Molly are weak. Let's get this guy," he said, chin pointing at Campbell, "and McGrath. We've already got half a million dollars that we can give back to the taxpayers, and we'll make another three or four million off Campbell's and McGrath's assets. Maybe more." Sawyer chuckled. "I'd say that's not a bad day's work for a couple of civil servants, Dave."

"I dunno," Dave said again. "I think . . ."

"Dave," Sawyer said, "I think you and I need to excuse ourselves for a moment."

Finally, DeMarco thought.

When Dave and Randy Sawyer came back to the conference room, Randy said, "We'll take the deal." Dave didn't say anything, but he had bright red spots on his cheeks. It looked as if he'd just had a major temper tantrum and been told to go stand in a corner.

Daniel Caine asked if anyone would like to have a drink while his secretary prepared a few documents for folks to sign. Doug Campbell instantly agreed. So did Randy. "Nothing for me," Dave said—his way of making it clear he wasn't going to attend the party.

DeMarco excused himself, saying he was late for another meeting, which was a small lie compared with the others he'd told in the past hour. As he was leaving, he took one last look at Douglas Campbell—a man who looked surprisingly content after just being told that he was going to have a record as a convicted felon and be relocated to some godforsaken place where he'd be working for minimum wage.

Poor Campbell. He didn't know it, but he wasn't going into witness protection; he was going to prison. And he was never going to spend any of the money that Richard Praeter had hidden away for him.

61

***

Billy was watching the marina while he played a pinball machine using a lot of violent body English to move the ball around. He was drinking a Coke. Billy was an alcoholic, but one thing Delray liked about him was that he never drank on the job. Delray was flipping through a golf magazine, wondering if maybe when they were finished here he could get in a few rounds.

"Here she comes," Billy said. "Finally. I thought that guy was gonna screw her forever. Not that you can blame him, the body she's got."

Delray looked over the top of the magazine and down at the marina. The guy's girlfriend was just *moseying* down the pier. If that girl didn't learn to move faster she was gonna have an ass on her the size of a boxcar. But he had to admit, she was one good-looking woman.

As soon as McGrath's girlfriend drove away, Delray rose from his seat. "Let's get this over with," he said.

They walked down the pier, taking their time, and Billy asked why most of the boats were named for women. "I mean, don't these guys think ahead?" Billy said. "They get a girlfriend, it'll piss her off every time she sees the wife's name on the boat."

Delray just shook his head.

It was twilight. There was one guy, a couple piers over, doing something on his boat but not paying any attention to them. McGrath was on the bow of his boat doing something, too. People who owned boats were always fiddling with them.

Delray had never had any desire to own a boat. Everyone he knew who had one hardly ever used 'em. They'd sail them maybe three, four times a year but most of the time they just *fussed* with things, fixing shit, polishing shit.

"Are you sure you can drive a boat that size?" he asked Billy.

"Yeah. Quit worrying about it."

They reached McGrath's slip and Delray said, "You Rusty McGrath?" It never hurt to make sure.

"Yeah," McGrath said. "What can I do for you boys?"

Delray took off his sunglasses so McGrath could see his eye.

"Whoa! You just clumsy, or did you piss someone off?"

"I think I'm going to enjoy this," Delray muttered to Billy.

"What's a boat like this cost?" Billy asked McGrath.

"Why? You thinkin' about makin' me an offer?"

McGrath had moved over to the gangway of his boat as he was talking, and on the way there, he had managed to pick up a long, heavy wrench. People like Billy and Delray tended to make other people nervous. Even tough guys like McGrath.

"We were told it was worth close to a million," Delray said.

"You were told?"

Delray nodded. McGrath was a good-size guy, as big as him. And he looked to be in shape. He was gonna be a handful, with or without the wrench in his hand, and Delray didn't feel like tusslin' with him.

He took a silenced .22 out from beneath the windbreaker he was wearing and shot Rusty McGrath in the knee, the same knee that had been destroyed the first and only year he played in the pros.

62

DeMarco had just taken a seat when the phone on Mahoney's desk rang. Mahoney listened for a moment, grunted, hung up, then rose from his chair.

As he was shrugging into his suit jacket, he said, "I gotta go over to the White House. The president's thinking about bombing someone."

DeMarco sometimes forgot about the arena in which Mahoney played.

"Wait here until I get back," he said to DeMarco, "but give me the bottom line right now. Is my daughter going to be okay?"

"Yeah," DeMarco said. "She's going to be okay."

DeMarco figured Mahoney would be gone at least an hour. He left the Capitol and walked across Independence Avenue and found a hot dog vendor. The vendor had on one article of clothing for every team that played professional sports in D.C. DeMarco had just taken a bite from his hot dog, a blob of mustard just missing his tie, when his cell phone rang.

"Kay Kiser just resigned," Randy Sawyer said.

"Why?" DeMarco said.

"Why do you think? I cut her out of the meeting with Campbell and then agreed to a deal that set Molly Mahoney free."

"Is she going to go to the press?"

"I don't know. She might. She's really pissed. I thought she was going to hit me."

The story that had been given to the media matched the agreement that had been reached at the meeting in Daniel Caine's office: Campbell confessed that he and his old college pals had been pulling off insider scams at Reston Tech for years, the police were currently hunting for Rusty McGrath, and it was Campbell and his friends who committed the crime that Molly had been accused of. Daniel Caine, acting as Molly's spokesman—Molly didn't attend the press conference—said that Molly and her family were just relieved that the SEC had found the real culprits and Molly just wanted to get on with her life. She wouldn't be granting any interviews.

Randy Sawyer was the SEC's spokesman at the press conference and DeMarco had to admit that he did a good job of explaining everything to the news guys, leaving them no place to go with the few questions they had. Fortunately, insider trading, even if it involved Mahoney's daughter, wasn't a particularly sexy story and the media appeared happy to move on to more entertaining news. But if Kay Kiser started talking to the press . . . DeMarco felt once again like Richard Nixon trying to keep the lid on Watergate.

"What does Kiser want?" DeMarco said.

"What does she want? She wants to put criminals in jail—and that's all she wants. If you think you can bribe Kay Kiser, you're nuts."

"I wasn't thinking about bribing her, Randy."

He almost added: *Unlike you, me, and Mahoney, she has integrity.*

"So it's all settled," Mahoney said. "I mean, I saw the press conference but I want to make sure that there aren't any loose ends." Mahoney had returned from the White House five minutes earlier. He didn't bother to tell DeMarco what conclusion the president had come to regarding bombing someone.

"Yeah," DeMarco said. "It all worked out the way you wanted." He tried not to sound judgmental, but he couldn't help it. And he knew he was being a hypocrite because he was just as guilty as Mahoney since he'd gone along with the plan.

Mahoney had ordered DeMarco to tell Al Castiglia what Ted Allen had done, knowing that Al would most likely kill Ted. Al would kill him not just because Ted had lost Al's money; Al would kill him because Ted had lied to him. But Al would still want back the half million that Ted had lost, so Mahoney gave him Rusty McGrath.

Rusty McGrath had a custom-built yacht worth about a million and a ton of money in various offshore accounts. McGrath would have to be convinced, of course, to give up the codes to access those accounts, but DeMarco had no doubt that Delray and his pal, Billy, could be quite convincing. Then after they convinced McGrath, he and his boat would both disappear. McGrath would most likely end up in the Atlantic Ocean and his boat would go to a yacht broker who would paint over the name, sell the boat, and pass on the proceeds to Al Castiglia.

Campbell, of course, got completely screwed. He had signed a confession admitting not only to the crimes that he, Praeter, and McGrath had committed but he also took responsibility for Molly's crimes. But Campbell's deal was contingent upon him giving testimony leading to the conviction of Rusty McGrath—and so when McGrath disappeared, the only guy left to take the fall was Campbell. If Campbell tried to tell folks a different story—that he really hadn't had anything to do with Molly and that DeMarco had coerced him into taking the fall for her . . . Well, who was going to believe a man who had already signed a confession? And after Campbell got out of jail—or maybe while he was still in jail—Al Castiglia would most likely get his money, too.

Mahoney's plan had been brutal. And his only moral justification had been—not that Mahoney felt the need to justify anything—that Molly was his daughter.

It wasn't that DeMarco felt bad about what happened to Ted Allen and Rusty McGrath, and what was going to happen to Campbell. He didn't. He didn't feel badly about that at all. He knew Campbell was a killer, that McGrath had tried to kill both Campbell and his wife, and, although he couldn't prove it, he knew that Ted Allen had most likely killed as well. So he wasn't sorry for the misery that these people had brought down upon their heads. What he felt bad about was that he had undermined a decent person like Kay Kiser and corrupted the legal system to save a guilty a person: Molly Mahoney, the lesser evil.

And then Mahoney surprised him. Mahoney was normally too self-centered to be attuned to the feelings of others, but it was as if he knew what DeMarco was thinking.

"By the way," Mahoney said, "Molly's going to do the time for what she did, she's just not gonna do it in a jail cell."

"What do you mean?" DeMarco said.

"I talked this over with Mary Pat this morning. I . . ."

"You told her Molly was guilty."

"Yeah. Basically. I mean, I didn't tell her what happened to Ted or McGrath or any of that stuff. She'd never stand for that; she'd turn *me* in. But I told her that Molly had helped with the insider stuff and the only reason she didn't go to jail was because I pulled some strings. The funny part was, Mary Pat didn't act surprised. It was like she'd known for some time that Molly was guilty but was afraid to say it out loud or admit it even to herself. So me and Mary Pat, we sat down with Molly, and Mary Pat told her what she was going to do to make things right. She didn't give her a choice."

"What did you decide?" DeMarco asked, and Mahoney told him.

And DeMarco thought: *Yeah, I can live with that.*

"But there is one other problem," DeMarco said.

"Aw, Christ!" Mahoney said. "Now what? Won't this fuckin' thing ever end?"

"Kay Kiser resigned from the SEC when Molly got the deal. She might talk to the press."

"She can talk to them, but that won't change anything. Not with Campbell's confession. And Sawyer and the guys at Justice, they aren't going to admit to anything. But what really bothers me is her resigning. We need people like her, Joe. She's smart and she's tough and she's incorruptible. The government needs her. The country needs her. What does she want? What can we do to make her stay?"

The strange thing was that DeMarco knew that John Mahoney, a man who was corrupt in so many ways himself, actually meant what he'd just said: that the country needed Kay Kiser.

63

Barbara Jane watched the lawyer as he walked away from the pool. He was a few years younger than her, maybe ten, and he was a cutie. She'd told him to come to the house for the meeting, and then told the maid to send him out to the pool when he arrived. She wanted to meet him at the pool because that way she'd be able to wear a bikini and flash her tits at him when she put her top back on.

She was *proud* of those puppies, and every once in a while she liked to take them out for a walk.

She'd told her cute young lawyer that she was divorcing Bob right away, and explained to him that Bob wouldn't be contesting the divorce in any way. Her lawyer had probably been surprised that she was moving so quickly—Bob had been arrested less than a week ago—but not as surprised as Bob had been. Yep, she'd done nothing but surprise lawyers lately, including dumb ol' Bob who was a lawyer, too.

What an idiot. He hires a man in his seventies who'd had a stroke to kill Melinda Stowe, and told the man to kill DeMarco as well, because DeMarco had talked to Stowe and made a tape recording. Apparently the killer was supposed to find out where the recording was and destroy it. When DeMarco captured the geezer, it wasn't long before the cops found out that his gun had been used to kill Stowe and he made a deal and gave up Bob.

She met with Bob briefly after his arrest. She didn't ask him why he did the dumb thing he did, but he started blubbering about how he wanted the VP job and how he had to get rid of Melinda Stowe because if he didn't Mahoney would have eventually used the information against him and undermined all his plans. "I figured Orville Rate, being an ex-cop, would have been able to pull it off," Bob had said.

Then he said: "But we can still get Mahoney. You know, leak the information about the casino canceling his daughter's marker like we talked about."

And that's when she explained to Bob that there wasn't going to be any *we*. She wasn't about to have him hanging around her neck like a stinking, dead albatross. She said that as long as he didn't contest the divorce, she'd pay for his legal costs, which were going to be staggering. But if he did contest the divorce, and since he had barely any money of his own, some snot-nosed public defender might be the one representing him against an accomplice-to-murder charge.

As for Mahoney, she said, just forget about him. The charges against his daughter had been dropped, but more important, she'd read that the man who ran the Atlantic Palace Casino had disappeared—and without him, it would probably be impossible to prove that Molly Mahoney ever had a marker with the casino. She concluded by saying, "So you're just going to have to take your medicine, Bob. But I'll get you the best lawyer I can and maybe he'll keep you from getting the needle for killing Melinda Stowe." She wondered if tough-on-crime Bob was happy that Arizona still had the death penalty.

My God, what a scandal! The media went berserk: you couldn't turn on a television set without seeing pictures of her and Bob, and the phone had been ringing off the hook with reporters requesting interviews. All Bob's colleagues in Congress were saying how shocked and dismayed they all were. She saw one clip of Mahoney, shaking his head gravely, saying how the stress of politics could often drive people to do unimaginable things.

One of these days, but not right away, she might run for Bob's seat. And whether she was in Congress or not, she just might go after John Mahoney—and she was a whole bunch smarter than dumb ol' Bob.

64

It was ten p.m. and DeMarco was sitting on a stone bench on the terrace on the west side of the Capitol. As he sat, he sipped cognac from a Styrofoam cup. At his feet was the bottle of Hennessy that he normally kept in the file cabinet in his office. The cognac was for medicinal purposes—for moments like this, when he felt the need to heal his soul.

It was a clear, cloudless night, and the weather was balmy, and DeMarco had an unobstructed view of the National Mall, from Washington's obelisk, across the Reflecting Pool, all the way to Lincoln's bright, white, shining cube.

He loved Washington at night.

He took a sip of cognac, relieved he didn't have to tilt his head to the right. Delray's cousin—and now DeMarco's new dentist—had put a crown on his cracked tooth and charged him only six hundred bucks as opposed to the thousand his previous dentist would have charged. One thing for sure: he was going to pay the bill on time. He didn't need Delray showing up to collect; he didn't ever want to see Delray again.

Then there was Tina Burke, sexy mother of two. Did he want to see her again? Maybe Alice was right—maybe he'd reached an age when he should be thinking beyond the end of his dick. He thought about that a moment longer, took another sip of brandy, and pulled out his cell phone—but still couldn't decide if he should make the call.

"I want to talk to you," a voice said.

He turned his head toward the person who had spoken. It was Kay Kiser. He had no idea how she'd found him, but he suspected Kiser could track down just about anybody she wanted to find.

"Hi," he said. But he was thinking: *Aw, shit.*

"Are you proud of what you've done?"

"Do you want some cognac?" he said.

She started to say something, to spit out some stinging retort, but then she didn't. "Yeah," she said, and sat down next to him.

He filled up the Styrofoam cup he'd been drinking from and passed it to her. She took a sip, then another, and passed the cup back to DeMarco.

"So thanks to you Molly Mahoney gets a free pass," Kiser said. "And basically Campbell does, too. Well, are you proud of yourself?" she asked again.

"No," he said—and he wasn't. And his answer probably surprised her. "But Molly's not getting a pass, Kay. She's not going to jail but she'll be doing something a whole lot harder than a couple years in some country-club prison."

"What's she going to do?" Kiser said.

DeMarco told her.

Kiser nodded, just like DeMarco had done, probably saying to herself the same thing that DeMarco had said: *I can live with that.*

"But Campbell, he goes into witness protection. You call that justice?"

"He's not going into witness protection. He just thinks he is."

"What does that mean?"

"I can't tell you. All I can tell you is that Campbell's going to prison and he's never going to spend a dime of what he stole." He paused then he added, "And McGrath's dead."

"What? How do you know that?"

"I can't tell you that either. All you need to know is that Richard Praeter and Doug Campbell and Rusty McGrath won't be committing any more crimes, and Doug Campbell's going to jail and losing all the money he stole."

She just looked at him. He could tell she believed him—and she was smart enough to know that it wasn't in her best interest to know any more than she'd just been told.

"So it's all over, Kay. You won."

Kiser took the cup back from DeMarco and sipped again.

"I hate these people," she said after a while.

"What people? Campbell and McGrath?"

"All the people who game the financial system. All the Wall Street crooks. They steal billions more than some ghetto kid who knocks off a liquor store, and they destroy people's lives. And when they do get caught, half the time they don't get convicted because the cases are so goddamn complicated that the average juror can't understand them."

"Is that why . . ."

"My dad worked for a company called Clemson Fasteners. They made stupid screws and bolts and rivets, things like that. He went to work for them when he was eighteen, and along the way he got some education and rose through the ranks. He was the first person in his family to hold a job where he didn't work with his hands. But when he was sixty-two, just a couple years away from retirement, it comes out that the CEO had been understating expenses, hiding debt, overstating the profits. All the usual crap companies pull when they're trying to keep their stock price up and the company afloat. I mean, this wasn't Enron big. Only a couple thousand people were affected. But my dad lost his job and he lost his pension, and because he was sixty-two years old, he couldn't find another job. He went through his savings in less than two years. After he declared bankruptcy, he sealed off the garage with towels and started the car and killed himself, and my mother was the one who found him. She died of heart failure a year later. So I hate these people and I'm going to spend my life putting them in jail."

"I thought you resigned."

"You don't know what Mahoney did?"

"No. What are you talking about?"

"I've been at the SEC for a long time, but I never really wanted to be there. The SEC investigates and regulates, but when we find somebody who's committed a serious crime, the guys at Justice are the ones who prosecute. After I'd been at the SEC only a couple of years, I realized I needed to be over at Justice if I really wanted to make a difference, but I've pissed off so many people at Justice, I knew they would never give me a job. At least not the one I wanted.

"But today, I got a call from the attorney general. That wimp. He's going to put me in charge of their criminal division. The job just miraculously opened up. The guy who had the job—the guy who agreed to the deal that Molly got—he's going off to teach at Harvard. So I get his job, and it's the job I've always wanted."

"Congratulations," DeMarco said, and he was being serious. He also wondered how Mahoney had been able to make the attorney general do what he wanted, but he didn't really care and he wasn't going to ask.

Kay Kiser stood up, all six feet two inches of her, and looked out at the National Mall, her head moving slowly as she took in all the government buildings surrounding the Mall. She was probably imagining the corruption occurring daily inside those buildings.

Kay Kiser was looking at a target-rich environment.

While she was looking at the buildings, DeMarco was looking at her. She was a pretty woman, but what struck him at that moment was the character in her face. She was going to be *somebody*, somebody that history would remember. One day he'd pick up a magazine, and there she'd be on the cover, older, her hair gray, and he'd be able to say: *I met her once.*

"I just wanted to let you know, DeMarco," Kiser said, "that I'm going to be watching you and John Mahoney. And if I ever get the chance to put you in jail, I will."

DeMarco filled his cup to the brim with cognac.

65

Emma was sitting on her patio, surveying her domain. Her lawn was a lush green carpet, her trees were pruned, her bushes neatly trimmed. The heads of pretty flowers were pushing their way up through the soil.

Emma was pleased.

She turned her head when she heard her backyard gate open. Even the sight of DeMarco couldn't totally dampen her contentment.

He sat down in a chair next to her without saying anything.

"Is it all over?" Emma said.

"Yeah, except for one thing."

"Molly Mahoney," Emma said.

"Yeah."

"So what did you do?"

He told her. The complete truth this time.

Maybe Emma wasn't quite the Puritan he thought she was. She didn't seem at all disturbed by what had happened to Ted Allen or Rusty McGrath, and what was going to happen to Douglas Campbell.

"But what happens to Molly?" she said.

DeMarco told her. Emma didn't say anything for a moment, then she nodded. "Okay. But if you ever lie to me again . . ."

349

Epilogue

Molly pulled back the canvas flap and stepped outside her tent.

It was a beautiful morning, the air crisp and clean, and the mountain —that incredible mountain—was visible in the distance. By noon the temperature would be over a hundred and the flies would start to swarm and the wind would begin to blow, but the mornings here . . . She'd never experienced such glorious mornings.

She'd been in Tanzania for six months now. She had endured the heat and the flies and the dust—and the dying. So many people dying, every day, mostly children. But after six months she was . . . what? *Used* to it? No, not used to it—you could never get used to it—but she could accept it. She did what she could and that was all she could do, and she accepted that some Higher Power must have some reason for all the suffering.

She had gotten a job with UNICEF. That was the deal she made with her mom. Three years with UNICEF. More time than she would have spent in prison for insider trading. But she already knew that when her three years were up, she was going to stay with the organization. She was going to make this her life.

UNICEF focused on children and mothers, providing health care and education. Another thing UNICEF did was work with poor communities to build clean water and sewer systems and, being an engineer, that was her job. And when she couldn't do her job because she couldn't get pumps and pipe and everything else she needed, she helped out in the hospital. Some days all she did was hold the hands of children who were dying.

But for the first time in more than a year, she felt good—about herself, about what she was doing, about everything. She hadn't had a drink in nine months and would never drink again. Her complexion was perfect, her eyes were clear, and she'd gained back the weight she'd lost. Most important, she had peace of mind. She couldn't believe that she had been so addicted to two small plastic cubes.

All that was behind her now: the gambling, the drinking, the lying. Everything was behind her—and everything was ahead of her. One day at a time.

She walked toward the mess tent to get breakfast, wondering what breakfast would be this morning. Yesterday it had been rice and a plant that looked like a tomato but wasn't. The supply plane was overdue, as always.

As she entered the mess tent, she saw the new doctor, the Italian, the one who'd arrived a week ago. He had gentle eyes, a cute gap between his front teeth like Omar Sharif, and arms and shoulders that looked like he should be holding a pickax instead of a scalpel. She'd caught him looking at her yesterday and he'd actually blushed. An Italian who blushed. Will wonders never cease?

He reminded her of DeMarco.

Acknowledgments

I want to thank James Donahue, Greg Alwood, and Dee Henderson for answering various questions related to the SEC, subpoenas, e-trading, and insider trading. Any errors related to SEC procedures and other legal matters associated with insider trading are mine alone.

Daniel Caine, a friend and real-life lawyer, who graciously permitted me to use his name as Molly's lawyer in this book. I also want to thank Dan for being such a big supporter of my books.

Kay Kiser, in a raffle in support of the Jefferson Oregon Library, won the right to have a character in this book named after her. I want to thank Kay for allowing me to use her name and Linda Baker of the Jefferson Oregon Library for contacting me regarding the raffle. In the same way the government could use a few more folks like the fictional Kay Kiser, we can also use more people like the real Kay Kiser who support our local libraries.

Jamison Stoltz, my editor on all the DeMarco books, save two. He always improves my books, but his comments on this book were especially astute, and it's a much better book because of him.